Josiah Nisbet, a once-risi uncertain future. He's los reputation, and his relations father, Admiral Horatio Nel ⌣ered a covert mission, will Josiah be able to redeem himself in the eyes of the navy, and his stepfather?

Set against the backdrop of the "Great Chase", the Caribbean campaign preceding the more well-known Trafalgar, author Oliver Greeves un-picks the story of *Nelson's Lost Son*. It is a tale of skulduggery, slavery and unrelenting military daring-do, set amidst the beauty and the horrors of the Sugar Islands.

## Reviews for *Nelson's Lost Son*

*Nelson's Lost Son* is a fast-paced, gripping adventure set against a colourful historical background. It vividly brings to life the father-son relationship of Horatio Nelson and his 'lost son' Josiah Nisbet. Josiah, the hero of the novel, faces warfare on the high seas as well as moral issues regarding the keeping of slaves, family honour and the legacy of colonialism. I highly recommend this book to those with a desire to learn about a fascinating period of naval history as well as those simply looking to be entertained by a lively and amusing adventure tale.

**– Walter McIntosh (Film & Television Editor)**

Oliver Greeves explores with great insight the nuances of extended family life clustering around the history of Horatio Nelson. A fictitious journey based on historical fact which the author reveals as a great adventure.

**– Oliver Freeman (Publisher)**

*Nelson's Lost Son* is more than an action/adventure, though it certainly is that. It's also an exploration of how a once rising star, brought low, begins his redemption, and starts to develop into a man of real character. A minor historical figure, cast into the darkness by a brilliant, heroic, but sometimes cruel stepfather, is brought into the light, and Oliver Greeves turns him this way and that to examine his very human weaknesses and motivations, though with a great deal of sympathy.

This is a rollicking and enjoyable read. Greeves is understanding and realistic in his depiction of character – Josiah's, and the others who cross his path. He takes some licence with historical events, to the great advantage of the plot, but carries it through with conviction, so that, by the close of the novel, the reader has become invested in this semi-fictional figure and wants to know more of what comes next.

I hope Greeves will bring us more adventures, and I look forward to reading them. Highly recommended.

**– Diane Donovan (Senior Reviewer,**
**Midwest Book Review, USA)**

# Nelson's Lost Son

*— An extraordinary tale of Nelson's step son' —*

To: Tom

## OLIVER GREEVES

With best wishes

Oliver

First published 2022 by Oliver Greeves

Produced by Independent Ink
independentink.com.au

Copyright © Oliver Greeves 2022

The moral right of the author to be identified as the author of this work
has been asserted.

Cover design by Daniela Catucci @ Catucci Design
Edited by Sabine Borgis
Internal design by Independent Ink
Typeset in 12/16.5 pt Adobe Caslon Pro by Post Pre-press Group,
Brisbane

Cover images: Owned by Oliver Greeves and is considered to be a likeness
of Josiah Nisbet

 A catalogue record for this
book is available from the
National Library of Australia

ISBN 978-0-6450237-5-6 (paperback)
ISBN 978-0-6450237-6-3 (epub)

*This book is dedicated to the memory of my mother, Sigridur Gudmundsdottir, who was born in Iceland and, through the strange circumstances of war, met my father and settled in England. She was the constant inspiration of my boyhood and – with other mothers – sat patiently through the reading of my first play when I was ten years old.*

# CONTENTS

## PROLOGUE: DECEMBER 1801

The London coach dropped Josiah off on Merton High Street and he chose to go on foot the rest of the way. The night had been clear and star-filled when he left Harley Street. Cloud now covered the sky and the wind was rising. Josiah knew what was to come: below the fast moving cigar-shaped cloud was a sinister blanket of rain. *Any Captain worth his salt would have reefed his sails by now.* Clutching his hat to his head, he took cover in an old flint church fronting the road. The cloud was overhead and the squall followed on its heels. He sat in a quiet pew, the rain rattling the windows. If he had been on board *Thalia*, it wouldn't have worried him. What made him nervous now was his forthcoming meeting with Horatio. *So unpredictable. Sunny one minute, stormy the next. Never quite knew what reception awaited him.*

Years ago, on *Agamemnon*, he had been his captain. Sometimes kind, often distant, he made Josiah feel he was a nuisance. But, when they met last time, Horatio had been cordial. He said Josiah should have *Thalia* again – when she had completed her refit. He would make sure of it.

The affair with the Hamiltons had changed everything. *It was like walking on eggshells. Everyone knew what was going on at Merton, but Horatio needed to pretend the Hamiltons were but his 'dear friends'. Nothing more! Fanny's longing to restore her marriage added to the delicacy of the situation. If her name were to come up, even once, all would be lost. Still, Horatio was his father, and his patronage was the only card Josiah could count on if he were to become captain of a fighting ship again.*

He picked up the prayer book resting on the shelf of the pew and opened it at random. The wind was dropping now and the rain would end soon. He read the first words of a psalm:

'Wherewithal shall a young man cleanse his way: even by ruling himself after thy word.'

He shut the book, irritated with the admonition. The storm had passed and the sun emerged. Josiah left the church to resume his journey. A few minutes later he was at the lodge gate and marching down Merton's gravelled drive. It was smart with lush borders and the house emerged from a screen of elm trees, rain dripping from their branches. A gothic façade suggested antiquity. *Must have cost at least ten thousand pounds.* Rooks swooped about the eaves, cawing. He approached the steps leading to the front door and hesitated. This was Emma Hamilton's home, and it was undeniable she hated him and this would be his one and only visit.

His knock was answered by the butler, who took his visiting card and escorted him to an alcove in the hall.

'Wait here, sir,' he said, pointing to a chair standing alone on a cold marble floor.

He preferred to look around. From the hall a flight of stone steps led to an upper floor. Between two tall windows above the staircase there was a large portrait of the admiral posed heroically, hand on sword. It must have been painted recently, because Josiah had not seen it before. On another wall hung four crossed swords. Below them, on a small table, was a bust of his father, the head swathed with laurel. Small Union flags were on either side. On the opposite wall hung another portrait of Horatio and, behind glass, a framed work of embroidery that betrayed the creator's modest skills.

He read: *What greater thing can a man do than lay down his life for his country?* Below were the names of battles, separated by decorative anchors: *Cape St Vincent, The Nile* and *Copenhagen.*

A candle on a low table burned with a smoky flame.

Josiah turned away and took a seat.

A door opened and Uncle William strode towards him with his hand outstretched. 'My dear fellow!'

Josiah struggled to his feet. 'Very good to see you, Uncle.'

The Reverend Nelson was a fleshy man, with eyes that protruded as if he was perpetually startled. His portly figure was clad in an old-fashioned red velvet coat. His stomach bulged over his white breeches and silk stockings. The buckles on his shoes sparkled in the rays of the sun streaming through the vast window.

'To what do we owe this unexpected visit?'

*Heavy emphasis on 'unexpected'.*

'I've come to visit my father.' He paused. '… and the family as well. How is Aunt Sarah?'

'Well, everyone's *very* busy. We have a big dinner tonight – many Persons of Quality are coming. I am not sure if there is room for you.'

The words hung in the air.

'Where is Papa? I'll take no more of his – or your – time after we've spoken.'

He felt his face flush at his clumsy words.

'I see! I must talk to her ladyship first. Perhaps I could order you something – a dish of tea?'

'I just want to talk to my father.'

'Your *step*father,' William corrected. 'Well, come in and take a seat in the library. I believe my brother may be asleep.'

He sat and brooded. *Stepfather. Horatio was the only father he'd ever known. Why had he never adopted him?*

Time passed. A maid brought him a dish of tea, which he drank slowly. Then from his seat he saw two figures bustle along the hall. The butler opened the door, bidding the ladies goodbye. Aunt Sarah and Emma Hamilton. They both ignored him. He felt the slight but was grateful he would not have to talk to them. *Bitches.*

A few more minutes passed. He checked his pocket watch, and the hall clock chimed the hour. Then a figure appeared. Horatio? No, it was a taller, more elegant man.

'Josiah! It's me, Matcham.'

It was his uncle, Aunt Kitty's husband. He had always liked Aunt Kitty and loved to hear Matcham's adventures in the East India Company. When Josiah was young, *they* were the patrons of the family, the people with the money and connections. Now Matcham and Kitty were lesser stars in Horatio's firmament. Josiah knew Matcham was in Horatio's debt after a failed venture in New South Wales.

'Uncle! Good to see you.'

Matcham sat. 'How do you find Merton?'

'It's the first time I have seen the place. Neither a great house nor a villa. You know, my mother built a house in Suffolk. Smaller, but much nicer. This seems false.'

'I agree – hate the place. *Our* houses are always elegant. This one trades comfort for pretension – what the French call *bourgeois*. Still, old Sir William likes the fishing, and her ladyship flatters herself with a house big enough for Horatio's noble friends. We're never short of visitors.'

He paused and, leaning forward, he said in a quiet voice, 'Tell me, Josiah; how is Fanny?'

'How would *you* feel if your spouse deserted you for a tart, and the family cut you off?'

'It's ugly. She's a wonderfully kind and brilliant woman. I will always love her. Do give her my best, Josiah.'

'I'll not be your messenger, uncle. Write her a note or pay her a visit yourself.'

'Steady, old fellow. Steady on. Have you seen your father recently?'

'Met him before he left for Copenhagen and then again in September.'

'What are you here for today?'

'He says the Admiralty have a Command for me, but everything has gone quiet. I need his help to move things along.'

'My advice to you is to steer clear of talking about Fanny – or Emma. And he is devoted to his love-child Horatia. Better not mention I told you that.'

There was a cough in the distance, and they looked up. Horatio was descending the stairs. From afar, he looked old and bent. In contrast to Matcham, who radiated robust good health, he seemed like a man with little life left in him.

Yet his voice, high pitched and authoritative, was warm. 'Josiah. My boy. Good to see you.' He paused to survey his son. 'My God, how you have grown! Come, Matcham, come, Josiah, let me show you my new estate!'

They stepped through the hall, Horatio taking a cane from the umbrella stand, and they set off down a path towards a distant lake.

Matcham strode ahead, while Horatio walked with Josiah, his one hand resting on his shoulder. 'Have you heard from the Admiralty, Josiah? I have been putting in the word for you, and everything I hear is positive … though you do have your enemies.'

'Colquitt?'

7

'Yes, Lieutenant Colquitt has used his influence to blacken you. I had the chance in Copenhagen to meet Brierley too. Do you remember him? The Purser? You ought to have been more careful. The Admiralty takes complaints from warrant officers more seriously than from commissioned officers.'

Josiah flushed. The old lies were still being circulated.

'And St Vincent both likes and hates you. The trouble is the peace. If St Vincent becomes First Lord, he will cut the navy down to size. Get rid of the older frigates. Still, I fought for you and was told you will have *Thalia.*'

They walked on, steering clear of controversy, navigating the shoals of hurt and misunderstanding and recalling the best of times – *Agamemnon,* his fellow midshipman, Weatherhead, and the battle for Bastia. Without noticing it they had circled the lake and were approaching the house again. The sun warmed their backs while a gentle breeze played on their faces and views across soft green meadows and golden trees reached all the way to the North Downs. Josiah thought how the natural beauty would appeal to Horatio, who must be looking for peace and quiet after a long voyage. He doubted there was much peace within the four walls with Emma Hamilton in charge. Nevertheless, he felt elated. Despite all that had gone wrong, his father still wanted him.

Horatio said, 'What has happened to me and Fanny divides you and me, Josiah. It compels me to take sides. My friend, Lady Hamilton, is a woman of great beauty and even greater passion.'

Josiah stiffened. *Just when everything was going well, Horatio had to ruin things.*

They were walking through a grove of silver birch trees. A nursemaid carrying a child in a shawl appeared from the house.

Horatio called out, 'You there!' He marched towards them.

Matcham, who had been striding ahead, stopped at Horatio's words and watched him approach the nurse as he waited for Josiah to catch up.

Horatio's voice rose above the cooing of wood pigeons. 'Nurse! It's too cold for the child!'

The nurse stopped.

Horatio handed his cane to the nurse and took the baby. They turned towards the house.

Josiah shouted, 'Goodbye, Father!'

Horatio paused, his useful arm full with his bundle. 'I wish you well, Josiah. I look forward to hearing of your successes soon. Please don't come back here again.'

Josiah shook hands with Matcham. 'Give my love to Aunt Catherine.'

'And mine to Fanny!'

He continued on his way along the gravel drive to the gates. He did not look back.

# PART 1: APRIL 1802

# CHAPTER 1

The tavern, on the banks of the Thames at Wapping, was surrounded by warehouses. Over its bow-fronted windows swung a sign – a Yorkshire coal ship under full sail. The 'Prospect of Whitby' had claims to antiquity and fame as a haunt for sailors, the ale being strong and the female company welcoming. It was a haven for Josiah these days. He preferred the company of mariners to that of gentlemen. Besides, it was a cheerful place to while away time. John Yule had written to say *Thalia* was berthed at the Deptford navy yard nearby, and Josiah had replied, by return, suggesting they meet here. It was March 1802 six months after his visit to Merton. He had spent many days here since then.

The tap room was packed but a sheltered nook

in the far corner was still unoccupied. He called to the wench for a glass of ale. He was dressed in an old blue coat, a pullover and breeches, and his dark brown hair was wild. Grey clouds hung low over the river, and rain drifted in sheets and pattered against the windows of the inn. Through them, he caught distant glimpses of merchant vessels loading cargo at the wharves.

Months had passed since he had last seen Horatio at Merton Park. John Yule steered a course towards him. Dressed in a blue lieutenant's overcoat, he looked smart – shaved and combed, ready for duty. Josiah was envious. He stood and thrust out his hand. 'John!'

He signalled to a servant, who bustled over with an armful of foaming glasses. John Yule sat down.

Josiah said, 'It must be near three years.'

'I took my leave and went home to Somerset and waited for a letter. You?'

'I was offered the command of *Thalia*. Shameful what they have done to her. The ship's been turned into a damned auxiliary!'

'Was you indeed!'

'I made a mistake.'

'A mistake?'

'The peace wasn't signed back then. I thought there would be alternatives.' Josiah took a deep draught and drained his glass. He took up his next and said, 'I turned her down when I found she was no longer a frigate.'

The news of his unemployment stilled the conversation.

John tapped his fingers on his glass. At length, he asked, 'What happened then?'

'Colquitt said I was a flogging captain who mistreated the officers. Brierley too. Copenhagen gave him added credibility. Anyway, I was told *Thalia* was the only ship they would offer.'

'And there are more captains than ships …'

He had overstated his case. 'And you, John? I'm glad you have come through this unscathed.'

'Unscathed – first lieutenant of a troop carrier?'

'Pretty soon we'll all be on the beach, but in the meantime …'

The noise around them swelled.

'Look, would you like to see the old ship?' John said. 'Stay overnight? Meet the captain?'

'Anyone I know?'

'Maybe.'

'I'd like that.'

They lingered for a while, talking about the old days. By the time they finished their drinks, the publican, red-faced and swearing, was bundling troublemakers out of the front door. Josiah settled the bill. Outside, the sun peeked through heavy clouds.

A waterman picked them up at Wapping steps in a wherry. They sat in the stern as he raised his main and steered into the swirling waters of the Thames. As they approached Deptford, Josiah saw *Thalia*. He shivered. It was the frigate he had commanded all right. The rake of her mast and the arrogant bowsprit above the reclining figurehead were the same. But her guns were gone. Troop quarters in the waist and stumpy masts disfigured her lines. She looked a lot like *HMS Dolphin*, his old hospital ship.

He recalled *Thalia* at her best with a sense of pride in his achievement. Two hundred and fifty men had lived, fought and died there. Everyone's ambition is to command a fighting frigate, and he had done it! He had brought her home in glory, the crew proud to be *Thalians* and himself richer for the prize money. He had been *so* certain he would take her to sea again after she completed her refit.

He and Yule boarded from the dock. No sentry challenged them. The rain had begun again; water was streaming from the yards. Yule left him with the purser and went off the find the captain. The purser took Josiah to his cabin and later returned with an invitation from the captain for supper. He hung up his coat and lay on the bunk and fell asleep as the ship rocked on the incoming tide.

He awoke when someone rapped on the door. He

lay on the berth, his mind occupied with memories. He dressed, combed his hair and made his way to the great cabin. A tall, grey-haired man, silhouetted by the setting sun, held out his hand in welcome. The rain had stopped. The table was laid and candles flickered, illuminating the captain's face.

'Kent!' Josiah said. 'My God!'

The grizzled features of his old lieutenant from *Dolphin* broke into a broad smile. 'Josiah Nisbet!'

'Kent, what are you doing here?'

'I brought *Dolphin* home a few months ago. We were paid off. Then they asked me to take *Thalia*. Quite the coincidence to have succeeded you in two commands.'

'I can't think of a finer man.'

'I talked to the yard. They said her knees and timbers were weak, and the Admiralty decided to convert her.'

'I'm not sure that was right,' Josiah said. 'There's been too many ships taken off the list since St Vincent became First Lord!'

Yule joined them as platters of fresh bread with crumbly cheese and pickled onions were served. Their glasses full, they sat in comfortable silence.

The old man looked at Josiah affectionately. 'What happened after *Dolphin*? Things were said ...'

'I'm not proud of it. I made a great nuisance of

myself in Gibraltar – to get St Vincent's attention. I was banished to the finance office. A terrible boring place! I found fraudsters were looting the dock-yard – thousands every year. Anyway, as a reward, he sent me to Alexandria to take command of *Bonne Citoyenne*. I was her captain for a glorious eighteen months. Then *Thalia's* commander was sent home on sick leave, and I took over the ship in Malta.'

'My God, Josiah. The luck of the Irish! A fighting frigate. Were you yet twenty?'

'Nineteen. Privateers and blockade runners. We must have taken ten every month.'

The steward returned and refilled their glasses. Old friends. No pretension or seniority. Josiah turned to John Yule. 'John, do you remember that rescue off Malta?'

Yule said, 'We were on convoy duty, escorting two troop carriers with over a thousand soldiers aboard into Malta. A fierce southerly blew up and both ships lost their masts and drifted towards a lee shore. We made fast to the one closest and towed her out to sea and put the carpenter and sail makers aboard. They rigged a sail. It began to get dark. We returned for the other. By the time we found her it was pitch dark and she was rolling – out of control – like to capsize. We couldn't carry a line across by cutter, so we brought *Thalia* alongside, and I boarded her with a crew and a hawser. We could hear the surf on the rocks – damned close. We clawed off – just.'

There was a silence as they remembered. A storm. A lee shore. Panic among the troops, the risk of both ships on the rocks or smashing each other to pieces. Towing her back to safe harbour in mountainous seas. A fighting frigate needed every drop of a man's courage.

Josiah added, 'St Vincent never saw fit to thank us for the lives of a thousand men. Only Duckworth and Governor Ball. Horatio never mentioned it either.' He sighed.

Kent said, 'It's the way of the world – praise and glory to them what never played a part.'

Josiah said, 'Where is *Thalia* bound?'

'After victualling, we leave for Plymouth. Could be months on a mooring.'

Like the *Dolphin* anchored in the Tagus, her hull gathering weed and worms, the crew bored half to death while the sick recovered or died.

'What's next for you, Josiah?'

'Join the line of officers waiting at the Admiralty.'

'Can't your father help you?'

He shifted uncomfortably. 'No.'

'You worked for St Vincent in Gibraltar. You must have heard about his crusade against corruption in English dockyards. What about helping him again?'

'He had a big falling out with Horatio over a

share of his Spanish treasure ship. St Vincent has not forgiven him—'

'Could be a way to re-establish yourself.'

'If I did, could you help?'

'I cannot take risks. This is my last command. I scarce have money for retiring, but I'd be willing to find out the lie of the land for you.'

The waves slapped against the hull of his old ship as he lay in his berth, the candle fluttering in the damp breeze. For the first time in many a week he felt better. He fell asleep, the pleasures of friendship suffusing his dreams and dispelling his frustrations.

# CHAPTER 2

In the morning, two sailors and an elderly midshipman took Josiah ashore in the gig. The little vessel was as familiar as an old coat. From Tower Bridge, a cab took him to Marylebone, to the house he shared with Fanny and Edmund, his grandfather. Edmund, alone among the Nelson clan, was loyal. Josiah rang the bell, and the maid opened the door, taking his coat as he made his way to the parlour.

'Her Ladyship is calling on friends,' she said over her shoulder as she hurried back to the kitchen.

He was pleased to have the house to himself. It was quiet and there was much to consider. On the hall table was a pile of letters on a salver. He picked them up and took a seat, flicking through them and selecting one in a finely embossed envelope. An address in St James Square. It was Davison, Horatio's prize agent. An invitation to dinner tomorrow.

He sat in the parlour and thought about the successful factotum who traded in the risky world of politics and business. Davison, for all his money, was always hungry for social acceptance but had never gained it. Together with Marsh, the banker, and Haslewood, the lawyer, he was a loyal adviser. Although Fanny had managed business with each of them for the years Horatio was at sea, their loyalties had been tested when Horatio dismissed her. But Davison was also Josiah's prize agent. Perhaps the meeting was Davison's way of keeping that relationship alive in case he went back to sea.

After breakfast he read the *Times*. He studied the advertisements on the first page before turning to the News; rumours of war and the struggles of the government and its opposition. War would be good. He'd best make the most of his meeting with Davison if war was coming. In the meantime he would walk to the Admiralty and keep his name in front of their lordships.

The walk to the Admiralty took him through Whitehall to the great headquarters of the navy. He joined many other officers on the same mission. But, as on most other days there, hours of waiting yielded no result. Not even a meeting. He returned to Harley

Street late in the afternoon, downhearted, and decided to venture to Vauxhall Gardens where there would be distractions to take his mind off his failure.

❧

Josiah awoke. It was dark, and the room was cold. His mouth was dry from too much drink. He eased from his bed and groped for the chamber pot.

As he pulled up the covers again the clock in the parlour struck four times. He lay back on the pillow, thinking about the evening gone. He regretted drinking beyond his fill. If it had been port wine it would have been different. He had struggled home from Vauxhall much the worse for wear and, when he had reached Harley Street, the house was abed. It had taken a lot of hammering – and cursing – to rouse the maid from her bed on the top floor. Mama would have heard him.

Dandies' clubs whose members dressed up and dictated male fashion were the current rage in London. Vauxhall Gardens, though, had varieties of entertainments to distract a man: jugglers, tightrope walkers, fireworks and musicians. There were taverns where a fellow could drink until the early morning. If you dressed well and were young without being foolish you might be admitted for romantic assigna-tions. All discreet.

He admitted to himself with some shame that these prurient interludes satisfied him. The more immediate and anonymous, the better. The trouble was, when he cooled down, he knew he too was being used.

Since he was thirteen he had lived aboard cities of men, where women were a fantasy. At assembly room balls he was uncomfortable. He could dance, but conversation was harder, as mothers peered through lorgnettes, their daughters fluttering their fans, calculating his parentage, education and fortune to a decimal place. Cool appraising eyes said more than simpering conversation. There was no tenderness. He had never spent even *one evening* with a woman of his own rank who he liked and desired.

He fell asleep again, and plunged into a restless dream.

As he paced the quarter deck, the frigate was flying, studding sails set, her hull plunging through the advancing waves. The sun was high in a sapphire sky. A powerful French battleship approached to starboard. Josiah gave an order to clear the decks for action, but he knew it would be futile to resist such force. The ship overhauled *Thalia*, and the flash of her guns was followed by a deafening report. The broadside cut *Thalia's* sails to ribbons, and as she slowed Josiah unsheathed his sword. The impact of the collision shook her timbers, and her mast fell.

He clambered up the side of the Frenchman but there was no one on deck.

His father emerged from the great cabin, medals glinting in the sun, face white with anger. 'Damn it, you have ruined my ship and my career. You and your beastly mama!'

Josiah plunged the sword into Horatio's heart.

He awoke to the sound of rain on the window, and relief suffused him as he realised it had been a dream.

The clock struck the half hour. He was wide awake. He decided to walk off his hangover and, dressed in his sea coat, a muffler around his neck, he opened the door and stepped into the damp wintry fog.

His walk took him northward up Baker Street. It was still quiet, too early for the milkman or coalman.

He pondered the meaning of the nightmare.

Raised voices caught his attention. A man and his wife were arguing. They were poor, ragged – down at heel. To Josiah's surprise he saw the man was a Negro. Must have been a sailor, perhaps a runaway slave. He looked again. The woman was white. The man carried a load on his shoulder, and the woman had a wheelbarrow. Was that a child sitting on its heaped contents? The city was full of people who'd reached rock bottom and were sometimes close to starvation. Probably came from a wretched cottage and lost their rights of commons to the local landlord.

He would give them a shilling. He reached into his pocket. The ordinary seamen on *Thalia* came from the dregs of society too. Almost savages, some of them. The man took the coin and grunted thanks. They saw him look away and walked off, their raised voices dulled by the fog.

By the time he was back at the house in Harley Street his mind was made up. Visiting Davison that afternoon would be his first step in taking command of his situation.

He rang the bell, and this time the door opened quickly. From the kitchen came a welcome smell of coffee. He sat down in the parlour. There were footsteps on the stairs, and Fanny appeared. She was wearing a blue dress that matched her blue eyes. Her dark hair was interlaced with strands of grey. She looked better than she had in a while.

'Oh, it's you!' She put her arms around his neck and kissed him. 'Hello, son. You're up early.'

'Couldn't sleep, Mama, and I decided fresh air would serve me better than my bed.'

'I heard you come in late last night. A great knocking on the door roused everyone. Could you come home a little earlier in the future? Edmund needs his sleep, and so do I.'

She looked at him steadily, her eyebrows raised, and then smiled.

'I'm sorry, Mama.'

She sat down at the table and took his hands.

'I have been doing some thinking about my future,' Josiah said. 'I don't think there's any prospect for me at the Admiralty unless the war begins again.'

'It was the same with your father. He was at home for five years. He had upset everyone, and there were no ships for those who had offended their lordships.' She looked at him meaningfully.

'It must have been difficult for both of you.'

'I was pleased to have him at home. We were newly wed, and his unemployment gave us a chance to know each other better – to become husband and wife. He was very frustrated, though, and he couldn't abide the condescension of the Whig gentry in that part of Norfolk – him being a Tory through and through.'

'How are you faring, Mother?'

'I am very fortunate in having such good friends – even the King has told me of his regard and insists I attend the levees at court. Still, without Horatio, I feel embarrassed. Lost, if you want to know.'

Her eyes filled with tears.

Josiah stood and put his arm around her shoulders, holding her gently. 'I saw him, you know. I went to Merton. Saw Uncle Matcham and William too.'

'How was he?'

'Sweet and kind to me. Said he would help me. He … he has a baby – a girl …'

Fanny sobbed.

'There, Mother. Don't cry. Life is hard enough, but thank God you have adequate money.'

'I have no complaints about that.' She paused. 'I still love him, you know.'

'I know you do, and it is incomprehensible after all the shame he brought to both of us.'

'I don't expect you to feel the same way, Josiah. I want you to find a different future; find a good wife and live comfortably, well away from the navy.'

'Mother, the navy *is* my life. There is nothing else I want to do.'

'Then, pray God, you will find a ship. When you do, dear, don't make the mistakes of your father. Never believe your achievements entitle you to treat another person badly.'

# CHAPTER 3

Number 9 St James Square was a four-storey town house, distinctive in its glossy white Palladian finish, unlike its neighbours with their smoke-blackened red brick. Josiah paused and studied the building. The house flaunted his wealth and status. Horatio said Davison had made his money as a lawyer – in Quebec – and then another fortune from a fleet of merchant ships. He had a manufacturing empire too, working as a supplier of everything from convict uniforms to barracks – which he built for His Majesty's government all over England. Without any training, he had become a prize agent, and Horatio had given him the prestigious job of selling the ships taken at the Battle of the Nile.

Josiah looked up at the grandiose façade. Business: maybe that was a better career to consider.

Pilasters, surmounted by a capital atop the modest portico, swept the viewer's gaze to four stone muses who guarded the roof above the line of attic windows. Josiah climbed the steps to the freshly painted black door with its polished brass handle and rang the bell. The butler answered and, after taking Josiah's card, escorted him into a sitting room off the hall. Mr Davison was currently engaged, he said, and would join him for dinner at two o'clock.

Josiah took out his watch. Another fifteen minutes. He stood with his back to the fire and looked around the gracious sitting room. A portrait of Davison and his wife decorated one wall and a portrait of Horatio another. It was said that the commission for the Nile prizes had topped seven thousand pounds, three times more than Horatio had earned.

Josiah had missed that battle by a few days; otherwise he too would have shared in the prize money. In the afterglow of his victory, though, perhaps to make up for his disappointment, Horatio had given him command of *La Bonne Citoyenne*. It was to be the command in which he took most pride and satisfaction.

'My dear fellow, how *very* pleasant to see you!'

Davison had quietly entered by a door on the other

side of the fireplace and greeted Josiah in a polished Scots accent. 'My friend.' Davison touched his shoulders with both hands and looked him in the face. 'How nice of you to find the time to see me!'

'Oh, hello, Davison. Good to see you again.'

Josiah was aware of how their positions had changed since his parents had separated, but the agent was as welcoming as ever. Davison led the way from the sitting room to the magnificent dining room on the other side of the hall, where a table was laid for two.

Davison was nothing if not hospitable. He had a reputation for winning people's trust, a trait that, since she and Horatio had parted, Fanny said was all deception. But he was capable of charming almost anyone. Josiah could see that his charisma and intelligence served a cunning nature most effectively.

'How are you settling down, Josiah? I heard you had been offered *Thalia* again and have turned it down. Was that wise? Do you sense something else is in the offing?'

'It was not an offer that I *could* have accepted, Davison,' Josiah said coolly.

'The peace is on us and we are all out of work. Better, perhaps, to have stayed afloat?'

Josiah said, 'You're a busy man, Davison. Have you something to tell me?'

'I've watched your progress, Josiah. Your mother kept me informed while you were in the Mediterranean.'

Josiah scowled. 'I would have guessed it was my father who kept you "informed", as you say. After all, he made sure I was surrounded by his minions!'

The butler interrupted the flow, pouring glasses of a claret. Josiah sipped his wine, raising his eyebrows appreciatively, and smiled for the first time.

'I import the wine myself. I've agents to keep me supplied, despite the war,' Davison said.

The footmen brought in dishes, filling the table with roasted meats and fish enriched with savoury sauce. Josiah ate hungrily, his irritation abating.

'Josiah, I am in an unenviable position. I am your mother's friend, but I am your father's too, as well as being his agent. You may not know, but the cost of your mother's settlement and the new house Horatio has bought with Sir William has stretched him to a financial breaking point. I'm doing everything I can for Fanny – though she may not feel that way – as well as for Horatio.'

'I cannot find any pity for him. He has used and abused both of us! I thought he was going to help me get another command. Nothing has happened! Remember *I* was the one who saved *his* life!'

'Have some more wine, Josiah.'

The butler poured a large glass.

'I do have something to propose. But I need to know you are not my enemy.'

'Well, it's very decent of you to invite me to dinner, and if there is something I can do to help both of us, so much the better. What do you have in mind?'

'You must give me your word not to tell anyone about our conversation – even your mother?'

'You have my word. What is it?'

'I am in a certain amount of trouble. I was involved in buying into ... a "situation" – with two seats in parliament. I was not a candidate for the seats but, naturally, I would have a say in how the two members *would* vote, and that would be of great value to my business.'

'A rotten borough?'

'An unfortunate term, but ... yes. Anyway, I was persuaded that instead of buying the borough – all the land, houses and so on – it would be easier if someone secured the support of the hundred or so voters to vote in my men ... and that is what happened. Now I am being accused of bribery, of buying votes.'

'Sounds like you did.'

'You've always been blunt, Josiah; you have a reputation for it. I would have put it differently. Someone persuaded the voters to support *my* candidates, and the owner of the borough didn't like it. The fact that he threatened anyone who didn't vote for *his* candidates with eviction from their homes was neither here nor there, apparently. Some more fish? Your plate is empty, sir.'

'What does this have to do with me?'

'Nothing at all.'

'Nothing?'

'This is just background, to let you know I am under investigation in the parliament and if my enemies have their way … well, frankly, I will be destroyed.'

'What do you want me to do?'

'I'm coming to that. I'm also under investigation by the Treasury about my role as a contractor building barracks for the army. The whole thing is a huge misunderstanding. If it is not sorted out, I could be indicted for that as well. I have a reputation in the city and with the government. If my integrity is questioned—'

'And my role?'

'I need to get "runs on the board", as it were. I need the government to see me as indispensable and overlook what has happened – allow me to straighten everything out. Put things to rights. You don't need to worry about that. It won't affect what you do.'

'So you want me to undertake something – legal, I hope – which will put you back in good standing with the government so they will be lenient. Is that it?'

'Yes.'

'I see. Where and what will I do?'

'We'll start with your friend St Vincent!'

All kinds of possibilities ran through Josiah's mind. St Vincent towered over everything in the navy. He was the vindictive man who had offered Josiah the broken hospital ship *Dolphin*, and later turned *Thalia* into a troop carrier. It was all about his legal battle with Horatio. To make matters worse, he was now First Lord of the Admiralty. Everything within Josiah rebelled at the thought of St Vincent.

'He and I have never seen things the same way. I doubt he would give me an audience.'

'Come now, Josiah. Would I embark on something without considering how I would complete it?'

'Very well. I am willing to consider anything. But I know that if I am involved, St Vincent will be very loath to consider it. It'll be a waste of time.'

They were interrupted by the footmen bearing away the dishes to the sideboard and bringing glasses of jellies and nuts. A fine cognac accompanied them, a testament to Davison's skill in obtaining the scarcest of commodities.

Davison said, 'I know St Vincent's reputation, Josiah. Horatio was *his* creation. He plucked him from obscurity and gave him the squadron that won the Battle of the Nile. Yet he downplayed Horatio's achievements and cast sufficient doubt on them to put Horatio's peerage in jeopardy. In the end, Horatio was awarded the honour only after considerable self-promotion and with the help of powerful friends. St Vincent is tough, self-assured, conceited beyond belief, and should never be underestimated.'

'I am glad you said that, Davison.'

'Here's what we will do. I'm dining with Lord Minto next week. Until recently he was our envoy in Vienna. He has told me he does not subscribe to Horatio's view of you. In fact he is quite your supporter. A word from him to St Vincent will take care of things. He will recommend you help investigate the dockyards. And I know that St Vincent has already experienced your skills in finding solutions. Your colourful episode in Gibraltar is quite a legend.'

'Everything I know about the navy tells me I shouldn't touch this with a barge pole. Meddling with commercial interests in the Caribbean kept my father on the beach for five years. My own encounter with the contractors in Gibraltar added to my list of enemies.'

'Josiah, you can't make an omelette without cracking a few eggs. Do what you have to do. Your alternative course of action is to be idle, drink away the modest fortune you made from prize money and get under your mother's feet!'

'Now you're speaking plainly! I prefer that. What *will* I have to do?'

'You'll be operating secretly. You will have a new identity. We will set up ways of communicating with you, but otherwise you will be on your own. Am I clear?'

A surge of excitement. It would be war again. A different kind of war. It would mean being busy, having an important job. Rebuilding his career.

He said impulsively, 'I am your man.'

'Excellent.' Davison rubbed his hands together. 'I will pass your decisions to the right people. Remember, you work for *me*. I will set everything up and I will see you are paid. But you *must* place your complete faith in me.'

Davison pushed back from the table and stretched his legs out. He took a sip of his brandy. 'The government sources its supplies through contracting. A supplier deals directly with the government at a negotiated price or the contractor acts as the intermediary between the ministry and the various sub-contractors. Do you understand?'

'Of course. What's your point?'

'St Vincent is convinced half the ship-building and supply contracts are rigged between the contractors, with the dockyard commissioners getting bribes to keep their mouths shut. The result is shoddy workmanship and excessive costs. With the huge debt the government has run up there is public pressure. The new taxes on income are much resented and most of the tax is paid by the people who sit in parliament. Among them there is a sense that the government is bungling or complicit.'

'And you want me to …?'

'You will find a suitable dockyard job using a pseudonym. Get to know the contractors and find out what is happening.'

'What's my next step?'

'Wait to hear from me. One last thing: be very careful. There's a lot of money and reputation at stake. Whatever you find, be on guard at all times. Your life could be in danger if people find out what you're doing!'

The butler showed him out of the house, and Josiah decided to walk home. The main roads were bustling with tradesmen and servants. For the first time in many months he felt optimistic. Captain Kent would help him get a dockyard job, and Davison had influence with the Admiralty. He wouldn't need Horatio's help.

He recalled his months at the Gibraltar dockyard years ago. He had mastered the yard's finances quickly and found fraud; it had been enough to prod St Vincent to give him another chance. He would do the same again. The stakes for St Vincent were higher; he had to deliver on his promise to parliament to 'clean up the corruption of the dockyards'.

An oncoming wagon laden with barrels swerved to miss a pothole in the road. It lurched, spraying him with filthy water. He jumped back, cursing the driver. But it failed to dampen his spirits, and by the time he reached Harley Street he had already planned his next move.

Mama saw his smile and said lightly, 'My dear, this is the first time I have seen you smile for many weeks. Something very grand must have happened.'

'Mama, I have a job.'

'What? A ship?' she said in a dismayed tone. 'I was hoping you had decided to pursue the law.'

'No, Mother. I have a chance to redeem my reputation with the Admiralty. It is a secret mission.'

She brightened. 'Will you be in London?'

'No, Mama, I will be elsewhere. I will be travelling "incognito", and we will have to invent a story to explain my absence. I will keep in touch with you. There's no need to worry about me.'

# CHAPTER 4

Three days of bone-shaking travel on dusty roads, and nights at down-at-heel coaching inns along the way finally brought Josiah to Plymouth. The journey gave him time to adapt to his disguise. He was a seaman on shore leave. His 'estuary English' was passable. It helped that the other passengers ignored him – too common for their liking. After three days of pretending, he had become an ordinary seaman.

Davison had made the arrangements. The naval records for Joss O'Brien had him working at age thirteen at the Chatham dockyard, followed by service in the Channel and then an honourable discharge from the navy a few months back.

Josiah took John Yule's letter from his pocket and read it again.

*My dear Josiah,*

*We are anchored in Plymouth Sound. Our crew is reduced by half and we wait for our orders. It looks like we will be here for many months. Our captain wants me to convey his greetings to you. Also, he says, mindful of our conversation, he has connections in the Royal Dockyard and he is sure he can help you get a job. Please contact me at the Seaman's Mission after you arrive. I hope to hear from you soon.*

*Sincerely yours,*
*John Yule, First Lieutenant,* Thalia

Josiah climbed down from the roof and stretched his legs. The sun warmed him, but he was stiff and tired. The coachman threw down his knapsack. *No tip for him!* He glared at the driver and marched through the archway to the street, stopping a passer-by to ask directions.

'On foot, are you?'

'That's right, sir.'

'Take King Street, then in half a mile, take Molesworth to the end.'

He tipped his cap and slung his knapsack over his shoulder, pleased to be on his way. It would be walking from now on. No more cabs or carriages. Arriving an hour later at the dockyard gates he cast around looking for somewhere to stay. The Queen's

Dock Inn was a mean waterside tavern. The publican eyed him suspiciously when he asked about a room.

'They're upstairs. Gentry take the front and the others are at the back.'

'How much?'

'A shilling a night. You share the bed.'

'I'll need to find a more permanent place to stay, bed and board. Anyone you'd recommend?'

'No. You want the bed? Money up front.'

Josiah took a shilling from his pouch and threw it on the bar.

'Supper is at six. Bed by eight.'

Josiah left his knapsack at the inn and crossed the road to the yard. A sentry stopped him.

'I'm looking for work.'

'Come back tomorrow morning five-thirty sharp.' The marine pointed to the wall opposite the gates. 'Casuals over there.'

'I have a friend on a navy ship in the anchorage. Any idea how I can find him?'

'If you was an officer I'd find out, but you ain't, so bugger off!'

No point arguing. He decided to search for somewhere to live. The mean streets around the dockyard were unpromising. How far away? About fifteen to twenty minutes' walk, he reckoned. In his mind he described a semi-circle with a diameter of a mile and set off.

As he walked he thought about this new life. The excitement had worn off. The disguise worked well enough, but it also placed him at the bottom. As a single man he would be viewed suspiciously. Where was he from? What was he up to?

He thought about the meetings with Davison and St Vincent. Once Davison had had Josiah's agreement he'd seemed to lose interest in the details of Josiah's mission. He was evasive, and when Josiah pressed him for instructions in the event he found things, he said Josiah should 'write to him' if he had seen evidence of corruption or other malfeasance. What Davison would do with the information was unclear, and that made him nervous.

St Vincent, on the other hand, was the bully he remembered him to be. They had met at Whites' Club and taken coffee in a small cold room at the back.

St Vincent had attacked him the moment they sat down. 'I never thought you'd amount to much, Nisbet. When I sent you to Alexandria with despatches, I was killing two birds with one stone. Getting you out of Gibraltar for your own good and giving you to Nelson to handle. You're his protégé, not mine. I told him to keep a close rein and I hear you resented it.'

'Sir, you're right about me resenting the minders. But you also know that when they were gone I was very successful. As good as any junior post captain.'

'Maybe. But you have burned bridges and made enemies. After turning down command of *Thalia* after her refit, what do you expect from me?'

'If I can help you root out corruption, I want to command another frigate.'

'With your father suing me in court why should I help?'

'I have a source in Plymouth at the Royal Yard. My plan is to work my way in secretly. Gain credibility without raising suspicion. Your inspectors will never find the truth of the matter. I will find what you are looking for.'

'I have no doubt, since the dockyards are all cesspits. The nation is being bankrupted and the ships are behind schedule and badly built. Root and branch I will sweep them clean – the whole stinking lot of them!'

He was obsessed. He had cleaned out the Mediterranean fleet of time-serving admirals and weak post captains. Now he would sift the dockyards. For a moment Josiah was taken with the picture of a grand overhaul resulting in efficiency and better ships.

'I take it that you accept my proposal, then. If I were to work for you undercover, when would it end?'

'At the point I present your findings of corruption to the commissioners of the navy board and parliament. No sooner or later, sir!'

He had no other cards to play. There would be no

guarantees, and with his tenuous connections with his father ... he paused and then said, 'If you are wrong about corruption in the docks, your enemies will want to hear about that too.'

A threat.

St Vincent scowled. 'You young pups are all the same. You're too big for your boots. Be careful, sir. I have my enemies, but I run the navy. I'm a man of my word, but don't cross me!'

The meeting was over. The admiral picked up his coat, leaving Josiah staring bleakly at his empty cup.

Number 10 Fishponds Street was a terrace house about fifteen minutes from the Queen's Dock Inn, at the top of the hill. It had a sign in the window: 'Room for Let. Good Company only need apply'. It was an ambiguous welcome. Did it mean there was no room for bad company, or that good company was to be found at 10 Fishponds Street?

His curiosity aroused, he knocked on the door, which fronted onto the street. A good-looking woman opened the door with a smile. After the coachman, the publican and the memory of St Vincent, her friendly face cheered him up.

'I'm looking for a room, missus. Your sign outside said—'

'Yes, sir. Come in.' She ushered him into the front room. 'I'm Mrs Lippett. And you are?'

'Joss O'Brien, ma'am.'

'Have you come far, sir?' She had a nice voice.

'I came from London. I hear there's work at the dockyard.'

He was suddenly finding it difficult to hold onto his new accent and paused, squaring his shoulders more like a seaman.

She looked at him appraisingly and said, 'I have a free room.' She had a West Country accent. Her eyes were soft and she had smooth skin and a nice figure. Perhaps thirty. There was something arousing about her. 'Come with me!'

They climbed the steep narrow stairs. The room was on the first floor and had a surprisingly good view over the dockyard to Mount Edgcumbe.

He nodded as he took in the narrow bed, the small table and single chair, a jug of water in a basin on a table with the chamber pot beneath. There were three or four blankets on the bed, which was made up with clean sheets and pillowcase. The room was drab but clean.

'Three shillings a week with breakfast. Five shillings full board.' It was cheap compared with London. 'We have breakfast at five, and supper is at six in the evening. No drinking allowed. No smoking. I live here with my mother, who is a Methodist, so she takes offence at bad language. But you don't look the sort to give any trouble,' she added.

'I like it and will pay a week in advance. Full board.' He reached in his pocket for his money bag and counted out the shillings. 'I'll be here tomorrow in time for dinner. Is that good with you, missus?'

'Funny, you sound like a Gent but you look like a sailor. What was it you said you did?'

'Nah. I'm a working man. No other side to me.'

'Well there's plenty of work to be done with the all the ships brought back home for refit. It's a good time to find work – as long as you avoid the Press-Gang.' She opened the door to let him out. 'I'm glad you came. I'll see you tomorrow!'

He made his way back to the Queen's Dock Inn. By now it was late afternoon and the shadows were longer. It was warm, the sky heavy with rain clouds. The roads around the pub were busy. The shift was over, and labourers were pouring through the gates on their way home, some stopping at the inn for a drink. The bar was packed and smoky.

The publican glanced at him. 'Do you want a drink?' he asked, pulling the pump handle for another customer.

Josiah stood near the empty fireplace, a pint of powerful cider at hand. A couple of labourers nearby were discussing their work. They were young and powerfully built. They had already drunk a glass or two and were ready for another.

'Let me buy you a drink,' he said. 'My name is Joss. I'm looking for work at the yard.'

'I don't mind if I do. "Never turn away a free one" is my motto. A pot of cider if you please.'

'You too?' Josiah asked the other man.

'Yes.' He was taciturn, suspicious.

Josiah waved to the barman, three fingers in the air.

'You two men work at the yard?'

They nodded.

'I'll be there tomorrow morning. Looking for work. What can you tell me?'

They looked uncomfortable. He was a stranger.

'There's plenty of work. You'll have no difficulty.' It was the younger of the two. Big shoulders. A strong West Country accent.

'What do you do there?'

'Rope yard. It's the best place. Indoors. Skilled work. I'm a machine fitter.'

'Machine?'

'We have a new steam engine. Does the work of fifty men.'

'Fifty? Are you joking?'

'It's all different. Steam. That's all the job is – driving engines.'

'You think there could be an opening?'

'When you get the nod tomorrow morning, tell them I said you should be at the rope yard. Taylor.

That's me. This 'ere is James. And who might I ask is you?'

'I'm Joss O'Brien. Ashore after years at sea. Want a dockyard job now. No more sea.'

'Joss, thanks for the drink. I best be on my way now. Her highness expects me home.'

After supper, following directions from the publican, Josiah made his way to the Seaman's Mission. He left a note for Lieutenant Yule with the man at the front desk and then returned to the inn for the night.

Early the next morning, bathed and dressed, Josiah ate his meagre breakfast. The air was cool and salty, and birds were twittering as he stepped from the inn. Fifty or sixty men stood opposite the dock gates. In a few minutes, a horse and cart came through the gates and stopped.

The driver took a box from the cart and stood on it. He waved the waiting men to gather around. 'Righto, men. We need forty today. Stand in two lines and I'll take a look at you. Any with trades over on my right. The rest of you wait until I'm done with them.'

Thirty minutes later he reached Josiah.

'Taylor sent me,' Josiah said. 'Said they need a man in the rope yard. Any chance of that?'

The overseer looked him over and said, 'You're in luck. They want someone there – hatchelling work.'

Soon the men with jobs were mustered and marched into the yard. Josiah and five others were led off towards the long building a few hundred yards away that housed the rope works.

They walked briskly across the yard, passing familiar sights – bales of cloth, piles of logs, coils of rope, barrels and anchors – and all around was a smell of brackish water and hundreds of gulls. He felt at home. But as he walked, he asked himself what he had done. He had given up everything to become just another labouring man. A 'nobody'. He was facing weeks of menial work. The image of his father at Merton crossed his mind, his grandiosity, ambition, wealth and power. He, the son of a viscount, the most famous admiral in England. At the bottom.

When they reached the yard they were brought into a building where the others were directed to different departments. Josiah looked around and was impressed. He had never been in a rope yard before. The building was at least two hundred yards long, disappearing off into the distance. It was long and low, and he could see immediately that one long machine occupied the whole structure. A rope twisting machine, the foreman said. It twisted individual strands of hemp yarn together to form a single rope.

Josiah saw that at one end the individual strands that would form the rope were fed through spools to a sled mounted on a rail. What a brilliant invention! *Thalia* had twenty miles of rope in its rigging and carried another ten miles as spare. Its ropes were everywhere, from the great anchor hawsers a foot in diameter to the six-inch cables for towing and the halyards, stays and the ratlines the crew used to climb the masts.

'Hey you! Stop daydreaming. Come with me!' It was the foreman. The others had gone. 'I've got work needs doing in the hatchelling department. Let's have a look at you. Take your coat off. Show me your hands.'

Josiah held out his hands.

'You look strong enough, but your hands are too smooth.'

'I was an able seaman, sir. I'm strong. I'm fit. My hands is smooth 'cause I was in a hoffice, wasn't I? No disrespect, sir. I can do a day's work like the next man.'

'I dunno. I'll give you a try but if you're not up for it by dinner, off you go!'

They left the rope yard and crossed an alley to another building. It was small and the air was full of dust. Josiah sneezed. The room was filled with tables topped with iron pads that had nails protruding from them, four or five pads to a table. The foreman gave Josiah a pair of heavy gloves and what looked like a rake. Then he put a square of matted hemp fibre on the iron pad, and with the rake brought it between the protruding teeth as he drew the rake towards him. The action straightened out the fibre as it passed between the nails. Josiah watched carefully, and then it was his turn. He put an armful of fibre on one side of the pad and, picking up the rake, drew it towards him. It brought out a sweat.

He looked at the foreman, who was grinning. 'Yeah, that's right. Now do that for the next three hours and we'll see how much work you've done.'

The foreman walked away. Looking around the room, Josiah saw there were twenty men doing the same work. They were all heavy-set, with big shoulders.

At dinner time, they had thirty minutes to eat. Josiah filled a tin mug and unwrapped the bread he had taken from the breakfast table. He sat with the other workers. He was exhausted. Every fibre in his body ached. His back and shoulders felt as though he had carried a ton of sand up a steep hill.

One of the others working near him looking at him curiously. 'What's wrong with you, mate? You look buggered.'

'This is very hard work. You have to agree.'

'You have to pace yourself. You'll never make it the way you're doing it.'

'I have to keep this job. The foreman said he'd turf me out after dinner if I hadn't made a go of it.'

'He's just got your number, hasn't he? He needs you! No one in their right mind will do this work.'

'What about you? You look like you have your mind right.'

'I got used to it. Didn't I? I got this job after I left the sea. They can't press you once you have your papers here. I learned how to do this. It's a shit job but leastways I have money in my pocket and the missus at home.'

'Do you know two fellows – Taylor and James? Met them at the pub last night. They told me about this.'

'Yes, they work over in the twisting room. Bleeding h'aristocracy!' Then the man laughed and stretched out his hand. 'Comey,' he said. 'They call me Bluey on account of my eyes.'

His eyes were sapphire blue, penetrating. He was tall and strong. In another life he could have been a captain or a lawyer. What was he doing here?

Dinner over, Josiah returned to the hatchelling works. He had passed the test. Now he had to make sure he blended in. Better not do too much work and attract the attention of the other labourers, who would be expected to match his output. But it was deadly dull and there was nothing happening here that would show how contractors made their money.

At five a bell rang and everyone put down their tools. Josiah had never worked harder in his life. He washed his face and hands in a bucket and put on his coat. Together with Bluey and two others they made their way to the Queen's Dock Inn. Mindful that he must be sober when he reached Mrs Lippett's place, Josiah declined Bluey's offer to join him for drinks; instead he recovered his knapsack and made his way to his digs. He lay on his bed trying to ease the pain in his shoulders.

At six Mrs Lippett announced that supper was on the table, and he made his way down the narrow stairs. There were two other men at the table. He wondered which one was her husband. They looked up as he entered.

One of the men stood. 'You must be O'Brien. I'm George Gaines.' He spoke with an unusual accent and he was well dressed.

Josiah looked enquiringly at the other man, who remained sitting. 'And this is?'

'Rockford.' His firm voice carried authority. 'We're here to carry out the navy inquiry into the dockyard. You may have heard that the First Lord is examining the workings of the yards. And what about you, Mr O'Brien?' He looked searchingly at Josiah.

'Me. I'm here for the work, mate. Just got a job in the rope yard.'

Rockford ignored him.

Mrs Lippett pushed open the door with her hip and put the stew on the table. 'The plates are on the sideboard, gents, along with glasses and water. Help yourselves. I'll be in the kitchen if you need anything.'

The three men set to. Josiah was very hungry and the food was tasty; he had to resist the temptation to refill his plate before the others had finished.

As he ate, he racked his brains. This was too much. The officials investigating the yard at the same lodgings? It was probably a coincidence; their work was to audit the yard, while he was there to find any suspicious doings in the day-to-day operations. It all pointed to St Vincent's compulsive pursuit of the guilty.

'Landlady seems a nice person,' he ventured. 'Is there a Mr Lippett?'

'She's a widow,' said Gaines abruptly.

Josiah could see they had no intention of engaging with him. He was beneath their station. Mrs Lippett must be short of business to have him stay in the same house as these gentlemen. He warmed to her at the thought.

'How long are you gentlemen staying?'

'We'll be here for a while,' said Gaines. 'It's a nice time of year but I wouldn't want to be here in winter.'

Josiah decided he must keep his distance while allaying any suspicions they might have of him. 'I'll be here a while myself. This place looks pretty well run to me. Might even decide to stay.'

# CHAPTER 5

The next morning Josiah woke when the knocker-up rapped on his window. A few minutes later, Mrs Lippett called out that breakfast was in half an hour. Josiah climbed from his bed, his back aching. He lit a candle, poured water in the basin and washed himself, towelled off and dressed in his working clothes as birdsong erupted with dawn's approach.

At the breakfast table there was no sign of the inspectors. Mrs Lippett said they were to be wakened at seven. She sat with him while he ate his eggs and toast, serving him small ale from a large brown pot.

'How did you sleep, Mr O'Brien?' she asked.

'Very well indeed, Mrs Lippett, but I'm as stiff as a board after a day in the hatchelling shed,' he said.

'Drink your tea, my dear.'

To his surprise she rose, stood behind him and placed her hands on his shoulders. Her hands were strong. He bowed his head and closed his eyes. His shoulders and upper arms, then his neck again. Then she sat down, and looked for his reaction. He felt better, but she had been too familiar. She didn't seem to think anything of it.

He was confused. 'I heard from your lodgers that you're a widow.'

'Yes, 'tis true. David died a year ago. An accident at the yard. A good man – we were married nigh on ten years. He had paid off this house by then and I am able to survive, but I miss him.'

'What happened?'

A tear moistened her eye. 'He was crushed to death in an accident. They were loading a cannon. The ropes snapped and the gun fell on David. He died instantly. Afterwards, the coroner's court that found the rope yard was to blame, and they fixed things up. But it is a shoddy business. They care for profit more than their workers' safety.'

From the direction of the yard he heard the bell announcing thirty minutes till his shift began. Josiah put on his coat and thanked her for breakfast.

'Call me Janet, and I'll call you Joss.'

'Thank you, Janet. I feel a lot better. See you tonight!'

She waved and closed the door behind him. He walked down the hill to the yard, whistling. For the first time in many months he felt optimistic. What a woman! But he and she were from different classes. And he would be there for only a short time ... still, she was gay, pretty and disposed to be friendly. He wondered how friendly.

At the yard, he showed his papers to the sentry and made his way to the rope yard. The other men were eating their breakfast and brewing tea. Soon work started on the pile of hemp beside his station. It was just as hard as yesterday. His body ached and time hung heavily. The air was dry. He wrapped his face in a length of rag to avoid breathing dust into his lungs. He paced himself, moderating his output to the speed of the other workers. The pile of combed fibre grew, and he replenished his stock of raw hemp, pausing to drink from his flask and keeping lookout for anything unusual. But nothing caught his attention. The sun rose higher in the sky, its beams lighting up the dancing dust particles.

Paddy and Sean were two Irishmen whose jocular banter had amused him the previous day. 'Come over here and eat with us, Joss,' called Paddy.

It was ten in the morning, and they'd been at work for two hours. He sat on a step next to them and opened the small linen bag packed by Janet. There was bread and cheese and a bottle of small ale, which he had bought from a vendor outside the dock gates.

'Ah, Paddy,' said Sean, savouring his breakfast 'Fine Irish bacon! You can taste the shamrock in it!'

Their daily ritual was greeted with laughter. Joss ate, enjoying the coarse bread and country pickle.

'Sean, what makes this place tick? See, I'm here as an outsider but I know there's a system. Do you know what I mean?'

'I know what you mean, Joss. Yes, there's a system, and if you don't buck it all will be well. It's been the same for the five years I've been here. It's smooth and the bosses have every reason to be happy. But we've heard there's a government man, an inspector about the place – from London. They're here to check on us. They're rocking the boat, by Gor. Is that not right, Paddy?'

'Now, Sean, our friend here is new, best not bother him with the polyteeks.'

Joss could sense Paddy's uneasiness. Sean had said too much. 'They're living at the same digs as I am. The inspectors, I mean. I can tell they're here because they suspect something.'

The bell rang and they returned to their tables and back-breaking hatchelling. And day after day it continued. By the end of the first week Josiah had settled uncomfortably into his routine. He had not heard from anyone outside the yard. Yule had not replied to the letter he'd left at the mission, and Josiah realised he must be at sea. Nor was there news from London, even though he had sent his address to Davison. Yet despite the lack of progress, Josiah had a sense of meaning that he welcomed after the weeks and months of purposeless meetings at the Admiralty and his mother's continued grief.

His friendship with Janet blossomed. She had an interest in him and he sensed flirtatiousness and a willingness to take their friendship further. He liked her forthrightness and her hospitality. The two inspectors kept to themselves, rarely saying anything of interest and making him aware of the unbridgeable social divide.

It was the tenth day at the rope works. Dinner had come and gone. Everyone was working steadily. Josiah was bored.

Then, *boom!* The building shook. He heard yells and a scream of tortured machinery. The workers dropped their tools, and the supervisor rushed from the room. The men looked at each other. Josiah led the way to the twisting shed.

A man was writhing in agony, blood spilling from his torn body. A helpless crowd gathered around him. It was the section foreman who had sent Josiah to the hatchelling shed. The man was unconscious. His arm below the elbow hung by a thread of flesh, and he was losing blood fast. Josiah threw his jacket down, tore his shirt off and ripped it into strips. He tied the tourniquet above the elbow, staunching the flow of blood. He bundled his coat under the man's head.

He looked up at the crowd standing around him. 'We must get this man to hospital. Get a horse and cart. Quickly!'

Two of the men ran for the door.

'What in all hell happened?' Josiah shouted.

'The sled left the rails. The poor bugger was by the machine. The loose end of the rope wrapped around his arm and …'

The rope machine was still working. Josiah took command. 'Someone. Stop the engine!' It was instinctive. Seven years on battleships had taught him to issue orders.

The engine was still attached to the bobbins. Someone pulled a lever and the bobbins stopped turning. He called for a check to see if anyone else was injured. There were four more, but none as seriously hurt. Men returned with a horse and a wagon. The injured man was carried on a make-do stretcher and gently loaded aboard. Three workers who knew their way to a doctor set off with the patient.

A new supervisor appeared and took over from Josiah. A mechanic appeared to repair the machine and, with everything back in order, Josiah returned to the hatchelling shed. He drank some water and put on the torn shirt and coat. He was about to begin work when a messenger told him to report to the main office.

He made his way there uneasily, aware that he had broken cover.

The yard manager sat behind a large oak desk. He was middle-aged, dressed in a morning coat, his hair sparse and plastered to his head with oil. Thin wire-framed spectacles sat uncomfortably on the bridge of his bulbous nose.

'O'Brien,' he said, 'you seem to be a man who knows how to give orders. What are you doing working on the shop floor?' His tone was curious.

Josiah remembered to talk like a working man. He touched his forelock. 'Well, sir, things was chaotic. It was natural. Someone had to take charge before the poor man died.'

'I didn't ask you that, O'Brien. What is your background? What's a man with your authority doing in a labouring job?'

'Yes, sir. It was like this. I was a midshipman in the navy for many years. No chance of promotion. Came from the wrong family and no patron. I was given my discharge papers when the peace came, and I've been living in London doing this and that. I have a friend on a ship in Plymouth who told me I might find work in the dockyard since I have no career at sea. Cheaper to live here, he said.'

'Well, O'Brien, you did a masterful job saving the foreman's life. I'm very grateful to you.'

'It was the least I could do.'

'I need someone with your initiative in this office. Can you read and write?'

'I can and I'd be very happy to take any position you have.'

'What's the name of the ship your friend serves on?'

'It's called *Thalia* sir. Old frigate fitted out recently as a troop carrier.'

'Is your friend Captain Kent?'

Josiah nodded.

'He was in touch a few weeks ago about someone he knew looking for work. That must be you. Said he knew you before and that you'd fallen on hard times. Recommended you highly. Seems he was right.'

A hint of a smile crossed the manager's face. He stood up and walked around the desk with his hand outstretched. 'My name's Robarts. It's good to meet you, Mr O'Brien. Tomorrow, come directly here and I'll let you know what we have for you to do. Is that satisfactory?'

A job in the office that held all the secrets of the yard. The best thing that could have happened. 'Sir, I'd be very happy to fit in wherever. I'll see you here at six tomorrow.'

'Not too early, O'Brien. The office doesn't open until eight. We'll meet then.'

Josiah made his way back to the hatchelling shed. An incredible turn of events. The accident, the chaos, taking charge and sorting things out and an offer of a job in the yard office. And Robarts knew Kent and had heard about *him*, Josiah. Much better to meet Robarts this way. Then, to ensure his work was above criticism, he set to on the hemp fibre and put in a good afternoon's work until the bell signalled the end of the shift.

At dinner that night, George Gaines was full of news about the accident at the yard. Rockford stayed silent. They didn't know about Josiah's role, and he decided to say nothing and see how the conversation unfolded.

'This is the second accident in the rope yard. It shows how weak the management is. Perhaps that points to something worse. The contractors are selling poor quality hemp and the yard is cutting corners. The yard management is in it as well!'

Rockford said: 'You've said enough, Gaines. Mr O'Brien here's not interested. Or is that *not* the case, Mr O'Brien?'

The insinuation was unmistakable: Josiah should tell them what he knew was going on. He looked at Rockford steadily. 'I'm a working man and I keep myself to myself. I need to keep my job at the yard … and they all know what you are about.'

'That's as it may be, Mr O'Brien, but we would expect you to let us know if you saw anything questionable.'

'Thank you, Mr Rockford, I'll bear that in mind.'

Janet came to him that night. He had taken off his working clothes and sponged off the sweat and grime of the hatchelling shed before getting into bed. He saw the glimmer of the candle through the partly opened door. She was wearing her dressing gown. She paused at the door and then, without more ado, took off her robe and slipped into his bed.

Their lovemaking was intense and very satisfying. She needed no prompting; he followed her movements and responded without saying a word. She came quietly, muting her cries in his shoulder, aware that a few feet away were rooms that housed the other lodgers.

He said quietly, 'Janet, you are the sweetest woman I have met. I believe I do love you dearly.'

'Oh, Joss, Joss,' she murmured.

But she was gone before he awoke. He asked himself if it had been a dream.

# CHAPTER 6

It was Thursday evening. Josiah had told Janet he would be back late and asked her to leave his supper on the table. Robarts had asked him to meet a hemp contractor from Belfast, a Mr Bulwer of McDowell & Bulwer, in town to negotiate a new supply contract. Robarts told Josiah that he had a meeting at the Masonic temple and could not be available himself. But Josiah suspected the Masonic meeting had nothing to do with Robarts' decision to send him as replacement. The two inspectors were still around, and Robarts was keenly aware they were watching and waiting to pounce.

Three weeks had passed since Josiah had been transferred to the yard office. What a relief from the drudgery of the hatchelling shed! It had gone quickly, as there was plenty of work for Josiah, especially once they knew he understood the basics of bookkeeping. But he had to be careful that the new boss continued to believe his story. Although he was proud of his copperplate writing, he made sure his script was juvenile. He felt more confident about the numbers because Robarts was aware he knew how to navigate. And after a time he gained Robarts' confidence, and it was clear that his probation was over; he was a fixture as long as he wanted to stay.

The two inspectors were also frequent visitors to the office. Initially surprised by Josiah's presence, they soon ignored him and went about their work reviewing lists of contractors, contract documents and the ledgers of receipts and payments. They had found discrepancies, and Josiah could see they were confident they had found evidence of the corruption that they had been sent to discover.

The hemp contract was their main target. Robarts told Josiah they considered the two accidents at the yard – involving Janet's husband and the rope-yard foreman – had been caused by rope breakages. They were evidence of the poor quality of the ropes, which the inspectors believed resulted from using inferior hemp. And they had found the contractors' prices had been rising steadily at the same time, which raised their suspicions further.

Josiah said nothing, but asked himself if there wasn't a simpler explanation.

When Josiah arrived at the Three Ferrets, Bulwer and his assistant Jones were already in their cups. They'd been there since early afternoon. Robarts had given Josiah funds from petty cash and warned him to pay for his own drinks, but Bulwer insisted on buying. He was a big Ulsterman with thick, fleshy features and short-cropped brown hair. Not a man to take 'no' for an answer. Tufts of eyebrows jutted from his forehead. He had a surprisingly high-pitched voice. His assistant was the opposite. Undistinguished features but with a deep voice. Josiah was confused. Who was the senior?

Bulwer saw his inquiring look. 'Come in, come in and take your seat! Where's Mr Robarts?'

'I am here as his replacement. He has an important meeting at the Masonic temple. He sends his apologies and asks you make do with me.'

'Sure that's disappointing. We've come a long way from Belfast, and I like Mr Robarts. But I suppose we have done our business with him, and you look like a bright young man who could do with a drink! Now young man, you are Mr ...?'

'O'Brien.'

'Irish, is it? Catholic, I assume. From the south?'

'Nah. I'm from London.'

'Well, that's good, is it not? Not that I hate anyone, but the power of the priests in Irish life is a fearsome thing!'

He signalled to the barman, who brought three glasses of whisky, together with a flask of water. Then their supper arrived and there was silence for a while.

'Mr O'Brien, we get the feeling that our visit is the subject of investigation. We saw two men in the office who were going through the books, and one of them asked Mr Robarts about his hemp. Navy board auditors?'

Josiah thought quickly. If the Irishmen had tumbled to the investigation, there was no point in denying it. 'Yes, they are trying to discover fraud in the dockyards. We had accidents recently, and the inspectors suspect the hemp is poor quality and over-priced.'

'Now I understand! It's been a puzzle. The yards have never been busier, but it seems as if everything has to be triple-checked. We've had to supply Robarts with our figures and invoices to prove our margin is fair.'

'What do you contractors make of all this?' Josiah asked.

'It's bloody nonsense, man!' Bulwer drank down the whisky with a single swallow. 'The truth is, there's a shortage of hemp,' he went on. 'The Russians supply most of the fibre and we were almost at war with them. Now everything's disrupted – timber, iron ore, hemp. You name it! Our ships are stuck in the Baltic ports. Lord Nelson has given the Danes a thrashing and they're all coming to their senses, but in the meantime the navy has to rely on Irish and English hemp. Expensive, it is. And to be first in line to meet our contract we have to give money to the merchants on the side. The investigation is going to make everything very difficult. We won't get paid on time and you won't get the hemp on time.'

'What about the accidents, the quality?' Josiah asked.

'That's nothing to do with us. The fibre isn't spun when we deliver it. The hemp is hackled and then twisted into rope on the rope machine. Something's gone wrong in that process. That's someone else's business, not ours. Any more questions, Mr O'Brien?'

He looked at Josiah sceptically. There was silence. Josiah broke it, saying, 'What do you hear from your other friends in the trade? Is this investigation happening elsewhere?'

'Yes, delays are causing a crisis. The yard managers are running scared. It's natural. They're being watched. The system is seizing up. Refits are delayed, invoices unpaid and no one is talking. Whoever is in charge is an idiot. Do you know who it is?'

'St Vincent. The First Lord of the Admiralty.'

'Tell Mr Robarts that I understand why his Masons are more important than we are, and we won't hold it against him. And as for you, Mr O'Brien, it has been my pleasure to meet you. Let me know if – and when – you're in Belfast. We'd like to entertain you the Irish way.'

He shook hands with them and watched as they left the tavern. He sat down with his unfinished whisky. There were major problems not just at this yard but in the whole ship-building industry. It seemed to him there were two issues – a shortage of good hemp and a crisis of trust caused by the investigation. Everyone was scared. And where did that leave him? This was becoming far more serious than he had ever thought. And dangerous too. Someone was going to pay. With St Vincent's obsession about theft, corruption and fraud, they had to find a suspect. But the problem was that the crisis was being caused *by the investigation itself* – and if he, Josiah, reported *that*, St Vincent's enemies would bring the First Lord down. This was not going the way he planned; the more he thought about it, the more he realised he might even be in danger.

The next morning he reported on his evening with the contractors. Robarts smoothed his hair carefully as he listened. 'They're right. There's nothing wrong with their hemp. The problem with the rope is in the yarn spinning. We're trying to reduce our costs by cutting the hemp with jute from Scotland. It's a lot cheaper. It ought to work, but our experiments may have resulted in problems. Just keep that under your hat, will you?'

'Where does the jute come from?'

'It comes from Dundee. Don't know much about it. One of their merchants is in town at the moment. He's brought one of the landowners with him. Lord Minto.'

Josiah bit his tongue. Better not admit he knew Minto.

~

Josiah's relationship with Janet continued to flourish. After their night together, a little embarrassment had hung in the air when they met in the dining room. While the inspectors were around she was very formal, calling him 'Mr O'Brien'. And there was little opportunity to get together. Between the inspectors and Janet's mother, they could rarely find a time to be alone at the house. Instead on Sunday, which was her day off, Janet arranged to meet Josiah at a country tavern a few miles away.

They tramped over the hills near Devonport, enjoying the late summer sun. Josiah found her fascinating; her chatter obliged him to open up. His main problem was how to dissemble, to avoid telling her lies while keeping his secret. The more time they spent together and the more they explored each other in the remote dells and fields amidst waving barley lit by poppies, the more his secret life weighed on him. And he realised he was falling in love. He could not get her out of his mind when he was at work. The impossibility of their relationship weighed on him. He loved her company so much he asked himself what life would be like without her.

Minto and his merchant partner visited the yard a few days after Josiah's conversation with Robarts. Josiah sat at his desk, uncomfortably aware that Minto might recognise him, although it was a few years since they had met. Thankfully, it seemed he remained undiscovered.

Later that day, Robarts called him into his office, closing the door after him and pulling down the blind.

Josiah sat uneasily, wondering what had happened.

'I have something important to say to you. It's as I thought. There is an unjust investigation in progress. We are by no means the only place being examined. Every yard in the country is being scrutinised by St Vincent's men, but our production is down and a backlog of work is building up. I had to be very careful what I said to Minto, him being a high government official.'

'What did you talk about?'

'The price of jute, and the opportunity jute provides us to keep rope prices from going through the roof.'

'Did you tell him about the accidents?'

'Yes, I did. I managed to get their prices down. Now, Mr O'Brien, can I trust you with another mission? I want you to meet with Lord Minto and pass a message along to him. I couldn't do it openly in the office and I have to be very careful about anything that would raise suspicions elsewhere, if you know what I mean. I'm sure I'm being watched.'

'Am I the person to do that? After all—'

Robarts interrupted. 'Mr O'Brien, you are a person of considerable ability. Your naval experiences have served you well. I trust you with the message I want you to carry.'

Josiah thought quickly. He'd have to count on Minto's memory failing him, or raise Robarts' suspicions by refusing. 'Very well, Mr Robarts. I'll carry the message for you.'

'Here's the envelope with my note. Minto knows the government people. It's an opportunity I can't afford to miss. My note gives a franker opinion than I was able to say when he was here. Be sure to show his lordship due respect. Take off your hat when addressing him and remember to bow. Don't drink too much if they ask you to stay! Find out as much as you can about this investigation. Explain that the yard is seizing up. We can't deliver the ships the navy wants on time, and already I'm under criticism for that.'

'Yes, sir. I'll be very careful. Will I see him alone or will his factor be there too?'

'I've passed the message on that it would be better if you see him alone. That way you'll learn more. Just be careful. Now, are there any more questions?'

'Where will I meet him?'

'At his hotel in Plymouth. I'll arrange for someone to get you there.'

It was still light when Josiah set off, although it was after seven in the evening. A cab took him to The Duke of Cornwall Hotel in Plymouth. Minto was waiting in the lobby.

Josiah approached and bowed. 'My lord, I'm Mr O'Brien from Mr Robarts' office. I'm here to give you a note from Mr Robarts.'

'Mr O'Brien, why don't we leave the hotel and go for an evening stroll; what do you say?'

The two men descended the steps of the hotel, Minto leading, and together they walked briskly towards the Hoe.

'How are you, Josiah? More to the point, what are you doing masquerading as Mr O'Brien?' Minto laughed, a chuckle spreading and expanding into a full and unseemly guffaw. He spluttered, 'Really, Josiah, I have a better memory than you think. What the devil are you doing working as a clerk at the dockyard?'

Josiah blushed. 'You are surely confusing me with someone else, my lord.'

'Nonsense, man. I have seen through your disguise. You can't deceive me. I would have recognised Fanny's boy anywhere.'

Josiah sighed. There was no point clinging on. Minto was more amused than upset. Best be open. He looked at the ground, rubbing his ear, and said, 'You're right, my lord. I *am* Josiah Nisbet. I'm working for Davison, trying to root out evidence of corruption in the dockyards. Davison is passing on my findings to Lord St Vincent. There are inspectors here as well – as you heard from Mr Robarts – but they don't know who I am or what I'm doing. My job is to see what is happening from the inside.'

'Why, Josiah?'

'I'm an unemployed captain, sir. In times gone by I would have had Father's help, but he is preoccupied. If I give St Vincent what he wants he will help me find command of another frigate and get my career back on track.'

'Do you have what he wants?'

Josiah paused. Could he trust Minto? He couldn't tell a barefaced lie, especially after all Robarts had shown him. 'Not yet.'

'Josiah, let me explain a few things. St Vincent is First Lord of the Admiralty for the Addington government. They came to power to make peace with France. St Vincent is navy through and through, and what he is doing – in *his* mind – is strengthening the navy by rooting out corruption. He has credibility too, because he built the most successful team of fighting men as commander of the Mediterranean fleet. He has convinced Addington and the others that his efforts will reduce government expenditure and improve the quality of the ships built.'

Josiah shook his head, trying to make sense of it all. St Vincent was no doubt trying to strengthen the navy, but from what he'd seen so far, his efforts were seriously undermining it. 'My lord, St Vincent's inspectors have slowed the yards to a crawl. Everyone is looking over their shoulder, afraid to be seen and unable to tell the truth. If this carries on the navy will be very short of ships.'

'My colleagues in opposition – Mr Pitt in particular – are convinced Napoleon is set on destroying us. This peace is a sham, an opportunity for Napoleon to re-arm. If we are ruining our yards and undermining our capacity to build ships, that is an explosive accusation.'

From the Hoe, the ships in the harbour were glistening with lights as the sun darkened in the west.

There was an uncomfortable silence. Then Minto said, 'Josiah, I am very fond of Fanny. I have never for one moment doubted her, and I admired her resolve to separate from Horatio rather than dishonour her reputation. She is admired at the highest levels of this country. As her son, I respect you too. You have much of her and Horatio about you. If you are willing, I will take this message to my friends in the opposition. Mr Pitt will want to know what you have learned. I am sure you will earn *his* gratitude.'

Josiah thought for a moment. Davison had set him the task of rooting out corruption for St Vincent's benefit, but instead the utter chaos he'd found in the industry reflected badly on St Vincent's management. If the news got out, it would spell political disaster for the man whose cause he was supposed to be supporting. When St Vincent found that Josiah had betrayed him, what then?

'Good evening, Mr O'Brien!'

It was Rockford, the inspector.

'Oh, hello, Mr Rockford. A nice evening to catch a sea breeze.'

Rockford lifted his hat and walked away in the direction of Devonport.

'Who was that?'

'Most unfortunate! The senior inspector. He thinks I'm a working man. His suspicions will be aroused.'

'Don't worry too much, Josiah. I am available any time.' He passed his card to Josiah.

They had reached the hotel.

'I will say farewell. Fear nothing. Your career will resume – soon, I am sure. In the meantime your secret is safe.'

He climbed the steps while Josiah returned on foot to Fishponds Street, worried that his future hung increasingly in the balance.

# CHAPTER 7

The next morning Josiah told Robarts that Minto had asked him many questions about the yard. Robarts, he could see, was pleased that this 'back door' had been opened. When Josiah saw Rockford later at the lodgings he said nothing about the chance meeting on the Hoe. Had he forgotten about it? When, a week later, Rockford and Gaines returned to London, Josiah was confident his cover was still intact.

It was a great shock when he arrived at the yard office one Monday morning to find Robarts packing up his office.

He seemed very upset. 'They fired me,' he said. He'd been warned that a warrant for his arrest was pending. His nervous hands ruffled his untidy hair and beads of sweat ran down a sallow face. 'They claim I'm embezzling the yard's funds!' he said weakly. 'I have no idea what they've found.'

'What will you do?'

'I'm suspended pending further investigation, and a new manager is arriving tomorrow to take over my job. That's all I know. This is what I get for thirty years of loyal service!'

Josiah attempted to comfort him. 'It's probably a precaution while they finish their investigation. You'll be back in the job in no time.'

'No, I'm out of work. My pension is suspended, my prospects hopeless. You'll be asked to give evidence to the Constable. I hope you will vouch for me, Josiah!'

'I certainly will. You've put your trust in me, and I won't let you down.'

Robarts took a large handkerchief and mopped the sweat from his brow. 'I better get on with this. You know where I live. Keep in touch, won't you?'

The following day, Josiah's new manager arrived. Cripps summoned Josiah into his office. He was a little man with cold eyes behind small wire spectacles. He wore a black worsted suit with a starched stock wound tightly around a scrawny neck.

'I will get to the bottom of this pervasive corruption.' His voice was civil but querulous and assertive. 'You are not above suspicion, O'Brien. As Robarts' assistant, you are aware of the illicit payments made and his dealings with the contractors. I expect you to be at the forefront in rooting out malpractice!'

Josiah started. He could hardly believe his ears. *He's threatening me, to get more evidence against Robarts!*

Later that day the head of each department was fired with a warning. They shuffled from office, complaining loudly. In their place came men from London. None of them, it turned out, had worked at a naval yard before. They were builders, carpenters, iron-workers pleased to find work and eager to do Cripps' bidding.

Josiah told Janet about them that night. 'The yard's already in trouble,' he said. 'It will fall apart unless something is done.'

Cripps gave Josiah instructions to uncover more evidence of theft and overcharging. He was able to point to a few irregularities, though loathing what Cripps was doing.

Janet was become anxious too. Perhaps she suspected he might leave. She urged him to look for another job and settle down. Her implication was plain enough, and he thought about it. Janet had shown him there was an alternative, a simple life – with her. It was strangely tempting. He loved her, and for the first time in his life was learning what it meant to be looked after by a fine woman who cared about him.

Conditions at the yard were chaotic. It had happened quickly. It used to be a good place to work. Now the opposite was true. Everything was sacrificed to meet the new standards. The slow decision-making meant that the yard employed fewer workers. A line of unemployed labourers grew longer by the day. The two Irishmen in the hatchelling shed lost their jobs. Janet's rented rooms were unfilled. Only the inn was busy – with angry men, intoxicated on cider. The constables were called in. There was fighting and arrests.

*Thalia* returned to port. A note arrived at Fishponds Street from Yule.

*My dear Nisbet,*
*We are back in Plymouth, taking on supplies before departing for Gibraltar. Captain Kent and I would like to entertain you aboard. Are you free this coming Sunday? Yule.*

It was at this point he made a mistake that he was to regret. He was careless. He dashed off a letter to Davison. He felt he owed an explanation for his change of heart. He knew now that finding corruption was the least of the difficulties this yard faced. The change in management on top of months of auditing and checking was the final disaster.

*Plymouth Docks*
*September 1803*

*My dear Davison,*
*I am writing to let you know my recent findings at the yard. In my last letter I told you that there was evidence of corruption, but that it was much exaggerated and largely money under the table to facilitate and expedite the otherwise unwieldy processes faced by the management. Now, however, everything has changed. The yard manager Mr Robarts has been relieved of his duty and replaced by someone with no experience. All major works have halted, including the production of new ships. In view of the possible outbreak of war, this is nothing short of catastrophe. If you have influence with St Vincent you must convince him to change direction before it is too late. The yard was visited by Lord Minto, who came with his Scottish connections to promote the sale of Scottish jute. He recognised me and we had a conversation in which, to explain my presence here, I had to mention your work. He seemed to understand what was happening. I thought that you should know this because he has strong connections with the opposition in parliament. They are building a case against St Vincent. God knows he is providing them with all the evidence they need!*

*Sincerely,*
*Josiah Nisbet.*

On Sunday afternoon he and Janet met at their country pub on the outskirts of Devonport for a picnic. He was to dine on *Thalia* that evening, so they did not linger at the tavern as they usually did, but set off along a country lane that led to a wood where they could be alone.

The sun was up and the leaves were changing colour. It was a lovely day and Josiah looked forward eagerly to their lovemaking. But there was something wrong. Janet had something on her mind that she was not telling him. She was silent and broody.

He tried to make up for her silence by talking about the yard. 'Cripps is the greatest disaster I've ever seen, and I've worked for some terrible admirals,' he said.

She was taking no interest, walking a little slower than he, perhaps half a pace behind, looking at the ground. It was a grand day, though, with the autumn sun warm on their backs, the birds singing and the wheat awaiting harvest waving in the slight breeze.

He stopped and she walked past him. 'Janet!' he called. 'What's wrong? What's upsetting you?'

'You're *not* who I thought you were.'

His mind raced. 'Come on, Janet, what do you mean?'

'You aren't Joss O'Brien. You have another name and you're not a working man; you're "quality". You took advantage of me, you did. And I thought we was a couple!'

'Who told you this tale?'

'Doesn't matter now. All I want to know from you is the truth.'

'It does matter who told you this. It could make all the difference to me.'

They'd stopped walking. She stood a distance away from him as if she hated him. Her hands were on her hips, her straw hat on the back of her head, her face red and wet from tears.

'Come, love, don't be like that. I'll tell you all there is to know. Let's be lovers.'

'No, Mr Josiah Nisbet! I know your name now. I'm onto you!'

'Janet, it *is* my name. But I had good reasons for adopting a cover name. Let me—'

'No, let *me* explain to you. I had an agent of the government call to see me. He asked all about you, about your "job" at the yard. He said you were a spy. He said you were the son of the famous Lord Nelson. He said you were angry that you'd been overlooked for promotion and were now working against our country. And he asked me all about you. And I told him everything!'

'Janet, let me—'

But she was now in full flight. She gathered herself and with a steady voice closed off any chance of him explaining himself. 'You're a repulsive French spy, sneaking into my house, sneaking into my bed!'

'Janet, who is this man? How did he convince you? Is he following us?'

'When he gets his hands on you, you're a dead man. As for me, I never want to see you again!'

She turned on her heel in the direction they had come. Josiah was stunned, but he realised the danger he was in. She was working with *them*! She had chosen this remote spot on purpose.

He heard approaching footsteps. He looked around nervously. The footsteps had stopped as if some pursuer had seen his reaction and was considering the next move. He was standing at a five-barred gate. With a bound he was over, picking himself up and sprinting along the edge of the grain field to a copse. Thudding footsteps followed him. He jumped over the stone wall and ran into trees. There was a river running through the forest, and he waded upstream in case there were dogs. After the copse there was another open field and then a larger wood. He was panting, his mind racing with a burning sense of betrayal. Davison! St Vincent must have told Davison to clean up the mess, and Davison had found someone to do the job.

He paused to gain his breath. Panting heavily, he listened. There was only silence. He had thrown them off the scent. He had left his pursuers behind. He surveyed the horizon from a hilltop, searching the Sound for *Thalia*. The grey-blue waters reached out from the port city towards the English Channel on the horizon. He could make out Mount Edgecumbe and St Nicholas Island and the forts guarding the mouth of the harbour. Over to the right were the chimneys and cranes of the dockyard, his home. There was *Thalia*, anchored on the far side of the bay, her lines unmistakable. He remembered Yule telling him that they would sail the following morning. They would bring her into the quay tonight to board the troops. That's when he would make his move. But whoever was following him would be there watching for him.

He stooped and rubbed his hand in the red Devon soil and rubbed it into his beard. He took off his coat and ripped out the lining. He fashioned the silk into a crude scarf and wrapped it round his throat. He needed a hat. Approaching the town, he stopped two youths and offered to buy a cap from them. He left them laughing at their good fortune while he pulled the brim low over his face and made his way towards the docks. He found a public house opposite the quay, full of sailors the worse for wear. It would serve his purpose, as it had a clear view from its bow windows.

As he sat there, with a glass half full of cider, he saw *Thalia* making her way towards the dock, as he had predicted. Outside, the regiment were formed into lines. They would be boarding soon.

Just as he began to feel that things were progressing nicely, he saw a heavy-set man enter the pub and talk to the landlord. He raised his tankard to cover his face. Josiah looked scruffy, like a sailor. His pursuers weren't looking for sailors. The man looked around the crowded saloon. Had he been spotted?

A press-gang came into the pub, and the publican angrily told them to get out. Josiah started to his feet, a plan in his mind. Outside, the gang were stopping sailors and offering sign-on bonuses.

Josiah walked up to the leader. 'I know someone interested. Can you come around the corner and talk?'

The man looked at him sharply and nodded his head. They walked around the corner from the pub.

'Someone's following me,' Josiah said. 'I owe them money. They'll kill me. I have to make out that I've been press-ganged. I want to get to *Thalia*, over there. I'll pay you!'

'How much?'

'I want to look like I'm being taken against my will. I'll give you ten pounds.'

'Make it fifteen and we take the bonus for pressing you too.'

'Very well. I'll go back into the pub and you come and get me there, all four of you.'

It went as he had suggested. It was dark now, and the pub was still heaving. Josiah sat down and picked up his glass.

The four men in the gang burst in. 'There he is. That's the bastard that jumped ship. You, sir.' He pointed to Josiah. 'Come quietly. Put up a fight and it'll be the worse for you!'

Josiah jumped to his feet as if to make a run. A billy club came down on his shoulder. Another tripped him and hit him on the head. They carried him out fighting and cursing. He was bundled across the road and past the marine sentry.

'Take him below!'

They dragged him down the companionway to the bottom of the ship and into a dark room on the orlop deck. A lantern flickered dimly. He gave them their money, complaining that they had hit him too hard. They left, laughing at their easy pickings. The door slammed behind them and a cross bar was put in place.

Josiah sat on the floor, listening to the sounds of the ship readying for sea. The excitement drained away and the enormity of what he had done began to dawn on him. Everything had gone sour. He had given information to St Vincent's enemies by talking to Minto. He had misjudged the situation. Worst of all was the break-up with Janet. He missed her. Was he guilty of trifling with her? He *had* intended to let her know who he was the moment he could do so safely. But she had decided he was a blackguard. Could he blame her? She had declared herself the moment she came to his bed, and he had not dissuaded her then. He loved her now. It was too late.

His failure swept over him. His prospects were worse than they had been two years ago. And, depending on *Thalia's* movements, he might be away from England for months – or even years.

# PART 2: OCTOBER 1803

# CHAPTER 8

He woke up as the ship pitched. They were underway, out in the Channel. He could hear familiar sounds: timbers creaking, footsteps on the deck, shouted orders and, from somewhere in the distance, a thin voice singing a sea shanty. The lantern was flickering, its candle low. He rose to his feet, his head aching where he had been struck. He felt the bruise; his hair was matted with blood and there was a bump the size of an apple. He asked himself why no one had come to get him. Where was Yule?

He lay back on the short bunk and fell asleep. When he awoke, the door was still locked. He wondered, and then realisation began to dawn. This ship was not *Thalia*. He knew *Thalia* from its keel to its tops. This was different. She rode the waves differently.

The sounds she made were different. She smelt different. What had happened since the Press-Gang brought him aboard? They had left him alone all night. Why?

Something had gone seriously wrong; they'd tricked him. He was not on *Thalia*. It was some other ship. If he was on a navy ship it could take months to sort this out. It occurred to him that pressed men often dived over the side and swam for the shore. Should he try that? He rationalised; he was a commissioned officer in the navy, a post captain on half pay; they could not press him! There would be hell to pay if they tried. He would demand they put him ashore.

His fit of anger subsided and he considered his situation calmly. He was still in serious danger. He had no doubt that the man who had interrogated Janet meant business. His pursuers would try to kill him. This was not a matter of mistaken identity; he knew enough to ruin the First Lord of the Admiralty, and even to threaten the government itself. Davison would be put on trial. He thought about the warning poor Janet had given him: 'When he gets his hands on you, you're a dead man.'

The day passed slowly. He was very hungry, and his mouth was dry. He lay on the bunk, his mind rambling. Why so many enemies? He was too ambitious. Horatio had pushed his promotions through ahead of his peers and perhaps faster than his experience warranted. He reviewed the events of the last two years. Before *Thalia* he had had the ship that was all he had hoped for, all that a young captain could desire: *Bonne Citoyenne*. But it had not been enough – he *had* to be a post captain and have his frigate. In consequence, surrounded by enemies who reported his every mistake to his father, he had been trapped between disloyal officers and critical admirals. Only Duckworth, the last of the admirals, had approved. And then they had turned *Thalia* into a troop ship and he had gone on that mad expedition to uncover corruption in the dockyard. He must be insane. He curled up and sobbed.

꩜

'When he awoke he resolved to gather himself; ten years at sea had taught him never to surrender to self-pity. Survival required acceptance – no matter how bad the situation was. Without doubt the best of his career in the navy was in the past. The glory of the past would remain just a memory. He must rebuild, and the first step was to resolve to do so. His father had done it. He too had been on the beach, despised by his enemies and all the senior admirals. Before *Agamemnon*.

It was dark. He rattled the door again and called

for water. Silence – other than the creaking of timber, the rushing of the sea as it swirled past the hull and the sound of a rat scurrying for the bilge. The ship was running smoothly. Then it dawned on him: he was aboard a merchantman. There were too few crew aboard for it to be a navy ship. He'd heard about seamen seized to make up the crew of merchant vessels. It was rare because the captain could be accused of kidnapping. To take that sort of risk the voyage would have to be a lengthy one. Was the ship a convict carrier, bound for New South Wales? Not likely – it would be packed. No, this one was carrying a different cargo. Then he realised: the ship was running high in the water. Lightly loaded. Why would a large merchantman be half empty? Couldn't be an Indiaman. That would be packed with goods and machinery. It must be on a trading route in which the cargo was loaded at the other end and brought back to England.

He sniffed. The faint smell that permeated the ship made him think again. It was a smell of the stable. If it was on a journey to the Indies there would be a scent of spice. That was why the idea of a convict ship had occurred to him.

But this was no convict ship; this must be a Slaver.

A filthy trade. Only owners and the captains grew rich from it. The crew were scum. They slept on the decks while the cargo was packed in below, and often met their end at the hands of desperate slaves. How had this happened to him? He decided he *must* not reveal his identity. The captain would surely toss him overboard rather than risk the consequences of kidnapping a post captain.

The door swung open, and a figure silhouetted in the light said, 'Come with me!'

Josiah put on his coat. They climbed the steps of the companionway to a cabin at the stern. He guessed it was the master's. Smaller than his own on *Thalia*, with a view of a white blaze – the ship's wake.

'Sit down!' the seaman said.

He sat, and the seaman stood behind him. They waited. The door opened and two men entered; a small, bearded man wearing a buff-coloured coat, accompanied by a thin tall man.

The bearded man had thick black hair and steely grey eyes. He took his seat at the desk and stared at Josiah, stroking his beard slowly. 'I am Captain Bacon and this is Mr James, my first mate. You are on the merchantman *Amelia* bound for St Kitts by way of the Guinea Coast.'

'This is a slave ship, ain't it?' His accent, perfected by months in the dockyard, had not deserted him.

'Clever! That tells me you are a seaman.'

'Yes. I am. Joss O'Brien, formerly of the Royal Navy, lately of the Plymouth Dockyard. Why am I prisoner on a slave ship?'

The captain nodded to the mate, who gave Josiah a painful smack on the ear with his knuckles.

'You are here to do my bidding; not to ask questions. Any trouble and you'll have a watery grave. Hear me?'

Josiah said nothing. Another blow – this time the other side. It stung but he kept quiet, burning with anger. He must keep his temper.

Bacon said, 'If you play the game you stand to do well. I can be generous to those who obey orders. Now, answer my questions. How old are you?'

Josiah thought quickly. If he told his real age, he would appear inexperienced. He needed a proper job without telling them all he had done. 'I'm twenty-eight.'

'You look young. Tell me about the navy.'

'I began as a captain's servant. I fought in frigates, ships of the line – you name it. I was a midshipman until my discharge two years since. I'm known for my seamanship. I'm a good navigator and can lead a crew in a fight.'

'Ever been a gun captain?'

'Yes – I started as a powder monkey and worked my way up.'

'Very well. You sign the papers and I'll make you a second mate. One pound a week. You'll get paid when we get to Nevis, with a bonus when we get the slaves to market there. You agree?'

'Yes, sir.'

'Very well. Sign here.'

He put the papers on the table. Josiah read through the simple document, picked up the pen and signed his adopted name with a scrawl. The captain dusted the paper with sand and put it in his drawer.

'Good. We are beginning to understand each other. I warn you, though: don't fight me or I'll break you. Mr James'—he nodded to the first mate—'take him to his quarters. Give him a meal.'

James took him to a small cabin on the main deck. 'We'll outfit you from the ship's store tomorrow. At the change of watch we'll have dinner. You mess with Mr Wishbone, ship's carpenter, Mr Allenby, boatswain, and Surgeon Smith. Got it?'

His voice was brusque, but Josiah knew he had gained some respect.

'How did I get here? I thought I would be taken to *Thalia*.'

'The Press Gang. They knew we needed a mate and a gunner. We paid them. They seemed to know you. *The Press Gang seemed to know me. Davison's men?* Now, take a look around the ship and I'll see you at dinner.'

Josiah sank onto the bunk, his head in his hands, confidence ebbing as he considered the situation. The slapping of the water on the hull and the ghostly emptiness preyed on him. He climbed the companion-way again.

The ship was running on a broad reach, canting in the breeze. She was fast. There'd be no convoy. She'd have to be able to outrun French or Spanish warships. He imagined her fully laden, stinking to high heaven, being chased by his frigate. He'd stopped Spanish slavers. He remembered the cries of chained slaves and the vile sicknesses they had. He usually took them to the next port of call and left them for the prize agents to dispose of in the slave market.

He continued his exploration, picking up a lantern as he made his way to the lower decks. There was no one to be seen other than two hands at the wheel. She was a three-masted barque, twelve guns – sleek lines for a merchantman. The stern quarters, where Josiah's cabin was located, were separated from the slave quarters by bulkheads. On the main deck were crew quarters, the galley, carpenter's shop, surgeon's cabin and hospital, cattle and sheep pen and a food storeroom. Below the crew quarters was another deck with cannon on each side and room for guards to sling their hammocks.

There was iron grill covering a companionway that

sealed off the slave quarters on the deck below. He pulled up the grill and descended, carrying the lantern. He calculated there was room for a hundred slaves on each of two decks. Above each tiny slot, barely enough for a man to lie full length, were ring bolts to secure the chains. The empty quarters were occupied by cargo that would be traded – guns, knives, bales of clothing, lamps and kitchen utensils. The whole thing was gruesomely efficient and reminded Josiah of the *Dolphin*, the old frigate-turned-hospital ship he had commanded years ago.

Nevertheless, after a few days he realised he was pleased to be back at sea, even on this horrible ship. The sea was his home. He thought about the voyage – to Africa and the West Indies. The Leeward Islands, where *Amelia* was headed, included Nevis – the home of his father, who had died when he was an infant, and his mother's family too. He'd heard all about the Nisbet plantation from his mother. His grandfather and his great-uncle had been island magnates. Slavery was an important trade, Horatio used to say. It supplied the sugar islands with labour, and sugar was vital to the prosperity of Britain. Everyone knew that if you owned sugar, you were as rich as an Indian nabob.

That night as he lay on his bed, he counted his losses and wondered what would happen at the dockyard.

The bitterness of Janet's parting words clung to him. And Fanny. What would she think when he didn't write? His father disowned him. His mother had been deserted. And he was captive on this filthy slave ship. He had been chewed up and spat out. There was no option; he must survive, return to England and deal with the unfinished business there.

## CHAPTER 9

On his second day aboard Josiah met the rest of the crew. They were the refuse of the ports of England – feared by naval Press Gangs or sly enough to stay beyond their reach. With no fear of the lash, they mingled mutinous contempt of authority with surliness toward each other.

At his first mess, James had introduced him to the officers as 'Mr O'Brien, formerly of the Royal Navy'. It was awkward. They all knew *how* he had come to be aboard. Josiah studied them quietly. The carpenter and the boatswain were men of few words. The surgeon looked familiar. His was a most difficult job, keeping two hundred slaves alive. And – Josiah recalled – under law, he was the only man who could challenge the captain on the condition of the ship.

His log would be reviewed by government inspectors as well as owners. It was the interest of the latter that gave the surgeon his authority; the more slaves who survived the middle passage, the more profit there would be. There was no like 'incentive' paid for keeping the crew alive.

They told him the Slaver had been newly copper-bottomed and was very fast. She had been captured from the French the year before by another slaver, the *Kitty*, and condemned as a prize. The Liverpool slave-ship owners had bought her and re-equipped her for the trade. *Probably the Colquitts*. This was her first voyage under new ownership.

On watch the next day, Josiah mused how his life had changed. One minute a dockyard worker, now second mate on a slave ship. If this had happened a year ago, he would have made such a fuss – and he would probably have been thrown overboard. After months at the yard he had a different outlook: less privileged – more realistic. He was making a fresh start – though where it would end was anyone's guess.

After months in England he loathed the indolent aristocratic London society. And he refused to 'make friends in high places', as his mother had urged. Merton was a stuffy museum satisfying his father's endless demand for praise. He was disgusted; he had promised he wouldn't think about Horatio and Emma

Hamilton. He would not allow them to torture him with the memories of their liaison in Palermo.

On the horizon was the outline of the French coast as they headed into the Bay of Biscay. Two weeks before he was seized, the Peace of Amiens had collapsed and Britain and France were at war again. There could be a skirmish at any moment. Napoleon had assembled a huge invasion army, but he didn't have the fleet to get them across the Channel. For years he had his army on the French coast, waiting to attack. How would he get them across the channel when the Royal Navy blockaded his ports with every available frigate and sloop? The threat was real enough and rumour had it French yards were busy building a new invasion fleet.

He felt vulnerable on this merchantman. Common sense said a lightly armed sloop could take a ship like this. There weren't enough men on *Amelia* to man her guns, sail the ship and fight hand to hand at the same time. He looked up at the rigging above; all sails were set, and in this breeze they were drawing nicely.

Off to port he saw a silhouette of a vessel. He put his glass to his eye. A frigate whose course would converge with *Amelia's*. He ran to the ratlines and sprinted to the tops. Yes a frigate, showing no flag. It had to be a Frenchman. He yelled to the seaman at the helm to signal the alarm. The bell rang and the crew assembled sluggishly in the waist of the ship. The captain was on the quarterdeck by the time he was back on deck.

'What the hell's going on, O'Brien?'

'A French frigate. They've spotted us and are preparing for a chase. Recommend you bear away to gain speed. We won't outrun them, but I have an idea.'

'What's that?'

'We'll fool them into believing they've got us and then give them a pounding and make our getaway.'

'What?'

'Raise as much sail as possible when I signal. As we near the frigate, take her as close under their stern as possible and wear to port. I will do some serious damage to their stern with the smasher. Then we'll haul up sail and make our escape while they're sorting themselves out.'

The captain looked at him narrowly, assessing what he had said. He smiled slyly. 'You done anything like this before?'

'I know what I'm doing.'

It must have been the tone in his voice. Bacon about to argue, turned to the first mate. 'Mr James!'

James was climbing the steps to the quarterdeck. 'Sir?'

'Assemble two gun crews for Mr O'Brien, at once,

on the foredeck. Get a party to carry powder and shot up from the armoury.'

Fourteen crewmen crowded around Josiah.

'Do whatever he tells you,' said Mr James.

'Anyone here fired a gun?'

'Yes, sir,' a boy spoke up. 'I have.'

Josiah's heart sank. 'Anyone else?' No response. 'Right, let's run them out and have a practice.'

There was enough time to explain the basics of firing the guns, but not enough to show how to reload. One round from each gun would have to do. There would be no second chance.

The frigate was closing. Josiah's team slowly hove the two carronades to the starboard side of the forecastle and loaded the first with powder and ball. The French ship was a mile away. *Amelia* had the advantage of the wind. Barely three hundred yards and they were within range of a broadside. A lesser captain would have hauled down his colours by now. At the last moment, and with almost naval precision, Bacon wore *Amelia* to port, presenting his carronades to the Frenchman's stern windows.

'Fire!'

The first gun launched its deadly cargo smashed into the frigate, wreaking havoc on the enemy's gun deck. A minute after, *Amelia's* second gun, primed with powder and grapeshot, followed suit, firing through the shattered windows of the great cabin. It was too fast for the enemy to respond. She would have to wear about amid the chaos of dying men and damage to their steering.

At Josiah's signal, sailors released the top gallants and studding sails, sheeting them home with an urgency primed by fear. *Amelia* shot forward like a greyhound. But as they passed the frigate's port rail a chaser fired; its ball flew across the deck of *Amelia*, striking the capstan, and bounced into the foresail, tearing it to shreds. A splinter of the wood hit Josiah in the chest, and he fell to the deck. He struggled back to his feet with a sense of triumph he hadn't experienced since his days on *Thalia*.

They carried him below to the hospital on a piece of the torn sail, his blood soaking the canvas. Surgeon Allison was in his empty ward, wearing a white apron. They lowered Josiah carefully. He stared up at the surgeon's red sideburns.

Allison gave him a portion of whisky to drink and a piece of rubber to bite on – for the pain. 'You're lucky, son. You'll live to fight another day,' he said.

*There was something very familiar about that voice.*

Josiah knew his injuries were less serious than the risk of infection. So many men died from gangrene. Josiah struggled from his berth as soon as he could and had a crew member sluice him with buckets of seawater. Then he put on a clean shirt and lay back down again.

Captain Bacon visited him and said, 'As fine a demonstration of gunnery I have ever seen! Where did you go to school?'

'Years of practice, sir. I studied under some of the best gunners in the Royal Navy.'

'You saved us from that Frenchman. Crippled him, you did. You've earned your pay. Take it easy and recover. Take a few days off.'

⌒

The wounds healed rapidly, and within a week Josiah resumed his duties. James had assigned him the roles of navigator and gunner. It was apparent to both of them Josiah excelled in each department and could be relied on. Between James and Josiah, respect fostered new trust.

In due course he was invited for dinner in Bacon's great cabin. Josiah looked enviously at his spacious accommodation. Hardly as grand as his captain's cabin on *Thalia* but much superior to his own cramped quarters. They dined on roasted lamb and potatoes, vegetables and gravy – all accompanied by a good claret.

He studied Captain Bacon. He was an educated man. He had worked his way up from the lower deck by hard work and demonstrated ruthlessness enough to command this slaver.

Bacon was unshaven and his cabin untidy. His eyes were dull grey, flecked with black. Dead eyes. They started menacingly from beneath bushy eyebrows, but tonight he was in a good mood. He thanked Josiah again.

Josiah said, 'The French have fine ships, but ever since they guillotined their aristocratic captains, their officers lack authority and they've become lazy.'

'How did *Amelia* come to be in Plymouth?' asked Josiah. 'You're Liverpool, aren't you?'

Bacon's face changed. He folded his arms across his chest and glowered.

Josiah reassured him. 'You don't need to worry about me. I needed to get on a ship. This was as good as any.'

The captain relaxed. 'We lost our second mate overboard and we were short-handed. Needed a gunner too. We stopped in Plymouth to see if we could find sailors with navy experience.'

'What's Surgeon Allison's background?'

'Like you, Royal Navy. Served in the Mediterranean. This is his first passage on a slaver. This is a dirty business for a man like him. There's a big difference between this ship and any other. It's important he and I see eye to eye. You too!'

Everything will change when take our 'cargo' aboard. The ship will be a dangerous place and you and Allison will need your wits about you. All the time – got that?'

'Aye Sir.'

'Good. Now let me tell you what will happen when we get to the Guinea coast.'

Josiah discovered he now had the one essential ingredient needed by any officer – the trust of his crew. He had shown his courage, and now he showed willingness to undertake any necessary tasks around the ship. While he did so, Josiah observed the crew, deciding who would be reliable in a tight spot, who was lazy and who liked mischief.

It was a very different from life in the navy. In the navy, a ship could be at sea indefinitely, stopping only to pick up supplies of fresh food and water. Josiah had served on ships out of sight of land for weeks and months. A warship was like a town, packed with men needed for the fight and always on the hunt for the enemy or the enemy's merchantmen. *Amelia* was undermanned, and those serving on her were slack in their tasks; they might go missing when it was time to put their lives on the line.

They ran south past the familiar coastline of

Portugal. Josiah remembered his time aboard HMS *Dolphin,* the hospital ship which was his training ground for command. Months and months moored in the Tagus with plenty of time to resent his father and St Vincent for abandoning him.

When they passed Santa Cruz on the island of Tenerife he recalled that terrible night when his father, underestimating Spanish defences, had commanded the squadron to seize the port at night. The Spanish had been waiting. Horatio and Josiah had accompanied the sailors and marines and Horatio was badly wounded. Josiah bound his arm in a tourniquet and carried him to the launch. They rowed to the ship beneath fire from the Spanish cannon on the mole above.

Horatio had never forgiven Josiah for saving his life. He was just a lad, a foolish boy. His father's reward was command of that awful hospital ship. But, as he thought about it, watching the island silhouetted against the morning sun to larboard, it was the loss of Weatherhead which had changed everything. Weatherhead was his closest friend in the years they'd served on *Agamemnon* as ship's servants and midshipmen. He'd been like an older brother. His death had changed everything. There were no longer two of them against everything the navy served up. Josiah was alone. An awful loneliness dogged the next three years until he learned to survive on his own.

Something been taken from him with Weatherhead's death. He was distant even to those who loved him. And angry too.

As they approached the coast of Africa, he learned about the Guinea coast and the 'Castle'. That was what they called the trading post where the slaves were gathered by the company's agent. It was said slaves had to be captured many miles inland because the coastal areas had been denuded of people. Caravans of traders went inland where the chiefs sold their captives, their delinquents and, sometimes, anyone who would fetch a price.

Josiah had been duped and dragged aboard the *Amelia*. These black people were in a similar predicament; one minute living in a village, tilling the soil, raising a family; the next moment caught, shackled and marching to the coast, their worst fears bedevilling every minute.

*Amelia* approached her destination and anchored amid a fleet of merchant ships and other slavers. It was hot as hell and humid, and a strange smell pervaded the sea where they dropped anchor. Lighters came alongside and took their cargo ashore. Josiah and the crew were not allowed off the ship. Mr James was left in charge as Bacon visited with the Agent and supervised unloading of the goods they brought from England.

After two days, shackled captives were dragged aboard by the slavers – black men themselves, armed with whips. They were a miserable lot of slaves. Men and women. They were stripped naked of their rags, both men and women. They were hosed down and given fresh slops to wear. Surgeon Allison, with the help of an assistant, inspected each of them carefully for signs of the flux or smallpox. A few were returned ashore. Then the batch was marched below, wailing and screaming, to be shackled to their berths with lengths of chain and manacles. All the time shouting. The African guards shouted back in their own language. The cacophony of voices, cries, screams and curses, was deafening.

Josiah watched from the quarterdeck, reminding himself he too was a prisoner on this ship. He felt sick with horror and shame. His journey had started well. Now it was another matter. He considered his options. Perhaps he could swim ashore? Get another boat back to England. But doing nothing in the face of the few hopeless choices was the only sensible course of action.

They turned the ship around efficiently and were soon on their way with the cargo of two hundred slaves. Bacon and Allison argued publicly for the first time. Bacon wanted to carry another fifty. Allison insisted they stick to the number in their licence. It seemed for a moment that the dispute might end in something worse, but Allison had the final say. He would write the report for the ministry.

When Josiah went below to see the conditions for himself, he got no further than the first steps of the companionway before being overcome by the heat and the smell and vomiting in the scuppers. Acting out of self-preservation more than sympathy for the slaves' plight, he found and installed wind chutes. As the ship gained speed a current of air wafted through the lower decks, alleviating the fug, but causing the smell to pervade the whole ship. The captain complained and ordered them removed, but Allison supported him.

Seeking to learn more about the slaves' condition, Josiah visited Allison's cabin. The door was open, and Allison lay on his berth reading.

He knocked and Allison looked up. 'I've been expecting you. Come in.'

He was a short man with a bald head and ginger sideburns. He was wearing a loose cotton shirt stuffed into breeches.

'Expecting?'

'Yes, you know we've met before? You just can't remember where you saw me, but I remember you.'

'Was it on the *Dolphin?*'

'No, it was *Agamemnon*. I was the assistant to

John Roxburgh until she was sent home before the Battle of Cape St Vincent. You were just a lad, the Captain's boy.'

Josiah examined his face for sarcasm.

Allison continued. 'You were quiet, always trying hard to impress your father. But he was the Captain, and no matter what you did, it was never good enough. You and Weatherhead stuck together. Must have devastated you when he was killed. That right?'

Josiah hesitated. Allison knew his secret, but it seemed he hadn't told anyone. Why? Would he want something in exchange?

Josiah said: 'I'd prefer you keep my identity to yourself. It wouldn't help me if people knew who I was, and I am content with what I'm doing.'

Allison smiled and stroked his chin. 'Well, none of us is here because we want to be – except the Captain.'

'Why are you here?'

'It's a job. I need the money to support my family. I do it well.'

'What do you mean by "do it well"?'

'Keep them alive. As many as possible. Keep them healthy so they fetch a good price at the slave market at the other end.'

'Doesn't this filthy trade bother you?'

'I tell myself, so long as I keep them from dying

I've done my job. The rest is not my responsibility. They are on others' conscience after that.'

He was not sure that Allison was being honest with him. Was he really doing this for money?

'Whose consciences?'

'The plantation owners.'

'And *they* live comfortable lives, mostly in England.'

'What do you know about the trade, Josiah?'

Josiah was about to tell him that his own family were in the plantation business. He caught himself. 'I know very little, but I hate to see what we're doing. And I despise those who benefit from it and care nothing for these people.'

'You seem to have done pretty well. You navigate, train the crew in gunnery and help the purser with his figures. You seem … happy.'

'Well, that was until the slaves came aboard. I figure, like you, I'll get this done and be back in England before long. Forget about this.'

He swept his arms around, a gesture that took in the slaves, the ship and everyone aboard.

As he sparred with Allison, he reassessed his opinion of him. They had much in common. Neither of them was like the other officers. Allison had a conscience and he despised Bacon and the mission of the *Amelia*. Yet he had his price and so did Josiah.

They were a week's passage from the coast, and the hot north-easterly winds carried them towards the destination. They had a routine. Allison insisted that the slaves were exercised every day for an hour. The slaves were divided into cohorts of ten or fifteen, and, for twelve daylight hours, they were brought up and marched round in a shambling circuit, chains jangling, while crew members stood by with truncheons, and sailors armed with muskets watched them cautiously from the foredeck. When the slaves appeared from below, blinking in the sunlight, they were hosed with cold seawater. Women received the same treatment but the women were partitioned off in a separate area of the deck and given a longer time there. The crew shouted appreciative comments at them until Bacon told them to shut their mouths or risk a flogging. The lower the tension on board, the better. He wanted no unnecessary provocation.

# CHAPTER 10

In a dying breeze the slave ship *Amelia* crept along, carrying as much canvas as possible while baking sun bathed its deck. Three weeks had passed since they had left Africa. Tempers were short and arguments became frequent. Morale among the crew was at its lowest. Conditions below were bad and getting worse by the hour. Allison argued with the captain about the slaves' diet. A miasma of stableyard stink clung to everything.

Then, when it seemed they would never find a breeze again, a powerful southerly blew up. In a matter of minutes, sails were shortened, the slaves were taken below and hatches battened. Josiah made sure the cannon were all double-lashed. Within the hour the stiff breeze had become a roaring gale. Hands took in sail while the helmsman struggled to keep *Amelia* from rounding up. At last, when sails had been reduced to a small storm jib on the forestay, the ship righted itself and was smashing into mountainous waves. Two of the crew were posted below as guards, to watch for trouble. Josiah imagined the scene. It would be chaotic – terrified slaves attempting to brace themselves, manacles chafing, vomiting from sea sickness; a small lantern chasing its shadows would be the only light in the awful blackness.

From the quarterdeck, where Josiah stood with the helmsman, the view was of endless roaring seas: white-capped rollers marching towards them, carrying the ship to the sky and plunging its bow into each trough, waist-high water roaring across the deck, and spume drenching the men at the wheel. Josiah had lived through too many storms to be scared, yet he wondered how they would come through this. He recalled a terrible storm off the Sardinian coast when they lost their main mast and were a drifting on a lee shore. They had jettisoned everything to keep the ship afloat – the cattle and sheep, heavy guns, even furniture. They couldn't afford to do that now. They had to keep these slaves alive, and they needed all their supplies.

At that moment, Surgeon Allison appeared on deck. 'Joss, we have problems below! They're getting a battering down there. Broken limbs and worse. Can we change course, find better weather, at least reduce the tossing?'

'Believe me we're safer heading into the wind than running before it. We'll be in this weather for another twelve hours at least!'

Allison hurried off to talk to the captain, but Josiah doubted the captain would order anything different. He was right.

Bacon emerged on deck with Allison. 'O'Brien, how is the ship handling?'

'We'll be fine as long as the weather stays like this. If the hurricane gets worse, we'll have problems.'

James came on deck. His normal stolid demeanour was gone; he was ashen faced – a frightened man. 'We've some choices to make, captain,' James said.

'What?'

'We must ditch half the guns and throw stores and half of the slaves overboard. The sooner we get on with it, the better!'

Allison said, 'This is madness. These are human beings! This is murder that you're proposing.'

Bacon said, 'Mr Allison, you have no voice in this decision. I am the captain and I have the final say on matters affecting the safety of the ship!'

'*I* am the one who'll have to report on this in court, for a trial will be inevitable. I have my duties to consider!'

They glared at each other.

Josiah intervened. 'We're in a bad situation, true, but the ship is robust. Let's not abandon our principles to fear. What's needed is the very best seamanship on the part of the crew. Captain, make sure the men know that we need their complete dedication. Promise them extra shares if we get through this. When the wind drops I'll wear her around and we'll run before the seas.'

Bacon considered the proposals. 'Very well, O'Brien, but if we lose a mast then we'll ditch cargo, slaves included! Carry on. Mr James, assemble the crew and tell them they'll be rewarded if we get through this, but we need their obedience to every order. No grog will be served until this is over. Anyone disobeying your orders, put them in irons.'

The wind, which had dropped slightly as they spoke, picked up again, and Josiah asked himself if his advice made sense. He had jettisoned guns and supplies when he was captain of *Thalia*. But on that vessel, no bigger than this one, he had had a crew of three hundred and fifty and supplies for three months. *Amelia* was a lighter vessel. But they would be safe as long as the crew worked together.

Twelve hours passed by. The hatches were still closed. There was no food, just biscuit and water. Josiah remained on watch. He was wet and exhausted, eyes bleary and legs stiff. But he needed to be here. He knew more about this than men twice his age and, he admitted to himself, he enjoyed the danger. This was his world. Since he was thirteen, the sea had been his life, and he had learned to command a ship under any conditions. He plotted their route as they slowly travelled south. He had the confidence of crew and captain. He had kept them from panicking. So long as this was over in a day or so they could recover. Any longer and there would be deaths.

Soon after he noticed that, while the wind continued to howl, it had lost some of its power. The seas were still mountainous. Later on, as the wind backed, Josiah wore the ship around to run before the wind. He deployed a sea anchor of spars, lashed together, to slow the ship. The wind continued to move to the east and they changed course, putting up sail and surfing the steep waves. At last, forty-eight hours after the storm blew up, things were calm enough and James grudgingly took over. Josiah retreated to his cabin to catch a few hours of sleep.

When he awoke, the sun was setting and the seas were calm. He washed and dressed in fresh clothes. When he emerged from his cabin he saw that the decks were full of crew and slaves. Two separate groups of slaves, one male and the other female, were being exercised; they were shuffling slowly around the hatches. Seamen with muskets perched in the crosstrees, while guards armed with cutlasses and whips herded the men and women to different stations to be washed and fed. Evidently there was a cleaning operation going on below decks; great buckets of human waste were being passed hand to hand and tossed over the side of the ship. A line of detritus stretched hundreds of yards in the ship's wake, and gulls were swarming and crying.

The slaves were mostly quieter; only a few were complaining. What could they do with a crew so alert and armed? Allison was examining individual slaves. Josiah could see they were exhausted and starved. When they took their gruel, they gulped it down. Many of them had welts in their skin – raw, bleeding wounds – and some could barely remain standing. A few sat down – but were immediately threatened with whipping. A great sense of revulsion swept him. For a moment he thought he might vomit. The smell, the terror, the starvation, the injuries were so prevalent that he could not fail to be moved. He thought about the punishments he had meted out in his time. He had given sentences of twenty, thirty or forty lashes many times, sometimes to old men or youths. It had been part of his duty; to do otherwise would have been to put the ship and hundreds of men at risk. But *this* was about *trade* – trade in humans.

A filthy business. The sooner he could get off *Amelia* the better.

The following day things were back to normal, and he dined with the others in the wardroom. After dinner he and Surgeon Allison walked the deck together. The ship still stank to high heaven, but the slaves were being exercised, and the cleaning of the ship was continuing unabated.

'I was asleep most of yesterday,' Josiah said. 'What happened when you opened the hatches?'

'It was worse than you can imagine. The conditions were disgusting. We lost ten slaves – dehydration, starvation, suicide. They were over the side long before you came on deck. By that time we'd sorted out the sick from injured and had given them all food and water.'

'And the crew?'

'A few injuries and a couple sick. Thank God.'

'Have you spoken with Captain Bacon?'

Allison grunted. 'Yes, the man is like a stone. He's concerned only about profits – the costs of additional food and the loss of the ten slaves. He rebuked me for refusing to take more when we left Africa – said it would have made up for the numbers lost. The man is a complete barbarian. The sooner the Parliament bans this Trade the better. It's uncivilised.'

'Do the slaves have a leader?'

'Captain Bacon would have me clapped in irons if I encouraged any such thing. But the answer is yes. They do have a leader. His name is Onabarsha, a forty-year-old man. A man I'd say could be the Captain of this ship in another life.'

'Have you spoken to him?'

'I've tried to, but he refuses to speak to me. Understandable. But he rallies the others, speaks to them in their dialects. He seems to speak many languages.'

'Is he a danger to the ship?'

'He could be if things go the wrong way.'

'Allison, what *is* a man like you doing on a ship like this?' Allison wasn't the usual alcoholic ship's surgeon, Josiah thought, but had the tact not to say it. 'You're an educated man and you care for these people. Given the choice, I think you'd let them all go free.'

'I could ask the same about you. I know you were kidnapped, but you've become a leader on this ship. You're wiser than your years. What are you, twenty-three or twenty-four?'

'I was a foolish young man, overly ambitious and greedy for promotion. I made it my ambition to be as successful as my father. Instead I made enemies everywhere. On my last ship I was in an impossible situation until my Admiral saw me in a true light and helped me. But on returning to England they did for me. I've been on the beach ever since. It was a sad time for me – full of bitterness. Now I'm learning to lead a different life: accountable to no one and free from my father. I have a chance to learn about life outside the navy. I'm grateful that I can help this ship through skirmishes and storms even though I hate its purpose.'

'We must keep talking. I have an agenda. When we're back home I want to introduce you to some people who want to abolish the Trade.'

Josiah paused. Allison's remark smelt of conspiracy – something he could not tolerate. And it reminded him of the mess he had left behind at the dockyard. 'Allison, I'm not your man. I want to find a good Command in the Navy, make money, marry a wife, have children. Your mission is your own business. I want none of it!'

'As you wish, Joss, but remember this conversation. A time will come when you'll have more to do than tend your own garden. When that happens, perhaps we may talk again.'

It was his last conversation with Allison. They avoided each other afterwards; the surgeon had raised too many questions and emotions. Josiah went about his affairs, concentrating on recovering the time lost in the storm. He had the gunners continue to practise and helped update the ship's ledger. Josiah kept himself to himself. His only regret was the lack of books. To fill the time he spent hours writing a personal log in which he reflected on the events in the dockyard – and on Janet. Who had been behind the plot to kill him? The stakes must have been high. And what was happening to the dockyards now the opposition knew the outcome of St Vincent's crusade? What was Janet doing now? Their parting had been so bitter. Was he at fault?

He considered his future once he got off this wretched ship. Perhaps he would resign his Commission and get command of an East Indiaman and make a fortune. Until then, he asked himself, might he visit his family in Nevis? Perhaps there was something for him there?

He was on the dog watch one morning. It was a dark night and the stars sparkled brilliantly, the Milky Way stretching luminous across the cloudless sky. Suddenly there was a cry from below and the sound of running feet. Bells rang, and the whole ship awoke. Hands poured on deck in answer to the alarm.

Bacon appeared. 'What the hell, Mr O'Brien?'

'Don't know, Captain. Something is afoot. Better break out the arms.'

A crew, armed with cutlasses and pistols, was quickly assembled by James.

From below Josiah could hear shouts and angry voices.

'Mr O'Brien!' Bacon shouted. 'You lead them below and find out what's going on. Remember, boys, we have to get our cargo to Nevis. No unnecessary killing!'

Down on the slave deck it was dark. The smell overwhelmed him. He gagged into his sleeve, gathering himself as his eyes adjusted to the dimness. A group of slaves had got free of their manacles and made to attack.

'Men, shoulder your muskets and aim above their heads!' Josiah ordered.

There was a pause as the men raised their muskets. Then one slave lurched forward, waving his hands in the air. His hands were free, but his legs were still shackled. He could barely move, but it was clear from his proud expression that he was the slaves' leader. What had Allison called him? Onabarsha.

The crew waited for the signal.

'Hold your fire!' An unfamiliar voice came from the darkness – clear but accented.

Josiah turned towards the voice and yelled, 'Order these men to sit on the deck. Immediately!'

There was an exchange between the leader and the voice in the dark.

The crowd of men around Onabarsha began to shout threateningly.

'Aim above their heads,' James shouted. 'Fire!'

The crackle of musket fire reverberated. There was a cry as someone was hit by a musket ball. Josiah stepped forward and struck the leader hard on the side of his head with the flat of his cutlass. The slave lost his balance and fell to the deck. There was a melee as the captives threw themselves at the crew.

'No killing!' shouted Josiah.

Five slaves had freed their hands from manacles, but they were still shackled about the legs. Soon they were on the floor, overpowered and manacled once more.

'Mr O'Brien,' James said. 'Over here!'

He pointed to the lifeless body of a man in the shadows. A crew member lowered his lantern. It was Allison. His broken body lay in a pool of blood, his clothes torn and his face barely recognisable. He had been strangled and beaten with chains.

# CHAPTER 11

They carried Allison's mangled body to his hospital ward. There was nothing more to be done. Josiah returned to the slave deck. The captives had regained their voice, hurling threats and abuse at their captors. Josiah ordered the crew to withdraw, and the grating at the companionway to the slave quarters was chained and locked.

When the officers assembled in Bacon's cabin Josiah explained what he had found. Bacon was silent, as if brooding on Josiah's command of the situation.

'What have you done with his body?' asked Bacon when he had finished.

'It is in the hospital ward.'

'We'll bury him as soon as we can, then we'll deal with the slaves.'

Josiah said, 'Deal with them?'

'We'll wait until they get hungry and thirsty enough to lose their appetite for rebellion. Then we'll hang the ringleaders from the yardarm!'

Josiah remembered Horatio's even-handedness when he handled the *Theseus* mutiny: *Deal with the issues, show mercy where possible.*

Something else was bothering him. James. Where was the first mate?

'Who is the officer of the watch?'

'Mr James.'

'But there was no one out there besides the helmsman.'

'What do you mean? You men; have you seen James?'

They looked at each other. Josiah tried but failed to remember whether he'd seen the first mate since the riot.

Wishbone said: 'Maybe in the head or in his cabin?'

'Go find him. Get him here immediately!'

Wishbone left. Josiah stroked his forehead worried about what Bacon would do. 'Have you had trouble like this with slaves before?'

'Yes. A troublemaker in the crew once convinced the slaves they'd be tortured and eaten when we reached land. Twenty of them, chained together, jumped over the side during exercise. All lost.'

Josiah shuddered. Bacon said, 'They have nothing to bargain with. We hold *all* the cards. Without victuals they'll come to their senses. But *someone* will pay for this!'

Wishbone was back. His voice trembled. 'There's no sign of Mr James! We searched the main deck and his cabin. The helmsman said that he went below decks. Hadn't seen him since. He must be down there still.'

'But we chained the iron grid at the companionway,' said Josiah.

There was a silence. Bacon said, 'Then he is a captive to those savages. He's a dead man!'

Josiah thought rapidly and coolly. He was used to the chaos of battle, used to thinking on his feet to keep his ship under control while they fought. Mutiny and reprisals. He'd seen them too. It needed calmness, firmness, a willingness to take risks to recover control. Reprisals had to be weighed against the need to regain trust. In truth, he saw, authority was based on trust earned in the thick of things.

Then he remembered the voice in the dark: 'Hold your fire,' the man had said. A man with authority, a military voice. The man had spoken English. It had sounded like he had an American accent.

Bacon was speaking. 'We have no alternative but to get Mr James out. I need volunteers. I would go myself, but …' He spread his hands. 'Do I have a volunteer?' He was looking at Josiah.

'Captain, I am ready to talk to the savages, but I am not willing to lead a reprisal. I will meet with their leader man to man.'

'Talk with them? Are you mad? Even if they understood what you were talking about, why should they come to terms? They have little to lose and nothing to gain.'

'If you want me to deal with this, I have to do it my way. Do you agree?'

Bacon stood. 'You are insubordinate, O'Brien.' He gripped the edge of the table, his voice loud and threatening.

'I have gained more experience in handling men in my years with the Royal Navy than you have had in your entire career as a master. Believe me, I know what I'm doing. But I will not take orders that I believe will lead to disaster. Do what you will!'

The bluff worked. Bacon sat down. 'Very well, but you will bear responsibility if matters get worse.'

Josiah led a dozen armed sailors to the companion-way to the slave quarters. He unlocked the iron grating and released the chain. The crew waited, bayonets fixed, as he stepped onto the deck. It took a moment for his eyes to adjust to the darkness. The heat, the smell and the noise were incredible. There was no sign of James … but he had to be in there somewhere.

'Men, raise your weapons,' Josiah commanded. 'Fire above their heads!'

An explosive rattle of musketry echoed through the darkness of the cavernous deck again. 'Reload! We will shoot anyone standing up!'

There was a pause in the racket.

A voice said, 'We are willing to parlay. We have your man. He's still alive.'

The speaker stepped forward: a short stocky man in a loin cloth.

'Very well; I am willing to talk with you, but not under threat. Release Mr James and we will parlay.'

The man translated what Josiah had said. There was an angry outburst from the listeners. The uproar continued for several minutes as the rebels discussed Josiah's proposal.

The leader spoke up again. 'I want no bloodshed. One man is already dead. We want no more killing.'

'Surrender Mr James and we will parlay.'

'You expect us to give you our only advantage?'

'I will give you my word that if you release Mr James there will be no reprisal.'

'No one trusts what you say. These men were kidnapped, brutally treated, chained, starved; you treat your livestock better than them. You are taking them to a life of perpetual brutality and confinement. Why should we believe a word you say? Many would sooner die than become the property of slave owners.'

*Perpetual, confinement.* Words of an educated man.

'I cannot do anything about that. These men are the property of the traders. They have a life of captivity ahead of them. If the situation is resolved without loss of more life, we will ensure they are treated more humanely hereafter.'

Even as he said it Josiah wondered how he could deliver on such a promise. He continued: 'I see you are a man of some education and reason. Can we parlay? Release James and I will see to it that some of your conditions are improved, and I am willing to witness that these matters were dealt with reasonably. There will be gratitude for that.'

The crowd were again restless, interjecting and arguing in their African languages. The temperature was rising. While the spokesman argued with them Josiah studied him. He looked older than the others. How could a man, educated and intelligent, be in this situation?

At length, they reached some agreement. The spokesman said, 'We are agreed to let James go. There is a condition.'

'What is it? Anything reasonable will be considered.'

'*You* will be our hostage while we parlay. We release James, but you stay. No weapons.'

This was absurd. He was likely to be torn limb from limb. He had no sure way of convincing Bacon of anything. He had no investment in this ship or its cargo. Yet how else could he save the mate's life and quell the revolt? He regarded the man closely. That voice. He could sense the authority. He could – he *would* – trust.

'Very well. I am willing. Release Mr James.'

'Tell the sailors to retreat and we will release him.'

Josiah turned to the crew. 'You hear the man. Back up the companionway. Now!'

His heart was thumping. It was so hot. He was drenched with sweat. From the dark a figure stumbled towards him; it was James.

'Mr James, a word with you.'

The figure swayed. He had a black eye and his clothes were torn. There had been a struggle.

'Mr James, they've released you in return for a parlay with me. I am going to trust you to deal with Captain Bacon. Any more violence and I am a dead man. I am going to negotiate with their leader, but I need you to convince Captain Bacon that the terms I negotiate will be honoured. Do I have your promise?'

James's eyes were wide, his mouth open. He was a

man back from the grave. 'My God, O'Brien, you have my word!'

'Perhaps I am being foolish, but we must avoid more bloodshed. Mr Allison would have wanted that.'

James stumbled up the companionway with the other sailors, and the prison gate was locked behind them. Josiah was alone, the lives of the crew and the slaves and the future of the ship on his shoulders. Why he had he agreed to do this? Was he trying to prove something yet again?

It was the voice of the man in the dark. There was something about that man. Fluent in English with an American accent – intelligent, well-spoken. Who was he? Why on Earth was an American Black a slave on this ship?

They sat down on either side of a mess table. Josiah asked for water, and the jug was filled. His opponent sat opposite, clad only in a loin cloth, an overpowering smell emanating from his soiled body. He needed a bath. No time for such things; he must seize the initiative while the slaves were willing to talk.

'Are you American?'

'Yes, I was born there. My name is John Jefferson. I am a former American slave and now a British citizen. I give you my word.'

'What are you doing on this ship?'

'I can ask you the same question. I heard the crew saying you were kidnapped.'

'A British citizen?'

'I was a slave on the plantation of Thomas Jefferson. Yes, the same hypocrite who wrote the Declaration of Independence.'

Josiah said, 'We hold these truths to be self-evident that all men are created equal, that they are endowed by the Creator with certain unalienable rights.'

'The very same.' The man continued, 'Joining the King's army during that rebellion was my only hope. I made my way to New York and enlisted in the British Army. I was promised my freedom. After New York was surrendered to the rebels, the American side demanded their slaves be returned, even the leaders who said they were fighting for American freedom! Washington and Jefferson both demanded their slaves, The British General refused to hand over any of his soldiers and shipped us Nova Scotia. We landed in Shelburne and were given passports signed by General Birch. We settled in Birchtown and were known as Black Pioneers. I got my schooling there – from the Quakers. Taught me to read and write. Introduced me to Thomas Paine and William Wilberforce.'

'How did you come to be in Africa?'

'I lived in Nova Scotia for five years. It was a damn cold country with poor agriculture and no money.

The promises made when we arrived were quickly broken, so we petitioned the government in London. In 1792 some of us boarded a ship for Africa and we were settled in Freetown on the African coast. We lived well for a few years in Sierra Leone. But again we were betrayed. The Sierra Leone Company refused to give us proper title to the land we worked. There was a revolt. Slavers, taking advantage of the uprising, kidnapped me. I am forty years old, a slave again.'

Josiah was shaken by his story. In the bowels of a slave ship was a man who had endured more hardship, more betrayal, more loss than he could ever have thought possible. His own preoccupation with restoring his fortunes was inconsequential by comparison.

'My friend, I will do whatever I can to help you regain your freedom! But what are we to do? You and I must prevent a bloodbath. The captain's interest will be in finding agreement. He will want his commission and his reputation to continue. But if blood is spilled or the crew is threatened he has the weapons to destroy you – and me too, for he cares nothing for me. He kidnapped me from Plymouth.'

Jefferson put his gnarled hand on Josiah's. It went beyond a gesture – it was a pact.

Jefferson said, 'I have explained to Chief Onabarsha what slavery is about. I have told him that the British are talking about banning the slave trade. I have told him the best thing we can expect is to be treated with humanity, but I need some sign that my promises are supported by *your* actions. When we get to our destination I will be protesting my illegal detention and hope I will secure my freedom. But what will become of these others? They will be put on the auction block and sold to plantations throughout the Caribbean. They'll be forced to labour under the hot sun for the rest of their working lives.'

'My friend, for I am already thinking of you as such, I will do whatever I can to ensure that you are all treated well when we arrive. But first we must reach an agreement to prevent this ship from being destroyed.'

'The situation of my fellow slaves *must* be improved. Their shackles must be removed and proper food and more plentiful water provided. We want the women to be free to move about the ship. We must clean up this terrible filth and deprivation. If we can do that we will take your word that when we arrive we will be treated as human beings, though illegally enslaved!'

Josiah considered his demands. The crew of the ship were outnumbered five to one. If they allowed the slaves to do what Jefferson suggested, they would quickly take over the vessel. Bacon would never agree.

'I think what you're asking is impossible, Jefferson. We can release you. We can increase food supplies.

We can improve conditions for the women, but we will not allow the slaves to go free and take over the ship!'

Jefferson turned and spoke to the others. There was a growl of anger.

'We are ten days' sailing from Nevis and St Kitts,' Josiah said. 'I will do all I can. Also, the captain expects you to surrender the slaves who killed Allison. He will surely hang them.'

'Very well, then you must provide surety until we reach our destination. The Captain must improve conditions. And we demand that the conditions for the women are improved.'

'I will talk with the Captain.'

'You may do that only if you provide another man to take your place.'

'Will you accompany me to see the captain? Your testimony will help.'

The American seemed drained. A look of despair crossed his face. 'Very well.'

'Come, let me talk to the guards.'

Jefferson turned to his fellow captives and spoke to them in Creole – or 'Krio', as he called it. They were restive and some were clearly opposed. But the chief nodded his head and spoke vehemently to Jefferson. It was clear that he too trusted him.

Jefferson and Josiah went to the gate. 'Tell Bacon

we need someone to take my place while we talk to him,' Josiah said.

The guards levelled their muskets threateningly.

'You are joking, mate. No one's going in there!'

It was a gunner, one of the crew who had helped fight off the French.

'*You* will take my place. Now get this gate open or Bacon will have your guts for garters!' His voice was stronger and firmer than he felt.

To his surprise the gate opened and the gunner walked down the steps and into the slave hold.

'I saw how you handled the guns when Frenchy tried to take us. I don't trust Bacon an inch, but I trust you. Have your discussion and make it quick, would you!'

'I guarantee that if we reach no agreement I will return and replace you.'

Josiah shook the gunner's hand, and he and Jefferson climbed the steps to the main deck. There they were greeted by the party of crew bristling with muskets and pistols. The sails were full and the sea calm. Must be making eight knots.

Josiah said to Jefferson, 'Let's get those manacles off your wrists and give you a quick wash and clothes before we see the captain.'

He beckoned a crew member, who went for a towel and clothes. While he was gone, other crew pumped fresh sea water over Jefferson. The crewman returned and hammered the pin from the manacles and the chains from his ankles. Another gave him a towel to dry himself and then shirt and breeches, which he donned. Then, with the guard watching them vigilantly, they marched to the great cabin.

Bacon was at the door when they arrived. He signalled for Josiah to enter and sit down, leaving Jefferson and the guard outside the door. 'What the hell are you playing at, O'Brien? I was pleased to see you got James back, but you are *negotiating* with them.'

'They have their lives to gain, and as long as we deal with them with fairly they will calm down and accept their fate.'

'We need to find the bastards who killed Allison and hang them!'

'To what end, Captain? Allison was on their side. He would never have wanted that! What can be gained by showing we have the power to destroy them?'

There was a pause. Bacon glowered as he tapped a fat finger on the desk. 'If I am known as a man who lost control of his ship, I am finished. I need to show I took action, I found the ringleaders!'

'Call James in. He'll support me.'

Bacon went to the door and spoke to the guard, who despatched one of their number to find James.

'I have with me the man I am negotiating with,' Josiah said. 'He is a former American slave, illegally captured. Speaks fluent English. Has British citizen-ship. A man of some education and reason. Bring him into the conversation too!'

'Have a Black tell me how to run my ship. Are you mad?'

He was going to have another fit, thought Josiah.

There was a knock and James came in. He had recovered himself, bathed and dressed his wounds. A bandage was wrapped around his forehead.

'Mr James, O'Brien has asked for you to help with the situation.'

Josiah said, 'I am asking we admit Mr Jefferson to our discussions. Tell him, Mr James!'

'He's a savage, but he speaks good English. He stopped the others from tearing me limb from limb. We should listen to him.'

'Bring him in. We'll have the guard here too.'

'No. If we are going to include him, we will show him the respect he deserves. No guard. He stays outside.'

James, Jefferson and Josiah sat around the Captain's table. For the first time it seemed Bacon might be persuaded.

'Now, Mr Jefferson,' Josiah said. 'You tell the captain what we discussed below.'

'Very well. Captain. I and my fellow slaves want no more violence. No more deaths. We want better conditions for ourselves and our women and we want no repercussions from the recent death of the surgeon.'

'You have no grounds. You and your fellows are guilty of a foul murder and taking hostages. I will never agree to what you have demanded!'

Bacon stood up, the veins on his head standing out, his eyes bulging.

Josiah held out a hand. 'Sit down, Captain. We're trying to save a situation from getting worse. I can persuade my fellows that their captivity is certain, but they will be dealt with humanely.'

Bacon sat down heavily. It was clear he had lost. His first and second mates were against him. There was a hostage. He had illegally taken a British subject as a slave and he had kidnapped another.

'And I have given my word to a fellow crew member that if we cannot reach agreement I will replace him down there,' said Josiah.

Bacon knew he was beaten.

# CHAPTER 12

As the crisis diminished Josiah separated himself from the negotiation. He had no taste for supporting the slave traders against their captives. He listened to Jefferson, who kept him abreast of the negotiations and busied himself by plotting the ship's route through the Windward Islands to their destination. The balmy breezes of the Caribbean trade winds were a welcome relief from the heat of the middle passage.

Under the pact negotiated between Jefferson and Bacon, women were on deck during the day. Males were still shackled to their berths between exercise periods, but manacles were removed from their wrists. The quarters were cleaned and washed every other day. The number of meals increased from a single ration to two meals per day. African women spiced the food with supplies discovered in the cargo – to everyone's added pleasure. There was more time to exercise on deck. No reprisal was taken against those who had killed Surgeon Allison.

At Josiah's insistence, Jefferson was released from the slave deck – pending an inquiry at their destination. He was provided a hammock with the crew. But it was an uneasy peace. The number of guards was doubled, and they were to be seen at all hours patrolling the ship. Grog was limited to one ration a day. No one was permitted on the slave deck without an armed guard. The crew were resentful, but everyone knew the voyage was nearing its end. Everyone had a reason to put their differences aside – to get through the remaining days so that the horror would be over.

But what would happen, Josiah asked himself, when they arrived in port? How would the civil authorities react? It would be impossible to keep the rebellion a secret. What about the slave market? Would the captain and his agents deliver on Josiah's promise that they would be treated humanely? What might become of Jefferson? Would the authorities agree to his permanent release and compensate him for his indignities?

Josiah kept to himself. He was popular with the crew for defusing the riot and admired for his skills and his bravery. Yet his aloofness caused some to suspect he had something to hide. His leadership in the battle and the storm and now the riot belied his rank. He heard rumours he was on the run, that he had murdered a rival in a love match and that he had killed an eminent figure in a duel.

When he was off-duty, he found a comfortable spot on the foredeck out of the wind, dreaming in the shade of the broad sails billowing above him. He had had no time until now to consider what would happen when they arrived. His role in the uprising would be debated. Once the ship was discharged he would find another way home. He had had more than enough of Captain Bacon.

They passed Martinique and Dominica, sails set for a broad reach, stays straining in the robust north-westerly. *Amelia* scythed through the calm seas like a horse scenting home. Josiah's spirits rose. The Caribbean was a sea he had never sailed in all his years in the navy. When Josiah was a small boy, Horatio had regaled him with magical tales of *HMS Boreas* patrolling these waters. He had hunted down merchantmen breaking the American blockade and thwarted Frenchmen trying to seize Britain's richest sugar islands. When Josiah was seven years old, every night, before blowing out the candle, Horatio would read him a chapter from *Robinson Crusoe*. Crusoe's island was surely near Nevis, the island his mother came from. And she too had enthralled him with stories: grand parties, the planting and harvest festivals, her pony rides on the island, the friendly people and her cheerful African servants.

Jefferson discovered him one afternoon as he relaxed in his hideout. The sun was low on the horizon and the winds were blowing steadily. The slaves had left the deck and were taking their supper, their women attending the men. Josiah beckoned him to sit, and they remained in companionable silence for a while.

'Do you know these seas, Josiah?'

Josiah considered the question. Could he confide in Jefferson? Was he reliable? He had trusted him with his life, but could he trust him with his secrets?

'No, I don't, Jefferson. But my family and I come from these parts.'

'Plantocracy?'

Josiah looked up sharply. Jefferson was smiling.

Josiah continued. 'I used to think a great deal about these islands. My father and I have had a falling out! He and my mother separated, so we don't talk much anymore. I've put all this aside rather than live with uncomfortable memories.'

'Tell me how you came to be living here and why you left – if you don't mind, that is.'

'No, I don't mind telling you. My mother's parents

settled in Nevis long ago. Grandpa was a lawyer who became the island's senior judge. Grandmama was descended from the Earls of Pembroke. They left England when the Civil War broke out a hundred and fifty years ago. Supporters of the King left Cromwell's England to settle here.

'My grandmother died when my mother was a young girl. Her father also died when she was in her late teens. Then my mother married a doctor, but soon after he took ill and died as well, leaving her a widow with an infant – me. Then she married a sea captain and went to live in England, where I was raised – until I joined the navy.'

'So you have relatives on this island, Nevis? Do you plan to see them?'

'I'm not sure. It will be complicated. You know what families are like!'

'Not my family. I would love to know where my relatives are.'

'You didn't have a family in Virginia?'

'No. I was brought to a plantation in the Carolinas with my mother. The plantation family put me up for sale and I was taken to Virginia. Never saw my mother again. I don't know where she lives or if she is still alive.'

Josiah shifted uneasily. His story about his mother, tragic though it was, did not compare. 'I had no idea.

And Monticello. We all know about that. The strange mountaintop home of Thomas Jefferson, the man who wrote the document justifying the American insurrection!'

'Yes, that's right. He called himself an "enlightened man". But I was a chattel of his. The British weren't in the war to liberate slaves, but they offered us freedom in return for our service in their army. It was an easy decision.'

'Are you concerned about me? After all, I am a member of a slave-owning family.'

'You are from that class, but you are so much more. When a man is willing to examine a situation with fresh eyes and draw his own conclusions and then acts upon them, he is a civilised human being. You could have easily ordered the crew to fire on us, and you could have refused to trade places with James. The new world will need men like you. People ready to reject the vices of slavery and all its savagery. There are other British and Americans who have reached the same conclusions as you have, but they need to band together to end this terrible trade. I hope you will continue to do so when we arrive and we encounter opposition from the people on the island.'

As they spoke Josiah saw land on the horizon. He studied it through his telescope. A peak rose steeply from the blue ocean. Clouds hovered over the mountain like a blanket of snow. *Nieve*, a Spanish word, Fanny had said, meaning snow, had become 'Nevis'. A magic name for the magic place Nevis had occupied in his childhood imagination, a contrast to the island adjacent with its humdrum name: 'St Christopher' – better known simply as 'St Kitts'.

The upper slopes of the mountain came into view, swathed in lush tropical forest, and then the plains beneath with fields of waving cane. Nevis was blessed with the finest volcanic soil in the world. In Italy, fine grapes would have been the crop; in Norfolk, the best wheat. Nevis grew sugar cane – in such abundance and of such value, they said, that even the riches of India could not compare. A plantation on Nevis was the equal of five English estates of the same size. It had taken a hundred years, wars with the French, dedication of settlers who often succumbed to tropical diseases, capital and, not least, thousands of slaves, to make Nevis so rich. It was an island which 'minted' fortunes.

He became aware Jefferson was still waiting for his answer.

'Sorry! Daydreaming.'

Jefferson was on his feet. 'Better get back. I am on duty in a few minutes.'

'On duty?'

'The captain gave me a job helping the cook and

carrying water for the crew on guard duty in return for my food and board. I don't mind.'

Josiah leaned back comfortably and put his feet up. For a while he nodded off. Jumbled thoughts ran through his mind. He had the sketchiest of plans. He must get ashore and find his mother's family. He would ask them for help to liberate Jefferson and deal with the aftermath of the riot. And then what? The sea was his home. Whether it was a fight with the French or an unruly crew or bad weather, he was on familiar territory. Could he become anything else? A planter, a lawyer? He nodded off.

They anchored in the narrows between St Kitts and Nevis. Bacon summoned Josiah to the great cabin. In a strange way they had come to respect each other, despite their many differences. Josiah continued to believe slave trading was despicable, a business dealing in human misery. Yet he had grown to respect Bacon's ability to be flexible, to accommodate the demands of the slaves and to keep the ship on its way.

'I want you to stay with me, O'Brien. You are a rare talent. I could make you a rich man. What can I do to persuade you?'

'I'm not like you, Bacon. I've learned from this

voyage the trade is unworthy of our nation. We are a nation of free men.'

Bacon stood angrily. 'Listen to me!'

Josiah held out his palms, gesturing for Bacon to be calm. 'We British conduct our trade from the barrel of the gun. We learned from our Spanish enemies, from our wars with the American Indians and the Company's wars in India. We all want to become like aristocrats and live on the backs of the poor. We have learned to make money trading commodities or through conquest and theft! Wealth and privilege are everyone's goal. And our navy is there to protect the flanks of this great economical machine. Times have to change. We must learn how to become civilised.'

'Now listen, O'Brien. You sound like a young fool or a Jacobin. We've worked for our empire. We've died on the battlefields, in the deserts and jungles for it! It's our destiny and, as an Englishman, I am proud of it! I don't like the dirty work anymore than you, but I feel better when I consider I'm part of a greater enterprise. You are young and you'll learn soon enough that I'm right. In the meantime, if I were you, I would be careful what you say in company!'

After this exchange, Bacon changed the subject to what would happen when they landed. He promised that his agent would see to Josiah's pay and said he would recommend a bonus for his role in settling the riot. In return, Josiah agreed not to sue the company for kidnapping him and agreed to testify that the surgeon's death was no one's fault. With this done they shook hands and Josiah left to pack his meagre possessions, pleased to be done with *Amelia*.

Bacon stood by his word and later, when they had discharged the slave prisoners and the crew had thoroughly cleaned the ship, the agent came aboard and paid Josiah in gold coin. He was rowed ashore, feeling like a free man.

But not everyone was free to go. The slaves were taken to the slave house in Charlestown, where they were to be quartered before the auction. Jefferson was arrested pending a coroner's court hearing on the riot and, despite Josiah's pleading, locked in the town jail.

With money in his pocket, Josiah sought friendly accommodation at the small port of Charlestown. He found a room in the Bath Hotel, an old but charming inn. His first order of business was to find a lawyer to represent Jefferson. Having done that, he decided to explore the island. He rented a horse from a livery stable and made his way up the west coast, stopping at plantation houses to discover more about the island. At first he felt uncomfortable after all the time he had been at sea. At the first plantation house he visited, he described himself as 'acting first mate on *Amelia*, soon to return to English Harbour on the neighbouring island of Antigua to rejoin the navy'. People seemed very friendly, and he quickly learned about the island. The wars with the French were on everyone's mind. There was the same fear of invasion he had seen in England. As soon as people knew he was in the navy he was warmly welcomed.

Sugar prices were very high owing to the war, and everyone was prospering. To get more production the planters were forced to offer incentives to the slaves – they fed them more and gave them privileges if they showed willingness to work longer hours. Gradually he began to form a picture the island's slave system. New slaves like those on *Amelia* were slowly introduced to island ways. 'Seasoning', it was called. It meant getting newly arrived slaves to accept their new life, a life of labouring in the fields under a hot sun. It meant crushing the spirit and destroying any residual hope. At the same time, the idea was planted that hard work might have its rewards – marriage, a house, a domestic role for a wife or daughter, an opportunity to move to a softer occupation in old age and perhaps even – the ultimate prize – freedom. In the first months, the slaves would resist, become violent or even attempt suicide. Older, tougher slaves and those who had proven their loyalty would be assigned as their overseers. On smaller plantations where there was little margin in the business it was a more violent enterprise. They didn't have the time to break their slaves. As he plodded along on his horse Josiah saw an overseer flogging a man with a horsewhip while the owner watched from a distance. It was a man called McPherson, he discovered. A brutal man with large estate. People said he took pleasure in his cruel work.

In Charlestown Josiah struck up conversations with merchants staying at the hotel, and with lawyers and doctors he met at the Parish Church on the Sabbath. They were men little older than he was. It seemed few were more than forty years. People died young or made enough money to return to England. As a result the island had a transient air. Few would be here for ever, although some old families had lived on the island for generations. Most committed to achieving a single goal: a heap of money to invest in a historic pile in Norfolk or some other county and a life of contentment in the English shire, their money safely invested in government stock.

On one ramble on his horse he paused at a white stuccoed church sitting above a plantation nearby. Idly wandering around the empty building, cooling breezes rattling the shutters, he came upon a blackboard bearing the names of the Sunday-school children. To his surprise, three quarters of the children had the same name he bore – Nisbet. He was intrigued to find such a large family with his own name – until he spoke to the verger. They were the slave children who had taken the name of the owners, as was the tradition.

The Nisbet plantation itself was a low-slung house built from coral rocks in the style of an English cottage, lawns sweeping down to a black sandy beach, white coral gleaming on the offshore reef, and all set before an azure sea. Tall coconut palms waved languidly.

His horse carried him up the long drive. He rang the bell and was invited to tea by the woman of the house, her husband being out in the fields. She was young, like most others, perhaps no older than thirty. The tea was borne in on a fine silver tray by a servant, an older black woman with the same sweet demeanour he had seen everywhere on the island.

After the lady of the house had spoken for a few minutes, Josiah asked about the family. 'I once knew a Nisbet,' he began. 'Nice enough fellow, son of an admiral in the navy. I think he told me he had connections in these parts—'

'I think you are talking about Josiah Nisbet, son of my husband's late uncle. He was born here, but he and his mother left long ago.'

'Did you know anything about his father?'

'You mean his father by birth, or the admiral?'

'His father by birth.'

'A most unhappy man. A doctor who was much

161

loved throughout the island. He had barely returned from his studies in Scotland and married when he fell desperately ill and had to return to England, where I believe he died.'

'What became of his son and his inheritance?'

'There was a dispute over the will. His father – the admiral – argued the estate was *his* property through marriage. There was no end of bad blood. The will was in probate for years. My husband can tell you more.'

'Thank you; it was just a casual inquiry. And now I must go. Thank you kindly for the tea.'

The elderly servant gave him his hat and his riding crop, and he left, waving genially to his relative, who waved back from the front step. He decided it had been wise to keep his identity secret. It was getting easier; he was even beginning to think of himself as 'O'Brien, the Irish Londoner, seaman and adventurer'. He liked that.

Travelling east from Charlestown he found Montpelier, home of the Herberts, where Fanny had lived for many years. Again he was invited in for tea. It was very different from the Nisbet plantation. It sat high on the hill with a commanding view over the fields and villages. It felt like an English country house, presiding grandly over the island. No expense had been spared on its lavish gardens, flowered borders or the house itself. It had an air of antiquity, dignity and old wealth.

Herbert's son-in-law and his daughter were home. Josiah had never met them, though he knew more about them than the Nisbets. He knew that his mother, the owner's niece, had been slated to inherit this estate when there was a breakdown between father and daughter. But they had duly reconciled, and the estate had passed to Herbert's daughter when her father died. Fanny had been compensated with a modest legacy.

The new owners were welcoming enough, but had a condescending manner and were incurious about Josiah, while making efforts to impress on him that they were the pinnacle of Nevis Society. Josiah did not mention his mother. He could see why she had chosen not to maintain the relationship after she returned to England.

Two weeks had passed quickly, Josiah feeling increasingly at peace. Then a letter arrived at his inn ordering him to appear at two scheduled court hearings in Charlestown. The first was the coroner's hearing on the death of Surgeon Allison and the second was to be a magistrate's hearing about Jefferson's status as slave or citizen. The second was slated to occur after the coroner's court in case there were charges against him. It was at this point that Josiah realised he had to make his mind up about his name. If he gave his name as O'Brien and his true identity was later discovered, he might be found guilty of perjury. If he maintained his disguise he would have to be careful no one recognised him.

It was with concern that he read in a London paper, now months old, a story about a missing relative of Lord Nelson. It was entitled 'The missing captain'.

*The son of Viscountess Nelson, Josiah Nisbet, has gone missing. Reports have been given that he was undertaking a special mission to investigate corruption in the nation's dockyards. He was last heard of in Plymouth where he had been working. A local woman where he lodged said, 'He disappeared last February, and I have no idea where he has gone. Good riddance, if you ask me!' When she was asked to explain this remark she said, 'He was working in the dockyard under an assumed name.'*

Thankfully the reporter had not asked any more questions. Josiah also noticed his mother's new title. Horatio must have been given a higher rank in the nobility.

Captain Bacon was the chief witness when the coroner's court convened. Josiah's role was to confirm what Bacon said. The coroner was a magistrate, who was assisted by the island's doctor. Since Allison's body had been buried at sea the medical report was secondhand. The questioning was *pro forma* rather than an investigation of the riot. An open verdict was returned with the stipulation that those responsible for the surgeon's death be prosecuted if 'they were identified'. Josiah considered this was meant to reduce the danger of someone's 'property' being arrested. It met with general approval.

Jefferson and the court meanwhile waited for news from Jefferson's lawyer, who had written to his correspondents in Nova Scotia to establish the *bona fides* of Jefferson's claim to be a British subject. Josiah met with Jefferson each day at the town jail to bring him food and to buoy his spirits with gossip learned from his travels around the island.

The date approached for the slave auction. Josiah's promise to the slaves worried him increasingly. He had no power to effect his promises. He racked his brain, but no new ideas offered themselves. His desperation grew and, with that, despair. To break his word would be to betray everything he stood for.

# CHAPTER 13

It was Sunday morning. Josiah awoke early and decided to take a walk before breakfast. He strolled through the lanes of the small town. No one was around. Birds were singing lustily in the palm trees, which offered shade from the rising sun. He thought of attending Morning Prayer at St Thomas's. He had been there two Sundays ago and met a good a cross section of the town's inhabitants. The parson, an old Englishman with a tired sallow face, read his sermon from a book: a treatise which may have excited clergy years ago when it was written, but as dry as sawdust now. Like most navy men, Josiah was sceptical of churchmen – seeing them as idle in duty and diligent in pursuit of position and opportunity. Uncle William was the perfect example; while Horatio put himself in harm's way, William pestered and pleaded for lucrative sinecures.

The parish was the local government, and the church administered as much as it preached. It was supposed to be on the side of the poor, but the irony of its position, in a place where people were property, was unmistakable. It occurred to him then his views had changed. When he was the successful son of an Admiral and an up-and-coming Captain, he thought slave owning was morally sound. Slaves were the property of the planters, and everyone knew property was an Englishman's right – blessed by God, a bulwark of an Englishman's freedom. Now, seeing the world differently, he was beginning to feel the church was being hypocritical, supporting slavery which its own teaching condemned. The thought jarred. He wondered at the changes in his thinking.

He reached the end of High Street and was about turn back to the Bath Hotel for breakfast when he heard a single bell tolling in the distance. He followed the sound. He turned the corner, and a well-worn track branched off to the right. In a clearing was a small building thatched with palm branches, its tall, shuttered windows open to the breeze and a simple wooden cross at the apex of the roof. Its bell rang, announcing it was a church. People were streaming toward the building from different directions. Most were black but there were a few whites too. At the door stood an African minister in a white surplice. He was tall, young and vigorous, pumping the hands of the men, at ease with the women and laughing with the children.

Josiah approached.

'Welcome to St Barnabas.' The minister shook Josiah's hand and looked into his eyes. The man had an intelligent face and a disarming smile. Josiah felt he had looked right into his heart, and was embarrassed by his thoughts. For a moment he asked what he had let himself in for. He had not yet had breakfast. He should apologise and retrace his steps. But curiosity won. This was the first mixed crowd he had seen on the island. This was something different.

'I … I am looking for the Church of England. Am I …?'

'My dear fellow, you are thinking of St Thomas on the High Street. They have a meeting at eleven in the morning. Would you prefer to …?

'No, no. I am happy to be with you. Are you Catholics?'

'No, though there is a Catholic chapel here too. We are the followers of John Wesley. Some people call us "Methodist", though I am certain that is intended as an insult!' He laughed heartily; a deep rolling sound from somewhere within.

Josiah smiled.

'We have no private pews here. Welcome. My name is Charles Grey.'

Josiah nodded and walked into the cool of the building, finding a seat near the door.

Dressed shabbily in their Sunday best the congregation filed in until the church was full. A few men and women stood at the back. A hymn was introduced by a small hand pumped organ, and the congregation burst into robust song. Such singing Josiah had never heard in church before. It was heartfelt and sung in fine harmony.

After prayers and a Bible reading the minister ascended to a small pulpit above his congregation and announced his text: Isaiah Chapter 61. 'The Spirit of the Lord God is upon me because the Lord has anointed me to preach good tidings unto the meek. He hath sent me to bind up the broken-hearted, to proclaim liberty to the captives, and the opening of the prison to them that are bound.'

Through his mind flashed the image of the slave revolt on *Amelia*, the promises he had made and the thought of Jefferson still languishing in prison.

It was as if the minister was talking to him, calling on him to examine himself, to repent and embrace a new gospel.

The congregation was at one with the speaker.

People cried and rocked in their pews. Yet the speaker was not a voice of insurrection but called upon the congregation, captives, even those in authority, to examine themselves. The sermon must have lasted an hour, but the time flew by. Josiah forgot his empty stomach and was transfixed by the fervour of the words and the congregation's response. His heart swelled with emotion. His despair at finding any way to resolve the fate of the slaves mounted within him. Suddenly he could listen no more, and he stood and worked his way through the crowd to the door, tears flowing.

A sidesman stepped up to him. He was a well-dressed black man with a quiet voice. 'Brother, it is not often we have visitors. May I ask who you are?'

'I was the first mate on the *Amelia*, the slave ship which arrived a while ago.'

'We all need God, no matter what our condition. Wait here. We have a gift for you.'

Josiah waited, wondering if he should escape while he could. In the church the sermon was over and the last hymn was being sung. The sun had risen and was beating on his back and shoulders. He took off his coat.

The sidesman returned with a small book. 'Brother, this book is our gift to you.' He looked at Josiah steadily.

'Thank you. I have enjoyed being at your church.'

Josiah reached out his hand. The man had a powerful grip.

Josiah said, 'Your name is?'

'I am James Nisbet.' Josiah's heart turned over. 'I live in Charlestown. I am an attorney, if you need any help.'

'I ... I'm Joss O'Brien. Good to know you. I must go ...'

He strode off up the track as the congregation poured out of the church behind him. Thank goodness he didn't have to talk with the minister. Back on the main road he paused under the shade of a tree and examined the book. It was by W. Wilberforce and had a lengthy title: *A Practical View of the Prevailing Religious System of Professed Christians in the Higher and Middle Classes in this Country, Contrasted with Real Christianity.*

Blacks and whites, together. Was that the future? He walked on, engrossed in his thoughts. Being a practical man, he reduced his speculation to one question: having heard the sermon, what was he going to do about the slaves of the *Amelia* and John Jefferson, his friend?

He quickened his pace. He had no answer.

He was very hungry and took breakfast immediately upon his return to the Hotel. Later, he found a letter waiting for him: an embossed invitation to dinner at the home of Mr Frederick Pinney, Mount Travers. Although he had never met Pinney, his mother often referred to her friend, the widow Mary, Frederick's mother. Mary had left Nevis twenty years ago with her husband, JP, and settled in a magnificent home in Clifton on the outskirts of Bristol. Why would a rich plantation owner like Frederick invite lowly O'Brien, second mate aboard a slave ship, to dinner? There could be only one answer: he had something to discuss with him. Something to do with the slaves.

On Monday he returned to the jail to see if there was any news from Jefferson. He stopped at Bell's Dry Goods and purchased a shirt and soap, and he bought groceries from the general store – fresh mangoes, a bag of oats, eggs and bread.

Jefferson was pleased to see him and delighted with the gifts.

'Now tell me how you are,' Josiah said.

'I'm bored stiff sitting here with only an hour of exercise each day. It's unbearably hot at noon, and only after it rains can I find any comfort.'

'What has the lawyer found?'

'Mr Beggs hasn't heard from Nova Scotia, and he tells me that three months is his expectation. I've been here a month now, so that means waiting another two! I hear that the other captives at the slave house are restless. They're saying the promises I made to them are not being honoured. I'm worried there may be more violence.'

Josiah told him about the invitation to visit with Frederick Pinney and his thought that Pinney might want something from him. He had heard there was little demand for additional labour on the island. Perhaps twenty or thirty men only. The other slaves might be sent to the markets in other Leeward Islands or even further away – perhaps to the United States. And yet – the invitation suggested other possibilities.

He could see the effects his words were having on Jefferson, whose reservoir of hope, like his own, was running dry.

'Look, I may have some other ways to resolve this situation. I do have connections on this island that I have refrained from using, but in the extreme I can bring those into the picture.'

'Well, my friend, whatever you do must be done soon. Time is running out.'

'I had an unusual experience on Sunday last, Jefferson.' He told him about the chance meeting with the Methodists and the lawyer, Nisbet.

Jefferson said, 'From what you say, this place seems unusual.'

'Yes, most ordinary people have lived here forever,

while the planters and the doctors and lawyers return to England when they have enough money.'

'In Virginia, some plantations were owned by the same families for generations and the slaves who lived there had some stability in their lives. It is a terrible thing when those plantations are broken up or sold. Their slaves are sold off to distant place and they lose all their family and connections immediately.'

The hour passed quickly and, as he departed, Josiah wondered how he would fare in Jefferson's situation. As he left he tried to reassure him he would be a free man again.

❧

The Pinney plantation, Mount Travers, was on the north side of the island a few miles from Charlestown. Josiah hired a carriage to take him there. It was already warm, with signs of a approaching storm as they set off. Josiah sat back in the chaise, braced against the seat as they rocked and swayed over the bumpy road. His mind switched back and forth between his own situation and his obligations to resolve the matter. He felt caught, trapped. Sooner or later someone would discover the truth about him, and that might make matters worse.

He considered what he had learned. The business of slavery was detestable, but there was something about this island that defied the popular view that plantations were gold mines for the owners and prisons for the workers. There was a sort of 'order' here, a culture that had resulted from years of cohabitation of the ten thousand Africans and Creoles and the thousand or so whites. Only the very rich, it seemed, lived as if the island were their business enterprise. The rest – people like Nisbet the lawyer – were settled. Yes, that was the word: settled.

The carriage rumbled up the long driveway to Mount Travers. As the horses sweated their way up the incline, Josiah saw the plantation's slave village on the left-hand side. It was set in a grid pattern of lanes. The single-storey houses sat on a quarter acre – perhaps thirty or forty in all. On the perimeter were tall coconut palms, swaying in the early afternoon breeze. The houses were not all the same; some were marked by care and expense – smart, painted, and tiled – while some had roofs of plaited palm leaves, greyed by sun and rain, and others were small or hastily flung together, with a poor, desolate aspect. Around each house were lemon trees and crops of yams and potatoes. There were a few goats and chickens wandering around. Josiah guessed that most of the men were out in the fields tending to cane.

Then the carriage turned through a small wood and he lost sight of the village. The road steepened as they climbed higher and higher until the horse was sweating and the carriage moved so slowly that Josiah thought he should disembark. But just then they sped up again and Mount Travers rose up in front of the carriage.

The house was bordered with gardens. Sweet-smelling tropical plants grew in profusion, offering a colourful backdrop to the grey pebbles and mortar in which the house was finished. To his surprise he recognised the Jacobean style, the sort of gentleman's house popular a hundred years ago. The great mullioned windows and tall brick chimneys towering above the square dwelling reminded him of similar houses in Norfolk. The carriage drove into the turning circle at the entrance and came to a stop. A uniformed servant appeared and opened the door.

Josiah stepped down and stretched himself. The view from the steps leading to the front door was magnificent. The ground fell away and there was no sign of the slave village below. Instead, rolling hills, dotted with distant houses and fields of cane, fell away to azure lagoons and the dark green of the Caribbean Sea.

'This way, sir. Mr Frederick is waiting for you inside.'

Up three steps and across the dark teak floor of the

hall Josiah could see a sunlit drawing room and four
or five figures standing with their drinks.

'Ah, you must be O'Brien.' A tall, youngish man
stepped forward. His hair was thinning, and he looked
more like a lawyer than a planter. But his voice was
warm, and Josiah felt at ease.

'Thank you for your kind invitation, Mr Pinney.'
He must remember to be deferential – to be aware of
his lower station without being servile.

'Let me introduce you to my guests. This is Colonel
Smith.' A man dressed in civilian clothes bowed. 'And
this is Chief Justice Daniell.'

The man looked at him curiously, as if he was
familiar. He was short, with sallow features and
glasses.

'Good day to you, sir.' Josiah bowed uncomfortably.
It seemed manners among the rulers were slow to
change on this island.

'And this is Parson Groves and Mr Morton,
son-in-law and heir to the late Mr Herbert of
Montpelier.'

Josiah recognised him as the supercilious man
he had met when he paid a visit to Montpelier. He
bowed politely.

Pinney said, 'The ladies are not joining us today, as
I would like to talk about business after we have had
dinner.'

A servant approached with a tray of drinks. Josiah declined the champagne, choosing a fruit juice instead. He must keep his wits about him.

'Gentlemen, shall we adjourn to the dining room?'

Pinney led the way and settled his guests around the oval table. Fans were revolving in the high ceiling. *Must be powered by slaves*, thought Josiah as he took his place in a high-backed chair opposite Pinney. The others seated themselves around him.

The first course appeared as soon as they had taken their seats – a tureen of turtle soup. It was delicious. Josiah tried to remember his table manners – whether he was supposed to dip the spoon from the front to the back, or was it the other way? It had all seemed to be so important in London. It was obvious, though, that Beau Brummell, the dictator of fashion, was unknown on Nevis.

The parson asked, 'My dear sir, what are your thoughts on the Methodist chapel? I did not observe you at St Thomas's and heard that you had been to the Methodist chapel's earlier service Sunday last.'

'Upon my word, Parson, you have good intelligence! I came upon the chapel on my walk, hearing the bell and the seeing the people crowding in. It was very interesting for me to see Negro and white peoples worshipping together.'

'That is as may be, Mr O'Brien. The so-called

Wesleyans are growing rapidly in numbers at our expense. But they are still only small in number compared with the congregations of Negro people who attend worship at the Church of England.'

Delicate mousse of fish was served with a fine white wine. The conversation turned to the war and the weakness of the British fleet in the Caribbean. Josiah's fellow diners asked him politely about his background, but it seemed as if they all knew who he was – or at least, who he was pretending to be. Josiah was not surprised. Word got around quickly on this island. He replied with general observations about the invasion threats to England to explain the reduced fleet operating in the Caribbean.

It was clear, though, that the invitation to join the most prominent men on the island was not about the generalities of wartime Nevis. It had to do with him and his role on the slave ship, or perhaps both. He was certain that his real secret was safe. They did not know of his family's long connection to this island – his mother the 'society hostess' for JR Herbert, whose son-in-law was sitting there, his grandfather a predecessor of the chief justice sitting on the other side, his father a member of the Nisbets and a leading doctor before his untimely death. Indeed, some might have gleaned from the conversation that Horatio was more revered than any Nesbit – a hero who had married the richest man's niece at Montpelier. He too was part of the fabric of this place. But it was all alien to Josiah. He had no desire to claim it as his birthright.

At one time he might have considered buying a small estate and making a fortune in sugar. No longer. Despite the peace and calm of the island, it was still a wretched business, a constant compromise between the competing rights of freedom and property. Nonetheless, he had obligations to Jefferson and the Africans imprisoned in the slave house. These gentlemen could help him discharge those – if that is what *they* wanted.

When the port began its journey around the table, Pinney spoke his mind. 'Mr O'Brien, you must be curious about the purpose of this meeting.'

Josiah flushed, struggling to keep his composure as the attention of the group fastened on him.

'You see, we have done our homework, and we know what happened on the voyage of the *Amelia*. We heard how you came to be aboard as second mate. We learned that you have had a career in the Royal Navy and your experience was called on when *Amelia* was attacked by a French corvette. We have investigated the revolt of the slaves and how you negotiated with the ringleaders. And, not least, we have your account of the wrongful seizure of a British citizen and former soldier in the British Army.

I refer to the Negro, John Jefferson, entered in the books of the slave ship as number 119.'

Josiah interrupted. 'Excuse me, I am not sure *why* we are holding this conversation. The matters are before the court. Jefferson has a lawyer who is checking on his status in Nova Scotia. If he is not charged for his role in the slave revolt – for there is no evidence other than his important role in defusing matters – I demand he is freed through a writ of *habeas corpus!*'

In the silence, Josiah realised he had offended Pinney. But Pinney held up his hands in a calming gesture. He said, 'You have every right to be indignant. But we who have made this island our home are not "savages". We are law-abiding Englishmen, and we try to do what is right and proper. But we also have responsibility for the security of this island and its people – including the slave population. Are you willing to listen to what I have to say about that?'

There was a moment's silence. Josiah could see from the expressions on the faces around him that he had overstepped his mark. He realised how he appeared: a young sailor, presumptuous and getting above his station. It was time to retreat.

'Look, I'm not used to these situations. On board ship we speak our minds. I apologise for my strong words. I am ready to listen to anything you have to tell me.'

It seemed to work. Pinney exchanged glances around the table. The chief justice nodded and Pinney gestured to Colonel Smith.

Smith cleared his throat and dabbed his lips with his napkin, his bright eyes fastening on Josiah. 'The security of this island against French aggression is of the highest interest in London as well as here. The French will take all measures to disrupt Britain's commerce. Creating a slave revolt and ransacking the island is not above them. But for all of us who live here – slave or freemen, and there are many hundred former slaves who are freemen – this would be a disaster. We are unanimous in believing that defending our island against French attack is our highest priority. Our present weakness is a reminder of the danger of putting all our eggs in one basket – reliance on the British Navy. But the Leeward Islands Fleet is reduced to little more than a squadron. The Admiralty says it must ensure there are sufficient capital ships to prevent Napoleon invading England. That means defence of these islands is now *our* business.'

He paused and looked at the other men at the table. They were nodding. Josiah could see that they were nervous. The French had been defeated in the east by Horatio's amazing victory at the Nile, but now, perhaps, they were on the way here. The people of Nevis stood to lose everything. He realised his position was not as hopeless as he had thought. Indeed the cards he held might be of the highest value.

Colonel Smith continued. He was a military man. His words were short and his manner abrupt. 'O'Brien, if we asked you to help us defend the islands, would you be prepared to do your duty?'

'Colonel Smith, my country's defence is my duty. However I have other obligations of which you are aware. How those are met will determine how I may help you.'

'Perhaps I can do something about that, O'Brien.'

'I will be happy to listen to whatever you suggest. You may be aware that John Jefferson served in the Royal Artillery during the American wars.'

'Yes, I had heard something to that effect.'

He looked around the room. There were faint nods from several of the gentlemen.

Colonel Smith said, 'O'Brien, I believe I may have something that you and John Jefferson should consider.'

When the lunch was over, Josiah said his thanks and farewells clumsily. His manners were rusty and he had an overwhelming desire to leave this home where he felt so out of place. As the chaise clattered down the hill past the slave village, Josiah pondered on the two problems – the freedom of the slaves and the defences of the island. He nodded off.

A bath in the hot springs helped him to relax upon his return to the hotel. His landlady, Elizabeth Darling, invited him again to join her at the dinner table, but he declined politely and ordered a small supper to his room. He was tired after his long day and the ride in the hot sun. He needed to think.

But he was distracted by her. She had caught his attention. He admitted he liked her interest in him. It was expressed in many ways – small things, which added to his comfort. He was always invited to sit at her table together with her latest guests. She had given him one of the best rooms in the house. She had introduced him to the joys of the mineral springs for which the hotel was named. She had even offered on one occasion to rub oil on his sunburned arms when he returned from his ride. He had politely declined. Her smiles had a hint of flirtation. *Once burned twice shy*, he reminded himself, determined to keep his 'seemly' distance while avoiding any suggestion he was rejecting her advances.

The next morning he made his way to the town jail to discuss the meeting at Mt Travers with Jefferson, but Jefferson had his own news. 'Listen to this, Joss.

A French fleet was here only a few months ago and threatened the island. The Assembly had to pay "tribute" of four thousand sterling in bullion and sugar to the French admiral.

'And the guards told me it has happened *before, only twenty years ago* – the worst time being a hundred years since when the island was completely sacked and many slaves were taken to French islands. Seventy years ago the French attacked and tried to seize all the slaves. The planters were powerless, and a large body of the slaves organised themselves to defend the island. The planters armed them, and they held off the French.

'*That's* why they wanted to see you. They know you and I are trusted by the Africans, and I wager they want to enlist us to help defend their island. It'll save having to second their own slaves. That's why the colonel was at the dinner.'

'I agree they need us as much as we need them,' said Josiah.

'Of course, a condition would be that I get my release and serve until this war is over. And you?'

'It gets me past this current crisis. I don't want the slaves to be sold off the island. This is a better place than many others. Here they can at least serve a useful purpose, and after they've earned their freedom they can return to Africa or settle here. The women too.

I feel it could work … but you and I might be stuck here for some time. It also depends whether the slaves themselves will agree. If they're not satisfied with the terms, they'll be poor soldiers.'

'Joss, get me my release and I will talk to them.'

'When I meet Colonel Smith again, that will be the first item on the agenda.'

# CHAPTER 14

Jefferson had been in the airless prison for two months. At first, he had felt it was endurable – a step towards freedom, knowing Joss O'Brien was working for his release. But when Beggs the lawyer interviewed him before writing to the authorities in Nova Scotia, his optimism waned. The lawyer patently disbelieved his story. He was making inquiries only because Joss had commissioned him to do so. If his lawyer thought he was lying, what chance was there?

His jailer was a grumpy old man who'd been in his job for too long. His two slaves brought Jefferson his food and took him out to exercise, watching him carefully to make sure he didn't abscond. His days were boring, and at night mosquitos tormented him.

When Joss visited the jail that morning his hopes

rose again. He craved conversation. They talked about Jefferson's past life and what he would do when he was released. Joss was meeting the plantation families, assessing the men who controlled the affairs of the island. They could talk about these things for hours. The only conversational boundary seemed to be around Joss himself. If Jefferson broached the subject of Joss's personal life, he would get an answer that raised more questions than it answered. If he persisted, Joss became taciturn. He would change the subject and ask about Monticello, about Jefferson's escape to New York, his life in the British Army and the events after Britain lost the American war. He was a master of diversion and deflection.

Josiah stretched out full length on the bench, his arm behind his head, his shoes propped on the windowsill. He said, 'When I heard your voice in the dark, speaking English, it was like a miracle.'

Jefferson said, 'I was like Squanto to you. Do you know that story?'

'No, I don't. Who was Squanto?'

'He was an odd Indian man who emerged from the woods that first summer at Plymouth Rock, when the English pilgrims were hungry, facing a brutally cold winter without any crops to harvest. What a shock when he spoke the King's English! He taught them about Indian corn, how to fish and trap game and build shelters to withstand the cold months to come. He taught them how to trade with the tribes, how to read the skies and foretell storms by looking at the colour of the sea. Best of all, to those old pilgrims, he was a Christian man who had spent years living in London!'

'What prodigious good fortune for them!'

'He had been captured by Portuguese fishermen and sold to Spanish friars in the Cadiz slave market. The friars gave him his freedom. Years later when he wanted to return home they sent him to London, where he lived for years until he found a ship. When he got to his village everyone was gone. It was deserted. They'd all died of smallpox. He lived there, alone. Then one day, ships arrived carrying white men.'

'Amazing! Such stories give me faith in Providence. *You* were providential. I knew when I heard that American voice.'

'And I felt the same.'

'Tell me about Thomas Jefferson. How could the American write so brilliantly *and* continue thinking of his slaves as property?'

'Let me tell you about Jefferson. A strange man, in some ways a benevolent master. American independence was his rational solution to all the contradictions of British democracy. His duty was to challenge the King of England in the name of an ideal – liberty!

Imagine that. And he was brave, too – he faced a traitor's death if he was captured. Yet, strangely, he was unaware of his own hypocrisy: owning slaves, having children by slaves who then became slaves. He is a man who prefers ideas to people. In the end his 'ideas' were more important to him than his people. For those like me who lived in his house it was sickening. Like all the others I had to pretend that we had a kind master. When the real opportunity came ... it was a simple decision.'

Joss left, promising to return again on the next day. Jefferson spent the rest of the morning pondering about those long-ago days of his youth in Virginia. Since then Thomas Jefferson and the other leaders had written a constitution that gave Virginia and the other states in the south relatively more seats in Congress because the calculation of their populations were based on the number of citizens *and* slaves in those southern states. As a result the slaveholders had equal or greater power in elections than those who opposed slavery. The franchise was based on people who would never be allowed to vote. He shook his head. A country with so many possibilities, unable to address its own flaws, while bitter at injustices done to them by the English King.

Twenty-five summers and winters had passed since then, and Jefferson didn't think much about America any more. Yet he still loved it. To love your native country and to hate some aspects of it led to despair. It was better not to think too much about these things

From outside he heard a voice he didn't recognise. He looked through the window. Another visitor. A slave. He was a black man, dressed presentably in coat and breeches. A gentleman's personal slave. The guard opened the gate, and the man entered his cell.

He took off his coat and held his hand out in greeting. 'Nisbet is the name. Joss O'Brien sent me to see you. I am a lawyer.'

Jefferson stood and shook his hand.

Nisbet said, 'I gather that one of my colleagues, Mr Beggs, is working on your behalf to establish your identity. In the meantime you are being held on a charge of leading an uprising against the captain of the *Amelia*.'

'Who *are* you?'

'Not every black man on this island is a slave, Mr Jefferson. Over the centuries many of us have gained our freedom. The aged are often manumitted; others have earned freedom by their labour. Occasionally a person may be a "natural son or daughter" of a planting family. This was my case. The Nisbets are an old established family here, and my father married my mother when his English wife died. I met your friend O'Brien at the Methodist church Sunday last. He has asked me to review your case and give him another opinion.'

Jefferson recalled Joss mentioning the church. His visitor seemed genuine – if a little earnest and youthful. Nisbet asked the guard to unlock the gate to the yard where they could not be overheard. Then they sat on a bench under a spreading poinciana tree, whose bright orange flowers and deep green leaves gave them shade.

'I am going to launch a suit for *habeas corpus* on your behalf – to demand your immediate release. You were detained on two grounds: first as an instigator of a slave uprising aboard *Amelia*. The Crown has no evidence of this, as many of the crew aboard *Amelia* have testified that without your intervention great loss of life and property would have ensued. The second ground for your detention is that you are the property of the agents of the *Amelia*. Mr Beggs, who has represented you until now, has been trying to secure a document from Halifax to prove you were freed long ago for your services to the British Army. It has taken too long for your papers to appear. I am going to the local court tomorrow to plead your release on the grounds of *habeas corpus*. Is that acceptable?'

'I am amazed.'

'Things are changing. The old plantation owners are retiring, and new people are trying to do things differently. The island depends on sugar, and all of us know our livelihood is tied up with that trade. Without it we would starve. There is a sort of unspoken agreement to live with what we have and hope things will change. The slave trade is almost done for. I hope and pray that slavery goes with it when it is abolished. But if and when it does, we must do things better than the Americans.'

'I know what you're talking about,' Jefferson said. 'The American Revolution was meant to bring freedom and liberty. Everyone talked about it when I was young. But in the end, property rights turned out to be more important that the ideals of the leaders. If they don't resolve it, I fear much blood will be spilled there.'

'There *is* fear of blood on this island too. Saint Domingue has everyone terrified of slave uprisings. But the Island Council has a typically English view that a few concessions will be enough to keep everyone happy for a while. I tell them they have only a few more years left to make serious change, but they mock my youth. In the meantime they're also very fearful of the French, who are threatening the island again.'

Nisbet paused for a moment and then changed the subject. 'What do you know about Joss O'Brien? Who is he? He was most solicitous to me when we met at the church last Sunday; said he would look me up, and here I am representing you. What can you tell me about him?'

'He is more than he makes himself out to be. He told me that he had been in the Royal Navy for many years at some lowly rank. He obviously has his reasons for keeping his story quiet. He is a man of strong character. From the moment I met him in that stinking hold of the slave ship, he has dedicated himself to achieving the noblest outcomes for the slaves and for me. Something in his past life has made him this way.'

'I am told that some of our leaders met with him and are determined to seek his services. I am basing my case in part on that assumption. If the leaders of this island need something, they will make concessions. Your freedom may be one of those.'

~

The courthouse in Charlestown was an old building next to the jail. It was small – like a toy model of a London court, its walls clad in a dark wood and pervaded by a smell of mould and old books. The room had tall glassless windows fitted with wooden blinds, which were open to the sky. In the ceiling two punkah fans moved the humid air back and forth.

The court was already assembled except for the judge. Beggs and Nisbet sat just below the prisoner's dock where Jefferson sat on his own. Jefferson could see Joss at the back of the room in the public section.

The clerk tapped the floor with his rod. 'All rise!'

The judge entered through a small door and mounted the steps to the platform, where he took his seat in a tall carved chair. The British coat of arms rose majestically above him. He adjusted his wig and addressed the prosecutor.

'Are you ready, Mr Gravel?'

The prosecutor said, 'I am, Your Honour. A writ of *habeas corpus* has been issued on behalf of John Jefferson, who is accused of fomenting a slave revolt aboard the *Amelia*. You will hear indisputable evidence that Jefferson is the property of Smythe and Smythe, merchants, who legally bought him as a chattel in slave markets of West Africa. This is the only germane fact in this case. A slave is *not* permitted the benefit of *habeas corpus*.

'Was he legally acquired? You will see from the documents that he was. His lawyer will give you some poppycock story that he is actually a British subject, legally a citizen. But they have no proof. Dismiss this writ, Your Worship, and the prisoner will be restored to his rightful owner and face possible charges of fomenting a slave revolt aboard the *Amelia*.'

He resumed his seat.

Beggs rose. 'We will give you chapter and verse as

to how Mr Jefferson came to be aboard that slave ship. He is a British citizen of American birth who was kidnapped by a gang of slavers at his home in Sierra Leone, a British colony in West Africa. He has already endured more than any Briton should be expected to. We know he faces subsequent charges, but we dispute these. In the interim we wish this court to free him from custody. *Habeas corpus* matters as much in this colony as it does in the mother country.'

Jefferson looked at the public benches. They were all men. Three of them were paying attention, nodding as each point was made. He glanced at the judge. It didn't look promising.

The case was slowly presented. Documents were produced and handed to the judge to examine. It seemed to be an open-and-shut case. The defence had nothing to offer in their support. The Crown's case lasted all morning and was followed by a lengthy break for dinner. Late in afternoon the defence was called.

Nisbet stood up. He said, 'I call the second mate of the *Amelia*, Mr Joss O'Brien.'

Joss entered the witness stand. He took the solemn oath to tell the truth. Then, step by step, Nisbet asked him to recount Jefferson's story. The court was silent, hanging on his words. Joss was cool, factual, controlled.

The judge interrupted.

'Mr O'Brien, I have a simple question: Why do you believe this man? He's a slave, and it is a well-known fact that the word of a slave cannot be depended upon.'

'Your Worship, I am a navy man. On a ship, the captain is judge and jury. Yet it is important for discipline that there must be sound evidence and fairness, and this must be seen and understood even at the level of the lowliest seaman. I have spent many hours with Mr Jefferson. I have talked to him about the place where he was born. His name is not an accident. He was born on the plantation of Thomas Jefferson, who is now the President of the United States of America. During the American war, Jefferson escaped from his master and fought on the British side. He was freed by the British in return for his services and went to Canada, and from there to Africa, where he was illegally kidnapped and sold to the merchants who claim he is their property. It is time for British justice to prevail and Mr Jefferson to be recognised as a British citizen and released.'

There was a stirring in the court. The judge brought down his gavel and chastised the courtroom for the interruption.

He called on the prosecutor to sum up, and Mr Gravel said, 'Your Worship, this is a simple question of fact. Is the person in the dock issuing a writ of *habeas corpus* a slave or a freeman? I think you have seen today that all the evidence points to the fact that he is a slave. We have seen the documentation, heard from the legal owner – and what have we heard from the other side? Unsubstantiated claims! The only evidence they have produced is a wildly improbable story and the fact that this slave speaks English. What is so unusual about that, I ask? Don't your slaves speak English too?'

He resumed his seat. It was time for Nisbet to sum up. 'Your Worship,' he said at the conclusion of his speech, 'we may live in a colony that practises slavery, but we are a colony that respects justice, even when it comes to the rights of citizens with a different skin colour.'

The judge rose and retreated to his chamber, but not for long. He returned within minutes. 'The writ is denied. John Jefferson is the rightful property of the merchants, Smythe and Smythe.'

Jefferson felt his knees give way. He had been standing for the verdict, but now he stepped back and sat. The jailer jerked him back on his feet.

The judge looked over his spectacles, holding the attention of the courtroom as he fumbled with his papers.

He addressed the lawyers: 'Thank you, gentlemen, for your *hard* work.' He said 'hard' in an acid tone. He turned to Jefferson. 'You have applied for evidence from Nova Scotia that you believe will ratify your status as a British citizen. I believe it is taking time to get here. I will release you on the recognisance of the witness Mr Joss O'Brien until such time as these papers are received. The bail will be set at ten pounds.'

The clerk called all to rise while the judge left for his chambers. Jefferson looked across the room and caught Joss's eye. He could have sworn he winked.

⤙

Two days later the auction for the slaves from *Amelia* was held at the market next to the slave house. Jefferson, Joss and Nisbet attended, along with a modest crowd, some of whom Josiah recognised from the courtroom. There were a dozen potential buyers at the slave market; they had been examining the slaves, making notes and adjusting their prices. After the slaves were examined, they were taken back to the slave house.

The auctioneer stood on his block. 'We have a very valuable cargo of West African Negroes for sale today. I welcome to this auction the local planters and our visitors from other Leeward Islands. I also welcome old friends from the United States. The auction will be in four stages: female and young slaves; strong healthy males prime for the great gang; others with special skills; and, last, older and sick slaves. Now, let me begin. Bring in the first group.'

The women and youths were ushered into the ring and, one by one, they approached the auctioneer's block.

The prices were bid up until a final price was reached. The first slave was sold. It was soon apparent that while there were several bidders, one party kept bidding when the others gave up. The other bidders tested his resolve with attempts to keep the bidding alive, but each time they failed. After a while they lost interest and the sale moved more quickly. After an hour had passed, the sole bidder was called to one side by the auctioneer and a discussion took place.

Finally, the auctioneer said, 'I have talked to my principal, and he has agreed to accept a single bid for the rest of the slaves offered today. They are now all sold.' He banged his gavel on the table and shook the hand of the successful bidder.

Josiah and Jefferson looked at each other and smiled. It had been arranged. The charade was a pretence of a fair market. But the deal to which everyone had agreed – including the slaves themselves – was done. The West India Regiment had its new recruits.

Josiah thought about the way his navy ships were crewed: ten percent volunteers, ten percent commissioned officers or midshipmen, thirty percent seized from merchant ships, fifty percent from the general public. Did they have any rights either, so long as there was a war? It was hardly fair, but who said that fairness had a seat at this table?

# PART 3: JULY 1804

# CHAPTER 15

Josiah was breakfasting with his landlady, Elizabeth
Darling. The bright morning promised a hot day.
Their table in the courtyard was shaded by a fragrant
magnolia tree, home to red and green parrots, flitting
to and fro in search of crumbs. Jefferson was not there;
he had told Josiah he wanted to keep out of the public
eye and was paying for his lodgings with an elderly
couple who were former slaves, freed after a lifetime
of service.

Elizabeth's cool blue dress showed off her figure,
and she wore a charming lacy bonnet over her
fetching black curls. A breakfast of delicious mango
and papaya was served together with fresh bread and
conserves. They had eaten their fill and were sipping
their coffee.

'Mr O'Brien, I heard that you were successful in releasing the American slave from the jail.'

'Mrs Darling, perhaps I should ask for your guidance regarding my future, for I have learned that you are the source of *all* useful information on this island.'

She laughed. 'I should have thought a man like you would stay on the island. Buy a small plantation. Knowing you, you'd turn it into something special. Make a fortune, marry a local beauty and retire.'

'That is far too conventional, Mrs Darling. I'm disappointed in you. I am used to being at sea, never in one place for long.'

'And with a sweetheart in every port, I'd be bound.'

'It used to be so, I admit. But I was deeply offended by someone dear to me who lived that sort of life, and I have to say that I am trying to be a better man than he was.'

'And who might that be?'

He overlooked the question and continued. 'Jefferson and I will be here for some time. But I will be moving to St Kitts. I will be back frequently, I hope, and count on you for a room when I am here.'

'St Kitts?'

'Yes. Jefferson and I will be joining the West Indies Regiment under Colonel Smith. The slaves on the *Amelia* – perhaps I should say former slaves – have "volunteered" to become soldiers. Our work is to train them in the art of war. Jefferson will be the infantry sergeant and I will be the artillery sergeant. Together we will turn these men into the finest soldiers in the West Indies.'

'Brimstone Hill – that's where you are off to.'

'You have hit the nail on the head, Mrs Darling. Brimstone Hill it is. Tell me about it.'

'It's a mighty fortress above the town of Basseterre. Guarding the approach to the Narrows. Built to defend us against the French forty or more years since. Now the French are back.'

'We're going to train these men to be proper soldiers: arm them and show them how to use their weapons.'

'In the past, the most anyone would give them would be a cutlass or a pike. Worried about them setting on their masters, see. Makes sense, doesn't it?'

'Mrs Darling, slavery is hopefully going to end soon. I sense everyone knows it, but they don't know how to undo it. They hate the thought of freeing the slaves because they would have to pay them to work. On the other hand, they fear a French attack even more. I tell you, slavery is not the way of the future. Trust and fair play is the only sensible path for the colony.'

'And how do you control someone you've treated so badly in the past?'

'I always found that if discipline is fair, everyone on my ship agrees it's necessary except the poor villain who is about to be flogged. If it is not fair the ship is usually in trouble. I have no concerns about that.'

'Well, rather you than me, is all I say. Running this inn is enough for me, but I do agree with you that winning people's trust is better than relying on authority. You are most welcome to stay here at any time. Call me Elizabeth, would you? I would like to think of you as a friend.'

'Perhaps one day—'

He was about to get to his feet when a young slave ran into the courtyard. 'Mistress, mistress,' he panted. 'Colonel Smith says that the gentleman should come *now*. Something is happening at the slave house!'

Josiah scrambled to his feet, smiling apologetically and, waving farewell, followed the young lad. Outside the slave house a crowd was gathering. An agitated constable, armed with an old musket, prevented the crowd from approaching the building. From within the barred windows came the sound of a furious argument.

Josiah asked a man in the leather apron of a blacksmith, 'What's happening? What's going on?'

'Seems like they had a visitor. It were that American who was released a few days ago. He went in there and said he wanted to talk with the slaves. Pretty soon there was a lot of shouting and disagreeing. It's still going on. Seems to me we'll have to call out the militia if this gets out of control.'

Josiah strode to the door, but his way was barred by the slave keeper.

'Keep back, sir. This is not your business. It's just a lot of shouting and complaining.'

Josiah looked over the man's shoulder. Within the cage he could see Jefferson. He was calmly holding his own in a shouting match with four young slaves. Then one of the older slaves took one of the young men aside and spoke quietly to him. He made a crude gesture, which struck them as funny. Laughter melted the moment. The banter continued a few minutes more while Jefferson made his farewells and called for the slave keeper to release him from the cage.

Josiah, impressed with Jefferson's imperturbable smile asked, 'What's going on?'

'It was time to speak the truth. They had little idea what's going on and what it means for them.'

'What did you say to those men that roused them so?'

'I was telling them what would happen – what it means to join an army, what it means to take an oath of loyalty and obedience, and all the things they will have to endure to become proficient soldiers. Some of the young men are still resentful and angry, but even they could see that this is the best chance for them. They came around, as I thought they would.'

As they passed the door of the lawyer's office it opened and Nisbet stepped out. 'Jefferson, I hear you started a riot. Why don't you come on in?'

He opened the door and ushered them out of the sun into a quiet book-lined study off the entrance hall. 'Take a seat.'

They sat in armchairs in front of his handsome Chippendale desk. He opened a cupboard behind his desk and took out three small glasses and a decanter of port. He poured a measure.

'Gentlemen,' he said solemnly. 'Raise your glasses with me and toast our dear friend John Jefferson, British subject, distinguished soldier and a great leader of men!'

Jefferson covered his face with his hands.

Nisbet sat behind his desk and took out a letter from the drawer. Attached to it was a document of two or three pages. 'My colleague passed on this letter.'

He read:

*My dear Beggs,*
*We have investigated the case of the man who is presently in custody in the Colony of Nevis and who claims to be John Jefferson, British subject and freed man.*

*We have examined the records of soldiers landed in Nova Scotia who were previously slaves enlisted in His Majesty's armed forces during the American war. I affirm that John Jefferson is included in the ranks of those given their freedom and citizenship in return for their faithful service to the Crown. With this letter is a notarised fair copy of the page from the Book of Negroes to that effect. I also draw your attention to the fair copy of the register of decorated loyalists, which shows that the said John Jefferson served with considerable distinction as a sergeant in his regiment and was awarded a medal for his services. The citation was signed by General Sir Guy Carleton.*

*General Carleton was a man of great honour. The terms of surrender required the British to return all American property, and George Washington, the American President, had determined that 'property' included all former slaves. Indeed three of his own slaves had joined the British Army. As a matter of honour, Carlton refused to break his agreement with his troops and instead shipped them to Nova Scotia.*

*It will not have escaped your attention that the former slave owner of John Jefferson is now the President of the United States. It is therefore with special pleasure that I affirm that John Jefferson is a freeman and a British citizen.*

The two men looked at each other while Nisbet poured another glass of port.

'This changes everything,' said Josiah.

'How so?'

Jefferson had been looking modestly at the ceiling while the letter was read.

'You have the endorsement of a great British general who defied none other than George Washington to preserve British honour. This letter provides support to anyone who needs to be assured of your loyalty and your accomplishments.'

'Like most old soldiers I had forgotten most of it. But I'm proud of what I have done.'

Nisbet said, 'People on this island will see this as a justification of the decision to expand the West Indian Regiment. It will give them confidence. It makes me proud to know you, Jefferson. I've always felt privileged as a son of a planter, but as a coloured man I have every sympathy for the slaves. I am grateful to be a free man, considering how easily I could have been a slave if my father had not acknowledged me and stood by me. He was a good man and he encouraged me to be unafraid and to consider myself the equal of everyone.'

While they were talking, Josiah had been silent, struggling with his own secret. Was it time to tell his friends? What these men had told him made him realise that his own struggle to free himself from the shadow of his stepfather was of little consequence. At the same, how could he keep up his deception with these men, who were heroes as well as friends?

The moment passed. It was not the right time.

The sun continued to rise in the sky and Nisbet drew down the blind. The temperature rose but no one noticed. It was an hour of reminiscence for Jefferson and Nisbet. Josiah sat silently, listening. It was what he was accustomed to doing. He liked the company of these men. Their generosity of spirit made him see that a lack of love defined him. He was a reserved and friendless man, like his father and many other captains too. Their ambition ruled them. Friendships were the victim of their self-sufficiency. Perhaps, he might recover that part of himself – before it was too late.

# CHAPTER 16

The message, which ordered Josiah and Jefferson to present themselves at the Charlestown barracks to take the oath of loyalty and receive their warrants, presented Josiah with a challenge. He was a serving officer in the Royal Navy on half pay. He would commit a felony if he took another enlistment oath. He pondered on the matter. He was not ready to disclose who he really was; nor would he commit a crime. He would have to talk with Colonel Smith and persuade him to accept him as a mercenary – at any event, on a temporary footing. At the same time he would have to explain his dilemma to Jefferson without lying to him.

He decided he would tell Smith that he had a continuing obligation to the Royal Navy but was unable to disclose the circumstances. And he decided he would ask Jefferson to trust him. He had already talked over the enlistment with Jefferson. The army said it would eventually free the soldiers they had 'bought', offering manumission after seven years or the coming of peace, whichever was first. Jefferson, feeling he had an obligation to his fellow captives, said he would make the same seven-year commitment if they would. Josiah knew Jefferson had no family, no desire to return to Nova Scotia or Sierra Leone, and no other place to go. If home was anywhere, it was Virginia: a place where he would always be at risk. The Africans had become his family and Nevis his new home.

Josiah's meeting with Smith was satisfactory. Smith lived at the Nevis Club, a gentlemen's haven styled after great London clubs – ideal for a bachelor on the move, as Smith was. They met for dinner there, amid the comforts of an attentive staff, leather chairs and an indefinable peace, which a member of a club had once told Josiah was due to the absence of females.

Having eaten well and drunk a full bottle of claret, they sat in deep rattan armchairs on the balcony overlooking the sea, stretching their legs on the extendable flaps designed to ease the circulation.

When Josiah asked him about the regiment, Colonel Smith said, 'My responsibilities are comprehensive and my resources are stretched. I have a hundred ill-trained troops on St Kitts, a troop of twenty on Nevis, and a few dozen more on neighbouring islands. Discipline is very weak and training is negligible. If the French landed tomorrow we could scarcely resist for long. Our hope lies with you two: an experienced sergeant with battle experience and a former naval gunner who can teach us how to fight. If I can give the French a bloody nose and deter them from invading the islands – without massive support – we will have done our job.'

Josiah said, 'Colonel, I am not in a position to accept a commission or a warrant from the regiment. I was on "leave" from the Royal Navy and, you know, I was then kidnapped. I must resume my responsibilities eventually. In the meantime I am more than happy to be of service to you and the regiment.'

'My dear fellow, I had no idea! I will enquire no further, trusting your word, as a gentleman, that no crime has been committed. If you are able to assist us to train these new troops to fire a cannon, that will be very satisfactory, and I will arrange a stipend for your services.'

'Thank you, Colonel. I will do everything possible, but my friend Jefferson is the man you must build your hopes upon; he has the experience and he is a free man with a common bond with the Africans.'

'I cannot agree more. His knowledge and skills and character are evident to me. He is trusted too. We've been lucky over the last few years. We have had greater naval strength than the French for many years and we've taken several of their islands. But our intelligence says they're returning with a mighty fleet. We have to be ready for them.'

After dinner, a contract was agreed which provided Josiah's services 'until such time as His Majesty requests and requires said Joss O'Brien's services for the Royal Navy.' As he signed the agreement, Josiah reflected he had perjured himself by signing in his assumed name – but under the circumstances in which the agreement was likely to be enforced it was unlikely to be an issue. To Josiah's delight, Smith then told him the Methodist minister he had met at the small church – Charles Grey – was to serve as a chaplain to the new troops, and attorney Nisbet had taken leave from his law practice and accepted a commission as a lieutenant.

Jefferson took the King's shilling at the courthouse the next day, signing up for seven years or for 'such period in which war with France ceases'. He took the oath with his hand on the justice's Bible and received a warrant as Sergeant Major John Jefferson. He wore the brown uniform of the West Indian Regiment, while Josiah chose the plain blue uniform of a naval warrant officer. Nisbet and the new chaplain took their oaths at the same time and were commissioned, Nisbet as lieutenant and the chaplain as major.

The same day, Nisbet, Josiah and Jefferson moved to their new headquarters at Fort Charles' barracks outside Charlestown. The colonel wanted the troops to complete basic training before transferring to their permanent base on Brimstone Hill on the neighbouring island of St Kitts.

Josiah and Jefferson divided their responsibilities, Jefferson taking the older men, and Josiah the younger. Routes for separate morning runs and afternoon marches were mapped out with the help of Nisbet, who decided he would alternate between the two groups. In the evenings the men would return to camp for supper. Jefferson would teach classes on basic tactics until drums and bugles signalled the end of the day.

The first exercise was a three-mile run, beginning early one morning before the sun rose. It was a challenge. Josiah had not run for years, Jefferson for decades and Nisbet ever. Puffing and panting, calves and thighs aching, Josiah did his best to disguise his pain. The Africans could not understand why they should wear clothes under a hot sun and discarded their shirts and boots. They had covered half a mile before Josiah noticed and ordered them to return.

It was a sober and sore regiment that slunk back to camp that first day. Fortunately, most of the men had grown up in African villages where hunting put meat on the table. Despite the deprivation of the Atlantic passage, they quickly reached fine physical condition. Plentiful food and rest between their exertions led to a marked improvement after only a week.

Then they drilled. For two days they practised forming a line, turning about, quick marching and slow marching. Their new sergeant major had a powerful voice with a rich vocabulary of insults and oaths, which the Africans quickly learned and turned on their instructors. Getting them to understand that it was a matter of 'speak only if spoken to' required punishments as reinforcement. Laps of the camp and push-ups were meted out liberally. Jefferson ruled out flogging from the start. Drilling accomplished little at first, and then, just as the friends were despairing, the new recruits found their rhythm; the lines became straighter and a model of disciplined command and response emerged. Morning runs became longer and steeper, and the afternoon marches became a pleasure for everyone. To maintain rhythm and morale, the men learned the marching songs of the American war – first in broken English, and then with newly improvised chants.

*I don't want the sergeant's shilling*
*I don't want to be shot down:*
*I'm really much more willing*
*To make myself a shilling*
*Living off the pickings of the ladies of the town …*

Their march began in the lowlands on sandy lanes and undulating paths through the sugarcane fields. Then they headed for the uplands until, finally, they conquered Nevis Peak and descended its slopes to the camp one afternoon as the sun dipped slowly into a purple sea.

While the men were on route marches, the women learned to manage the camp – to cook, clean, launder the clothes and serve food. Managing the twenty-three women were two matrons who had served at Brimstone Hill. Eager to ensure that the men received the best comforts from their exertions, Josiah recruited Elizabeth Darling to supervise the kitchen. Together the women created a menu of local island food and African dishes. Delicious fruit juices greeted the thirsty men on their return to camp. Later, tables were filled with steaming food, and the men, tired and hungry, ate their fill.

On Sundays they rested at Fort Charles. Church parade, conducted by the chaplain, was followed by a football match organised by Josiah. It became the event everyone looked forward to, and soon rival teams were formed and began to compete. Afterwards the men had time to themselves but were ordered to stay near the barracks. There were few discipline issues, most of the soldiers being content in the company of their friends.

Leaving the troops in Jefferson's charge, Colonel Smith and Josiah visited Brimstone Hill, crossing over the narrow passage between the two islands. The massive stone fort perched nine hundred feet above the sea with a supremely commanding view to the south-west. Nevis Peak was visible ten miles to the south. Eight miles south of the fort was Basseterre, the principal town on the island. Smith said that it had been founded by the French and then had become a condominium of French, English and African, and recently a wholly British town in which the people spoke a Creole patois combining all three languages.

Josh asked: 'How did Brimstone Hill come to be constructed so far north of the major town?'

Smith said: 'Back at the beginning of the century, the island was divided between the French and English Settlers – this was St Christopher and the French part of the island was St Christophe. The frontier ran from the east of the island to the west just south of here. At that time, Sandy Point was considered one of the best anchorages in the British Empire and the town was thriving. At that time Fort Charles – not to be confused with Charles Fort on Nevis- was nearer to the coast and was the principal fortification of the British but it was vulnerable to bombardment from enemy ships, so they moved higher up the hill to this position. Then the island came under British control after the War of the Spanish Succession and Basseterre took over from Sandy Point as the biggest town on the island.'

'Does that mean the fort is too far away to be of help defending Basseterre? It does but don't forget the French will never take control of the island as long as we hold Brimstone Hill. But it does mean that we have to have a plan to defend Basseterre from attack too.'

The fort was guarded by a squadron of troops of the existing West Indian Regiment. The artillery platoon had only ten men. Smith explained that most of the gunners had been sent to other islands. The troops were armed with swords and pikes, it being accepted wisdom that arming them properly would be an inducement to mutiny. Discipline was lax. The buildings were green with moss, and a smell of latrines pervaded the whole fort. There was no officer present, the fort being in the charge of a fat sunburnt Welsh sergeant.

Josiah was dismayed and said so. 'The place has a

magnificent defensive position, but the troops … I'm at a loss for words.'

'I cannot disagree, but when they are trained with your men they will improve.'

'No, sir – that must not happen. Any gains we have made in training and morale will be lost the moment we mingle our Africans with this very sorry group of men. We will take the fort with vacant possession.'

'But we cannot afford to lose men. We need them.'

'Perhaps Nisbet might take command of them? Shake them up. We need a coastguard. I want to maintain our Africans' high standards by keeping them separate from the Regulars.'

'Very well. I agree and I'll speak with Nisbet.'

Smith and Josiah agreed the three platoons from the fort would be redistributed to Basseterre and Charles Fort in Nevis under Lieutenant Nisbet's command. Before they departed, Smith had the troops prepare Brimstone Hill for the new occupants. Josiah was sure little would be done if they left before the work was completed.

As the ferry returned to Charlestown, Josiah's spirits were high. Later, seated comfortably in the snug at the Bath Hotel with Jefferson and Nisbet, he explained his optimism. 'Brimstone Hill is the most amazing redoubt. I have rarely seen any better. I liken it to Gibraltar – smaller, of course, but with the same impregnable aspect. I cannot believe the French captured it but twenty years ago. Having spent the money and the labour to erect such a fortification, Smith told me the garrison was allowed to fall into such a state of decline they were forced to surrender after a short siege. This is the problem with these colonies. Britain needs all its best soldiers to fight in Europe, and these rich sugar barons aren't willing to dig into their own pockets to support local troops. They claim it's the job of the British Government. Well, this time they know they may lose everything and are finally stumping up the money.'

'Where will the French attack?'

'The French will want to retake Basseterre, but they know that to do that they have to take Brimstone Hill as well. We can try to protect Charlestown and Basseterre from landings, but a large enough force of French will mean we have to fall back to the fortifications of Brimstone Hill. I am confident that with these new soldiers we can drive off the French and set a new standard for the defence of these islands. Now tell us your news. What has happened in my absence?'

Jefferson said, 'I have rarely seen a finer body of recruits. I already knew the leaders and I've set about creating corporals who will eventually become our next sergeants. We have great men. After months of incarceration their enthusiasm knows no bounds.'

Nisbet said, 'I have good news too: we are expecting a cargo of muskets and artillery pieces from Jamaica garrison, and everyone is excited about weapons training.'

'When I was at Brimstone Hill,' Josiah said, 'we reviewed the garrison. It is as pathetic a squadron of soldiers as I have seen, Nisbet. Smith and I agreed that you should be the one to take them on and improve their discipline and morale.'

'Are you joking? I'm barely able to march and salute, never mind take on a battalion of inferior and ill-trained men. Do I have to?'

'Nisbet, I have seen you in action. There is no one on this island as organised, determined or persuasive. These men have been neglected and allowed to descend into disarray. Create an incentive. Breed a healthy rivalry among them. Can you do that?'

Nisbet nodded despondently.

'Don't worry, Nisbet, I will help you,' said Jefferson, smiling. 'We need all your men, but they must be better than they are now.'

'Come along, boys! I have a table ready.'

It was Elizabeth Darling. She too was excited to be a member of the new regime. She sat with them as they ate and explained what had been happening with the women. She was excited about their hard work and their experience. 'They've all come from villages where the women are used to working together for the tribe. There is so much public spirit among them.'

'Who is looking after them? Where are the African women lodged?'

'The Methodist church has cottages for visiting missionaries, and they have loaned these to the women. That way we keep them safe. We must be careful to ensure they continue to feel safe. When we move to St Kitts, we will do something similar. And I am very glad to report that they have all become Methodists!'

Josiah noticed that both his friends were enjoying Mrs Darling's company, perhaps too much. He felt a pang of jealousy, checking himself with the reminder it had been *his* decision not to pursue her.

He distracted his thoughts by changing the topic. 'And how are you, Jefferson?'

Jefferson settled back and took a gulp from his mug of ale. He looked like a new man; the nervousness and frustration gone, he was healthy and fit. 'I had forgotten how much I enjoy the life of a soldier! To be outside, with my men, exercising, marching, singing, training, is good for the soul! I have left the horrible things I endured behind me. I feel excited. I want to create a war machine the like of which these islands have never seen. My men are fit and pleased to be out and about after so much incarceration. There are some who are bitter, who miss family and village, but the majority are finding their new life suits them. Rather do this than be a labouring slave on a plantation! When we get to Brimstone Hill and train with weapons and artillery, they'll know they're trusted and their future is assured. And having the women to cook for them – a stroke of genius. They're eating their own wonderful food. An army marches on its stomach, and this army is well fed!'

Jefferson's laugh was infectious – a deep baritone rumble starting with a giggle and rising to a crescendo of barking mirth. It was impossible to refrain from laughing with him.

As Josiah lay in bed afterwards contemplating their move to Brimstone Hill the next day, he felt a great sense of satisfaction. It reminded him of those years on good old 'eggs and bacon' as they called his father's ship *Agamemnon*. Those halcyon years spent with his friend Weatherhead returned to his thoughts. They had been inseparable. Whenever they landed, the ship's master prescribed route marches to toughen his sailors after weeks at sea. How he and Weatherhead had hated those marches at the beginning. But as they became fit, they had learned to enjoy them. He remembered hauling guns up the mountains of Corsica. By God, they had been strong.

The memories of his friend haunted him that

night, and for the first time in many years his sleep was overtaken by a nightmare about Santa Cruz and Weatherhead's premature death. He awoke the next morning disturbed by the events that could still shake him, even now. As the light filled his room and dispelled his dreams, his dark thoughts were replaced with pleasant memories of the night before with his two friends and Mrs Darling. He felt a sense of purpose for the first time since he had left his command of *Thalia*.

The French would soon be here. He felt it in his bones. Bonaparte had planted the seed of his own hatred for the British in his soldiers. When the French fought, they were fuelled with a zeal unknown in the British armies. Josiah must be ready for them. He got out of bed and dressed, determined to ready his troops for the day of battle.

The largest body of the troops, including Jefferson and Josiah prepared to set off for Brimstone Hill. Nisbet was to remain behind at Charles Fort. They left after breakfast. Dressed in brown worsted with white breeches, white hats and shoes, led by the Union flag and accompanied by fife and drum, they formed up in a column, two by two. Colonel Smith was there to greet them and tell them they were as fine a body of soldiers he had ever seen. Then they shouldered their knapsacks, buckled on their swords or carried their pikes over their shoulders and marched out of the camp to the cheers of the women, who were left to pack the field kitchen and load it onto the baggage carts. Colonel Smith led the column through Charlestown, mounted on his white mare, while Josiah, and Jefferson marched behind him at the head of the regiment. The music brought out the townspeople, who cheered them on, children and barking dogs running alongside.

They marched all morning until they reached the Narrows. Then they sat and waited for the baggage train. The last time he had crossed the Narrows, he had been rowed across in a large dinghy with a dozen passengers. This time they were to be taken across the two-mile channel by a lugger, a spritsail barge with drop keels. Josiah's nautical interest was aroused. He asked the burly waterman, 'A Thames lighter *here*. Amazing. Where did it come from?'

'It's not from the Thames, sir. The owner is a Dutchman who lives on the next island, St Eustace. These narrows are full of sand bars and shallows and these 'ere barges are perfect. We can raise or lower the drop keels and hoist as much sail as we can carry without leeway.'

'So the narrows separating the islands aren't navigable?'

'That's right. Nothing bigger than a dinghy or one

of these luggers can get through. There may as well be one island.'

It dawned on Josiah that the west coast of St Kitts and the north-west of Nevis were protected from the east by rocky shores and these shallows. The fort was perfectly positioned to protect the more vulnerable approaches by sea to Basseterre and Charlestown in the west.

The baggage carts had arrived, and now the troops and the women came aboard. They cast off, reached the other side within five minutes. Then once again they carried everything off the boat and reloaded the carts. Forming into lines, they set off up the hilly track to their new home on Brimstone Hill ten miles away, singing their regimental song.

# CHAPTER 17

Josiah was back in the navy; at least it felt as though he was. He was saluting, he was reporting, he was demanding information, he was 'on top' of everything. His habits changed. He awoke with the sun and retired early. At day's end tiredness overcame him and, exhausted, he fell into dreamless sleep.

Jefferson likewise had reconnected with his inner soldier. It showed particularly in his attention to detail. He wanted military order to prevail; everything had to be done by the book. He wore a smart uniform and expected the same from his men. He was quick to upbraid carelessness or insubordination. On occasion he was tart with Josiah, when he felt he was slacking.

Nisbet was unused to military jargon. Josiah realised he was lost in this new world, but he was doing his best to navigate it. Colonel Smith had recruited two other planters in addition to Nisbet and had given them both the rank of captain. But they were useless. Josiah drew a line at teaching them their business. He noticed they respected Jefferson's skills but were unable to moderate their condescending superiority. He suggested to Colonel Smith that he might find them work to do elsewhere.

The new African regiment was now housed in the barracks at Brimstone Hill, while Smith and the captains and a squadron of old regulars found quarters in Basseterre. Each morning the three officers rode up to the fort, where they were outsiders; 'supernumeraries', Josiah called them.

The fort had been tidied up, but its condition was far from satisfactory. Jefferson took command, organising details to clean the quarters, to paint and repair the broken floors and windows until whitewash, paint and carpentry produced the desired result – a clean, efficient building. The parade ground was marked out with chalk, the sentry boxes were freshly painted, and troops stood duty at the gate. Lookouts were posted, and the training runs and marches resumed.

Jefferson didn't want the African women to live at the fort, and arranged to clear an area nearby, where he put up tents for them until a small barrack was complete. They too worked hard, riding down with a quartermaster corporal to buy food. They picked up the local patois and, in the market, traders realised quickly there was a penalty to be paid if they tried to cheat.

Josiah and Jefferson had their own rooms high in the fort. Breezes kept them cool in the day, and at night they could close the shutters and burn herbs to keep the mosquitos at bay. They were clean and thoroughly spartan in their furnishings. Josiah had a bunk, a table and two folding chairs. He had brought a few possessions, including a miniature of his mother which he had found for sale in Nevis.

At dinner he ate with the captains and occasionally with Colonel Smith. They talked about island life: the price of sugar, the landowning families and the latest news from the neighbouring islands. They asked Josiah about London, about the Admiralty, the famous Lord Nelson, Vauxhall Gardens and the King and Queen. Josiah answered their questions as best he could. Nisbet was full of stories about his troops and how he was easing himself into his role commanding coastal defence. His troops had resented being moved out of the fort, and Nisbet was harnessing their competitiveness with the Africans. He said they were envious that the new troops had officers with such experience. Josiah and Nisbet agreed to teach his soldiers how to improve their football. They also worked out a system of sending messages to the troops deployed around the island – by flag during the day and by beacons at night. In the evenings, when the officers had left and the troops had eaten their suppers and gone to bed, Josiah and Jefferson met in the small mess room to light pipes and talk about the day's events.

When they talked about their early lives, they found they had some things in common. Jefferson's mother had raised him. He never knew his father. Josiah said he also knew little about his own father, who had died when he was a small boy. His stepfather was a sea captain who had taken him to sea when he was thirteen.

Josiah wanted to find the strongest and most willing of the group to train with the five cannon that remained at the fort. He had interviewed soldiers from the platoon of artillery who were already at the fort and chosen three. The other forty he had selected were from the younger men he had trained on Nevis. Meanwhile he arranged to import another ten cannon, including two carronades from Jamaica. The order had been taken to Kingston by a trading ship that plied between Jamaica and the Leeward Islands. The guns were expected within a few weeks. In the meantime Josiah practised with what he had studied ballistics, using Benjamin Robin's book as a primer.

*Agamemnon* had had twenty-six 24-pounders, twenty-six 18-pounders and twelve 9-pounders. He remembered details of the gun crews too: the grizzled veterans – muscular men, fiercely proud of their gun and their team. He remembered the drills, the commands, the split-second decisions, the necessary rhythm of arming and firing a gun, and the personal discipline demanded from each member of the gun crew. As a boy he had been a powder monkey, running back and forth to the magazine. He recalled the smoke, the howling of guns firing, the tremendous vibration that shook everything. Enemy balls would penetrate the hull, ricocheting across the deck, taking off heads and smashing bodies to pieces with showers of splinters as deadly as the balls. No time for terror. Life depended on a cool head. He had become a gun captain, calling the shots. Then as he rose in the ranks, he had lost touch with the guns. As captain he could call for practice, practice, practice and measure the results in the rate of fire and accuracy, but the responsibility for firing the guns belonged to others.

The guns he ordered arrived at Basseterre together with a warning from Kingston that the islands be on lookout for a French fleet on its way to the Caribbean from France as they were likely to pass there first. Josiah discussed the news with Colonel Smith, who said he would put the islands on alert for any sign of the fleet. Later, after supper, Josiah said to Jefferson, 'We are by no means ready. We've barely taught our gunners to load and fire. They're too slow and unaware of the risk of accidents.'

'How much time do you need?'

'Well, let me see. First we need to haul the new guns up here from Sandy Point. That will take days. Then we need to complete training. I'd say three weeks as a minimum.'

'We may not have three weeks. Here's what I suggest. You keep training your gunners. I'll detach men from my squadron to drag the guns up here. I know the basics. We will also have to move some of the smaller guns from here to Nevis. I'll take care of that too. I suggest we work against a deadline of two weeks maximum, and in the meantime I hope you can get your boys into shape.'

'Jefferson, are we fooling ourselves? A frontal assault straight off the beach would carry us away in a few hours, I reckon.'

'Well, that's possible, but we can harry them when they try to land, and if we have to fall back to the fort we'll hold them until help shows up.'

'And where would that be from?'

'The Leewards Island naval squadron is our only hope.'

'I haven't seen them yet. I hope you are right.'

The two friends went to work. Josiah wanted to try his skills in relocating the guns, recalling nostalgically how he and Weatherhead had hauled guns from *Agamemnon* to the heights above Bastia in the Corsican campaign. He set about drilling his artillery. Up early at dawn they set off on a morning run, up the steepest of the hills, then gymnastics and other exercises until breakfast. Between breakfast and lunch, they practised loading and running out the cannon. Their speed could not compete with the weakest of vessels he had known, but they were much better now than they had been. In the afternoon they fired the guns. They couldn't afford to waste ammunition, but they worked with each gun until he was satisfied that they could find the range, fire and reload.

Meanwhile, Jefferson was bringing up the new guns. He worked methodically, using teams of horses loaned from the surrounding plantations to heave the heavy gun carriages up the hill. At times, when the gradient was too severe Josiah was called on to assist with blocks and tackle.

They met their two-week target and summoned Colonel Smith to a parade and a demonstration of the new guns a few days later. It was a humid day, the sun high in the sky and the towering white cumulus clouds signalling a storm was in the offing. Smith was accompanied by several planters from Nevis as well as

St Kitts. It was a passing-out parade, and everyone had a heightened sense of the occasion, accompanied by necessary nervousness that something would go wrong.

Jefferson's men marched with precision from the fort to the parade ground a short distance away to the accompaniment of snare drums, the slapping of hands on muskets and crisp orders from Jefferson's sergeants. There was a scattering of applause from the onlookers. Then it was time for the artillery display, and Josiah's men were detached from the rest of the troops and marched back into the fort, taking their positions by their cannon. Josiah told the assembled guests what was about to happen, cautioning them to block their ears when the guns fired. Then he gave his orders. The guns were run out, the charge tamped and the ball loaded. There was a target area half a mile away, and Josiah explained that for the purposes of the demonstration this should be seen as a ship. The orders given, the guns fired. A signal flag in the target area gave the score. It was little enough but it impressed the onlookers.

One of the planters asked Josiah about the range of the guns.

'Maximum range is three miles, but they're effective for only a mile or so. We're high up here and we might be able to reach as much as four miles, but at that range it will be difficult to achieve any accuracy.'

'How do you know what angle to set the guns?'

'I have a mathematical table. If we know the distance to the target, the wind speed and a few other details we can make a fair estimate. It's far easier on dry land. When I was at sea we had the movement of the ship to consider as well. That's why we liked to get as close as possible to the enemy.'

Impressed with the progress made, Smith addressed the troops, congratulating them and inviting them to Basseterre, where he would arrange a football match with Nisbet's troops, followed by a dinner. This was greeted with a hearty cheer.

Later, Josiah and Jefferson discussed the day's work.

'I was waiting for a mistake, but it never happened,' said Jefferson with a smile of satisfaction.

'I was just hoping we could get through one broadside without a gun exploding. Sometimes you need luck. It was satisfactory, but you and I know that when the time comes it will be up to these men to do whatever is necessary. Will they do that? I don't know.' Then Josiah thought for a moment, and added: 'Actually I do know. I have rarely if ever been with a group fellows with a greater sense of morale. They're not committed to these islands, but they *are* committed to each other, and that's what's important. Even the troublemakers have caught the spirit!'

On Saturday the regiment left behind a small

detachment of disappointed men to guard the fort, promising to return with a victory in the football match. One of the captains remained behind with two of Jefferson's four sergeants. Josiah's men were all invited to Basseterre, but Josiah made sure that if there was a surprise attack everything was ready; balls were stacked by each gun, and the ammunition and powder, though under lock and key in the magazine, were ready in pouches. He left a trusted corporal in charge and a good runner ready to carry a message to Basseterre.

As they marched through Basseterre all the town's people came out to greet them. Flags were fluttering and children ran around the marchers, whooping and laughing. Everyone blended together with equal enthusiasm. The town was twice the size of Charlestown and was jammed with visitors from the plantations eager to see the promised football match.

The troops on each side had a tent in which the players could change, while the others ranged themselves on the grassy banks surrounding a pitch marked out with chalk. Two posts at each end signified the goals. The team captains agreed that it would be fair if they had the same number of players on each side. They agreed on twenty men each. There would be no fighting except for the ball, and a goal would be counted if the ball passed between the posts. A referee was appointed.

The Regulars, as the older regiment called itself, had played on the pitch before, and it was no surprise that when they won the 'toss' they chose the direction to play. With the wind at their backs, they had the advantage, and soon they were three goals ahead. Jefferson's Africans, disadvantaged by the wind and angered by the opposition's success, began to fight. The referee and onlookers separated the men, and a half-hour break was taken. The match began again, and the Regulars scored another two goals before it was time for a break. In the second half, with the wind favouring the Africans, they recovered, scoring two fast goals, but the players were weary, and a halt was called. The two teams stumbled from the pitch, the one enthusiastic and happy, the other licking their wounds.

The colonel gave a speech, applauding the winners and thanking the losers, and then the two teams together with their supporters and the town's people sat down at tables loaded with food.

Josiah caught sight of Elizabeth Darling and made his way through the crowd towards her. She was talking with Nisbet but, seeing Josiah, she broke off her conversation and they strolled together as they talked.

'Did you get my letter?' she asked, linking her arm in his as they ambled down Bay Road towards the harbour.

Josiah said, 'I did get the letter, and have been meaning to write to you but I've been too busy. I would love to meet you at the cottage at Hackett Point ... but we do need to talk about *us* before we do that.'

'Josiah, there's going to be a battle. Who knows what will happen? I want to enjoy being with you a short time – while we can. We'll be away from the public eye. We don't need anything else.'

'I'll think about it,' he said carefully. He remembered the hurt he had caused Janet – how terrible it had been. He didn't want to do the same to Elizabeth. 'I don't know what's going to happen to me and I cannot say I will stay here – happy though I am at the present.'

'Don't ever worry, love, we will always be friends ... and perhaps ... *more*. Is that too much?'

'Write to me when you make the arrangements, and I will meet you there.' He took a deep breath. 'I truly care for you, Elizabeth.'

She gave his arm a squeeze and he held her hand, searching her eyes. They both knew this was the point of no return.

Later on, Josiah and Jefferson were guests of

Colonel Smith. He had arranged a private room, and a fine dinner was served to them as the soldiers feasted on the parade ground.

'I'm happy with what happened today,' Jefferson said. 'The men are beginning to understand they're on the same side. The Regulars have a new spirit. Nisbet has encouraged them to draw on their knowledge of the islands as well as to learn new skills. They're eager to use the cannon, and now that they're armed they feel like soldiers. Our men are all in this together!' Jefferson raised a toast to the two teams. 'I'm so pleased that a bond – even of rivalry – has been forged today. If the French attack, we need the Regulars to defend the beaches. We must batter the attackers at sea and defend this fort – to the last man if necessary. We need each other, and working together will be the way we will defeat the French. Here's to the men in our regiment!'

Josiah felt they expected him to say something as well. He recalled those moments as his ship prepared for battle. He said, 'I too thought the match today showed that the Regulars are a fighting force and together with the Africans will push any French back into the sea.'

As he said this, he was thinking about Corsica – about how they had outmanoeuvred the French – and he thought too about the disaster at Santa Cruz and the important role that the Regulars might play in defending Basseterre.

⁓

Two weeks had passed. True to her word, Elizabeth sent a note to say she had the small house at Hackett Point, a few miles away to the north. On the agreed day they met at a hotel in Basseterre. Josiah had hired a horse and trap with a driver. They awkwardly shook hands and Elizabeth gave him a peck on his cheek. Then they set off. The horse was old and slow, and they plodded their way through fields of cane, glimpsing the turquoise waters far below. Josiah felt awkward and sensed Elizabeth's nervousness too. When they arrived, they unloaded their bags, tipping the driver and arranging for him to return two days later.

The cottage was very simple yet beautiful, set amid palm trees on the top of a cliff with a view to the north. It belonged to a family who came here for holidays, and they obviously had children because there was a rocking horse and a top lying idle on the veranda. The owners said the servants who lived nearby would cook for them, but there was no other sign of life.

Josiah could wait no longer. As soon as they crossed the threshold he caught hold of Elizabeth and held her in a deep kiss.

To his unspoken question she asked, simply, 'Darling, why wait?'

They undressed each other, feeling a warming breeze fan their ardour. Then they fell into each other's arms, losing all sense of self and feeling only the other. Elizabeth was a generous lover. He saw she knew the arts of love, and her gentleness and lack of inhibition aroused him, but he was aware too of her needs and made sure that, in spite of his intoxication, they remained together throughout their explorations and lovemaking.

Then in a moment of calm satisfaction, they held each other before falling asleep, their legs and arms still intertwined. Satiated, loved, fulfilled.

After supper they sat out on the porch under a huge swathe of brilliant stars, feeling no need to talk, only to savour the sweet after-effects of love, holding hands and luxuriating in the pleasure of the moment.

'Oh, my darling,' Elizabeth said. 'I wanted you from the moment I saw you at the Bath Hotel. I am so bored with life, so entirely fed up with the people who rule our lives on this island, pretending that they're the elite of the world because they have sugar estates. Then you came.'

Josiah said, 'You have awoken me. Sometimes I felt like a corpse, a piece of rubbish that has been discarded, tossed on the scrap heap. You welcomed me for who I am ... and now you have given me something precious. Pray God we have some time to live it.'

It was as if the fates were listening, because the next day as they sat in the same spot, enjoying a dish of tea, Josiah saw the masts and hulls down on the horizon. They were far off, and at first Elizabeth had difficulty seeing them, but Josiah could make them out: French frigates, scouting ahead of the fleet.

He jumped to his feet. 'I must go. I must go now.'

'But dear, he's not coming to pick us up until tomorrow.'

'Wait here for him here. There's going to be a battle.'

# CHAPTER 18

It was a good five miles from the house to the junction where the road to Brimstone Hill branched off. He pounded along on foot, short of breath and grateful for a breeze and for his training runs. He passed a carriage taking a planter's lady home, a gang of labourers returning from the cane fields, then three boys playing cricket in the road. They pointed at his sweating red face, laughing. Josiah smiled and waved as he passed by.

By the time he reached the road to Brimstone Hill he was thirsty. He slowed to a walk and forced himself to climb the hill as fast as he could. It would take hours for the early ships to approach the island if they intended to attack it. He thought about Elizabeth back at the house at Hackett Point. What was she thinking as she watched the sun go down – a lonely night ahead waiting for the jogging cart to pick her up? Would she be furious with him? Had he used her? The question was painful to consider. Why had they succumbed to these feelings? It occurred to him that Janet had been a widow like Elizabeth. Then an absurd thought: *is* Elizabeth a widow?

By now he had crested the hill, and there was Brimstone Hill fortress before him with Mount Misery towering above it. The Union flag was fluttering high above the battlements, the sentries were posted and there was activity – soldiers marching, sandbags being filled, and signal flags flying. He approached the fort, panting.

'Halt!'

The sentry knew him, but would not let him proceed without correct identification. Josiah approved. He was following procedure. When he had climbed the steps to the main floor of the fort, he found Jefferson sitting behind his desk. He looked up as Josiah came into the room and smiled when he saw Josiah's red face.

'We are ready,' he said. 'Better get into uniform and have something to eat. Colonel Smith is on his way, and we'll have a conference as soon as he arrives.'

'Thanks, Jefferson. I left Elizabeth on her own at Hackett Point. I hope she'll come to no harm overnight. The driver is picking her up in the morning.'

'She'll be fine. Now go and clean up.'

Later, when Josiah and the other officers met around the mess table, Smith said, 'A French frigate was sighted off the north-east coast just before sundown. It was accompanied by two frigates and a corvette, and their course took them past the north of the island. They will check to see if there are any British warships about. I believe that we will be attacked. They know about Brimstone Hill. They want it as a base for their attack on our islands. They were here twenty years ago for the same purpose. We must be prepared for a landing tonight, and a full-scale attack tomorrow morning.

'I want us to consider every aspect of an attack, beginning with our deployment of the Regulars and then the deployment of the Africans, and then lastly I want to hear from Josiah on the readiness of our gunners.'

Nisbet stood and, using a rod, pointed to the map of the islands. 'Sir, I already have my coastal platoons deployed here, here and here, on St Kitts.'

The rocky east coast had few beaches, and the hills rose steeply from the shoreline to the range that ran like a spine bisecting St Kitts into east and west. On Nevis the shoreline lent itself to more choices for invaders, with the island ranged around the cloud-capped mountain. It was an unlikely target, being distant from Brimstone Hill. Nevertheless, Nisbet had a lookout there with bonfire and signal flags to pass messages back to Brimstone Hill if landings occurred there.

Jefferson said he anticipated a French attempt to haul cannon to Mount Misery overlooking Brimstone Hill and was locating men on its ridges to prevent attempts to overlook the fort. Josiah took the floor and described the likely targets of his gunners – ships attacking the Sandy Point from the west. He described how he had been in touch with the Dutch owner of the lugger that carried passengers between the two islands, and the Dutchman had agreed in the event of an attack that he would make his ship available for in-shore operations.

The hours crept passed. A flow of information from lookouts began to come in. Messengers reported the French were approaching. Jefferson moved more troops north to Mount Misery.

Josiah worried about Elizabeth on her own at Hackett Point. That area was vulnerable to attack, but he was reassured that Nisbet had a platoon nearby. Tired after his long run, he decided to take a rest, leaving instructions to be woken if anything happened. He inspected guns one last time before returning to his room and then fell asleep, fully clothed.

The first light of dawn broke, and he woke with

a start and hurried to the mess to see what was happening. He was there when a messenger from coastal defence arrived from the north-east of the island. Puffing and panting, the messenger reported sighting French troops ashore with a cannon. They had succeeded in landing on a small beach on the east coast and were manoeuvring their cannon up the slopes to the north. Coastal defence were trying to find the frigate. It seemed to have landed the troops and then stood out to sea.

'They won't get far with that! They have no idea of our defences and the troops we have,' said Jefferson. 'They're thinking we're in the position we were last time they came – underarmed and poorly organised. I have my men deployed. But I don't want to alert the French yet – otherwise they will call for reinforcements. Let them think we're unprepared until we're ready.'

The dawn light grew, and the night mist that had cloaked the hills began to fade in the strong sun. A single battleship was heading towards Sandy Point.

Josiah took a telescope and climbed to the highest point of the fort before returning to report. 'It's a monster – at least a hundred gun first-rater. This is definitely the fleet from France. It's still three miles away. When she gets into range – perhaps a mile from the coast – we may have a target.'

Breakfast arrived: coffee, bread and hot porridge. They ate quickly. Then Colonel Smith said he wanted to return to Basseterre to review the situation there. Between breakfast and midday all was quiet. The observers reported that the French sweating with the cannons on the hills were making very slow progress. Their goal was a plateau at the heights above. The defenders kept under cover so the French would not know they were being observed.

More battleships appeared on the horizon – smaller but no less threatening for that. By dinner time the French ships had anchored. The watchers saw a cutter lowered from the battleship and making its way towards the town, a white flag fluttering from the stern.

A few hours passed, and Smith returned from his inspection. 'The French have given us two hours to respond to their conditions or they'll open fire on the town. The planters they met are divided in their opinion. The French want supplies – cattle, water, firewood and provisions for their fleet. They say they'll post a small force here to ensure we give them what they want. The older planters remember what happened last time and think we should accommodate them. The younger want to resist. I've told them matters are out of their hands and called for volunteers. I expect hostilities to begin within an hour, gentlemen.'

Josiah remembered the disastrous attack at Santa Cruz. There was similarity between both situations: underestimating the enemy. At Santa Cruz the British had underestimated the ability of the Spanish commander to repel a landing from the sea.

'Colonel Smith, I suggest that we minimise any intelligence about our strength. We should disguise our guns to make it appear we have few, keep our troop movements to a minimum and wait until their ships are close enough for our guns.'

Smith said, 'Jefferson, I want the French who are already ashore to believe they have not been seen. Let them get as far as possible before taking them.'

Josiah said, 'When we fire on their ships in Sandy Point Anchorage, we have to expect they will move their fleet further South and attack Basseterre. I'll ride down to Basseterre and see if Nisbet is ready for that.'

The minutes ticked by. As the deadline for a response to the French offer expired, Josiah and Nisbet were constructing a deadly trap for the invading force. Josiah was impressed by Nisbet's handiwork and returned to the fort confident they could drive the French back to their boats. He heard hear muskets firing in the distance. A messenger, sweat pouring from his face, stumbled into the fort to report that Jefferson's men had taken the cannon and five prisoners. An eye to his telescope, Josiah estimated the range to the leading ship – about three quarters of a mile. The battleship lay further out, keeping its distance from the guns of the fort– he estimated a mile. It was unlikely the French admiral had learned the fate of his landing party. He made some calculations of the range, consulting the tables he had made earlier. The frigate, he could see, had anchored by the stern and was winching itself into a position to deliver a broadside to the town. He would take that one first.

The balls were heated, the cannon were loaded and the matches lit. They awaited Smith's orders. Smith had delivered the news of a likely French attack as late as possible to the townspeople, urging them to flee to the hills.

Finally Smith decided he had given everyone enough time to leave Basseterre and Sandy Point. He gave the order to Josiah: 'Fire at will.'

Josiah mounted the steps to the gun platform. His men were waiting impatiently. Josiah gave them the coordinates of the frigate and then watched as the men manhandled the guns into position. He checked his calculations again: the wind speed, the humidity, the breezes at sea level. The frigate was a long way off.

'Fire!'

The thunder of fifteen guns rumbled through the surrounding hills. Smoke and acrid smells surrounded him.

'Reload!'

He waited for the smoke to clear. Already the guns were being reloaded. The gun crew were working together smoothly. His telescope was glued to the frigate far below, unaware of what was about to happen to them. The balls would reach them before the reports from the guns.

He saw splashes and estimated the distance to the moored ship. At least fifty paces. Really not bad, and the pattern was good. He could see that the crew on the frigate were already aware of what was happening. He recalculated the elevation and made adjustments.

'Fire!'

This time at least three balls reached the ship. One skipped on the water and struck the hull, another hit the deck and bounced into the sea. A third reached its target. Through his telescope he saw men reeling, running, falling. The ship was in disarray, its sails afire, bodies strewn on the decks.

'Reload! Keep the same elevation.'

He turned his attention to the flagship further out to sea. There was activity on the deck. *They can't elevate their guns to reach us here*, he thought. *If I can calculate the distance, they'll be sitting ducks as well.*

The African gunners were enjoying their work, sweating hard as they reloaded and fired, cheering each other on, powder monkeys running back and forth to the magazine.

He returned his telescope to the frigate. It had managed a broadside at the town. A building had caught fire. He saw figures running about with buckets and hoses, trying to extinguish the blaze.

And now the frigate was cutting its moorings. It was leaving! Another round of balls flew towards it, and the mast shattered and toppled overboard. A cheer went up. A sail was being hoisted on the mizzen mast and it was slowly moving. Not a good target. Better not waste their ammunition.

'Cease fire!'

He could just about reach the flagship, which was still manoeuvring to anchor by the stern. He studied his numbers carefully – distance, wind, humidity. More adjustments. He called out a new direction of fire and elevation.

'Fire!'

The guns fired, smoke billowing from their barrels. Deafening. The flagship. It was a mile and a half away. Enough to give them a scare at least.

He had his eye to his telescope and saw the first balls splash into the sea twenty or thirty yards beyond the ship. The crew began to busy themselves as if to move the ship. It seemed they knew his guns could reach them if they stayed where they were.

'Reload!'

Two or three balls struck the ship at the stern. Not enough to do any serious damage, but someone was down. Perhaps the captain, with luck. By now the sails were being hoisted, the anchor was being raised and the ship was making its escape. Time for one more round.

The guns fired. He felt the reverberation through his feet. The smoke cleared. The frigate was well out to sea now. Beyond his range. The final round struck the battleship amidships. There was confusion aboard, but Josiah admired the disciplined way the crew continued to work to get her underway.

No point in using any more ammunition. It was over.

～

Another council of war. Smith presided again. Josiah noticed how he was growing into the role. Smith was untroubled by what had happened. A month ago he would have been counselling caution, and no doubt his fellow planters were even now counting the cost. But his blood was up. His words were short, his tone sharp. Any sense of superiority was gone. They were his team, his men. This was war. Josiah wondered where he had fought in the past. Perhaps in the American war. That might explain why he had taken such a liking to Jefferson.

'We've blooded them, caused some damage,' Smith said. 'Honour will demand they return and extract a price. They cannot do otherwise, or this story will travel around the world. We can expect another five or six enemy ships, perhaps an invasion force. They'll attack the town and the fort. Seizing the fort will remove the threat to their ships, and taking the town will enable them to force the island to surrender.'

'I'm sorry, sir, but I disagree.'

'Josiah, speak your mind.'

'The fort is a distraction. If they're able to secure the town, the fort will come next. Dividing their forces is *not* what they'll do. And if they keep their ships out of range, what damage can the fort inflict on them once they land? We must concentrate our forces in Basseterre and be ready for them tonight. We can fall back to the fort if they overwhelm us.'

'I agree with Josiah,' said Jefferson.

'Very well. But Jefferson, you will man fall-back positions in case of retreat. I estimate an invasion force of perhaps five hundred. We have only two hundred troops and perhaps another hundred volunteers.'

Jefferson said, 'Colonel, we have fewer men, but we know the terrain. I'll set up a diversion to let them think we're hunkered down at the fort.'

It was agreed. Josiah had time to eat and to take a short rest before returning to Basseterre. Meanwhile he had the smashers brought out and loaded to cover the approaches to the fort in the event they had to retreat. Apart from a small garrison of ten men, the fort was emptied of its troops. As promised, Jefferson set up a small body of men to cover a potential retreat, and the rest of the men began the two hour march to Basseterre.

The point of landing would surely be the quay. Further out there were exposed beaches. The French would most likely make a head-on charge down the quay to the cover of the warehouses and then into the town centre. The French would plan for it to be over in a matter of minutes.

Darkness fell, and with it a gentle breeze sprang up. Everything was done efficiently and quietly. They had to give the impression of inactivity, of incapacity. Josiah checked the gunners. He had brought down his best men. The cannon were positioned to sweep the quay. They were concealed in a timber yard, the logs piled high enough to provide a screen. The logs were to be released when the order was given. These would then roll down the steeply sloping street, making it hard for the enemy to charge the guns.

By eleven o'clock Josiah was ready to concede the French were not coming that night. And then: a faint splashing. Oars. They had muffled their rowlocks, but the stillness of the night amplified any sounds.

From their hiding place they saw marines land. The invaders slipped over the edge of the wharf and into the shadows of the warehouses. Soon they had satisfied themselves no one was about and gave the signal. Dozens of sailors and marines came ashore in minutes.

To the north, firing broke out. A few shots in response, and the illusion was destroyed. The French troops marched briskly towards the town square. When they were a hundred yards away, Josiah gave the order, and Jefferson's men released the logs. They rolled towards the approaching men.

'Fire!'

The guns were loaded with bar and chain. The first rank of the French, perhaps fifty or so, fell immediately, like wheat before a reaper's scythe. To Josiah's right, another gun fired, catching the French in crossfire. Jefferson's sharpshooters were in the upper windows of the warehouses, picking off the officers. The invasion force hesitated, and Josiah fired his deadly smasher, glass, shrapnel and stones mowing down the enemy. The French fell back. Then there was pandemonium as they fled to their boats. Jefferson's men cut off their retreat and took prisoners, Jefferson himself calling for his men to spare the prisoners' lives. They took them into a warehouse and set up a guard.

The French filled their boats with their injured

and rowed back to their ships, the Regulars and the Africans firing at them as they disappeared into the dark.

Then there was a hush but for the screams of the wounded.

The attack was over; now there remained the awful business of dealing with the wounded and dead.

❧

'They won't be back today,' Josiah said. 'But tomorrow is another day.' He was exultant, as proud of their fight as any he had witnessed.

Josiah and Jefferson returned to the fort. Colonel Smith, satisfied with his night's work, lit a pipe and handed glasses of whisky to each of the officers. 'We lost twenty men. Their casualties were over fifty dead, fifty taken prisoner and another hundred injured. Surely they cannot feel it worthwhile to return for more?'

'Colonel, we have given them every reason to return,' Josiah said. 'Their honour is at stake. To retreat from a mauling by the troops of a small island is impossible to accept. They will be back with a larger force, and they will try to take this island tomorrow night.'

'I suspect Josiah is right.' Jefferson was tired but triumphant. 'The question is what are we going to do?'

Josiah said, 'We have to go on the offensive. I'll take the lugger, mount a small cannon, and drift through the shallows to the French fleet and upset them. They are licking their wounds. I could be there in a couple of hours. Let me take a handful of men. We'll be back by dawn. By the way, where is Nisbet?'

'He's out inspecting his positions around the island, checking on any attempts by the French to get a foothold on the remoter beaches.'

Four soldiers loaded the small five-pounder cannon, powder and ball onto the cart, and Josiah and the party set off towards the Narrows. By now it was three in the morning. They'd have another three hours of darkness. Fortunately there was a good moon to light their way, and a breeze blowing from the east would assist them too.

The lugger was tied to the wharf as promised. Its sideboards were raised. There was no one about. It was easy to load the cannon and secure it in the prow. They hauled up the single huge sail and cast off the lines. Without its side boards, the lugger drifted rapidly through the shallows. Josiah stood at the wheel and gave orders to lower the side boards halfway. Then, working from memory, he steered the ship towards the anchorage, which he estimated was three miles to the north. The others lit a fire in the brazier and fed it with wood. They had found old sail down below, cut it into ribbons and poured tar from a barrel onto the rags. Then they balled up the rags and put shot inside each bundle before tying them up with spare lines. As they drifted they piled up their home-made bombs.

Josiah saw the French ships in the distance silhouetted by the dying moon. He steered for the nearest, a two masted sloop.

'Get those bombs ready. Light them as we approach.'

They coasted up to the stern of the corvette. No one was on watch. The French knew there was no threat from the sea; the island had no naval ships.

Jefferson lit his bomb and heaved it aboard. It flew through the open window of the great cabin and exploded in a shower of sparks and flames. They moved on to the frigate anchored nearby. Again there was no watch – or if there was, they were asleep. The same strategy. Three bombs through the stern windows.

Now that they'd made their presence known, they only had time to fire the cannon twice at the flagship before they turned tail. A second corvette, wide awake, pursued them. The corvette's sails were up and its anchors away before they had fired the last round. The lugger responded sluggishly as they jibed and headed for home. The corvette was only a few hundred yards behind them, and its speed gave it the advantage.

Josiah steered for the shallowest water. Swinging

the lead, a voice called out from the depths. 'By the mark, five. By the mark, four, by the mark, three.'

Josiah said: 'Haul up the keels!'

The lugger picked up speed, skimming over the waves towards the centre of the Narrows. Behind them the corvette, under full sail, overhauled them until it ran out of depth. As it struck sand it pivoted and lay over on its side, men, guns and cargo spilling into the sea. Further off, efforts to quench the fire on the second corvette failed, and as it burned furiously towards the magazine, the crew of over a hundred men hastily abandoned ship. With a huge explosion, it blew. The blast echoed in the hills. The devastating sight reminded Josiah of *L'Orient* at the Battle of the Nile.

As dawn broke Josiah and his men returned triumphantly to Brimstone Hill. But as they looked over the ramparts at the bay, they could see that the French had supplemented their numbers with more ships. In addition to the smoking wrecks of the ruined corvette, there was the battleship and its two frigates, but now a second battleship and a third frigate as well rode at anchor.

They looked at each other uncertainly. 'They'll be back tonight,' Colonel Smith said.

Josiah searched the horizon. In the distance, perhaps twenty miles away, he saw more sails. His heart sank. The odds were against them.

He said, 'Colonel, there are more French ships on the horizon. There's nothing to be done other than gather ourselves and prepare for another assault – one we will be unable to withstand. I, for one, need to sleep a few hours. At the speed they're travelling it will be another four hours at least before they arrive.'

Jefferson said, 'I will prepare a plan to defend the fort.'

They agreed that planning for a robust defence was their only remaining option. Without admitting it, and despite their achievements, they knew their new plan had little chance of success.

# CHAPTER 19

Josiah awoke. He rose and washed himself in the basin, sponging his aching body and drying himself with a towel. He dressed in a freshly laundered shirt and breeches, which his servant had left out for him while he slept.

As he made his way to the mess, he passed his men hard at work. They were filling sandbags and passing them along a chain to bolster the battlements. Piles of cannon balls were stacked beside the guns. It was hot and soon he began to sweat. Jefferson had the place humming – men running to and fro, a squad of men at the firing range and others busy preparing for what was to come.

He sat at the table and his orderly brought him coffee, bread and fruit. He was hungry. No one came to see him, and as he ate he thought about the day ahead, the preparations he must make. He dismissed the thought that by the next morning he might be wounded or a prisoner. Then he thought about his men. These men who had endured a terrible ordeal had been saved from a life of slavery. For what? To be killed or enslaved by a superior French force?

For the first time in many months he thought about his father. Where was Horatio? *He* always prepared for battle knowing he would be victorious – or in his grave. Surrender or defeat never crossed *his* mind. Josiah thought about his famous saying: 'Westminster Abbey or the House of Lords!' Well, sooner or later his luck *would* run out. He knew what Horatio meant, and how it motivated him. He needed to adopt that attitude. 'Westminster Abbey or the House of Lords.' He chuckled as he repeated it to himself.

The orderly returned, placed an envelope on the table and then gathered the breakfast things.

'For you, sir. Delivered by messenger. Colonel Smith says to tell you that he will be meeting with the officers at dinner in the mess at two o'clock.'

He saluted, picked up the tray and left Josiah with the letter.

It was from Elizabeth.

'My dear Joss,' he read,

*I have stayed on at Hackett Point. After you left, the family whose cottage this is said it was too dangerous to return to Nevis. I am still here and would like it very much if you could help me find a safe place.*

*Truly yours,*
*Elizabeth.*

His immediate reaction was to dismiss her fears. Yet he felt responsible for her, alone on the edge of the battlefield. If the French landed in force she might become a victim of their lust. At least he must bring her back to the fort where she would be safe – safer than at Hackett Point.

He went to find the colonel, but Smith was away with Jefferson. It would take a maximum of two hours to ride there and back. He hurried to the stable to saddle the colonel's white mare. He was interrupted by the groom, who helped him attach a second pair of stirrups for his passenger after he explained his intention.

Mounting up, he rode slowly down the hill to the junction and, turning north, broke into a canter. It took him only thirty minutes to reach the Hackett Point cottage. He tied his horse to a rail and strode up the path, and was about to knock when Elizabeth opened the door and threw her arms around his neck, kissing him with tears of relief. He told her of his plan to take her back to Brimstone Hill.

While she packed her bag he took a cloth and wiped the sweat from the mare and gave her a drink. Elizabeth closed the blinds and shut the door behind them. Then he mounted the mare and pulled Elizabeth up behind him, and they set off for the fort. By now the sun had disappeared behind clouds, while the close air and rising wind were portents of a storm. As they trotted along the road, she asked him what had happened. He told her about the attack on Bassetere, the terrible destruction and the retreat of the French marines.

She said, 'Joss, I want to say something very important.'

He held his breath as she said;' I've thought and thought about you, and I realise that you love me ... but I know – in my heart – you will soon be gone.'

'Elizabeth, I have planned no such thing, I assure you.'

'I know you haven't, but I've seen enough people coming and going from these islands to know who stays and who goes. You are destined for other things, and you do not like life on this island. If you stayed here you *would* become a wealthy man because you're so capable – but you don't want that.'

They rode in silence for a while. As the fort came

into sight, Josiah said heavily, 'As usual, Elizabeth, you are right. I am *not* a planter. I cannot abide the "slave society". It makes me sick to see the wealthy English living in such luxury while their slaves labour under the hot sun. In England the poor are everywhere to be seen and their lives are very, very, hard, but at least they're free. No, I could not stay here. Yet I do not have any other plans. All I know is that I do love you.'

They had reached the junction, and Josiah dismounted. He led the horse up the steep track with Elizabeth as its passenger. When they reached the fort, Josiah took her to his room and said he would move in with Jefferson. He left her, after explaining to her that tonight there would be an attack. He asked his orderly to find an African woman who would give her food and ensure her of necessary comforts. Then he said farewell, feeling impossibly formal and stiff.

He carried his kit into Jefferson's room and asked his orderly to set up another bunk. His heart was heavy, but he knew that no relationship could be sustained without complete truth. He asked himself once again why he did not explain himself.

He had lived his whole life under the shadow of his father. He had to learn to live outside, to know who he was and what he was capable of. And it was true, despite his deceptions: he did have a better sense of that than he had two years ago. Yet he was not ready to go back to living the life that everyone expected from him. In the meantime, he would guard his heart and avoid hurting people with his deception. Morosely, he thought: *perhaps this will soon be over and I will be dead.* The thought did not displease him and he began, for the first time, to understand Horatio's bleak commitment to the notion of Providence – that old-fashioned word for God – who would decide the matter one way or the other, no matter what one wanted.

At dinner the officers assembled in the mess. Josiah took Jefferson aside and explained why he had set up a bunk in his room. As he expected, there was no complaint.

Dinner was a simple meal of roast beef and potatoes. There was no wine and only a weak ale to wash it down. While they ate, Colonel Smith explained his new deployments. He expected the French to land a smaller force in the Narrows where it was easy to wade ashore and foray to the east of Brimstone Hill. Meanwhile the main body of French troops would attack Basseterre again, with beach landings to the north and south. He had deployed his artillery accordingly. Nisbet had guns and troops at the Narrows and had reconnoitred all the likely landing places.

Josiah asked, 'What is your plan if the French encircle Brimstone Hill?'

'In that case, we will fall back to positions to the north as well as the fort itself. Of course the fort *is* a formidable obstacle, and they will have to drag artillery up the road from Basseterre. That will not happen until they have us besieged.'

'How long do you think we could hold out?'

'That will depend on the strength of their attack and our resistance. If we give them a bloody nose tonight I am sure we will be in for a long siege.'

'What about the weather?'

'There's a big storm coming,' Colonel Smith replied. 'All the usual signs – the heat and humidity, the birds taking shelter, the gusting winds. The storm will help us and hinder the French. We must assume that they know that, so tonight may be their last chance for several days.'

Jefferson said, 'My thoughts exactly, Colonel Smith. We have to hold out until the storm gives us relief.'

'Have you prepared the troops?' the colonel asked.

'Yes, we've given the orders for tonight. We've distributed capes and sou'westers to everyone and tied down as much of our equipment as possible.'

Colonel Smith said, 'Very well; I think we have done everything we can. We will serve supper early so that the African women can return to their barracks.'

Josiah's orderly had taken dinner to Elizabeth in

his room. Later in the afternoon he went to see her. She dropped the book she had been reading, stood and looked at him inquiringly. 'Any signs of the French?'

'They will be here, have no doubt. Listen, a big storm is coming. Every sign is that it is going to blow very hard. We're hoping it will deter the French. When the storm begins, close your shutters and put your bed against the wall. If the roof comes off, get under the bed.'

Elizabeth laughed. 'Joss, I've lived through hurricanes. This won't be the last.'

'I won't be able to see you again until the morning. The French are unlikely to get to the fort tonight, but I promise if anything unexpected happens I'll come back for you.'

'Joss, I've been thinking. About the other day. You don't owe me anything. Your friendship is enough. I will always love you.' Then, covering her embarrassment, she hugged him and turned him towards the door and said lightly, 'Take good care of yourself, dear.'

He returned to the mess. Jefferson was there, but Colonel Smith had left.

'Jefferson, if you were the French where would you come ashore?'

'I would avoid the area within range of Brimstone's guns. The east coast is too rocky. So I would land in the Narrows and work towards the east of Brimstone

Hill from there. Meanwhile, as the Colonel said, the main body will attack Basseterre. We have Nisbet's two artillery units set up to defend the Narrows – guns one each side. Would you take a squad down there and reinforce him? We'll send more ammunition with you.'

'I will go immediately.'

Josiah quickly packed his knapsack, took his musket and saddled a horse. The afternoon sun had given way to a trembling grey twilight. The palm trees were bending in the stiffening breeze. As the mare trotted gently down the trail from the fort, Josiah considered how Jefferson had grown. At the beginning, Colonel Smith had always asked for Josiah's opinion first and seemed to think of Jefferson as the junior. Now Jefferson's superior knowledge of land battles and his great success at Basseterre had given him the leading role in the defence of the island. Josiah was third in the chain of command. The horse stumbled on a rock and Josiah pulled its head up. The strange thing was that he didn't mind. He was pleased by Jefferson's success. In years gone by he would have been jealous.

The horse crested a low hill, and before him in the fading light was the water dividing St Kitts from Nevis: the Narrows. A heavy sea was pounding the eastern shore and great rollers were piling up as they met the shallow seabed. He found Nisbet had prepared well. There were impressive earthworks thrown up around four cannon. The carronade's wide mouth and a stack of shrapnel and chain would be the most effective deterrent. Nisbet was pleased to see him, confident and relaxed in the face of the battle to come. Josiah thought he had never seen him happier. Nisbet's life as a lawyer was in the past. When he greeted Josiah, his voice was deep and he had that measured way of speaking of an officer in command.

After inspecting the gun platform, Josiah said, 'You've been hard at work, I see. There's no more advice I can give. The extra troops will be here shortly. I warn you, though: we consider this stretch of beach may bear the brunt of the attack tonight!'

'We've a commanding position here. We'll repel anyone approaching from the sea – as we did in Basseterre.'

'In the dark? You won't see them.'

'We have flares and rockets.'

Josiah felt proud of him. For a moment he wondered how things might have been if he had told Nisbet weeks ago that they were cousins. They would never have become such good friends. There would have been suspicions about his motives and awkward social moments. Other people would have been involved. But still …

By now it was dark. Sentries were posted along the beach and runners were in place to carry messages. They found a comfortable spot – two trees next to each other – and they rested their backs against them and settled down to wait. It was totally silent except for the sighing of the wind in the palms and the waves breaking on the beach.

'Do you ever regret not visiting Britain?' asked Josiah.

'Yes, I do. I have relations there – an aunt through marriage as well as Scottish cousins.'

'Did you ever dream of going to university?'

'If I had been born to a white mother I might have gone to Edinburgh University.'

Josiah laughed. 'When I was a young lad my mother wanted me to study there too, but my father insisted I become a sailor. We might have met up in Edinburgh if things were different.'

'I have no regrets.'

'Are you the owner of the Nisbet estate?'

'Yes and no. There are a few properties in the family, and I have two of them – both of decent size, but I still need to work as a lawyer. I have an entailed estate as well that will go to my son if I ever marry.'

'Interesting. At least your father looked after you. Mine – my stepfather, that is – disinherited me. I was difficult and I challenged him often. His unfaithfulness to my mother divided us and drove us apart. I find it hard to forgive him.'

'Sir!' A corporal was running towards them. He stopped and saluted. 'Our scouts report sounds of oars.'

'Well, this is it, Joss. We have to hold them – to the last man.'

Josiah embraced him. 'May God protect you.'

'And you as well.'

# CHAPTER 20

Nisbet addressed his men. 'When I give the signal, we open fire with our muskets first. We wait until they are no further than fifty paces before we fire. Then the carronade and cannon. Fight hard, and remember: the French are brutes. If they take the islands we will lose everything – our homes, our wives and loved ones: everything dear to us.'

Josiah said, 'A famous admiral used to say to me: "Westminster Abbey or the House of Lords." What he meant was "Death or Glory", and that's what I say to you: *Death or Glory!*'

'Death or Glory!'

Then they waited. The last rays of the sun disappeared. Twilight faded into heavy blackness – a moonless night. The strong breeze had died and there was a feeling of expectation – as if the storm were a third actor in the conflict to come.

A shout and the sound of voices. Bullets whined over the emplacement. Nisbet gave a signal and a flare rose in the darkness. The French marines searched for cover. Nisbet's muskets fired a volley. The enemy, surprised, fell back towards the beach. Several of them fell.

Nisbet raised his sword. 'Come on, men. After them!'

They pursued the French marines down the hill towards the beach. Shots rang out from their left and right. They paused. Then the French reformed and stormed towards them again. Nisbet's men took cover behind the emplacement. Then the smasher did its brutal work, and this time the French fell back in disarray.

Josiah, sword in hand, led the second charge. They pursued the French down the slopes towards the water, the Regulars firing their pistols and muskets as they ran. At the water's edge it was chaotic as the sailors pushed out the boats, and soldiers scrambled aboard with their wounded mates, while the pursuers hacked and shot at them.

Then the French were gone. Josiah made his way back to the emplacement. He found Nisbet propped against the wheel of a cannon. Josiah saw the torn shirt, the tattered sleeve and the missing arm, the head at an odd angle. He knelt.

'I'm done for, Joss. I'm finished. Kiss Jefferson for me. Give my love to my mother and sisters. Tell the colonel I died a soldier's death!'

'Nonsense! We'll get these wounds taken care of.'

Nisbet spoke in a whisper, and Josiah bent closer. 'Joss, you are my best friend. You took me with you.' He coughed. 'My life is done. Keep working to help the slaves get their freedom.' His voice was weaker. 'I leave it to you.'

Josiah said, 'Nisbet, you have challenged all I believed to be true. If only …'

Nisbet's breathing became lighter. He was bleeding from his wounds, and there was nothing Josiah could do.

He whispered, 'Joss. Promise me. The slaves …'

Josiah held him as he said the Lord's Prayer. Nisbet's eyes closed and his breathing stopped. He was gone.

The soldiers straggled back to them and reported that the French had returned to their ships. Josiah called the corporal to form a stretcher party to carry Nisbet's body to the fort. Then he posted a guard and gave orders to keep the watch.

He accompanied the stretcher as the men struggled up the hill to the fort. He wept as he walked; not since the death of Weatherhead had he felt so bereft.

In the distance came the crackle of gunfire and faint cries. The wind had risen again and a smoky moon flitted between the scudding clouds.

'Friend or foe?'

They gave the password to the sentry and passed through the gate; they took Nisbet's body to the mess and laid the stretcher on the floor and covered him with a sheet. Josiah went to find Jefferson.

He was on the ramparts, ebullient, and proud of the night's work. 'Another glorious night, Joss. We've repulsed attacks at five places on the island – You and Nisbet have a victory to celebrate.'

Josiah closed his eyes. 'Nisbet died fighting. I have taken his body to the mess.'

Jefferson sat, head in his hands. Tears ran down his cheeks. 'What happened?'

Josiah told him, describing the attack, Nisbet's robust defence, the counter-attack and the stray ball that killed him. 'He was valiant to the end.' He added, 'There will be a time for us to mourn.'

Jefferson breathed deeply and said, 'Our men acquitted themselves well – with great courage and determination. The French never anticipated our opposition. They had no idea. And we had the advantage of the higher ground. Our losses were light – four men dead – five including Nisbet – and a dozen wounded. And we have captured five of their marines.'

Josiah said: 'They will be back.'

From the darkness, a voice said, 'In the meantime, we must bury our brother.' Josiah looked up, startled. It was Colonel Smith; he had appeared from below. Smith, the *planter*? Smith the man who owned slaves, part of the island's establishment?

'He was a man of great courage,' Smith said, 'and we will give him a soldier's farewell. He is an example to all on these islands.'

He saw the look on Josiah's face. He flushed. 'You think we're all depraved, Joss.'

Josiah made to speak but Colonel Smith continued, 'Nisbet is from a good family, an old family of Scottish stock. He was man of great integrity who never nursed a grudge. Always the first to jump to and get things done. There are many like him on the islands, ignored for too long. In years gone by I scarcely knew Nisbet, though I knew his reputation. Since he has been my right-hand man commanding the Regulars, I've watched him grow and become … a leader.'

His voice faltered and he walked to the window and stared out. The only sound was the wind, sighing through the cracks in the shutters.

They did not go to bed that night; Josiah battled his grief alone on the rampart. It was the death of

Weatherhead again. This time, mercifully, it had been fast. Back then it was different: over the weeks, Weatherhead had struggled on, his wounds discharging pus, his agony extenuated by liberal doses of laudanum, until he expired in the arms of Horatio. Why did God take the just and good and leave the evil and incompetent? Guilt overwhelmed him. Why had *he* survived?

The morning dawned, the sky full of menace. The clouds were full, heavy, grey – ascending to black, with flashes of lightening adding to their menace. In the anchorage to the lee of the island the French battleships rolled in their moorings.

After breakfast, the officers reported the losses. Two dozen French had been killed and five of their own. Jefferson was not at breakfast and did not appear until mid-morning. Josiah, sick to the heart, revisited the guns of the fort and talked to his men. He scanned the horizon. The enemy fleet was still visible out to sea. The French squadron attacking the island was still anchored beyond the range of his guns.

At noon Jefferson reappeared and joined him in the mess. He had been out inspecting his units and talking to his men. He had news. 'We've been inter-rogating the prisoners. We've learned little. They're all Jacobins, and they seem to think we're stupid savages – except one: a black fellow from Haiti. I think there are possibilities. We've tried to reassure him we would not return him to the French if he talked with us. Problem is none of us speak enough French, and we've had to rely on a man from Basseterre.'

Josiah said, 'I speak the language passably.'

'You do?'

'Bien sûr.'

Jefferson ordered the sergeant with him to bring the prisoner up.

After a short while the sergeant returned with the prisoner and two guards.

'Sit down!'

The prisoner sat, with a guard on either side. His arms were tied. Josiah spoke to him and after an initial pause he began to respond, at first in monosyllables and then in a torrent of words.

Several minutes passed before Josiah said in English, 'I need to give him an incentive. I'd like to suggest we offer him his freedom and a chance to enlist with us. He's a slave. If we can offer better terms, I think he might talk.'

'Subject to complete cooperation and honesty. If we find he is lying—'

'Yes, of course.'

Josiah talked to the prisoner for several more minutes. Then he turned to Colonel Smith. 'I think we have an agreement. He's a marine, poorly treated by his fellow marines and willing to join us. He wants a promise in writing.'

'Who is he?'

'He's from Haiti.'

'Ah,' said Colonel Smith. 'A troubled place. His name?'

'Jacob Ricard. He's a marine private serving on the flagship.'

Now the conversation picked up speed. Ricard was angry and spoke quickly with many gestures.

At last, Josiah turned to Jefferson and Colonel Smith. 'This man has intelligence of the first order. Make sure he's kept separate from the other prisoners until we can finish our interrogation.'

Jefferson said, 'Sure, but what have you learned?'

'He was privy to some very interesting information as a marine guard posted in Admiral Villeneuve's cabin. He was present when matters of importance were discussed. Senior people often think the butler or the footman – or, in this case, the guard – are part of the furniture for all the care they take!'

'And? What did he tell you?'

'The French fleet is not here to take these islands. That is what they *want* us to believe. It is an invasion fleet – but their goal is to invade England. They want to convince our navy they are here to take these islands, to remain here. Meanwhile their fleet will backtrack to France, link up with the Spanish fleet and carry Napoleon's troops over the Channel to England – while the British fleet are preparing for battle here – in the islands!'

Colonel Smith said, 'That would explain the French attack. But this man may have been planted. He may be genuine in his hatred of the French, but they could still be using him as an agent to mislead us!'

As they were talking, the wind dropped. The whistling through the shutters stopped and a strange calm descended. Colonel Smith made arrangements for the prisoner to be taken to a secure room and to be fed and treated well. Meanwhile they went to the ramparts to see what was happening.

The sky was a metallic grey, and clouds towered above the distant peak of Nevis. The storm was all about them except in the small circle of blue sky above St Kitts. The French ships were preparing – tying everything down, lowering their top masts to the decks and removing anything that would move. Meanwhile another squadron had approached and was only a mile seaward of the anchorage: six ships in all.

'Must be at least two thousand men on those ships. If our prisoner's lying, we'll be mincemeat.'

The ships were signalling with flags. Josiah assumed orders had been given to prepare for the storm. He focused his telescope on the French ship that was in the lead as they approach the anchorage. Then he saw that they were clearing their decks for action; hammocks were being slung in nets in the rigging.

The leading battleship, a third-rater with seventy or eighty guns, changed direction as it wore round. Then the huge tricolour fluttering from the standard was taken down. Another flag was being hoisted. It was the Union Jack!

'What in the world?' Jefferson said.

Josiah said, 'They're British!. Classic move. Pretend to be French so they can get closer.'

Then as they watched, the French ships opened fire. But they were outnumbered by the British newcomers, and started hoisting sail. The sound of cannon fire reached Josiah seconds after he saw the flashes.

The wind had returned and continued to build.

'I hope everything is tied down, Colonel,' Josiah said.

'This will be a huge hurricane, Joss. We must bring everyone in and secure the fort. Give the order, Jefferson1'

The wind was now roaring. Josiah was finding it difficult to remain standing while he followed the fight in the anchorage. The ships were exchanging fire, but as the bigger gusts reached them they broke off.

By now the fort was crowded with soldiers –the

Africans and the Regulars, the African women, townspeople from Basseterre and planters who had enough influence to demand a place in the securest shelter of all. A population of fifty or sixty had grown to two hundred or more. Jefferson was to be seen everywhere, ordering ropes to be lashed on roofs and organising his soldiers to take care of the swelling crowd. Then he gave the order to close the gates. The crowd outside desperately hurried down the hill to find shelter elsewhere, complaining as they went.

The sky was dark with a greenish hue, and in the east great bolts of lightning lit up the heavens with continuous flashes. The rain began to fall, lashing down on buildings unprepared for its onslaught. The storm swept over the Leeward Islands in full force, sounding like herds of wild horses thundering down a mountain pass. The rain drummed on the tiled roofs, water finding its way through every crevice and crack until there were pools everywhere. Storm shutters vibrated as the wind battered them. Josiah thought of the crowds sheltering in the lee of the fort's thick walls. At sea, the only safe thing to do would be to run before the wind with bare poles and drogues, with every man aboard praying there were no islands in the way. He imagined the French ships and British out to sea, the battle delayed, survival the only consideration.

He left Jefferson and made his way to Elizabeth's

room. He knocked on the door and opened it. It was dark and crowded; people had been pressed into every room available.

He saw her comforting an elderly woman. 'Elizabeth, I've come to check on you.'

'This is the safest place to be in a storm like this.'

'The French retreated to their ships, but poor Nisbet … he has been killed.'

She gasped, hands to her mouth. 'That's not true.'

'It is true.'

She was dabbing her eyes, sobbing. 'His poor family.'

'Do you know them?'

'Of course. It is one of the oldest families on the island. Not the richest but good, good people.'

'When this is over, we will bury him on Nevis. He became a soldier and has died like a soldier. I am proud of him.'

He put his arm around her, but with the slightest of shrugs she let him know their affair was over – for now.

He returned to the crowded mess and Jefferson said, 'This has been a great victory,' though there was no triumph in his voice. 'We have lost only five of our men, captured twelve, obtained intelligence critical to the safety of the British fleet and developed a fine fighting force to defend the island against the French for years to come. And you can take the credit, Joss.'

'No, it has been *our* project. The four of us made this happen. What worries me is this storm; it's ripping the islands to pieces. The destruction will be terrible.'

'And that too we can deal with. I want my troops to become builders, to learn trades and be ready when the war is over.'

The storm raged for six hours, until its fury finally abated and the winds lost their power. By now it was dawn, and they could see the destruction. In the weak sunlight they inspected the damage. The barracks had lost its roof. Bed clothes were hanging from every window and a washing line was full of damp clothing. The smell of cooking and clouds of smoke from the fires filled the air. The troops were removing debris, and lines of townspeople were making their way back to Basseterre.

Josiah was helping restore order to the mess when he heard a shout. He rushed outside. A battleship was mooring off Sandy Point, the Union flag flying in the breeze. As he watched, a boat was lowered and a crew of ten pulled towards the mole.

Josiah pulled on his coat and ran to the mess. 'Gentlemen, the navy is here. I will go to the mole to meet them.'

'I'll come with you,' said Colonel Smith.

Josiah marched down the hill with Colonel Smith, his excitement rising. Whoever it was would have news: perhaps news that might affect his future.

They reached the end of the mole as the cutter approached. The crew raised their oars and a crewman jumped ashore. The boat was tied up expertly and the figure in the stern, a middle-aged captain in dress coat and hat, rose from his seat and climbed the steps leading from the water's edge. The crew formed a guard.

When the captain reached Josiah and Colonel Smith, he paused and pushed back his hat, hands on hips. 'Josiah Nisbet! What in the world are you doing here?'

# CHAPTER 21

It was Sam Hood – Sir Samuel. None other than the captain of *Zealous* at the Battle of the Nile – a man who had been friendly to Josiah when he had had many enemies, back in the days when he was a rising sun in the firmament of the Mediterranean Fleet.

Josiah's jaw dropped. He was at a loss for words. 'Sir?'

He stared at Sam Hood's bluff sea-worn face. He hadn't seen him in years. The last time was after the Battle of the Nile.

'What are you doing here?' the captain said.

Josiah saluted. 'Joss O'Brien at your service, sir.'

The captain turned to Smith with raised eyebrows. He said smoothly, 'I used to know someone who looks a lot like Mr O'Brien.'

Smith came to the rescue. 'Colonel Smith. Commanding officer of the Leeward Islands. And you are?'

'Captain Sam Hood, Royal Navy.'

Smith saluted.

Sam returned the salute and then put out his hand, gripping Smith's in a powerful squeeze.

''Pon my word, Captain,' Smith said, flexing his fingers when Sam released his grip, 'I am not familiar with this new custom of shaking hands!'

The captain laughed. 'Well, Smith, it's good to be on terra firma! That was a mighty blow we had last night. We came through it well enough, but there are casualties, and I daresay the French were savaged too.'

'You arrived at the turning point in our fight. Were we relieved! We repulsed two attempts to land, but we were outnumbered, and we would have had to retreat to the fort next time they came.'

'They're here to seize the most important of our possessions – the sugar islands. They broke our hold on the American states and tried again with India. Now once again they're trying to destroy our West Indies trade.'

'We have intelligence about that, captain. Mr O'Brien interrogated one of our prisoners.'

The colonel turned to Josiah. 'Mr O'Brien, why

don't you escort the captain to the fort? I have to survey the storm damage in Basseterre.'

He turned back to Sam. 'Captain, I will see you presently at the fort. Perhaps you will stay for dinner at two o'clock after noon?'

Smith took Josiah's arm and led him a little distance away. 'Don't worry, Joss. You are not a deserter, and you have your own reasons for your silence. I will not mention this episode to Jefferson, but you must take care of this matter yourself.'

Josiah said, 'Colonel, I apologise for any embarrassment. I promise to explain everything – at the right time.'

Colonel Smith set off on his inspection, while Josiah and Sam Hood walked to Brimstone Hill.

The hurricane had wreaked destruction on the town, even though the hills behind had protected it from the main fury of the storm. People filled the streets, clearing rubble. As far as the eye could see there was scarcely a warehouse or a cottage with roof intact. The street was a river of mud mingled with palm branches, broken tiles, timbers and shattered glass.

Josiah asked Sam, 'What happened to your squadron?'

'We took shelter further north. The hurricane was travelling from the south-east to the north-west. The hill to the north of Basseterre gave us some shelter, but even so we had a terrible battering. The French were blown away to the west. It'll be days before we see them again.'

They began the climb up to the fort.

'Joss, your resemblance to a young officer I knew years ago is remarkable. Good man, he was. Struggled under his father's control like many a youth. Saved his father's life, once.'

So his secret *had* been discovered.

'Everyone here knows me as Joss O'Brien, and I have *become* Joss O'Brien with time. But I am the Josiah Nisbet you knew.'

'Last time I heard your name, you were an officer on half pay. I heard you have enemies and the Admiralty was teaching you a lesson. Then I heard you had disappeared.'

'May I have your word that what I am about to tell you will remain confidential?'

'You have my word as an officer.'

'It's a long story. I was on a mission to find corruption in the Plymouth dockyard, under the misapprehension it would restore me to grace with the "powers that be" at the Admiralty. It rebounded on me. I was seized – in circumstances I don't yet understand – and put aboard a slaver. They brought me to this island, and I have been helping Colonel Smith. He doesn't know who I am. I don't see that it is necessary for *anyone* to know my stepfather is Horatio Nelson. So much of my time in the navy I was a symbol of nepotism. Now I am trying to be myself and not having to explain who I am.'

'I understand. It is difficult being the son of a great man. He treated you and your mother poorly. I say that as a man who admires him for his courage and leadership.'

They walked up the hill in silence for a while. Then Sam asked, 'Your colonel said you have intelligence on the French?'

'Yes, Colonel Smith wants to discuss the matter. But before I tell you, let me explain how we came to get it.'

They climbed up the track to the fort. Trees had fallen across the road and streams overflowed, spilling rock and sand everywhere. A part of the road was gone. They passed soldiers from the African regiment armed with spades and wheelbarrows, clearing the debris. As they walked, Josiah described how he had persuaded the planters to put up the money to bolster defences. He told Sam about Jefferson and how he and Nisbet had trained the Africans and the Regulars. He described the battles with the French: the bombardment of the French ships and the battle at Basseterre, the night attack on the French ships and the recent landings.

Sam listened carefully, interjecting with questions from time to time. When Josiah had finished he said, 'It makes me proud that a young naval officer has achieved as much as you have. We learned so much in the Mediterranean in those days.'

'I did draw on what I had learned – at Corsica, Santa Cruz and elsewhere, but I share the achievements here with others. Smith convinced the planters to put up the money; Nisbet, a young lawyer, took the Regulars in hand and whipped them into shape, and John Jefferson's knowledge from the American wars was just as important. We could not have succeeded without working together.'

'That is invariably true. It is the combined effort of the team on which battles succeed or fail – but still, your initiative is worthy of praise. Now, let's move on. What did you learn from the interrogation of the Frenchman?'

'At first we were certain that the French attacks were aimed at reconquering the islands. They are of such strategic importance to Britain. Even now the money made from the sale of sugar to the world fills the coffers of the government through excise and taxation. We pay our allies to fight with us. We lose these islands and our fight against the French will suffer—'

'Josiah, I understand this. When we were fighting

the great French fleet in Egypt, we were defending our trade with India. The French helped the Americans gain their independence for the same reason – to wound Britain, to reduce our power. And now we're convinced that the same stratagem is at play here. Horatio is firm in his conviction that the French are here to dislodge us from the islands. He's expecting the French fleet to do battle, just as *he* did at the Nile. Now, what have you learned that would change that view?'

Brimstone Hill was visible now, a stark mass silhouetted against the blue sky. The coconut palms on the crest of the hill had been uprooted. The landscape was bleak. The fort was like a battleship, anchored to the naked hill, cannons protruding from its ramparts, Union flag fluttering from its flagstaff. They paused.

Josiah chose his words carefully. It was apparent from Sam's tone that he was not going to find it easy to take in the intelligence Josiah was about to give him. No doubt, along with the other senior captains and Horatio himself, he was convinced there would be a replay of the Battle of the Nile – a titanic fight for the possession of these jewels: the islands and their sugar. Why else would the French send a fleet all this way? How could he challenge this conviction? For, if the Haitian marine *was* telling the truth, the very freedom of England itself was at stake.

'The French marine said the attack on the West Indian islands by the French fleet is a "feint," a deception to keep the British fleet occupied here while the French fleet quickly returns across the Atlantic to carry Napoleon's invasion army to England.'

'What? That would be the most fantastical humbuggery if it were true!'

'If he was lying, our offer of his freedom and an opportunity to join our regiment would be foolishness. He would be recaptured by the French and hanged as a traitor.'

'Josiah, we must take this to Horatio. It's no good sending this news through a third party. He has to hear it from someone who spoke to the source and can convince him. A great deal rides on this, you understand? *You* have to go.'

Josiah paused, feeling a rising sense of excitement. To play such a crucial role, to see his father …

'I am too junior, my motives and my judgement too suspect. Even if I could meet with Horatio – and he gave me short shrift last time – can I convince him?'

'Our fleet is refitting and taking on supplies in Barbados. You will see him immediately.'

'I still have matters to take care of here.'

'I will meet with your prisoner myself and I will make my own decision. It will take me at least two days to prepare a fast ship. You must take care of your business in that time.'

By now they had reached the gate to the fort. The courtyard was full of soldiers who were cleaning up and rebuilding. Jefferson was there too, encouraging them and directing events. He saw them approaching and walked over, saluting Sam when he saw he was a captain.

'Sam, this is John Jefferson – the man I told you about.'

Sam looked at the tall American with interest. 'My uncle fought in the American war. You fought on the British side?'

'Yes, sir.'

'A great deal of bungling. It taught Britain an important lesson: to treat the people of the colonies with more respect, and to defend the colonies carefully against rebellion and insurgency. And to deal with the pervasive corruption. I hear very good things about you, sir. Joss has been telling me how you have built this regiment from a shipload of African slaves. I congratulate you, sir.'

'I understand a happy ship is the best fighting ship. I have tried the same thing. No flogging, and we feed and house the men well and train them and train them until they're ready to fight. These men have been promised their freedom – a strong motivation for them.'

'A good few captains would do well to adopt your philosophy.'

Jefferson conducted the captain around the fort, explaining its purpose, describing the defences. Then they visited the gun platform on the ramparts and Hood saw for himself what Josiah had accomplished.

He said, 'My word! The French were faced with a challenge to take this place. It would have needed a long siege though. I'm glad we were able to relieve you of that terrible experience.'

Over dinner, they talked of the war. The conversation was convivial, but, as often happens to warriors when a battle is over, Josiah found it hard to keep focussed. A thousand thoughts followed each other remorselessly. Chiefly he thought about leaving the islands. He had never considered his investment in this place. It was not the place he had thought it would be. The gleam and glitter had proved on closer observation to be a cruel commercial factory for sugar, the island's natural beauty marred by the inequality of the society.

But against those thoughts were balanced the prospect of losing those he had come to love – Elizabeth, Jefferson, his troops and even dour Colonel Smith. The prospect of joining the navy again held no pleasure for him. How could he possibly fit in after his experiences here? His thoughts chased each other. Yet there was no doubt the navy *was* his duty. If Horatio had taught him nothing else, he had learned that truth.

'You're not saying much, Joss!'

He started. It was Jefferson. The room had fallen silent.

'I have a lot on my mind, John. I think Captain Hood and I should speak to the prisoner.'

The men stood.

Jefferson said, 'I'll have the Frenchman brought up immediately.'

They waited in silence, and then there was a knock on the door, and the prisoner and a soldier were there.

'Sit down,' said Sam in French.

Josiah said, 'Tell your story to the captain. Be honest. If you are not, you will be hanged as a spy! If we're satisfied, you will join the regiment on the island and be given your freedom when this war is at an end. You will be treated well and can make a new life here.'

'What choice do we slaves have? Whether French or English, we're compelled to serve without condition. What do you want to know?'

Sam followed with question after question in French. Josiah was impressed; clearly Sam had interrogated many prisoners in the past. He asked questions quickly – time and place, conversations, battles, time and place again, checking and returning, crossing back and forth to keep the prisoner from thinking too much.

Eventually he sat back and said, 'This man is telling the truth, Joss. We're the victims of our own convictions. Twice before, the French fought to take our colonies. This time they're depending on our belief that they're here to do the same again – and they know we'll swallow that because of their previous actions. This is a feint to keep us here while they return. We must get this to Lord Nelson as soon as possible. Make your arrangements, Joss. We're leaving on Wednesday.'

Afterwards, Josiah met with Colonel Smith and Jefferson.

To Colonel Smith, he said, 'Colonel, I beg you to arrange Nisbet's funeral before I leave. I could not depart without seeing my friend to his grave and speaking with his family.'

Smith nodded gravely and said, 'When you leave we lose a great leader – and one of our own. I'm so sorry and so grateful. I'll make the arrangements at once.'

Before they left for the funeral on Nevis, the chaplain held a separate solemn ceremony at the fort. The soldiers were formed up in lines, and the native women and the African women stood together. The captain and sergeants of the Regulars were present.

A hymn was sung, a reading from the Bible followed, and the chaplain said a few words of consolation. The sound of weeping arose from the group, interrupted by the firing of a ten-gun salute. The flag was lowered and then the coffin was put on a cart and led by Colonel Smith on his white mare. Josiah and Jefferson followed on foot. The party made its way to the Narrows.

Josiah at that point decided it no longer made sense to keep his secret. He was leaving the island. His secret no longer served a purpose. Better to be honest and leave the island with a clean slate.

Once they boarded the lugger, Josiah found a space to talk to Jefferson and the colonel at length. He had already told them the barest of outlines of the events that had led to his presence on the slave ship. Now he told them about his life before that.

Jefferson listened carefully, asking a question or two to clarify. There was no bitterness nor anxiety about his own future. It was as if Jefferson was Josiah's elder brother, as if their intimacy had been lifelong.

Colonel Smith was already prepared for Josiah's confession. He said, 'People will be deeply hurt by your secrecy. Your mother was well regarded on the island, and the men worship Horatio. They'll be asking themselves why you were not forthcoming. As for me – you'll always be "Joss", my right-hand man.'

After disembarking they marched to Charlestown as the sun dipped towards the western sea. Nevis, untouched by the fighting, had fared better than St Kitts in the storm. But there was destruction here too. Everywhere people were working to repair and rebuild. Most of the sugar cane had already been harvested and processed, but what was left lay flattened in the fields.

When they reached Charlestown, Colonel Smith said to Josiah, 'I will call a meeting of the council. They will consider what we can do for you in view of your many services. They will attend the funeral here in Charlestown.'

'I will speak to Nisbet's family,' Josiah said, 'but I think it should be held at St John's Church near the family plantation. Nisbet would have wanted that. And I would like Chaplain Grey to preside, if that is well with you? After all, Nisbet was a member of his congregation.'

'It shall be done. I will speak to the family and I will let you know of the arrangements. In the meantime, will you and Jefferson be staying at the Bath Hotel?'

'We will.'

Elizabeth had returned with them. She found them rooms at the inn and then she left them to help in the arrangements for the following day, promising to join them for supper.

Jefferson and Josiah went out for a walk through the town and past the Methodist chapel. The palm groves were silent. A soft breeze was the only reminder of the tumult of the previous day's storm.

'You must feel relieved to be leaving,' Jefferson said.

'I am at sixes and sevens about it.'

'I will miss you, as a brother in arms ... and for much more.'

'I don't know if I will ever return, but I *will* let you know what becomes of me – and I'll use any influence I have on this island to ensure you and the Africans are treated according to our agreement.'

The only other conversation he had that night was with Elizabeth. She said nothing when he told her his secret. When they had supper with Jefferson, she was silent, and Josiah knew once again he had hurt a woman badly. Their affair was over; the only question now concerned their ongoing relationship. Could they still be friends?

When they parted that evening, she said, 'Joss – for I will always think of you having that name – why didn't you tell me when we were at Hackett Point? That was the time to tell me. Not now. Not when you're leaving me.'

Tired and very sad, Josiah retired to his room, but despite his exhaustion it took him hours to fall asleep. He lay awake, self-criticism competing with regret.

He slept late and eventually Jefferson woke him up with the news that the colonel had been working long and late. He gave Josiah an envelope.

*My dear Josiah,*

*I have been in touch with the island leaders and the family. The council and many island families will be in attendance at the funeral, which is to be held at St John's Church at ten o'clock in the morning. The service will be conducted jointly by Chaplain Grey and the curate of St John's. There will be a light repast at the Nisbet plantation following, and you will stay on at the plantation for the reading of the will. In view of the very short time we have, the council has informed me that they will entertain you at Montpelier for dinner afterwards. Both you and Jefferson will be their guests of honour. I will see you at the church.*

*Sincerely*
*Col. (Edward) Smith.*

He read the note again. He'd never known Smith's Christian name until now.

# CHAPTER 22

Elizabeth joined them in the parlour once breakfast was over. Her black crepe dress and a silk turban edged with black lace highlighted the pallor of her face. Josiah asked himself if she had slept, dismissing the thought that she was grieving for *him*.

Josiah said, 'You look very well in black, Elizabeth.'

She turned away and said shortly, 'I wear this dress at least four times a year. So many of our people die from the sicknesses.'

In the silence, Josiah thought: *There is a moral sickness too – greed and the slavery.*

He said, 'My grandmother died here when my mother was seven years old, her father when she was eighteen and her husband when she was twenty-two.'

Jefferson changed the subject. 'Josiah, Elizabeth

and I have had a conversation. She will help us – she has decided to quit her job as proprietor of the Bath Hotel. She will arrange all domestic supplies for the regiment. I have yet to obtain Colonel Smith's agreement, but I am confident of the outcome.'

Josiah felt a stab of jealousy. The fraternity would continue without him – and so would Elizabeth. He said, 'Perhaps Elizabeth will command the artillery as well!'

They laughed, but Josiah knew that their good humour masked complicated feelings about his imminent departure.

After breakfast they took the jogging cart and began the journey to St James Church. Elizabeth had her parasol to shade her from the sun. Josiah took off his coat, and the three spent the time reminiscing about Nisbet and enjoying the peaceful island and the azure sea that surrounded it. The conversation was inconsequential, and Josiah felt guilty that his confession had divided them. The guilt and sadness made him forget the happy times and wish to be away from Nevis as soon as possible.

They arrived at the church to find the choir practising and the two clergymen busy making arrangements. The church filled as the mourners arrived. Josiah, Jefferson and Elizabeth took their seats in the public pews at the back, while local gentry and the families who owned their pews sat at the front of the church close to the altar, their slaves remaining at the back. At length the council arrived, the gentlemen filing in together and sitting on the front pew. The president took his place last, at the aisle. The coffin had arrived in a funeral hearse drawn by two black horses. Beggs, Nisbet's former colleague, was one of the bearers. He approached Josiah.

'I learned from Colonel Smith who you are. I feel misled – as do many others on the island. The colonel told me you had good reason to hide your identity.'

He paused, waiting for an apology. Josiah said nothing.

'I am the lawyer to the Nisbet family. As a member of the family, you must attend the reading of the will after the funeral. You are mentioned in it. More, I cannot say.'

He bowed and took his place at the opposite side of the coffin.

Josiah had conflicting feelings; he had no desire to become entangled with family, but at the same time his curiosity was piqued. He wrestled unsuccessfully with the feeling and conceded he would go to the reading of the will.

The service began with the vicar announcing the first hymn. Josiah and the other bearers raised the coffin to their shoulders and carried it slowly into the church, laying it on a platform before the altar. They were followed by the cross and choir. The two ministers took their seats. The hymn concluded and Josiah and Jefferson sat beside Elizabeth.

'The Lord be with you.'

'And also with you'

'Let us pray. Oh God, whose mercies cannot be numbered ...'

Josiah thought of the sailors he had buried at sea. When he was captain, he had had to read these words many times.

The choir stood to sing the anthem.

After prayers for the dead and the grieving, the Reverend Grey rose. He was wearing his white Methodist surplice. Used to speaking at open-air meetings, his voice resonated powerfully.

'This is no ordinary funeral. This man loved God. He showed God's spirit in his life and in his death. He was a member of the Nisbet family, who have been in this community of St James's since the beginnings. *But* he was also from a family of slaves, brought to these islands against their will, who form the very fabric of this place. Nisbet's life and his noble death point to a future when descendants of these slaves will take their rightful place on this island.'

Josiah looked at the front pew. Some shifted uneasily in their seats. The power of the pulpit.

'Nisbet's death was sacrificial. He died for his fellow islanders following Jesus, who gave his life for us all. We mourn him but we are grateful to God. We should each ponder his example and consider our own. Are we sacrificial? Do we consider the good of all who live on these islands, or are we only concerned with what we own and how much money we have?'

He sat down in silence, and then from the back of the church came a loud voice: 'Amen, brother! Amen.'

The vicar rose hastily and announced the final hymn. *Embarrassment*, Josiah thought, *dealt with in the English fashion: ignored.*

At the cemetery, tears spoke louder than the words. Nisbet had been dearly loved by all who knew him. His cousins and his mother wept as the coffin was lowered into the grave and the vicar intoned the final words: 'Dust to dust. Ashes to ashes …'

Even the president of the council dabbed his eyes with his kerchief. Elizabeth and Jefferson wept, but Josiah felt nothing. What was wrong with him? Why couldn't *he* weep?

The mourners dispersed, either to their carriages or on foot. The slaves were already gone. Jefferson and Josiah agreed to meet before noon. Jefferson hitched the horse to the cart and, together with Elizabeth, set off for Charlestown. Meanwhile, Josiah made his way to the Nisbet home nearby.

Josiah's identity was public knowledge by now. Josiah saw several resentful looks, and some people turned away as he passed. At the house he approached Nisbet's mother to give her his condolences. She gave way to tears as Josiah described how much Nisbet had meant to him and how he much had contributed to the defence of the islands.

She said, 'I knew your mother when I was a young girl. She was often here, especially when she and your father were courting. I admired her. She never put herself above others. She always cared for the young women of the island. We miss her still.'

Josiah's aunt, the doyenne of the plantation house, whom he had met when he first arrived, cut him when he approached her. Josiah tried to speak to his cousins, but they were formal and distant. At length, the guests gone, the family crowded into the drawing room to hear the reading of the will. Josiah stood by the window trying to be inconspicuous.

'I, James Nisbet, being of sound mind, hereby bequeath and bequest my worldly goods.'

Beggs had a plummy accent. Like most lawyers he enjoyed moments like these. There were bequests of money and possessions that Nisbet had accumulated. The majority went to his mother, but his treasured possessions were willed to his cousins. A codicil had been added: 'To my dear friend Joss O'Brien, I leave the miniature painted of me as a child, trusting he will cherish my memory every time he regards it.'

At length the reading ended. Beggs looked up theatrically, adjusted his spectacles and said, 'Now I will deal with the *entailed* estate.'

Josiah had already received what was due from his father's will. It had taken many years and ongoing disputes between lawyers in London and Nevis. What else was there? An estate in entail? When he was younger, like other young men, he had had fantasies of sudden wealth. A letter from a firm of lawyers would inform him that a distant relative with a title and land had died without a male heir, and that his estate had been entailed to him as the only one in the line of succession. But in Nevis?

Beggs was speaking, his mellifluous voice warming to the subject. 'Nisbet had two estates. He held one in freehold, and the proceeds of that were the subject of the will I have read out to you. However ...' His tone implied the news he was about to reveal was painful. 'Nisbet was also the current owner of an *entailed* estate. The entail goes back to the early part of this century. In Nisbet's case, his deceased uncle had no heir, and Nisbet was the closest in line of succession. The estate, in the south of the island, comprises four hundred acres of prime sugar cane and a plantation house. The slaves on the plantation were the personal property of the previous owner and were sold at his death. Since then, our dear departed friend did not farm the estate himself, but chose to rent it to neighbouring plantations. The entail has been the subject of some work on my part since I learned of Nisbet's death – work to establish the new owner. And I have found that the person in line of succession to Nisbet is'—he looked over his glasses, savouring the surprise, and then said—'Josiah.'

There was silence.

Someone said, 'Oh no!' and another sobbed.

Josiah, shocked and guilty, felt overwhelmed. The family dissolved into groups and Josiah looked for a way to escape.

Nisbet's mother came to his rescue. She said, 'You're a just man. You will do the right thing. James was so reluctant to be a planter. That is why he went into the law.'

Josiah said, 'I am touched – and amazed – by this turn of fortune. I promise whatever I do it will be something Nisbet would have wanted.'

Josiah could not linger, and was glad he had good reason to leave once he had discussed the legal aspects of the inheritance with Beggs. Nisbet's mother arranged for her chaise to take him back to Charlestown. Then it was time for him to depart. As the carriage rolled down the aisle of tall palm trees that led from the plantation house to the road, Josiah thought about how different his life would have been if his birth father had not died so young. He would have been living here. He would be *like them*.

But Fanny had taken him to England and Horatio had taken him to sea. The driver cracked the whip and the carriage gathered speed. It was still a fine, cloudless day. Such a beautiful place. Would he still leave the island? He knew what he ought to do. But first he must talk to Jefferson.

Dinner was to be held at Montpelier at one o'clock after noon. Mr Herbert had invited the Nevis Council to celebrate the victory over the French and to farewell Josiah. In the meantime, before they left the hotel, Josiah sought a moment to talk to Jefferson alone.

They met on the veranda of the hotel.

Josiah said, 'I have something to say, John. It's very personal and I would prefer if we took a short walk.'

'Have you decided to stay after all?'

'No. I am leaving tonight as we agreed.'

They made their way towards the little Methodist church. It was off the main road, and the shade beneath the towering palms and native trees was welcome in the afternoon heat. They walked in companionable silence.

'Jefferson, I have learned that I have inherited a substantial estate.' He recounted what Beggs had said at the reading of the will. 'What do you think of that?'

'I must say I don't see you as a planter, Joss – forgive me – Josiah!'

'I will continue to call you Jefferson if you agree to call me Joss. Is that agreeable? Good. Now listen to my news.'

He explained the meaning of the entailed estate and the implications of the inheritance. When he had finished, Jefferson nodded and said, 'And now. What is your decision?'

'I'm still leaving. I am a naval officer. I will pay a visit to my father and I may be posted back here – I know Colonel Smith wants me. But after that? It's impossible to predict. I don't see myself as a farmer, and definitely not as a slave owner.'

'Well, then you can continue to lease it out and collect the earnings. It will enable you to establish yourself well when you leave the navy.'

'I *could* do that … but I want to leave more than a memory behind me. I'm thinking that I'll transfer my interest – during my lifetime – which is permitted under the entail.' He stopped walking and put a hand on Jefferson's arm. '*You* could use the land to provide housing and work for the African soldiers who want to stay on the island once they've been discharged. If there are any profits, we can purchase the freedom of more slaves on the island.'

'Whoa there, Joss! You're asking me to do something that you've dreamed up in the few hours since you got the good news. I think you need to reflect. As for me, I have no home, and I might well choose to stay here, but I need to think about that too. And I wouldn't want a lot of enemies.'

'Well, think about it. If you don't know by the time I leave, it can wait – but for how long, I don't know.'

Josiah, Jefferson and Colonel Smith – still in dress uniform – met at the Bath Hotel just before noon and made their way to the great estate house of Montpelier in a carriage Smith had borrowed from the Nevis Club. Josiah said little, listening as Jefferson and Colonel Smith talked about their plan to combine the Regulars with the Africans.

*They have already forgotten me*, thought Josiah. *Such is the way of the world. Once people know you are leaving, it is an established fact.*

As if he had read his thoughts, the colonel said, 'When you get back, we will work on the artillery. There is still much to be done.'

Josiah said, 'In my experience, nothing is predictable once the war takes you to your next post.'

He fell silent as the conversation swirled around him. The news of his inheritance had changed everything. He had the means to advance in the world. He would have money that would enable him to marry and raise a family. Yet, even as he considered the prospect, he knew that the taint of slavery would mar his fortune.

The carriage was winding its way up the narrow lanes to Montpelier. A short glimpse of the house, and the carriage drew to a halt under the portico. Around the freshly painted porch bougainvillea bloomed, and a scent of lilies wafted into the carriage.

They alighted, Josiah awed by the views over the island. And the sight of the great house, redolent of history and wealth, tempted him to reconsider his decision. It was here his mother had presided over the social life of the island, setting a new standard for official entertainment. This was the house in which Horatio and Fanny had met. He had heard the family that lived here now was in decline, its family pride intact but its wealth undermined by poor management and its social position proportionately the less. Meanwhile Fanny had taken what she had learned here and built her own house in Ipswich. If her new home lacked the size and ostentation of Montpelier, it had something far better: the character of Fanny.

The butler waited on them. 'Gentlemen, your fellow guests have arrived, and Mr Herbert has told me you do not have much time. Kindly step this way.'

The drawing room opened onto a spacious veranda where the gentlemen, drinks in hand, stood talking animatedly. They fell silent as Josiah, Jefferson and the colonel stepped into the room. The new arrivals shook hands with Mr Herbert and the other planters. Josiah was introduced to Mr McPherson. He looked familiar.

Beggs had already delivered his news, and Josiah sensed the change in his situation. He was no longer an exotic visitor. He was a member of their hierarchy, and they showed this by cordially shaking his hand, clapping him on the shoulder and telling him how they could readily see a family likeness. Josiah's discomfort grew. It was worse when they sat down at the table and – as rivals in business usually do at these occasions – discussed the latest price of sugar, the cargoes recently despatched, the effects of the recent hurricane and the French threat. The conversation was interrupted only by the arrival of dinner and the wine. Delicious.

To Jefferson they paid scant attention. A cursory statement here and there and a polite question or two about the troops and the recent battles were tossed to him. But Jefferson was unperturbed. He was familiar with condescension.

Josiah realised where he had seen McPherson before. He was the man he had seen leaning against the tree while his overseer beat a slave. It had happened back when he went on his first ride around the island, and it had broken the trance in which the island's beauty had embraced him. He looked across the table at McPherson. He seemed an ordinary sort of fellow enjoying his dinner with his friends. There was no hint of the evil spirit within.

After dessert – a sweet, icy flummery – Colonel Smith brought the meeting to order. 'Gentlemen, be upstanding for the loyal toast.'

There was a scraping of chairs as the men stood. 'The King!'

'The King!'

'Gentlemen, I have brought my two fellow officers today so that we might offer them our gratitude for defending us and also to say farewell to Josiah, who leaves tonight to meet with Admiral Lord Nelson. Lord Nelson's fleet pursued the French hotly to these islands and is now, I am told, near Barbados. God speed, Josiah. May you and your father win a mighty victory over the French enemy!'

There was a long round of applause, and then the colonel called on Jefferson. 'Let's hear your account of the recent fighting, Sergeant Major.'

Jefferson's American accent, blunt delivery and authority were unusual on this island. Despite their obvious coolness towards him, the gentlemen listened intently. He talked about the fighting and the way they had kept the French at bay. His listeners applauded and then he said, 'We came here on a slave ship, not knowing what our future would hold. Only the grace of God and the hard work of Josiah have resulted in our present position. It is to him our thanks are due. I was merely using my skills as a soldier, which I learned long ago. My only concern, gentlemen, is what will happen once my friend leaves. Can I count on you to support me without his guidance and diplomacy?'

The host and the guests were silent.

Beggs stepped in. 'Gentlemen, we are civilised men. We keep the law of the land and have due regard for everyone who lives here, our slaves included. Jefferson, you have earned our respect, and I am sure that you will find your place in our society. We want you to stay.'

There was a flutter of applause around the table and Colonel Smith called for a toast to Jefferson and the Africans. This time there was a stamping of feet, and everyone drained their bumpers.

'Josiah, it's your turn. I'm sure we would like to know what will become of you.'

Josiah stood. Even though he had drunk very little, he felt light-headed. So much had happened, so quickly. What could he say?

'I would like to thank each of you for welcoming

me to the island. Even though you didn't know me, you opened your houses and made me feel welcome. And you helped to form the new African regiment and to pay for it. So you have made our victory possible.

'This morning Mr Beggs told me of my good fortune. Some four hundred acres of fine sugar-producing land, I am told. I'm sure you know it. But before I can assume any role in this estate, I have to leave you to undertake my duties as a naval officer. This raises the question of what will happen in my absence. I have talked the matter over with Colonel Smith and Sergeant Major Jefferson. I've suggested John Jefferson takes over the management of the estate so that when the Africans are discharged from their military service they have a place to settle. Each of them might be given land and money for a house, and I could build a school and a church. I would like this new village to anticipate life on this island once slavery is over – as I hope and believe it will be soon. This will be the starting point for a different way of life on our island. But it will only work with your cooperation. Jefferson and his troops have put their lives on the line for you. Now you must help them succeed.'

There was a silence, during which Josiah sat down. He flushed and felt a sense of failure, antagonism hanging in the air.

The butler refilled his glass.

'Gentlemen!' It was Mr Pinney; he had risen to his feet. 'I am amazed by our young friend. It is as if God in his mercy used him to deliver us from the French ... but a peril of a different order remains. And our peril is indeed very great. There are six times as many slaves on this island as there are white men. We have had enough slave revolts in the past to teach us that we cannot permit our vigilance to fail even for one minute. We know what happened recently in Saint Domingue. This peril to life and property will continue if we do not look to a future beyond slavery. I am going to say here and now that I have the greatest admiration for what you are proposing – and if I can help, I will.'

He sat down. The room appeared divided, half nodding vigorously while the other half frowned and muttered to each other.

Colonel Smith rose again and proposed a toast to Josiah and Jefferson. On this everyone could agree, and they stood as one man. A lukewarm hurrah – three times three – concluded the dinner.

The carriage rolled down the steep hill, the coachman straining to hold the wheels on the road with both hands on the brake. There was an uneasy silence and then Jefferson said, 'Josiah, a slave society is a society in the grip of fear. The slaves are terrified of repercussions if they try to assert even their most basic rights. The white owners know that their wealth is made on the backs of the slaves. Their lives depend on the maintenance of law and order and brutal penalties for any miscreants. Enforcement was the role of the Regulars.'

Colonel Smith said, 'You're right, Jefferson. My soldiers were charged with protecting the planters and the rest of our society. Talk about abolishing the slave trade and even slavery itself has simply raised the stakes. Only Mr Pinney and I are willing to take even one step towards change. I believe we *should* follow your plan, but I agree with Jefferson. It's risky. Your vision is ahead of its time, Josiah. You have done so much for these islands, but in relation to this matter I am afraid you have overstepped the mark with the majority.'

# PART 4: MAY 1805

# CHAPTER 23

The sun was setting as Josiah and his friends made their way to the Charlestown quay. They had dined together but the conversation was stilted, and his departure hung in the air. Jefferson carried Josiah's case; a few clothes and books and his master's uniform were all he had. Josiah was feeling both regret and anticipation. His regrets were at saying goodbye to his friends and to be leaving Elizabeth. The failure of his plans for the estate had left him disappointed that he could not effect change. The timing of his return – indeed, whether he even *would* return – was a matter he could not decide. Much would depend on his meeting with Horatio. That meeting gave him a feeling of anticipation.

The two friends talked of nothing consequential

as they walked to the quay. Colonel Smith marched ahead, and Elizabeth walked beside Josiah silently. She was a wearing white smock and a large straw hat that shaded her face. At one point he tried to hold her hand, but she gently withdrew. They reached the harbour, just a few minutes away, and saw that the cutter was already moored at the mole.

A young midshipman said to Josiah, 'Sir Samuel sends his compliments. He says we have no time to lose.'

'Patience, sir, while I say my farewells.'

But everything to be said had already been said. He shook hands with Colonel Smith and then Jefferson; he bowed to Elizabeth and then held her arms gently.

She looked at him tenderly. He wondered at how deeply her grey eyes penetrated him. He could think of nothing to say.

'Look after yourself, Josiah.'

He felt an overwhelming desire to embrace her, but as if she could read his thoughts she took a step backwards and raised her hand at the wrist, her fingers moving gently in farewell. He realised their affair was their business alone and she did not want to reveal it to Colonel Smith

He walked down the steps to the cutter that was bobbing below in the swell, and took his seat in the stern. The crew rowed expertly and soon they were out of the small harbour. Josiah turned and waved. They were still watching from the quay. He pulled up his collar against the breeze, turning away from the midshipman who was about to engage him in conversation. He saw *Centaur* ahead, a mile away: the ship that would be his new home. He was returning to his old life. The midshipman gave another order, and a sail was hoisted. The figures on the quay were small now. He waved once more and, turning to the younger man beside him, said in a gruff voice, 'What's your name, sir?'

'Midshipman Fellows, sir.'

'Now, Fellows, tell me about *Centaur.*'

'Captain Richardson is in command, and Sir Samuel Hood is the commodore of our squadron.'

'… and what is your duty?'

'Sir, I am in charge of this cutter. Also I stand watch. I was made up to midshipman last year.'

'How old?'

'I am fifteen, sir. I will be sitting the lieutenant's exam soon, I expect. Captain Richardson says he has every confidence in my success when the time comes. I've been on the list since I was eleven, so I have seniority.'

'What makes you so proud of being a "Centaurian"?'

'Since coming to Antigua we've been taking islands from the French. Last year we took St Lucia.

Now they have only Martinique left, and we've put a garrison on Diamond Rock to harass their ships as they enter their harbour. Did you know the rock was commissioned as a ship of the line? *HMS Diamond Rock.*'

'I've never heard of such a thing.'

Darkness was falling and the breeze chilled him to the bone. Waves were building, an opposing current sharpening their peaks and valleys. Josiah felt a spasm of nausea.

*Centaur* loomed out of the gloom, its masts towering. A 74-gun, copper-bottomed, three-decker to *Agamemnon's* two. The memories were returning. A young boy with a powerful father, learning the ropes. Just like this lad. Josiah was ten years senior but he felt like an old man.

'Ahoy, cutter coming alongside! Prepare to come about!'

The sail down, the oarsmen manoeuvred her alongside, keeping their distance from the heaving sides of the great battleship. A rope was tossed from the deck and secured. Josiah grasped the rope ladder with both hands and pulled himself up. A helping hand at the upper gun deck eased him over the rail, and he was looking at Sam Hood.

'Welcome aboard, Captain Nisbet.'

Was there a hint of sarcasm? 'Sir, it's good to be

aboard.' Then he remembered to salute. 'It brings back memories!'

'Lieutenant Richardson has found you a cabin on the poop deck, Josiah. I'll have your bag delivered. Wash up and change. We're dining in fifteen minutes!'

The ship was underway by the time he opened the door of his cabin: a small and poky place, but, he reflected, what ship ever has a spare cabin of any size? A seaman brought a bucket of warm water and he bathed himself and changed into his threadbare uniform. He noticed a stain from the dinner party the night before. He must have it cleaned.

The great cabin was lit by candelabra rigged in the ceiling and several lamps mounted in brackets on the panelled walls. There was a sitting area, a large dining table, the commodore's desk and a door to his sleeping quarters. *How well senior officers look after themselves*, Josiah thought. Rank must be accompanied by prestige, and fine living was part of that. It was the way of the British world. Else how could they recruit ambitious men for this dangerous life? For a moment he felt envy, but his appetite for these symbols of success had dulled.

'Captain Nisbet; Lieutenant Richardson.'

Josiah bowed.

Four other officers were introduced.

'Come, gentlemen, pray take a seat at my table and

we will get things underway. I have grown ravenous waiting for Captain Nisbet.'

A steward filled their glasses with champagne.

'Rescued it from the last French ship we took,' Captain Hood said by way of explanation to Josiah, whose surprise at the lavishness of his table was evident.

The champagne was chilled and served in the finest cut glass. A china dinner service from the Wedgewood factory and silverware of the highest quality decorated the table. They took their seats and dinner was served: a dish of parrot fish preceded the main course – a roast of pork with crackling and potatoes. Cheese with biscuits and fruit followed and then a pudding of crumbled peach with cream, with a fine dessert wine concluding the meal. Josiah felt a little drunk.

The commodore made conversation with the other officers. He inquired about their work and their relations with the non-commissioned officers and crew. Even about the books they were reading. The intelligence of the conversation was far above the normal musings of captains at their tables. Most used these occasions to pontificate or repeat their stories of glory.

'Now, Josiah, it's time to tell us of your valiant deeds at St Kitts.'

Josiah surveyed the table. They were all the worse for wear. How could he explain what he had been doing? He hesitated, his face flushing, and shifted in his seat. 'A very unfortunate incident in England resulted in me being kidnapped and brought to the islands. I used my knowledge as a naval officer to help defend the islands against the French.'

There was a silence as they waited for more. Sam did not interrupt. Josiah squirmed and found he had nothing more to say.

At last the first lieutenant said, 'I understand you are Admiral Nelson's son. Tell us about *Agamemnon* and *Captain* and the glorious battles you have fought.'

'Your own commodore distinguished himself there. I wager he has already told you tales of Cape St Vincent, Santa Cruz and the Nile. I was but a junior, and my role entitled me to a share in prize money though none of the glory.'

They laughed uncertainly.

'Come now, Josiah,' said one of the men. 'You are far too modest. I recall that you boarded the *San Josef* ahead of your father at Cape St Vincent. And you saved his life at Santa Cruz. Tell us about that.'

They wanted to talk about Horatio! He quelled his resentment and recounted the legendary stories about his father until the port was finished and it was time to retire.

He slept badly that night. The rich wine and food took a toll, and he woke as the ship rolled. Unable to sleep, he dressed and walked the decks. As dawn broke, the commodore appeared and they walked together in companionable silence. The watch changed and the drums beat to quarters: the daily ritual of getting ready for a daybreak attack. The ship came alive with the thump of running feet, bells and whistles. The great ochre sails filled with a strong breeze, and *Centaur* and the six ships of the squadron ploughed through calm seas south and west towards Barbados.

Two days passed – days in which Josiah slept for long hours, exhausted from months of hard work and fighting. When he was awake, he paced the decks and occasionally climbed in the rigging. These days of balmy weather and uncomplicated sailing gave him time to reflect. He compared the operation of *Centaur* with the many ships on which he had sailed. Sam was as blunt as Horatio, but his bluffness was tempered with empathy. The crew had imbibed his optimism, their confidence evident in their morale and in the ship's operation. Everything was orderly and efficient, from the trim of the sails to the smartness of the decks. The crew were proud of their ship. Even at the Sunday muster, as the commodore read the service, Josiah observed that the crew were attentive. Afterwards, the Articles of War were read and the punishment of offenders, usually loathed by sailors, was accepted meekly. There was no flogging. If only *Thalia* had been like this.

He knocked on the door of the great cabin.

'Ah, Josiah, come in, come in. Pull up a chair. Coffee?'

'Yes please, sir.' He settled in and addressed the captain. '*Centaur* works as smoothly as a fine clock. I have to congratulate both you and Lieutenant Richardson.'

'Well, thank you, Josiah. We have known each other a long time, and I appreciate a genuine accolade. Now, tell *me* about St Kitts and Nevis.'

He sipped his coffee, wondering how far he should go. 'My family on my mother's side have a long association with Nevis. My natural father was also from this island. However, I did not declare this when I arrived, preferring to form an independent view of that society. I was fortunate to become a close friend of John Jefferson, whom you met. An amazing American. A former slave. I began to see the islands through his eyes. Slavery, I now see, is abhorrent, and I cannot imagine how it can continue in an age where every enlightened Englishman believes freedom is an unalienable right.'

'I'm sure I agree with you. We can discuss that subject over dinner one day. It is *you* I want to talk about. The last time I heard of you was in 1800 when you returned to Chatham as captain of *Thalia*. By the way, do you know that *Thalia* is in the West Indies now – a troop ship, I hear?'

'No, I didn't know she was here. Her timbers were too frail to continue her life as a frigate, so she was modified to become a troop carrier. They offered her to me, but I was too proud. I felt the offer beneath me.'

'I heard you'd made enemies. One of your officers on *Thalia* was from that Liverpool family with good connections in parliament. I was told he gave a damning report on you, supported by letters from the purser. No one could understand why your father didn't pull your chestnuts out of the fire. Mind you, he had his own problems at that time.'

The coffee arrived and Josiah waited until it was poured. He was dismayed by Sam's news.

'I shouldn't be upset if I were you,' Sam said. 'These things happen. But losing Horatio's patronage ...'

'After he cut my mother from his life I could not bear to see him. I visited his home at Merton once only. I was told never to return. I hate Emma Hamilton – and Horatio, for taking up with her. I still love him, but we are divided by his affair.'

'Understandable. But it is a high price for you to pay.'

'If it means the end of my hope for another commission, so be it.'

'What happened then?'

'When?'

'After you turned down *Thalia*.'

'I was caught up in a scheme which I thought would restore me to favour at the Admiralty … but which failed.'

'And that was?'

'I must have your word that what I will tell you will remain between us.'

'You have my word.'

'Lord St Vincent encouraged me work as his agent – undercover – at the dockyard in Plymouth. I was to find corruption there and report the detail to him.'

'And?'

'There was nothing of consequence to be found – not of *corruption*, at least. Of mismanagement, plenty. St Vincent's men created such an atmosphere the contractors refused to supply timbers and other materials to the yards on the terms dictated by the Admiralty. The yard began to have serious problems delivering their ships, and the witch hunt for conspirators slowed deliveries to a crawl. The campaign to tidy up the docks achieved the very the opposite of what Lord St Vincent wanted.'

'It seems that your findings confirmed what the navy knew from the start – building ships is not the same business as fighting them. Our whole fleet is still suffering from St Vincent's "witch hunt" – as you call it. Your work in exposing it was of great benefit to the navy.'

'I realised that in revealing the … chaos … I had made an enemy of St Vincent, so my whole stratagem rebounded on me. I was about to leave Plymouth when I was attacked and kidnapped by the captain of a short-handed slave ship. That was where I met Jefferson.'

Sam shifted in his seat. 'Your intervention in the revolt on the *Amelia* calmed a very dangerous situation, I hear. But, at the same time, your sentiments about the future of slavery were not appreciated by those you spoke to at Nevis. It will be a while until things improve in that quarter – even if the bill in parliament to abolish the trade *is* passed.'

'I seem to be very good at making enemies.'

'You misunderstand me, Josiah. The opposition to abolition is powerful and has permeated our governing class from the King down. I agree freeing the slaves is the way of the future, but the reformers are faced with implacable opposition.'

'I am simply an Englishman who has come to realise the depths to which we have sunk as a nation and wants to do something about it. Now I have failed at everything – finding a command, the dockyard business and here too.'

'Come now, Josiah. You are too hard on yourself.

You're still young, and in time you will recover. I'll make a good report for you when we reach Barbados – and in London as well.'

The meeting over, Josiah made his way to his cabin preoccupied with the conversation, and fell asleep confused and depressed.

He dreamed he was lost and wandering London streets trying to find his way to the Admiralty. He awoke relieved it was only a dream. He wondered if it had to do with this ship. The commodore and his officers were gentlemen in the best sense of the word. The ship's record in battle was impeccable. Its morale was high. But it was beyond his reach. He really was finished.

When these dark thoughts dissipated enough to allow him to think of other things, he missed Jefferson. He missed his friend's dry wit. Even the colonel. Most of all, he missed Elizabeth. And Nisbet's death preyed on him. It was as if anything or anyone he touched would die or disappear.

Lieutenant Richardson asked if he would assist the schoolmaster with his midshipman's class and, for the want of something to take his mind off his situation, he agreed. He taught mathematics. Though he was rusty and struggled to keep ahead of his students, the boundless energy, curiosity and untrained minds of the boys at last distracted him and reminded him of happier times.

When the weather permitted he climbed the main mast and found peace in the tops, cooled by the breezes and the sea, which unfolded like a great green cloth to the horizon. Two of the three seventy-fours sailed either side of *Centaur* while a third, an old fourth-rated ship, struggled to keep up and trailed barely above the horizon behind them. Three frigates ranged on the horizon ahead.

He scanned the horizon, looking for sail. Horatio and the British fleet were out there somewhere. They might be close. But how would they find them in this enormous expanse of sea?

When he thought about Elizabeth he felt lonely for her company. His time alone gave him the chance to see things in better perspective. She was older by at least ten years and he liked her the better for that. She had seen more of life than all the younger women he had known. She had a straightforward way of dealing with him. He liked that too. Perhaps she was the woman he should marry. With that he again plunged into self-reproach. He had property now, but what use was it to him if he couldn't bring himself to live off it? His career was still a blank to him. How could he ask a woman to share his uncertain future? He thought about penniless officers he had known. They had no connections and no family to support them. Their wives lived in wretched cottages or apartments, struggling to bring up children in genteel poverty. He would not offer her that prospect.

Then he noticed that one of the frigates had changed course. It was wearing around and approaching them. A mile away it signalled.

He looked towards the helm, and he could see, far below, the Lieutenant and the commodore discussing the situation. Signal flags ran up and down.

'Course change one point. Keep up!'

The frigate approached. *Centaur* reduced sail. Time passed. Josiah asked himself if he ought to go below to see what was happening. A strange lethargy overtook him. They didn't need him. He was supernumerary. He leaned back against the mast and closed his eyes and fell asleep.

They were searching for him. He was in the dockyard at Plymouth. There was a strange half-light, and it was cold. He was trying to hide, but wherever he ran, their agents were getting closer. Then he was falling.

He woke. It was twilight and he was still in the tops. His back had slid from the mast and he was sprawled on the small platform. He climbed back down the shrouds and went to his quarters and tumbled onto his bunk, still clothed, and fell asleep again.

There was a thump on the door. He staggered to his feet, and there was the commodore's servant.

'Sir, please report to the great cabin as soon as possible.'

He straightened his coat and smoothed his hair.

'Come in, Josiah. Sit down.'

It was a council of war. Lieutenant Richardson, two other lieutenants, the captain of the marines and Sam, their faces lit by the fluttering light of the candles. They had a map of an island before them.

'Josiah, I have been telling these gentlemen about your feats at Bastia. You and one of your young friends … Weather … something.'

'Weatherhead, sir.'

'Yes, that's the name. You swarmed up that cliff and helped rig the blocks to hoist the cannon. Remember it well. Quite the talk of the fleet at the time.'

'Well, something that a young lad would do. Not sure I could still do that.'

'Listen, do you know Diamond Rock?'

'The rock that has been commissioned as a ship by our navy?'

'They are besieged by the French. They can keep Admiral Villeneuve's men at bay easily enough but they are running out of water, food and ammunition.'

'I'm not sure—'

'There's a man on that island who must be removed.

He is a man who helped us take Diamond Rock as well as other islands. We call him Monsieur Roche. He is a French royalist whose father and mother were murdered in the revolution. He hates all Jacobins. His knowledge of these islands and the French defences has helped us greatly. If the French take Diamond Rock we can arrange an exchange of our prisoners, but this man will die.'

'Why don't we attack the French besieging the rock?'

'Diamond Rock has served its purpose and is holding up the French fleet. Now we know that they will return to Europe it is more important we get to the rendezvous with Horatio. What I want is for you to land on the island and bring Monsieur Roche to safety.'

'Why me, sir?'

'You speak French, so you can explain to Roche why he must leave. You are senior enough to deal with any issues that may arise and young and strong enough to get on that rock and deliver my message. Are you willing?'

Josiah didn't hesitate. 'I am happy to volunteer, sir.'

# CHAPTER 24

Over the horizon another fleet was moving steadily through the pale dawn. Aboard the flagship, a strong westerly, moist and warm, blew puffs of spume across the deck. Somewhere ahead, perhaps a hundred or so miles, was Barbados. The sun rose over *Victory*, revealing a great fleet stretching as far as the eye could see in each direction. The flagship was making eight knots, its sails taut and its stays loose. The spars creaked as the twenty powerful sails stretched mast and tackle. The breeze whistled through the rigging. The sea pounded the bulwarks and splashed over. Although it was still early morning, running feet beat the deck like a roll of drums. Far above, dozens of sailors were aloft, furling and reefing to whistles and shouts from below. Deep in the bowels, the cooks stoked the fires, loading coal into the furnace to heat vats of steaming water, as daybreak brought the prospect of breakfast. On the poop deck, where the master paced back and forth to keep his ship on the wind, the compass was checked while two hands, moving like dancers, played the wheel.

It was a great city of men – nine hundred and a few extras – in total. Possibly she could be managed handily with a crew of fifty if she was on a day sail. But double that for the two watches each day and multiply that by nine if the great battleship were to engage in war – a likelihood that with each passing day seemed to the admiral was diminishing into a distant future.

The smoothness of everything and the stateliness of the flagship seemed, to those who had recently joined, befitting to a vessel whose admiral was Horatio Nelson. Yet almost everyone aboard knew *Victory* was like an old war horse ready for pasture. Her strength was spent. Two years sailing the north-west Mediterranean off Toulon, darting into a Sardinian bay to resupply, serving on blockade duty, tacking over to Spain to obtain intelligence from a British merchant with connections in Toulon, and back on watch. All this 'to-ing and fro-ing' had been in vain. When the French fleet was ready for sea it had evaded the *Victory* and her fleet. A furious chase had ended only when the French fleet, damaged in a great storm, returned to Toulon to recover and refit its damaged ships.

*Victory* had returned to her vigil. But again the French evaded the watchers. It was a dark day for the admiral. People said his luck had run out, that he was careless or tired or both – even that it was time for someone else to take over. But whatever might be said, his determination was not to be underestimated. East to Egypt and back to Gibraltar went *Victory* and her fleet – to no avail. The seas were empty. Salt was rubbed in her wounds when they ventured west beyond Gibraltar to learn, from Sir John Orde's squadron, that the French were sailing westwards for the Caribbean. Orde's squadron, in haste to avoid unequal conflict, had sailed northwards, neglecting to send word to *Victory*, still in the Mediterranean. To say that the Admiral was incandescent with rage would be an understatement.

Tired, frustrated, cynical woebegone though she was, her timbers were as resilient as the admiral's patience, and once more she stretched her legs for the long Atlantic crossing – following the Admiral's hunch that 'Bony was going to seize Britain's Crown Jewels': the sugar islands.

But, although the ship itself – patched and mended,

washed and scrubbed, hull supported with riders and sails down to the last set – maintained a dignity as suited such a vessel, the crew were only human. They were tired and sullen. They needed discipline, which was relentlessly imposed by the captain – Thomas Masterman Hardy. If the Admiral was a soft touch, sometimes going to the length of stopping the ship to pick up a young servant or mariner who had fallen over the side, Hardy had less compunction. He ran a tight ship, respectful of naval tradition and a philosophy that a good ship ran on generous helpings of the lash.

After the great mutinies towards the end of the century, fearful of sparking an English revolution, the 'powers that be' had decided twelve lashes would punish and subdue and keep a ship's discipline tight. But the crew, disgruntled by shortages of fresh meat and female company, and by constant demands to 'jump to' and no leave, sometimes cracked. And then they experienced Captain Hardy's unflinching retribution. Twelve lashes was deemed too low, all things considered. Twenty lashes were the more frequent sentence, but they too were now considered too lenient, and by the time *Victory* neared Barbados, thirty-five and forty lashes were standard at punishment details on Sunday after church and the reading of the Articles of War.

Fourth Lieutenant John Yule was officer of the watch. He was maintaining a north-westerly course and, in keeping with the Admiral's standing instruction, maintaining maximum speed –flying all her sails even at night. As long as they had a steady twelve-to-fifteen-knot wind all would be well. They had been spared the full might of the recent hurricane, but this had not tempered the Admiral's demand that they overhaul the French, so the masts and the rigging were still at risk. John had joined the fleet off Sicily, and it had been the same ever since. Once the admiral had decided on pursuit, nothing would let up. He had learned that from the great chase that had culminated in the Battle of the Nile seven years ago. Then, as now, they had failed to detect the French leaving Toulon.

John missed the sedate pace of *Thalia*, although his career had ground to a halt on that transport. Kent had moved on to take command of a sloop, and John had been overlooked. A young captain, five years his junior but with more patronage, had taken command. He had put in a request for a transfer to the flagship. Fortunately for him, Captain Hardy knew him from the days he had fought on Captain Ball's battleship, *Alexander*, and was more than happy to have him aboard. Rumour was there would be a great battle when they reached the West Indies, and John looked forward to that with keen anticipation. The opposing rumour said that the admiral was pursuing a will-o'-the-wisp. There was no French fleet in the Caribbean. Either way, John was happy to be sailing aboard *Victory*.

A bell rang. The sun was above the horizon. The seas were calm and *Victory* seemed to hover over the water as she raced ahead. He rechecked the compass and took out his telescope and surveyed the horizon. Too late now for a star setting. He made a quick calculation. They should be there within two days. He surveyed the fleet as the day brightened. He counted them and recognised them all by their silhouetted forms, each having its own character stamped by their builders and by masters who had decided which sails to fly and their set. Good – they had all kept up with the flagship. There ahead of them were two frigates keeping watchful eye on the horizon.

'Good day, Mr Yule!' It was Captain Hardy.

'Good morning, Captain.'

Hardy put his telescope to his eye and surveyed the fleet. 'You said something interesting at yesterday's meeting. You said when you were on *Thalia* there was conflict between officers. You will recall we were discussing a situation on *Victory* – an argument between two midshipmen which turned into a fight.'

'I do recall that.'

He also regretted his comment. Hardy was always

on the watch for slackness – in thinking as much as in practice. He should have kept his mouth shut.

'What happened?'

'It depends on who you talk to, Captain.'

Hardy's face darkened. 'Come now, sir. This is your captain asking you a straight question. I want a straight answer.'

'I left *Thalia* to join *Victory* – a new captain had been posted to *Thalia*, and I could see that it was better if I moved on. Very grateful to you having me.'

'Come now!'

It was time to get off the fence. '*Thalia* was no longer the frigate I fought on in '98 and '99. The old frigate fell victim to the Admiralty's decision to retire older vessels. She's a transport now. The old *Thalia* was a different ship altogether. When I joined *her*, she had a new captain – Josiah Nisbet. She was an unhappy ship, sir.'

'What was the reason?'

'May I ask why you are interested?'

'If I didn't know you better, John, I'd say that was an impertinent question – but I see that if I want the truth, I need to tell you what is on my mind. Our admiral mentioned *Thalia* the other day. We were talking about St Vincent's time as First Lord of the Admiralty and the mistakes … I mean … *changes* that he made. *Thalia* came up as an example of a ship that could have been fixed – riders would have done the job. He made some remark that he had arranged for Captain Nisbet to have the command again, but the yard had gone ahead and turned her into a transport. There is some mystery to the business, and I had a mind to pursue it – delicate though it is. Then you mentioned the ship at our meeting.'

'I met Captain Nisbet again when I joined the ship in Deptford.'

'You did, by Jove? You must be one of the last to hear of him. He disappeared years ago, you know. No one has seen hide nor hair of him.'

'He was offered *Thalia*, but when he learned she was no longer a frigate, he turned her down. By then the peace was on us and nothing else was offered. He visited us at Deptford –stayed overnight. The new captain, Kent, knew him too. They'd been together on *Dolphin* years before – when Josiah, I mean Captain Nisbet, was given his first command.'

'Let's go back, may we. To the unhappy ship you joined back in – when?'

''99 it was. Captain Nisbet was very young to take over *Thalia*. The crew were unhappy, and also the first lieutenant, Colquitt. I and two others were told to "keep a watchful eye" and "support" the new captain. Brierley and Bulkely took that as a sign they should keep reporting back to the admiral about the ship.

Captain Nisbet knew this and determined he had to get rid of all three: Bulkely, the captain of the marine, Brierley – who served as master and purser – and Colquitt.'

'What about you?'

'He never suspected I played any role other than being a junior lieutenant, and I never did. After these three were finally moved on, everything went well. Admiral Duckworth gave us all high marks. But when we returned to London, the others set out to destroy Nisbet. They wrecked his career.'

In the silence John knew he had said too much. But he couldn't stop himself from adding, 'That's the way I feel too. He was a good man. A bit too young for the job. God only knows what's happened to him since.'

'He was working in Plymouth – in the dock-yard – when he disappeared,' Hardy said.

'Yes, I know. We were the last to see him. May I ask if the admiral has tried to find him?'

'Thank you, John. That will be all.'

Hardy turned his back and continued his inspection of the ship.

In the days that followed, Yule returned to the conversation. He'd said too much. His comments would be relayed to the admiral. He tried to recall his every word. Everything was fair – and truthful.

Captain Nisbet *had* been inexperienced, and it was also true he would never have been considered for the position if he had not been the admiral's son. He recalled the skirmishes with privateers down in the Canaries, how the morale of the crew had risen once Colquitt left. Josiah had become better and better as he'd learned the ropes. It was a happier ship by then.

He was on morning watch when they arrived in Barbados. The relief on board was palpable. They had been at sea for so long. A few cables from Bridgetown's harbour, *Victory's* mighty anchors plunged through the clear green water to the sandy bottom. Yule watched with interest as the ship's boat took the admiral ashore; Yule had barely laid eyes on him the whole time they had both been aboard *Victory*. Loading stores consumed his time all morning as half of the crew were granted leave to go ashore. Rumours circulated. There were no reports of the French fleet.

A few days later it was time to take his half a day's leave, and the ship's boat took him ashore. The moment he landed at the mole he was besieged with offers to take him for tours, for every type of service, even to a 'hotel for gentlemen'. He made his way to the officer's club in the dockyard. There he had dinner and decided to rent a carriage.

The driver of the chaise introduced himself as Billy. He was an old black man with grey hair, dressed in the livery of the club. The club steward told John he had been a driver there for many years and knew everything about the island.

As they drove out of town, John said, 'I have but two or three hours at the maximum before we must return.'

'Then we will visit Drax Hall.'

'Drax Hall?'

'A famous plantation in these parts. My travellers love to visit it. The Drax family always welcome visitors.'

The roads were well made, and the island had a long-settled feeling. A piece of old England. Billy talked about life on the island, about the families that owned the plantations, the early settlers and the Africans who now were more numerous than the native British.

'Billy, the island looks like a little paradise. Everything is so tidy and the agriculture is so rich.'

'True, sir.'

Drax Hall was at the end of a long drive. Its age was no detriment because it was so finely preserved. It was a Jacobean mansion set amidst palms and luxurious tropical flowers.

The carriage rolled to a stop beside another. Billy said, 'Just go inside and say you're from the officers' club. They'll look after you.'

'What about you? Why not come with me?'

'No, sir, the folks there won't want me to come with you.'

'Well, at least come and introduce me.'

'No, sir. It's not permitted. You go alone.'

John Yule alighted, his complacency about the island upset by Billy's refusal. The truth began to dawn as he made his way up the stately steps of the hall. He rang the bell and a servant came to the door. John made his explanations, expecting to be refused, but the servant said, 'You are most welcome, sir. The family is away, but we are encouraged to entertain visitors. We're happy to offer you a tour of the house and some refreshment.'

They walked into the shaded hall, John realising the servant meant '*white* visitors'. The scent of flowers and beeswax floor polish infused the house with an air of calm luxuriance.

In the sitting room to the left of the lobby was a figure he recognised. It was the admiral.

'Yule, isn't it?'

He stood up, the light catching his face. The luxuriant black hair had greyed. His intelligent eyes and ready smile had not changed. All those months on the *Victory*, yet they had never met. He had had his own quarterdeck, his own great cabin.

'Yes sir, I am taking my leave with a carriage ride to see the island.'

'I was hoping to meet the owners, who I know from my earlier posting in the West Indies, but they are away.'

'Gentlemen, shall we begin the tour of the house?'

'I've seen it before. Perhaps a dish of coffee. Yule – you look around.'

'I'd sooner sit with you, if you are willing.'

'Certainly. Sit down. I was talking with Hardy the other day and he told me about your time on *Thalia*. I was moved by your loyalty to Captain Nisbet. A long time has passed since we last saw each other. We didn't have the best of relations in those years, but I feel I should have helped him more. Petty of me.'

'Captain Hardy told me about him going missing. I saw the better side of him and feel the loss too.'

'All the more difficult because his mother and I are not on speaking terms. Well, these things happen. Anything I can do for you, Yule?'

'Are we going to have another battle – like the Nile?'

'There are similarities. I am persuaded by the other senior officers that Trinidad's Port of Spain would be an ideal base for the French. We are heading there as soon as we have resupplied.'

The servant poured two dishes of coffee and placed a plate of biscuits on the low table between them. John watched as Horatio took a sip and bit into a biscuit.

To be in such an intimate conversation left him short of words. They drank in silence.

'Was he a good captain, Yule? Many people told me the opposite. He dismissed Brierley from *Thalia*. Brierley came with me to Copenhagen. The man had such seamanship. Without him we could never have negotiated those treacherous shallows. Why would Josiah have dismissed him?'

'He was young and overwhelmed by the officers watching his every move. He struck back, but that was all. When all was said and done, I have rarely met anyone with the skills he had – and nerve too.'

There was a warm silence. Horatio stood up. 'Yule, I like you. You speak plainly, do your job well and everyone trusts you!'

With that he picked up his hat and strode out into the hot sun. John waited for him to leave, and as he heard the sounds of wheels on gravel he made his own way to the chaise.

'Back to the ship, sir?'

'Yes please.'

He wondered where Josiah was now. Would he ever learn what happened to him?

# CHAPTER 25

It was pitch dark. Josiah clambered down a rope ladder to the jolly boat rocking gently below and took his seat amidships. Midshipman Fellows stood at the tiller. As soon as Josiah sat down he raised the sail and headed away from *Centaur*. Josiah noticed that a small barrel of gunpowder, a cask of water, muskets and flares and a basket of food had been stowed forward. Josiah took out the compass and opened the cover.

'Five degrees to starboard, Mr Fellows.'

The correction made, Josiah settled back for the journey beyond the horizon. Sam Hood was keeping his distance from Villeneuve's fleet.

At length Josiah saw a shadow towering indistinctly towards the night sky. Sam said it was six hundred feet high. It was nothing short of miraculous to have hoisted the guns up the sheer face to the top. He could make out two enemy ships lying five or six cables from the island. They would have lookouts in the yards, but they were looking for a supply ship, not a jolly boat. He signalled to Fellows to change direction.

They lowered the sail and Fellows rowed to the west of the rock where Josiah could make out a landing. Pulling closer, Josiah called out in a low voice. 'Ahoy there. *HMS Centaur*, Captain Josiah Nisbet. Permission to come aboard.'

There was silence. Then a voice called out, 'Tell me the name of our captain.'

'Maurice.'

'Come aboard.'

'Our boat will drop me and wait in the lee of the island.'

'Very well.'

Josiah stepped into the water and waded knee deep to the shore.

There was a sailor and a marine, armed with cutlass and pistol. A carronade was strategically placed.

'We have brought you a little water and extra gunpowder,' Josiah said.

'I'll take you to the commander. Others will unload.'

They set off up a steep path towards cliffs two

hundred feet above the landing place. An exchange of passwords and a cable descended. Josiah fixed a belt around his waist, and a tug signalled that they were ready to draw him up. Jumping from rock to rock, with nothing but a black void below, Josiah rose quickly into the abyss. At last, after what must have been three or four hundred feet, he found himself on level ground.

In the darkness, he could make out tents and make-shift emplacements. Two cannon pointed towards Martinique, whose outline he could see a mile away.

A tall figure appeared, dressed in a well-worn uniform. 'I am Captain Maurice. And you are?'

'Captain Nisbet, from *Centaur* – over the horizon.' He gesticulated to the east.

'We saw you. We're desperate for supplies, especially water. Villeneuve has a squadron surrounding us, with more keeping watch from Fort Royal. We cannot resist for much longer!'

'Commodore Hood says you must hold out for as long as you can. I have a letter for you. I've brought a small amount of water and gunpowder but there will be no more supplies. The siege will not be lifted. You are keeping the French fleet busy – and that is still of greatest value to us.'

'If you don't bring news of relief, why are you here?'

'I understand you have a Monsieur Roche here, a

French royalist? I am under orders from Sir Samuel Hood to take him off the island. If you are forced to surrender, he is a dead man.'

'He came here to help us when we took over the rock. Like many of his sort, he hates the Republic and Napoleon.'

At length Roche appeared, rubbing his eyes and trying to smooth unruly hair. 'I am Roche. What can I do for you?' he asked in a heavy accent.

Josiah spoke to him in French. 'I have orders to take you off Diamond Rock. Get your possessions ready. We leave in a few minutes.'

Minutes later Roche, the belt secure around him, was lowered down the rock face. He reached the bottom, and the line was drawn up and secured around Josiah's waist. He walked backward over the precipice. As he was lowered, he saw a flash out of the corner of his eye. A cannon?

There was a crack some fifty yards to his left, and a piece of rock fell, bouncing into the air as it hit the lower slopes. He must have been seen. Another to his right, and then all was silent again. The enemy had been alerted. When he reached the bottom a soldier released his belt and escorted him down the steep slope to the boat.

Roche was waiting for him.

'They were shooting at me!' Josiah said.

'They keep a look out for any movement.'

'Don't you worry, sir.' It was the soldier. 'We'll put the dummy in the belt and have them take it up. That way they'll believe it was an inspection. Lazy bastards.'

Sure enough, as they waited they saw a figure being drawn up the cliff, and more shots rang out.

Roche was already aboard as Josiah waded through the water. A brief wave to the guards. They pulled away.

With the oars muffled and in total silence, they took a wide berth around the squadron besieging Diamond Rock. Josiah kept a keen eye out for any sign the enemy had seen them. He thought about the men on Diamond Rock: dirty, short of water, completely committed. *HMS Diamond Rock.* The rock was now a commissioned navy ship. Why? No doubt some technical reason, some bureaucratic reason. But it *was*, in almost every sense, a ship with a captain and a crew, bursting with pride and ready to fight to the death. It reminded him of the days when he and Weatherhead clambered to the heights above Bastia and helped haul up the guns that led to the town's surrender. How he had gloried in the navy then.

Fellows gestured. A French frigate, shrouded in darkness, lay in silence, its outline blending with the towering cliff behind. If they passed seaward, they would be silhouetted by the light of the stars. They changed course towards the rocks. Roche replaced Fellows at the oars. Josiah steered as close to the rocks as possible; less chance they would be seen. He could hear waves breaking. Fellows gestured; they were in danger of being sucked into the swells and onto the rocks below the cliff. They went on. The boom of the surf drowned out every other sound. The jolly boat rolled and swayed as the waves struck it abeam. He looked at the frigate: it was a cable away, its gun ports threatening. But there was not a sound or movement aboard. He could see the watchman's lantern on the poop deck, he could hear the slap of the rigging against the spars. Slowly, slowly they crept past, and the rocky coast fell away and the rollers abated. They were through the cordon, and after another mile of rowing they pulled up the sail.

Josiah gestured to the Frenchman to sit with him in the stern as steered.

He spoke in French; he imagined Fellows' language skills would be minimal. 'Monsieur, at last we can introduce ourselves properly. I believe you are a man loyal to the royalist cause?'

'First, thank you for taking the risk of getting me off the island. If the French republican vermin took the island they would have killed me then and there. Captain Maurice knew that, and that was one of the reasons they resisted for so long.'

'How did you come to be on the island?'

'I fought for the royalists in France. I was in the French Navy based in Toulon. At the beginning of the war the British were there helping us to defend the indefensible. Napoleon's French force took the port and killed all the French royalists they could find. I found myself aboard a British ship with the commander of the Toulon forces. He sent me to his cousin's ship, *Juno,* commanded by Sir Samuel Hood. I joined as an ordinary seaman and I worked my way up to be a gunner. I fought in the Battle of Cape St Vincent and then Santa Cruz on *Zealous,* and after that at the Nile. I was always aboard ships commanded by Sam Hood. When he brought me with him to the Leeward Island Station he gave me the chance to serve as the officer in charge of the guns on Diamond Rock.'

'My God, how our lives intertwine.'

Josiah told him about *Agamemnon* and *Captain.* He was moved by Roche's loyalty to Sam Hood. Like so many others he had attached himself to a man who showed great leadership and care for his men. Would Horatio have done the same? Josiah had saved his father's life at Santa Cruz, but in Horatio's mind he had repaid all his debts to Josiah. There was no love or loyalty any more.

'Do you have any opinion of Villeneuve?'

'Villeneuve is a man without principle. He is an aristocrat who came to terms with the revolutionaries to keep his job. He is a creature of today's France – fearful of the mob, hypocritical and deceitful. Napoleon captured the heart of the army by his military genius. He has been able to channel revolutionary zeal into military successes, and his tactics cannot be resisted by the allies. But he has failed completely with his navy because he knows nothing about ships and the men that sail them. The French Navy's *esprit* is dead, its captains fearful, and its ordinary seamen believe they are in charge.'

'Why do you fight for your country's enemy?'

'I am not an aristocrat. I come from what the English call "gentry". I grew up accepting all the beliefs of the enlightenment from my father. He believed in the power of reason and inevitability of reform. In the Terror of Robespierre he was seized by the mob from the small town near our estate and butchered, together with my mother and sister. They had no guillotines there, so they hacked my father to pieces and hung him and my mother from the walls of the town.'

Josiah paused. The brutality of the lawless mob. There was something to be said for order and tradition.

'Will you return to France?'

'After the monster is dead I will return. My country

will be devastated, and they will need men untainted by the revolution.'

'Do you mean they'll restore the monarchy and the nobility to pre-revolutionary times?'

'No, we will never return to those days. If God wills it, we will become a country like Britain – moderate in policy, strong in trade, governed by men of integrity and religion.'

'What is it you like about Britain?'

'The English are a people full of contradictions – divided like the French between the power of the wealthy landowners and the poverty of the ordinary people. But the powerful in Britain do not fear or hate the poor. They share things with them. They are charitable and neighbourly. Go to a village cricket match and the players could come from any social background. Go to cockfight or a May Day celebration; everyone will be there.'

Roche pointed a finger at Josiah. '*Your* revolution happened when your leaders rid the country of the Stewart Kings in the Glorious Revolution a hundred years ago. Now kings depend on parliament, and parliament represents the people. The law is above politics. Would that the French Revolution had been the same.'

'We still struggle against privilege and patronage. Many seats in our parliament belong to rich men,' Josiah said.

'That's true, but your ruling elite *will* admit people to its ranks from below if they offer the country their best. Admiral Nelson came from an insignificant family but, *voilà*, now he is a viscount. There is always room for people to rise to the top in England. England is pragmatic. It has no interest in theory. Your Edmund Burke summed up the revolution in France as the dictatorship and terror that results when man make a religion of reason.'

At length they saw their ships lying at anchor and made their way to *Centaur*, at the heart of the squadron.

A short while later they were back at the flagship and sitting in Sam Hood's great cabin. Hood was delighted to see Roche and greeted him warmly. Josiah gave Captain Maurice's note to the commodore.

He read it quickly and asked, 'How long can Maurice last? Every extra day we delay the French fleet, the more chance we have Lord Nelson will catch up and destroy them.'

Roche said, 'We were short of water, powder and ball. We could repel any attempt to land, but thirst will defeat us. The occasional rain shower has helped, but the cistern is cracked. I estimate they will not be able to last more than ten days.'

'We will leave at once for Barbados. It will take us a day's sail. There is no time to lose.'

Over the next day, Josiah thought about Roche. He liked him and felt the common bond shared by men displaced by fate. He admired his style: forthright, without judgement or pretence. A bit like Jefferson.

Two days of sailing and they reached Barbados. Josiah scanned the horizon with his telescope, but there was no sign of *Victory* or the rest of the British fleet. At length a brig sloop flying the Union flag spotted them and made in their direction. A boat was lowered, and its captain came aboard.

When Josiah arrived at the great cabin, Roche was already there together with Lieutenant Richardson, Sam Hood and an older man, whose back was turned as he poured himself a drink.

'Come in, come in,' Richardson said. 'Sit you down! I have learned Admiral Nelson is not here. He was persuaded that Villeneuve would be found in Trinidad – at Port of Spain. I'm sure he was thinking Villeneuve was here to recover the islands and disrupt our trade. Port of Spain would be the ideal place base for that goal. We must find Nelson as soon as possible. I am sending you ahead on the corvette together with Monsieur Roche. Josiah, let me introduce you to the captain of *Rover*. Captain Kent, meet Captain Nisbet.'

The older man turned around to greet him.

'Kent!' Josiah said. It was indeed his old shipmate.

'Josiah?'

Sam laughed as recognition dawned. 'How do you two know each other?'

'We served on *Dolphin*, my first command. She was an old frigate converted to a hospital ship and lying most of the time in the Tagus.'

'Last time I saw Captain Nisbet, sir, was in London. I was captain of *Thalia*.'

'*Thalia?* Fascinating! You two will have a lot to say to each other on the way to Trinidad! Josiah, I have a letter for Admiral Nelson, and you are to take it to him immediately. When you meet Horatio, Josiah, I want you to repeat what we learned from the French marine on St Kitts. I have pressed Horatio to engage Villeneuve before he reaches Europe. I have told him the great things you have accomplished on Diamond Rock and before, Josiah. I am trusting that all of that will be enough to find you a command.'

'Thank you, sir.'

'I too will be returning to England, as I am to be replaced in the Leeward Islands' command. I will always be happy to have you sail with me.'

With this, they said farewell, Sam slapping Josiah on the shoulder in a parting gesture.

The full heat of the Caribbean sun bore down on the small ship as she raced southwards. Every sail in the locker was set, with studding sails and top sails flying. That evening, Kent took Josiah aside and asked him to dine with him alone. Roche was invited to the ward room to dine with the officers instead. As he dressed, Josiah reflected how Kent had grown in his years in command. He remembered him as an aging lieutenant, trapped on the dismal hospital ship. At their meeting in London he had been talking about retirement. Now he had the healthy glow of a man comfortable in his own skin, a man who had realised his destiny. A man who had found his niche at last.

They sat comfortably in wicker chairs, the windows open to the wake and the cooling breezes as the heat of noon turned into the softness of late afternoon. A gull trailed the ship, swooping and soaring as they spoke. They sipped their claret.

'My dear friend,' said Kent, 'our pathways continue to cross. I thought you were lost. People said you had been carried off by a gang of watermen sent from the dockyard. We searched everywhere. Even called out the constables, but no one heard or saw you again.'

'Before I tell you my story, where is Lieutenant Yule?'

'He was still lieutenant of *Thalia* under a new captain. The last I heard from him they were ferrying troops from England to Malta. A good man, indeed. If he was from a better family he would have advanced, but I fear like me he must be satisfied with fewer prospects.'

'Who is your commander?'

'I am attached to the Barbados station. My job is to patrol the island and keep an eye out for privateers and smugglers.'

As the sun made its path to the western sea, Josiah told Kent all that had transpired. As he spoke, he reflected that he no longer took pleasure in his successes and spent more time talking about his friends.

Kent, fascinated by Josiah's story, listened intently. By the time they retired it was late in the evening. Kent was worried they might pass the fleet during the night, and left to talk to the officers.

It was noon on the following day by the time they caught sight of their destination and, rounding the Western Cape, they passed the islands of the Dragon's Mouth towards Port of Spain.

Josiah anxiously scanned the horizon with his telescope. At length he made out a forest of masts in the distance. The battleships were anchored in the deep waters to the north of the bay. In the midst of the fifteen ships he could make out the mighty hull, the towering masts and distinctive yellow gun ports of *Victory*. As they approached he saw activity around the fleet. Barrels of water were being loaded, together with goats and cattle, pallets stacked with bags of flour and kegs of rum. Sailors were busily winching the produce from lighters and stowing them below. Lookouts were posted in the tops, and soon signal flags ran up calling for their identification. The helmsman brought her into the wind, and the anchor was lowered. Within minutes Josiah was in the ship's cutter being rowed to *Victory*. His father was less than two cables away.

# CHAPTER 26

Josiah struggled as he considered what to say. He'd be friendly – friendly, but not forward. *He would explain how he had come about the intelligence. He would give him Sam Hood's letter. No, he would greet him first, as 'sir'; he would greet him as 'Papa'. Others would be present; it had better be 'sir'.*

The flagship towered above him like a cliff painted in menacing ochre and black stripes. Last time he had been aboard was after the Battle of Cape St Vincent, when it was Jervis's flagship. The ship was a fixture of the navy, an ever-present reminder of the Britain's maritime power.

He raised his eyes to the deck. An officer was studying him through a telescope. Damn it, he was still wearing his warrant officer uniform. There would be no 'manning the side' ceremony today. The cutter bumped against the hull and a seaman held her steady. Josiah climbed onto a small platform and ascended the ladder to the main deck. The officer and two sailors lined up and saluted as one of the side boys piped him aboard. The officer had dark hair and a broad smile.

As Josiah returned the salute, he bowed and said, 'Welcome aboard, Josiah.'

It was John Yule. Josiah was speechless, thinking about their last meeting so long ago.

Yule said, 'I've been on *Victory* since May. Joined her in the Mediterranean. It's near three years since you disappeared. We waited for you on *Thalia* that night and you never came! We gave you up for dead!'

The greeting party was waiting for its orders.

'Party dismissed!'

Josiah gestured to his companion and said: 'This is Mr Roche, from *HMS Diamond Rock*.'

'Come on, gentlemen. The captain will see you in his cabin.'

It was orderly, spick and span as only flagships can be: the massive armaments of cannon and carronades with balls in racks beside them, sails neatly furled and not a stray rope or bucket to be seen. He looked up at the tops and took in the great mass of the ship. There was a time when he would have wanted nothing more than to be a senior officer aboard this ship. But how threadbare everything looked.

Yule said, 'She's thirty years old. They would have scrapped her if St Vincent had had his way. Thank God he didn't.'

'She looks exactly the same as I remember. Must have been eight years since I was aboard last.'

They reached Captain Hardy's cabin. Yule knocked. 'Come!'

The captain was at his desk. He rose to his feet. Josiah saluted.

'And you are?'

Yule said, 'Captain Nisbet, with a letter from the commander of the Leeward Islands for Admiral Nelson.'

Captain Hardy took off his reading glasses and put them on his desk. 'It *is* you Nisbet, by Jove.'

'And this is?'

'This is Monsieur Roche from *HMS Diamond Rock* – that's the place off Martinique.'

Josiah said, 'I am here with information. Would you take us to see the Admiral?'

'You have lost none of your plain speech, Josiah. I have a few questions of my own before I take you to him.'

'I have a letter from Captain Hood.'

'May I read it?'

'Very well.'

He took Sam's letter from his pocket and passed it to Hardy. Hardy scanned the contents quickly. 'I see what you mean, Josiah.' He turned to Roche. 'What have you to say?'

'The French fleet are in Martinique – in force. They will take Diamond Rock within days if they haven't done so already.'

'I see.'

'Yule, take Monsieur Roche and give him some food and drink. I want to talk with Captain Nisbet alone.'

'Aye, Captain.' Yule saluted.

'I'll see you later, Mr Roche.'

The door closed behind them. There was a silence and then Hardy said, 'I have been talking about you to your father recently – only last week. He has changed his opinions, softened a little.'

'A long time has passed – must be three years.'

Silence. Josiah stroked the polished table with a finger.

'It has been a gruelling chase,' Hardy said. 'Our men and our ships are worn out. We knew we could not afford a mistake. Villeneuve could devastate these islands. We have to get this right. That's why this intelligence is so important. I am going to see him now with Hood's letter. We will call you in later. In the meantime Yule will look after you in the wardroom.'

He signalled to his servant. 'Take Captain Nisbet to the purser and see if there is a captain's uniform aboard. If not, have one made up for him by the Tailor. Then take him to the wardroom.'

'Do we have time for this?'

'Nothing is going to happen until we are resupplied. We cannot sail until tomorrow at the earliest. In the meantime he will call for a council of war with the captains.'

Josiah followed the servant to the purser's office and tried on a spare jacket. It was uncomfortable – tight under the armpits. The purser promised the ship's tailor would let it out.

In the wardroom he found Yule talking to Roche and other officers.

Yule approached Josiah and said nervously, 'There has been such a conjunction of events.'

'What do you mean?'

'About a week ago I was talking about *Thalia* at Hardy's meeting – well, not about the ship, but about the unhappiness at the beginning until some of the officers left.'

Josiah raised his eyebrows.

'Afterwards Hardy asked me for more information. Your disappearance had been noticed – not least by your father.'

'What did you say?'

'I told him that after Colquitt and the others left, things improved mightily and you were a great captain.'

'Well, I don't see anything wrong with that. It's the truth.'

'Just letting you know, because my comments were passed along.'

Josiah said, 'He will have to make up his own mind about me. I am merely bringing intelligence.'

'Don't be like that, Josiah. This is your chance to make up with him.'

'It's up to him.' He listened to himself: harsh, defensive, resentful. It would not do. 'I'm sorry, John. I didn't mean it. It was awful. The break with my mother, flaunting the Hamilton woman in public, the loss of my ship. He abandoned me, his *only* child. I was his son, whether he liked me or not. A father wouldn't abandon his son, I thought.'

'I saw him – on Barbados. We met at Drax Hall and he said – I remember his exact words – "It was petty of me."'

Yule's words were cool water on the fire within. He was silent for a moment. Then he said, 'John, I like you.'

He laughed. 'Would you believe that's what your father also said?'

Horatio's servant collected Josiah and Roche and escorted them to the admiral's quarters.

Josiah gathered his thoughts and feelings as he went. *Petty of me.*

The door opened and he walked into the broad room. The great cabin was cool – its windows open, papers fluttering.

Captains filled chairs around the long table. The inner circle. Perfectly dressed and groomed. Finely powdered wigs.

'Sit down, Captain,' said Hardy, pointing to a chair at the end of the table near the door.

Horatio was at the other end. He sat down.

'I have called a council of war, Captain Nisbet.'

*The formality.*

'I have read Commodore Hood's letter. He tells me of your activities in the Leeward Isles and affirms intelligence was gathered properly and he believes it to be true.' He turned to the captains and admirals. 'Gentlemen, Captain Nisbet fought a bold battle against the French, defending the Leeward Islands against overwhelming odds and aided only by a few slave soldiers and hopeless regulars. Trained them and led them, says the letter.'

'You are too kind. The men were great soldiers, and my fellow commander was a man with experience in the American wars.'

'Yes, I read about him. Brave … but slaves, nonetheless.'

Josiah felt his face reddening. How dare Horatio use these words to describe those fine men? His blood boiled; it was too much. The officers were looking at him, uncertainly. A long silence.

Jefferson came to mind. How would he handle this?

With calmness, Josiah said, 'It was indeed an unequal fight, but everyone did their duty. You would have been proud of them.'

There was a spontaneous round of applause, led by Horatio. Josiah peered down the long table to the small figure at the other end, silhouetted against the stern windows.

'Gentlemen,' Josiah said, 'I interrogated a French marine we captured on St Kitts during their attempted seizure of the island. We learned he was a former slave from Haiti with no reason to love the French. He served in Admiral Villeneuve's Great Cabin, and from him I learned the intent of the Admiral. In short, they have succeeded in drawing your fleet away from the Mediterranean and the shores of Britain and, having done so successfully, they are even now returning there to carry Bonaparte's troops across the Channel to England.'

There was immediate consternation, with two officers trying to speak at the same time.

Horatio said, 'Come, gentlemen. Let us be orderly. I find this intelligence to be creditable. I would prefer to believe the French are here to fight – as they were at the time of the Nile – but we have some clear differences from that situation. First, they have no army with them, only a few hundred troops. Second, there are so many islands for them to attack it would take them a year and, by now, they know we have pursued them. Their failure at St Kitts and Diamond Rock will have further convinced them of our resolve. I was sure they would be here at Port of Spain and was hungry for a repeat of our glorious victory at the Nile. But they are not. Gentlemen, they have bluffed us and we are now at a disadvantage. I want to hear your opinions and hear your arguments.'

He looked at Josiah. 'Captain Nisbet, I am sure you are hungry and thirsty. You may leave now.'

Josiah rose amid scattered applause, feeling like a boy dismissed by the headmaster. His cheeks flushed, he bowed awkwardly and made his way to the door.

When he reached the wardroom no one was there. They must be on deck, he realised, and, thanking the servant, made his way up the companionway to the poop.

Valuable as his information had proven, he was not a member of the inner circle. Apologetic though his father had been to Yule, he had shown Josiah no sign he wished to reconcile. Yet even as these thoughts confounded him, making him feel low, he recalled Jefferson's counsel to be careful with his feelings.

Then he saw Yule and Roche sitting under the shade of a sail at the bow and he felt better. Soon he was immersed in conversation. Yule was telling Roche about St Vincent's witch hunt and Josiah's discoveries at the Plymouth yard.

Josiah asked, 'How did you discover I was missing?'

'When you failed to appear on *Thalia*, the crew searched for you. We met with your landlady. You and she had fallen out, I gather. But when she heard you'd been taken she was of a mind to tell us more – and that was when we realised there were people at work who didn't want your news to reach London.'

'Janet.'

'Who?'

'That was her name. I never told her who I was, but she found out and hated me for it.'

'I am sorry to hear that'

'And what happened with my news?'

'It reached the right people, and St Vincent was forced from office. But he salvaged his career and now commands the Channel Fleet.'

*Minto must have carried the message.*

'What about my mother? Have you heard anything about her?'

'I feared for her – losing her husband *and* her son.'

'Perhaps word got back from Nevis. Perhaps a letter.'

'I wouldn't know, but I would think that whatever follows, you should write to her now.'

They were interrupted by Horatio's servant. 'I have a note for you, sir.'

He handed a small envelope to Josiah. He ripped it open. An embossed parchment.

*Victory*
*Vice Admiral, Lord Nelson*

*My dear Josiah,*
*Many thanks for addressing my men. You will hear soon that we will be underway tomorrow morning. We have but a few hours and I need exercise. Meet me on the quarterdeck in an hour and we will take a walk up the hill to starboard. We have much to talk about. Please arrange to stay for supper.*

*Yours affectionately,*
*Father.*

# CHAPTER 27

*Victory's* launch brought Horatio and Josiah to the beach. It was mid-afternoon, and the languid mist that had draped the forested slopes a few hours before had burned off. They set off up the track for the summit, visible between the trees a mile or so away. While Horatio panted and puffed as the path steepened, months of training and the battle on St Kitts had toughened Josiah. He could see that their goal – Santa Anna – was but a modest foothill of distant peaks, their heads buried in clouds over the northern massif.

Josiah's pleasure was complete. *Papa must recall our walk in the hills above Lisbon when everything was different.* It had been before all those terrible things. It had been the last time he had loved his father unquestioningly. Since then great chasms had opened, chasms of suspicion, anger and hurt.

He had been too ready to give voice to his ambitions, too ready to boast of his paltry achievements, too ready to judge. He had been a young prig who knew. And Horatio had been changed by fame and success. The price was evident: a premature stoop, a shaking hand, weakness in the lungs and a voice with a distinct tremor. At the council of war Josiah had witnessed Horatio summoning his reserves, and his strength had given him command of the proceedings. Yet Josiah felt he ought to take him by the arm now and help him up the hill. Then the hill flattened out a little and they paused. Horatio sat on a rock and Josiah dropped on the ground.

'I feel weak these days,' Horatio said.

'Father, you are one of the strongest of men.'

'It has all changed. I am not the man I was. Still, as long as I am alive I have work to do, and I try to keep myself fit.'

He rose to his feet as if to make the point but failed to gain his balance and fell as he stooped for his stick. As Josiah ran to him, Horatio rolled and raised himself until he was kneeling. He planted his stick firmly and swayed to his feet. As he dusted himself down he said, 'I'm fine. Leave me alone. We will proceed.'

Josiah tied a kerchief around his neck and adjusted

his straw hat. How would he begin? He had been thinking about this opportunity for years: to get Horatio alone and tell him how abandoned he felt and how his mother had suffered; to ask for an explanation.

They reached the top without another word. The trees gave way to mossy rocks and huge boulders. Horatio sat down again, propping his back against a rock. Josiah stretched out on the grass, hands behind his head, and watched the clouds scudding across the sky.

Josiah said, 'Quite a blow today. A good day to sail.'

'Tell me more about yourself, Josiah. Sam's letter said you were commanding troops on Nevis?'

Soon he was deep into the story of his strange journey. It seemed a lifetime ago, but now, here he was. Together with Father. Home.

Horatio liked the story.

Josiah said, 'Father, may I speak openly?'

Horatio raised an eyebrow and gripped his stick.

'I wasn't the best son. I was young and stupid, part of a crowd of young men competing for your attention. I was jealous.'

'Jealous?'

'Of the others. I wanted you for myself, but you were doing your job, and you shared yourself and your time evenly.'

'Of course. I was your father and I had my duty.'

'You were fair. I'm sorry I was surly. You didn't deserve it.'

'Why now?'

There was an edge in his voice. Josiah raised his hand to his mouth. 'No agenda. Indeed, I wish to apologise for my *attitude* – then.'

A load slid from his shoulders as he said this – and in that instant he knew, whether or not the apology was accepted, he was free.

'Son, I am in shallow waters. I cannot navigate them. Are you about to give me a message from your mother?'

'No. I am sorry if I caused you heartache or even criticism. You gave me every chance, and I want to thank you and apologise.'

Horatio was standing up. Was he going to leave?

He turned his back and took a few paces before turning. He was wiping his face with a handkerchief. 'It was dreadful. I knew what I was doing to Fanny, and I couldn't stop myself. And you. You came to see me, and I turned you away. When I thought you were dead I searched *everywhere*. I heard you were in Plymouth and I spoke to the dockyard people. They remembered you well. They loved you. They had no idea. Disappeared off the face of the earth, they said. And now you are here … and *you* are apologising to *me*. I have not done my duty to you.'

Josiah put his arms round Horatio and sobbed. His father's back felt bony under his hands. Both men stepped back, holding each other by the shoulders.

Horatio consulted his watch. His voice was brisk. 'We must return. The fleet departs in less than two hours. You come with me on *Victory*. You will have your wish to fight again.'

'Father, I must return to Nevis and put things to rights there. Matters to discuss with the commanding officer, Colonel Smith.'

They made their way down the hill. It was steep, and Horatio took Josiah's arm.

'What else is there to do?' Horatio said. 'What is better than to fight our nation's wars, to earn glory and to retire thankful?'

'Papa, you and I belong to different generations. You are part of the world in which great landowners and their estates run the England you know. The world has changed. The Indian trade and the sugar business are in decline. Industry is changing everything in England. Machinery is winning the war against Napoleon. The canals transport coal and iron, and engines are driven by steam. In London Rothschild and Barings borrow and lend millions to the government. Landowning aristocracy is losing power to these new industries and the people who own them.'

Horatio nodded. 'The last time I travelled to south Wales I came back through Birmingham and inspected their workshops and foundries. Amazing what these buggers can do!'

'Mama wanted me to go to university, to study the law or medicine, but *I* want to study this new world. When this war is over and captains are not needed I want to have my own business.'

By now they had reached the bottom of the hill. They boarded the launch, and its crew rowed to the flagship. They sat side by side, silently. He wondered why he had turned his back on his career. Surely he had not made that decision – yet?

As they approached *Victory*, Horatio said, 'This will be my last battle. I have been pursuing the French fleet for over two years and I will find them and destroy them.'

He said these words with such finality that Josiah knew this *would* be the last chapter. He had witnessed it before on the deck of *Agamemnon* as Horatio had led the charge to board San Josef. He had seen it at Santa Cruz. This was the way Horatio made war.

'Father, I *do* want to be there, with you.'

'You can accompany me as a passenger. Or I can find some other useful work for you to do.'

Dispassionate, detached.

Josiah said, 'I still have to finish what I have begun

on Nevis … and *then* I will join you – if I have a ship to carry me.'

'I'd like nothing better, Josiah.' Horatio held his arm as he said, 'You and I have fought each other, but I'd prefer we fight the French together – side by side.'

Victory was being readied for the long sea voyage across the Atlantic. Loading was done. The last barrels of water and firewood had been lowered into the holds. Crew were in the tops, changing sails and testing the rigging.

Horatio took Josiah to the great cabin and ordered supper be brought. Then he summoned the fleet captain, George Murray. While they drank their tea, Murray updated Horatio on the preparations.

When he had finished, Horatio said, 'George, I need a sloop for Captain Nisbet. It will take him to Nevis, and afterwards he will rejoin the fleet at Gibraltar. What do you have?'

'Your lordship knows we are very short of frigates and sloops. We need everyone to keep an eye on Villeneuve.'

Horatio turned to Josiah. 'I remember when I was leaving Naples. I had to carry a queen and an ambassador, and Admiral Hotham, the new commander of the Mediterranean, said the same thing: the best they could offer me was an old frigate returning for a refit. Such a slight. That's why we returned by land.'

'We have an empty transport, sir.'

'A troop transport?'

'Yes, she's a converted frigate – *Thalia*.'

Josiah breathed deeply and thought about his resolution. 'That will be very fine. I am happy to command her.'

In a soft Scots brogue Murray said, 'Welcome, Captain Nisbet!'

Josiah smiled in acknowledgement. 'Where is she bound?'

'When we were in Barbados I received a letter from the commander of Jamaica. There's trouble on Saint Domingue – a slave uprising turned very nasty – and the French have been driven out of Haiti. There's been wholesale slaughter of the planters and their families. There's fear in nearby Jamaica that the new slave government will promote an uprising there too. It's been decided that *Thalia* will stop in St Kitts and Nevis to carry soldiers of the West Indian Regiment to keep the peace. If you take *Thalia*, then you must complete the mission. There will be relief ships returning to the Leeward Islands with Sam Hood's replacement, and when they arrive you will be free to return *Thalia* to Gibraltar and return to England. I am sure you will find a ship.'

After that everything moved fast, for the fleet was under orders to leave within the hour. Josiah sought out Yule to say farewell. He found him busy supervising crew, who were stowing barrels of biscuit and lemons.

He said, 'Yule. I am to return to *Thalia* as her captain. I will be going to St Kitts and Nevis and then return to the fleet. It's just temporary – a favour from the Vice Admiral.'

'I would love to ship with you, Josiah, but I am needed here.'

'John, I will see you in London, but please keep an eye on my father. He is not what he used to be. I'm worried about him.'

'I will, Josiah, but you know he will do whatever he decides. He is the bravest of the brave – and so far God has protected him.'

'May God go with you too, Yule. I wish you success in battle.'

☙

The launch was already stowed on board *Victory*, so Josiah took the cutter to *Rover*. Kent was in no hurry and was content to yarn with Josiah while the fleet prepared to leave. Signals were passed to *Thalia*, and it was agreed that *Rover* would escort *Thalia* past Martinique. With her limited armament *Thalia* would otherwise be fair game for privateers.

At length the fleet gathered itself. Signal flags fluttered between the ships. Sails were hoisted, and one by one the battleships moved out of the port and took up their allotted position in the convoy. There were more than twenty of them manoeuvring to their positions, hauling cutters aboard and then making their way to the west. The sun began its slow descent and the wind began to rise. Against the backdrop of the deep green, jungle-clad hills, the fleet set sail and, with *Victory* at its heart, slowly disappeared into the distance, leaving the two small vessels behind.

*Thalia* was empty, its troops distributed to the islands. Only the ship's master, Mr Mitchell, four warrant officers and twenty-five men remained to sail the ship that had once housed over three hundred sailors.

Josiah had no desire to insist on any change to the ship's routine. He took stock, nevertheless, and found it was well maintained and the crew experienced in their tasks. *Thalia's* previous captain had jumped at the opportunity to serve on the flagship of the departing fleet. Josiah recognised some of the attributes of that bumptious young captain. He recalled how bored *he* had been on the *Dolphin* and how grateful to return to Gibraltar all those years ago. Now, *Thalia's* crew seemed to breathe a sigh of relief after the young captain's departure. Josiah's evident familiarity with all the routines of the ship and his skill in seamanship was quietly observed, so while the crew mulled over the 'who' and the 'why' of his command, they showed their gratitude for the change and their respect for their new captain by working hard and running the ship smoothly.

In the three days it took to reach St Kitts and Nevis he had time to reflect on his friends on the island. He had been hasty to depart, reacting to the rejection of his plan for his estate by the island leaders. He had been perhaps too willing to hand over everything to Jefferson – and, most of all, he asked himself if he had been right to break off his relations with Elizabeth. It was her face that filled his thoughts.

Without a cargo *Thalia* rode high on the waves and was as fleet as the *Rover*. As a consequence they made good time and passed by Martinique within a day, without sighting a single enemy ship. At length it was time to farewell *Rover*, and he asked the master to make a signal. As he was rowed the short distance between the two ships, Josiah thought about his time as captain of a sloop the mirror image of *Rover*: *La Bonne Citoyenne*. It had been a perfect ship at a perfect time. Why had he demanded promotion? *Sometimes you get what you ask for, and it is not what you expected*, he thought.

The cutter bumped against the hull, and he sprang

up the rope ladder to be greeted by a bosun's whistle. Kent greeted him and escorted him to the great cabin. It was palatial compared with the cramped quarters on *Thalia*.

'My dear friend, let us drink to the renewal of friendship.' Kent poured a glass of port and the two friends silently toasted each other. 'I must leave you here and return to my station at Barbados. No doubt they are wondering where I am and will be anxious.'

'Kent, how I appreciate you. You taught me that having a lieutenant who was loyal and hard-working is the greatest blessing for a commander. And you are still a true friend.'

'What are your plans, Josiah?'

'I am still drawn to serving my country, but when the war is over I plan to get into business.'

'Nonsense, man. You are still young. You have reunited and made your peace with your father. One day he will be First Sea Lord.'

'Events have passed me by, and there's a different world arriving. First we must beat the French ... but after that there will be no need for a navy. Instead there will be a new world of industry, inventions and new sources of wealth in commerce. England will be a different place, and I want to be part of that new world.'

'Well, God bless you, Josiah. You are as talented

as anyone I've known, and I'm sure you will master whatever you turn your hand to.'

The two men sat back in silence. Josiah looked at Kent's kindly face, the leathery skin creased with wrinkles. He had spent too many years on board ships. It was good to see that his twilight years had brought him command of a fine fighting ship. Josiah stroked the arm of his chair absently and stretched his legs and sighed. He hadn't intended to say those things. They had come unbidden from somewhere within him.

Two days had passed since he and Kent had said their farewell. At Kent's suggestion, *Thalia* made for Antigua, fifty miles away and home to the Leeward Islands command. As they entered English Harbour, Josiah marvelled at the well-protected dockyard and its shore base.

Samuel Hood had left for England, and his replacement had not yet arrived. Josiah explained his orders to the dockyard commissioner.

'Your arrival could not be more fortunately timed,' the commissioner said, 'as we must transport soldiers of the West Indian Regiment from St Kitts to Jamaica. It will scarcely take you a fortnight, sir.'

'Jamaica? What about the defence of St Kitts?'

'Everything has changed. The French have gone. The threat is negligible. Moreover, not all the troops are leaving the island.'

'What is the problem on Jamaica?'

'That's not for me to say, sir; I am here to organise the shipment of the troops. You should be ready to sail for St Kitts and Jamaica tomorrow.'

# CHAPTER 28

Colonel Smith told Jefferson, 'You will lead the Regular Squadron to their new post – Kingston, Jamaica.'

Orders were orders, but everything within him resisted.

'They are to replace the British troops in Jamaica recalled to England,' Smith went on.

'Why are they recalled?'

'Our army has been decimated. Thirteen thousand men were lost to yellow fever in the Saint Domingue campaign. Bloody nightmare. Trouble is, without them, the bastards who run Haiti, as they call it now, will spread their poison to Jamaica. Planters are terrified of slave uprisings.'

'Why the Regulars?'

'The Jamaicans want white or Creole troops only. And with the French fleet gone we don't need all these men here.'

Jefferson reflected that since Josiah's departure, the promise of settling the soldiers on his plantation had withered and the morale of his African troops was low. And the massacre of five thousand white planters – including women and children – on Saint Domingue had brought the horrors of the French Revolution to the Leeward Islands. Stories of children's heads on spikes around the towns and villages, and of women being raped before being murdered along with the men roused terror in everyone. The Haitian revolutionary Dessalines was the Robespierre of San Domingue, and the fear of him had replaced the fear of French invasion.

And now Jefferson was to sail for Jamaica to protect the planters against their slaves. It was depressing to contemplate. Nonetheless, he could do nothing about it. He had taken the King's shilling. Earlier he had seen the French fleet passing on its way to France, followed days later by the British fleet. Josiah would be with them, he guessed – probably on the flagship. His father would have been eager to have him aboard. A cloud of loneliness descended on Jefferson. After the action of the last few months, he was uncomfortable.

It was a welcome distraction when a frigate was

sighted anchoring off Basseterre. He climbed to the battlements to see what was happening.

Colonel Smith was there with his eye to his telescope. 'To my untutored eye, it seems to be some sort of transport.'

He passed the telescope to Jefferson.

'Perhaps this is our ship. I wasn't expecting anything so soon,' Smith said. 'Let us greet the captain at the mole.'

The two men took their coats and hats and descended the hill together. Since the announcement of Jefferson's mission some of the warmth in their relationship had dissipated. He knew Colonel Smith understood him but had had no choice than to send his right-hand man. Nevertheless, it rankled.

At the mole they waited as the cutter pulled smoothly into the quay and the captain stepped ashore. He was smartly dressed in a new uniform and a powdered wig.

With a shock, Jefferson saw it was Josiah.

Josiah saluted, and the two soldiers returned his salute. Then Josiah took Jefferson by both shoulders. 'My dear friend, so much has happened to me since we said farewell. Are you well? Are our friends still attentive to their duties? Elizabeth: how is she?'

'Come, Josiah, let us walk with Colonel Smith and he will fill you in, and you too will tell us your news.

Only a few days ago when the British fleet passed by I was convinced I would never see you again. Yet here you are!'

By now Josiah had caught up with Colonel Smith, who was striding ahead. 'Colonel Smith, is all well? How are the soldiers?'

'My dear Josiah, I have news for you. I have determined that Jefferson will escort the Regulars to Jamaica. British troops are leaving for Europe, and the regular soldiers of the West Indian Regiment must take up the slack.'

'Is that wise? The Africans are devoted to Jefferson. Without him they will be leaderless.'

'The Africans are to remain here.'

Jefferson looked at Josiah. Their eyes met. Jefferson made a gesture with his shoulders. It said, 'This is not my decision.'

～

A stormy passage to Jamaica. For the first time, Jefferson quarrelled with Josiah. Neither was comfortable with their situation. The cause of Jefferson's discomfort was more obvious, but not so dissimilar to Josiah's. But the situation created tension between them.

They were sitting in Josiah's cabin as a tropical storm turned the sea into a boiling mass of white horses. *Thalia,* old and disfigured as she was, rode the waves with ease, her sails furled tight, a small bowsprit helping them to point.

Jefferson said, 'I cannot fight to maintain slavery in Jamaica. That was not my reason for joining the army!'

'We are both under orders. I have been obliged to sail this ship – a mockery of my seniority. It's the same thing.'

'No it is not, my friend. This is but a slight interruption in your career.'

'What do you want to do? I see you are in a difficult position.'

'It is time for me to leave the army.'

'Don't be hasty, Jefferson.'

Jefferson exploded. 'You have no idea! You have never suffered from this terrible fate and cannot imagine the passion it raises in my heart!'

❧

They sailed passed Haiti, both men sick with the story of that island. Hell on earth. By the time they reached Kingston, Jefferson had settled into rueful despondency. He made sure his men were settled in at the barracks at the dockyard and then he and Josiah made their way to the officers' mess. It was unpleasant when they were stopped at the door and told they might not dine there. Jefferson curled his lip when the marine captain suggested he should mess with the men. His sense of pride and justice battled with his loyalty. They left the mess with no further comment, and he and Josiah took a room together in Kingston.

The following day, Josiah was summoned to a meeting at the port commissioner's office. As he later told Jefferson, it was an amiable meeting, although the intent of the discussion was clear. Together with the commissioner was a British colonel.

Josiah recounted the absurd conversation later on:

'My dear captain, I understand that you are Lord Nelson's relative?'

'Yes, he is my father.'

'Dashed complicated situation we have on our hands.'

'What is that?'

'Your American man. Just won't do.'

'You are talking about Sergeant Major Jefferson?'

'That's right. Can't have a black man leading white troops. Just won't wash here in Jamaica.'

'He has an impeccable record with the British Army in the American war, and more recently he built a fighting force in the Leeward Islands.'

'That's as it maybe, but I am going to have to return him with you. This island is very different from the sleepy hollow you are from. Our relations with the freemen and the slaves are far from relaxed. Saint

Domingue has stirred things to a boiling point. We have hundreds of runaway slaves in the hills trained by people from Haiti. No, it won't work.'

'Why did you ask him to come in the first place?'

'Bureaucratic mistake. The name. Seemed obvious he was an Englishman to me.'

Jefferson was overjoyed, greeting Josiah's description of the meeting with a straight face which could hardly disguise his real feelings. To assuage Josiah's apparent ire, the colonel had presented a sword to Josiah to recognise his great father. There was no apology for Jefferson.

The following day, the two men were back at sea, rejoicing at the unexpected turn of events. But something had changed. Jefferson was no longer committed to his new career. He saw clearly that there were limits beyond which he could not go and dangers that could easily overwhelm him.

'I shall have no other choice but to return my warrant and become a private citizen, Josiah.'

'I understand and will support you ... but first we have something to do. We need to arrange the Africans' new situation. Convert them from their regular status to a militia. We need to settle them on my property in Nevis. When we have done that, then we can both consider what to do next.'

Jefferson said, 'That's what I like about you, Josiah.

Once you have set your course, you continue until you reach your goal regardless.'

*Thalia*, empty of troops again and driven by a westerly wind, sped back to the Leeward Islands. It was a cruise – an empty ship and a following wind. Upon their arrival at Basseterre they were again greeted by Colonel Smith on the mole. Colonel Smith's surprise was obvious, but less clear was what he thought about the situation. After all, Jamaica's rejection of his leading soldier reflected poorly on him. Josiah was pleased when Smith suggested they return to the barracks and let the African troops know that Jefferson was back.

But the next day, after breakfast was over, Jefferson requested a meeting with Colonel Smith. The latter, clearly surprised and discomforted by the request for a formal meeting, asked Josiah to join them. Overnight, Jefferson had considered what to say. It would have been easy to ask Josiah to be the mediator, but he rejected that as dishonourable; he did not wish to entangle Josiah in the matter. Instead he sat up late pondering his words, reflecting on his honour and considering what the reaction of his commanding officer would be when he told him. It would be so easy to appear disloyal, and he had no wish to undermine Colonel Smith's dignity by leaving him in an impossible situation. Only his loyalty to the Africans tugged at his heart. It would be a grave disappointment to them if someone else was recruited from another island to take his place.

When Jefferson had said his piece, Colonel Smith replied, 'The threat to the islands has diminished. I agree with that. However, Brimstone Hill needs to be manned in case the situation changes. I will have to discuss this when the Leeward Islands Council meets next in Charlestown. Jefferson, your decision has created a dilemma for me and for the leaders of the island. When you left for Jamaica I was already worried about the vacuum you left behind. Now I fear there will be more repercussions, which we will need to tackle quickly and decisively.'

# CHAPTER 29

Josiah knew he had only a limited period before he must return with *Thalia* to Gibraltar. Over a month had passed since he had seen Horatio. It was only a matter of time before a great sea battle against the French and Spanish fleet broke out. Josiah desperately wanted to be there when that battle was fought.

His conflicting priorities made him feel pressured to speed things up, to make decisions and achieve resolution. The slowness of island life was frustrating. He debated what he might achieve in the time he had left, and the outline of a plan took shape in his mind.

The next morning he returned to the Bath Hotel to see Elizabeth but there was no sign of her, and he was told she had not been at the hotel for several days. Perhaps she was taking a holiday. In the absence of anything else, he decided to retrace his steps to St Barnabas Methodist Church. When he reached the church, the door was open but there was no one there. The soft warm breeze blew through the opened shutters, giving the building a pleasant coolness. He read notices chalked on a board and saw again that among the children in the Sunday school there were several called Nisbet. *Relatives*, he thought. He wandered to the back of the church, where a door opened into a courtyard. On the other side was a small house built in the grey volcanic rock commonly used on the island.

'Can I help you?'

He spun around.

It was Charles Grey. He stretched out his hand. 'Take a seat. I was about to brew some tea, if you care to join me.'

'That would be very nice.'

They sat in his simple parlour and sipped a strong, unsweetened cup of tea. Grey looked at him expectantly.

'I have a dilemma,' Josiah said. 'I have an inheritance, an estate on the island.'

'I know you do. It has caused quite a stir among the great men here!'

Josiah stared at him. Grey smiled slowly. 'Your attempts to convince the planters to back your endeavours failed. They are all too terrified of setting a precedent. It has been ever thus. Sometimes their servants are loyal members of the family. Sometimes the planters believe they will be murdered in their beds. Some are worse than others, and when times are peaceful it's possible to imagine we will one day be free of slavery. Then the French threaten, or there is an atrocity on Saint Domingue, and everybody ducks. The overseers reassert themselves. It will never end until the wretched institution is ended.'

'What does your church believe?'

'We Methodists are completely opposed to the slave system. We believe it is abhorrent to God and man and it will, God willing, come to an end. Sooner, I hope, than later.'

'I'd like to talk to you about my plan.'

✒

Josiah returned to *Thalia* to check on the preparations for the long Atlantic crossing. He had arranged to meet Jefferson and Colonel Smith at the Bath Hotel the next night, but in the meantime he tried again to find Elizabeth. His starting point was the hotel, and this time he was able to discover Elizabeth's whereabouts. She had taken a holiday and returned to St Kitts – to the house where they had spent the days before the French attacked.

He set off immediately for Basseterre, where he

rented a jogging cart to take him to the cottage on the cliff. It was all so familiar: the peacefulness of the place, the beauty of the view over the sea, the lush trees and sweet-smelling flowers.

He approached the door and looked through the open window. Elizabeth was sitting at the table, writing. She put down her pen and dusted the letter. Then she looked up and met his eyes.

She started. 'Is that you, Josiah?'

He opened the door. For a moment there was a hesitation, and then she flung her arms around his neck and kissed him full on the lips. They held each other for a few moments, and then Josiah said, 'Elizabeth, I love you.'

Silence.

Then she was all briskness. 'Sit down. Let me put the kettle on for tea. Where are you staying? What happened with your father?'

He said, 'I love you and I want you to marry me.'

Elizabeth flushed. She said slowly, 'I'm surprised, Josiah. I thought you had gone back – to England.'

'I *am* going back, but I want you to come with me.'

She turned her back to him as she put the kettle on the hob. He heard her say, 'I cannot, Josiah. You see, I am already married.'

'Married? I never …'

She turned, tears in her eyes. 'Like you, I have secrets. I have a child to consider.'

They sat side by side at the table as Elizabeth told her story.

'I am the daughter of a Jamaican family. My father, who was very old-fashioned, arranged my marriage to the son of a Nevis planter. It was a bad marriage from the very beginning. My husband is an alcoholic. When he drinks he is cruel. We had a child together – a daughter.

'When I could bear it no longer I fled with my daughter to St Kitts. I was arrested, and Ruth and I were returned to Nevis.' She began to sob. 'He took Ruth. She is fifteen now. She lives in his house. I have no right to see her, but I have friends who tell me how she is. We exchange notes and sometimes I see her if he's away. My father bought an interest in the Bath Hotel and made me the innkeeper.'

Josiah said, 'Oh, my dear.'

He held her to him as she continued. 'You see, I couldn't tell you. It was too painful. Better we enjoyed being together while we could. When I learned you had inherited an estate, I felt for a moment that we could somehow make things work ... but I know that will not happen. I love you, Josiah. You made me so happy.'

She took his face in her hands and kissed him. But as he reached for her, she withdrew.

'We have said our farewell. Let's love each other from a distance. It's too painful otherwise.'

As the jogging cart took him back to Basseterre, Josiah thought about Elizabeth's story. Her courage, her determination and her ability to deal with the tragedy of her life made him realise the depth of his love for her.

But soon he would have to leave her. When he returned to Basseterre, he would join Colonel Smith in his meeting with the council the following day. He was determined to announce his plans for his estate and see that the council made the right decision. After that he would have a few days to put everything into place before he left for Gibraltar.

Elizabeth's story had confirmed for him that this place *must* change. Once the war was over the oppressiveness and unfairness could not be sustained. The power of the rulers was tyrannical. The 'stability' they offered came at too high a price, and it ought not – must not – be sustained.

His mother and Elizabeth had so much in common. They had loved and they had lost everything. But there was nothing he could do so long as the war continued. Horatio was right. Everyone's duty must be to defeat the French. But after the war was over, then these other evils must be defeated as well.

# CHAPTER 30

The weathered grey stone building had unfulfilled pretensions to colonial grandeur – columns and pediments and an elaborate coat of arms above the grand entrance lobby. The square before the assembly house filled as planters and wives and personal slaves arrived in carriages, ladies opening parasols against the sun as they stopped to exchange greetings with their friends. Everyone was dressed for the occasion – ladies in muslin and lace, men in sober black cutaway coats and, for some, uniforms. Josiah wore his new captain's uniform and a wig.

On the steps he met Colonel Smith and Elizabeth, and when they reached the lobby they saw John Jefferson and Charles Grey waiting for them. They all made their way up the steps to the gallery above, where a black usher escorted them to their seats. Below, in the well, the councillors took their places, some chatting informally while others strutted about, proud to be part of the august body.

Then there was a call for silence, and the governor of the Leeward Islands took his seat beside the president of the Island Council. The Lord's Prayer was read aloud by the chaplain and the president called the meeting to order.

'Gentlemen, we have a full agenda today. I will begin by asking the governor to address us, and then I will call on Colonel Smith of the West Indian Regiment, who has an announcement. Governor Leigh...'

'Gentlemen!' A red-faced, portly man in a blue colonial uniform rose to his feet with his cockaded hat beneath his arm. 'It is my pleasure to be with you today. I bring you good news. The French fleet have quit the West Indies. Sightings have been confirmed by trading ships coming from Europe. The enemy ships are under full sail back to France. I am pleased to say also there is no sign of any substantial military assets left behind other than the garrison on Martinique. I can also confirm that, as a result of the intelligence Captain Nisbet conveyed to our *own* Lord Nelson, the British fleet is in hot pursuit.'

There was a pounding of feet on the floor and cries of 'Hear, hear!'

'Yes, the noble lord has a strong connection to this island and to the West Indies. Nelson's fleet is pursuing the Spanish and French fleet, and we know that when they catch them, they will bring them to battle – and I have every confidence it will be a great victory.'

More shouts and applause greeted this announcement.

'In view of this change in our fortunes and the restoration of peace to the islands, Colonel Smith, the commander of the Leeward Islands, has an announcement to make. I want you to know that Colonel Smith and I have discussed what he is to say, and we are in firm agreement.'

He resumed his seat and the president called on Colonel Smith.

Colonel Smith stood. He gravely thanked the governor for his introduction. Then he said, 'Gentlemen. Thank you for this opportunity to address you. I am pleased to confirm what Governor Leigh has just told you. The French forces have departed. Over the last ten years we have worked to expel them from these islands – island by island. The last to fall was St Lucia. There remains Martinique, Guadeloupe and Saint Domingue. Saint Domingue, we can now say, is firmly in the hands of its former slaves. They are enemies of our people, but we do not believe they will attempt to invade our islands, although they will attempt to subvert our slaves. Britain has abandoned its goal of taking the island after a great loss of men from fever. In due course, we will remove the remaining outposts there. Despite Saint Domingue, however, it is fair to say we have won our campaign against the French enemy.'

He paused and mopped his brow. The temperature had risen, and despite the open shutters and fans, the room was losing the battle with humidity. Women were fluttering their fans, while men shifted uncomfortably in their black coats and dabbed their necks with handkerchiefs.

'As a consequence, I wish to announce that the West Indies Regiment is to be reduced. We have already removed the regular troops to Jamaica, and we will be discharging the African soldiers on St Kitts and Nevis, except for a small garrison to guard Brimstone Hill.'

There were murmurs of unease. The president interrupted and called for quiet.

Colonel Smith continued, 'As I said, the army will discharge its soldiers and thereby reduce the cost to us all. This means, under the agreement we have with these brave men, those discharged will be given their freedom.'

He held up his hand against the swelling dissent.

'They will still be part of our militia – on call to us, should we need them. Each soldier will be given a conditional discharge subject to recall in the event of a renewed threat. In the meantime, however, they are now members of the free Negro population of Nevis.'

By now the noise in the room made it hard for the colonel to make himself heard. In the visitor's gallery the agitation had several men on their feet.

Colonel Smith sat down and the president stood. 'Gentlemen, please be quiet. You have not yet heard how this matter is to be resolved. I now call on the Reverend Charles Grey of Nevis Free Methodist church.'

The minister stood and made his way down to the well of the house calmly. 'Gentlemen, your attention please. I have something important to say.'

The insults and angry shouts anger gave way to uneasy silence.

'As many of you know, I have been working with the free Negro citizens of Nevis for many years. I myself am a freed slave. Many, if not most, of my congregation at St Barnabas Church are law-abiding, hard-working people deserving of your admiration for all they have achieved. I know that some of you here have manumitted slaves, and you know that given their freedom these former enslaved people – like all of us here – are peaceably raising families and contributing to the wellbeing of our island.

'As well as my clerical duties, I am manager of a friendly society, which I established with other citizens. Our members put their hard-earned savings into this fund. In return it provides them sums of money in times of hardship. It pays for members' funerals and lends money to buy land and build houses. This is how we, as an island, have largely avoided the terrible trap of poverty that has afflicted former slaves after their manumission.'

There was a short pause in which could be heard a few shouts of 'Hear, hear.'

He continued, his thumbs gripping his lapels, his voice firm and confident. 'I have been fortunate to make a friend of Captain Nisbet. Now Captain Nisbet has visited with me and made a magnificent proposal. After discussing this with the president we reached agreement on a plan, which I would like him to describe. My role in this is to assume the leadership of this project and, with your cooperation and help, make this become a reality. And now I am going to ask the president to introduce Captain Nisbet.'

The room was abuzz. The decision to disband the West Indies Regiment at Brimstone Hill had been kept secret until now while the details of the discharge of the troops were discussed. The planters were angry the army would release its troops on the island without consulting them. Reverend Charles Grey had laid the groundwork to allay these fears, and now it was up to him to persuade the council to support the plan. Josiah walked down the stairs from the gallery and entered the assembly room. He looked around. The members were the same men he had met before. With trepidation he remembered their reaction last time he had spoken to them.

He breathed deeply. 'Gentlemen, when I left you last I was a ship's master. I return dressed rightfully in a post captain's uniform given to me but a short while ago by Lord Nelson, my stepfather. He and I had the opportunity to spend time together when I met him at Port of Spain, and I told him I would be returning here to talk to you about the future of the troops I commanded with Sergeant Major Jefferson and Colonel Smith. As Governor Leigh has told you, my father has returned to Europe to destroy Napoleon's fleet. I am under orders to accompany him in battle once I am done with my business here.'

'Get to the point. Speak plainly!'

Josiah saw the man who interrupted. It was the planter who had opposed his earlier plans. McPherson.

'I will indeed. Before I tell you my plan, you all know that at the next session of the parliament in London, the government will introduce a bill abolishing the slave trade. Unlike others introduced over the last ten years, this one *will* become law. It will prohibit buying captives from African Slavers and shipping them to the West Indies. The international trade in human flesh is about to end.'

McPherson shouted, 'No, never!'

'The question I would like to ask you is this: once the slave trade has been abolished, what will happen on these islands? I think you already know the answer: the cost of your labour will increase and the sugar trade that has made these islands so valuable will diminish. Once that happens, gentlemen, the reason most of you are here will disappear too. Eventually slavery itself will be abolished. Hopefully sooner rather than later. Delay it you may, but the change is inevitable. In the meantime, more and more of the citizens of this island will be free blacks.

'The Reverend Grey has already made a grand start to create an organisation – the Society for Free Africans – committed to the support of Nevis' free black citizens. He and I have agreed my estate will be leased to the society as long as I am alive. The land will be divided into small holdings, enough to offer room for a house and ten acres to cultivate food and other cash crops. The money paid to the society by its tenants will be accumulated into a fund to acquire more land, which will be leased as more slaves are manumitted. In this way, the plan will help the island to change and become home for the formerly enslaved people and any others who live here. What I want to do is to support the change that *is* taking place. No longer will the government be the supporter and the protector of planters alone. It will instead make sure that all free men are equal under the law, and the law is not used to oppress them because they are poor or enslaved.

'Some of you hate what I am doing. Others may be more aware of the change that is occurring in all spheres of life as a result of this war and the great industrialisation in England. You can choose whether to support us or to fight us. I hope sincerely it is the former.'

Amid silence Josiah mounted the steps to the balcony. He sat down next to Jefferson. Jefferson held out his hand and shook Josiah's.

The president stood and said, 'The announcement by Colonel Smith has my full support. These troops have put their lives on the line to defend us. Reverend Grey's church and the work he has done with the friendly society are of great benefit to our community. When we look at the terrible disaster of Saint Domingue and the problems of Jamaica, we must ask ourselves how we are to avoid a similar fate here. The future demands we accept that a larger and larger portion of our people are *free* black people. Captain Nisbet's generosity comes from the spirit of sacrifice and duty his father our noble admiral demonstrated in defending our freedom. Thank you, Captain Nisbet. I now declare this session will be closed to outsiders.'

*At last it was time.* Josiah knew that whatever happened today would determine the future of two hundred men and women whose destiny had become enmeshed with his own. He could see the different threads of his life and how they had been spun into this strong cord. The afternoon with Elizabeth had taught him a person has to accept responsibility for others and be willing to submit to the moral obligations that this realisation creates.

His new self-awareness was liberating. He felt free of resentment, anger and ambition. He had a fresh thirst for justice. Unimaginable wealth was created here but it all flowed to England, where it was invested in magnificent estates, the purchase of titles and rotten boroughs and even the new industries. The very blood of the nobility was mingled with and sweetened by the despicable business of this island and places like it. The bloom on the rose of England concealed an awful canker.

The trade had even paid for the war with Napoleon. England's freedom was being purchased with the money made here from the sweat of its black inhabitants. His conversation with the Reverend Charles Grey had convinced him of this. And now he had played his own part to change it. A small initiative, but a beginning.

～

The friends were at the Bath Hotel. Elizabeth had organised dinner – a salad with poached fish and roasted yams. The colonel had declined their invitation but sent a magnum of champagne, which had been cooled on ice in the hotel's cellars.

Elizabeth said, 'Josiah, I very am ashamed of my husband's insulting jeers.'

'I ignored him, Elizabeth.'

'I am so ignorant of the whole matter of slavery and those struggling to free themselves. It looks as if I don't care. But I do, I do. I feel shame.'

They were joined by Charles Grey at this point. Elizabeth toasted Josiah and Charles, though, as a man who abstained from alcohol, Charles drank none of the champagne.

She said, 'I had no idea about your society, Reverend Grey.'

'It was not my invention. I learned about friendly societies in London. I have friends there who are in constant touch me with me.'

Jefferson said, 'American freemen formed these

societies too. America has a long experience with mutual aid. Perhaps the best known are the fire companies in every city and town.'

Elizabeth turned to Josiah. 'I was amazed by your speech. It is as if you can actually see the future.'

Josiah said, 'It *is* the future. When I met my father, we talked about this. He is "old world". He thinks things will be as they always have. It made me ask if this was right. I am still learning, but I feel the best I can do for this island's leaders is to show them where things are going. And then, perhaps—'

Their musings were interrupted by voices on the other side of the partition. 'That bastard Nisbet! A damn traitor. It will lead to a slave uprising. We risk seeing our women and children killed in front of us!'

Elizabeth gasped, her hand to her mouth. 'It's him.'

But already Josiah was on his feet, striding out of the room.

Jefferson said: 'Stop, Josiah. Think!'

McPherson saw Josiah coming and struggled to his feet. 'Look at the great betrayer! The thief of other men's property.'

A quiet fell over the company.

'Come, Clive,' one of McPherson's companions urged. 'You have had enough to drink. Let us retire.'

'Get away from me! You, sir, are stealing my wife just as you are stealing the slaves of this island.'

'Sir, you are drunk and insult my honour. Retract those words.'

'You coward. Are you going to challenge me?'

Josiah's answer was to punch him in the face.

McPherson struggled to his feet. 'I demand satisfaction from you, you damned rascal!'

The lunch was over, and now a dark cloud settled over the friends. Elizabeth and Jefferson tried to talk sense into Josiah, telling him he must cool his ardour and think about consequences.

Charles tried to persuade Josiah that a duel was not the way to settle the matter. 'You should follow the example of the Saviour, who received insult after insult without responding in anger.'

And Jefferson added, 'This is a deadly matter. If he kills you, this island will suffer. If you kill him, *he* will be a martyr.'

But by late afternoon they had failed to persuade him, and McPherson's second arrived to make arrangements for the duel.

Josiah was unable to overcome the image of McPherson leaning against a tree while his overseer whipped his slave. He knew the man had treated Elizabeth similarly. Yet at the same time he could not forget that his affair with Elizabeth had an element of dishonour, even though he had been ignorant of the circumstances. He had simply not made it his business to ask questions. And, he realised, as a crack shot with a pistol, he held the advantage. He was uneasy with it.

They met in the early morning of the following day as first light crept over the horizon. The pistols were inspected by their seconds and presented to the combatants. McPherson was unapologetic when asked if he wished to retract. Josiah said it was too late for apologies. Jefferson, as Josiah's second, took his coat and pressed him again to consider whether this was the best way to settle matters. But Josiah was determined. This duel was more than the settling of personal differences, important though they were. This was not about honour. It was about duty. This was about McPherson's contempt and his violation of Elizabeth's rights and the rights of his slaves.

Then the two men were ready and, each armed with pistols, took ten paces.

The referee dropped his handkerchief.

Josiah turned as the bullet whistled past his head. He paused and raised his gun. McPherson was shaking.

Josiah waited – and then fired into the air.

The smoke cleared and the referee said, 'I am satisfied you have discharged your debts to honour. Shake hands, gentlemen, and we will breakfast together.'

McPherson was obdurate. 'No. I am not satisfied.'

'Then reload.'

The seconds cleaned the pistols and reloaded them.

The referee took his position again.

The handkerchief dropped again, and this time both men fired at the same time.

The round hit Josiah's shoulder like a blow from an iron bar. He staggered back, clutching his arm. McPherson was on the ground, moaning. All his passion spent, Josiah rushed to him, but the referee held him back.

'You are bleeding, sir.'

Jefferson inspected his wound. His heart was pumping. The doctor was working on McPherson. Drops of sweat blinded him.

He heard Jefferson say, 'The bastard will never abuse another woman or slave.'

The doctor said, 'He is dead.'

Josiah vomited.

They dressed Josiah's flesh wound as McPherson's body was carried to the waiting carriage. Jefferson took Josiah back to the horses and they rode them to the mole, where the cutter was waiting.

'I'll come to the hotel later in the morning when I feel better,' Josiah said.

'No, Josiah. Colonel Smith and the attorney general of the colony insisted that if you killed him you have to leave. You must get underway tonight. If you are here in the morning, you will be arrested.'

Sick to his stomach, Josiah considered his options. He needed to settle many things. He needed to complete all the details of the new estate with the lawyers and Reverend Grey. Most of all he needed to see Elizabeth. Instead of this, aboard *Thalia* he sat with Jefferson and a notary and signed the power of attorney for Charles Grey to represent his affairs.

'Jefferson, I feel I have let you down. I am fleeing and leaving you to fight an uneven battle.'

'What is done is done. I will see everything is put in place before you get to Gibraltar. I will write to you in London, and hopefully we will see each other again.'

The two men embraced, Josiah feeling he had allowed his pride to overcome his common sense. He was no better than these planters. Full of remorse, he wrote to Elizabeth and gave the letter to Jefferson.

'Look after her, John,' he said, sealing the letter with wax and his signet.

The cutter took Jefferson and the notary ashore. When it returned and it was hoisted aboard, Josiah gave the order to pull up the anchor. The sails were set. *Thalia* was bound for Gibraltar. A strong westerly blew as they sailed for the north cape of St Kitts. Josiah watched as Nevis grew smaller, its peak stark against a blue sky. Then they passed Basseterre, and Josiah looked up at Brimstone Hill. There were sentries on the parapets, and the Union flag fluttered in the strong breeze. At length they passed the northerly coast and, telescope at his eye, Josiah found the small cottage on the hill.

The islands far behind them, Josiah retreated to his great cabin, where his supper awaited him. A sense of finality overcame him. He was not meant to stay. He had done his work. The death of McPherson was like a full stop at the end of a sentence. He felt he had taken an irrevocable step. Now, his only thought was to join his father for the battle.

# CHAPTER 31

Late that night, Josiah met with the master and agreed on the course to Gibraltar and the watch schedules. He read the log and walked the ship on a tour of inspection. It gave him a sense of calmness. These rituals he knew by heart.

But, after he had eaten a simple meal, a crushing sense of failure returned. He put himself in the dock and prosecuted his case. He had murdered that wretch – in cold blood. There was no one to make a contrary argument, and so the jury was not out for long. His hot-headed action had undone his work – work in which he had found life-changing purpose. This might well be the excuse the planters needed to undermine all the painstaking efforts of Nisbet, Charles Grey and Jefferson. Their earlier sacrifices had made change possible. Then his impetuous action might have ruined it. To add to his distress, he had left the island as a fugitive from the law. He had run away from the consequences.

Now he had time to think, he realised how unbalanced the fight had been. McPherson was a dwarf. Yes, a dwarf with a deadly weapon and with conceit and pride, but still an empty, pitiful bully. Josiah had known that the very moment he had fired the pistol. Killing a dwarf was not something to be proud of.

He put his head on the pillow and fell into an uneasy sleep.

When he awoke, *Thalia* was listing and chopping through the waves. He struggled into his clothes and heavy sea coat and boots, a feeling of nausea in his throat, and made his way on deck. The master stood by the mariner at the wheel.

'Evening, sir. We're in for rough weather.'

'I know this ship through and through. She has been through far worse than this.'

'Aye, sir.'

'I killed a man. Shameful business. I cannot endure my own company. Will you stand watch for a while longer?'

'Not what I heard, sir.'

'What?'

'The crew told me what Mr Jefferson said.'

'But—'

'They said you rid the island of a rat. A bully of a man despised by everyone in Charlestown. Said you gave him a free shot at you and offered to settle the matter. He refused. Good job you was trained by the navy, sir. Proud of you they are. The rest of it is just for lawyers to argue over.'

'Thank you. You make me out to be a better man than I do myself.'

The two men stood together uncomfortably.

'You see, sir, when we're in battle, we do our very best to kill the enemy. Yet when 'tis over and we see our handiwork, we all feel we need God's forgiveness, no matter the situation. That's the way of things. You will feel better in a day or two.'

❧

The wind continued to rise. *Thalia* bore away to reduce the pounding on her hull. With sail shortened, the ship reduced speed amidst a sea of whitecaps. Rain beat on the decks, and soon Josiah was wet through. At length the master finished his watch and retired, leaving the bosun and Josiah alone with two helmsman who struggled to hold her on course. The wind whistled through the rigging. Gale force. The bosun gave the order to take down the topsails. Half a dozen men climbed the ratlines and, with practised speed, lowered the sails to the deck and swung down again.

Josiah watched them as they came. The first man was on the deck when his fellow still at the crosstrees lost his footing. His hand shot out to grab the halyard, but the ship hit a steep wave and came up into the wind. He lost his footing and, as the ship heeled, fell into the sea.

'Into the wind!'

The helmsmen swung the wheel as *Thalia* rounded up.

Josiah could see the man in the water disappearing as the ship passed him.

'Keep your eyes on him!' he screamed over the roar of the wind.

He stripped off his coat and seized a length of rope from the deck. He lashed one end to the mast, tied the other end about his waist, bounded to the gunnels and dived overboard.

The water was still warm, he noticed, his mind racing as he surfaced. The slack was not yet taken up, and he swam towards the stern. The crewman was twenty yards away. He struck out and swam for his life. He seized the panicked man by his armpits, and as he did so there was a mighty tug and he almost lost his grip. He was being towed by the ship.

'Hold on! I have you.'

The ship had stopped. A line with a noose secured by a bowline was thrown, and he caught it and put it around the man's waist and drew it tight. They hauled him out of the water, spinning and dripping and cursing. Then another line dropped and he pulled it over his head. It ran through a block attached to the boom. They hauled him out, dripping and shaking with exhaustion. What a crew.

Mitchell was back on deck.

'How's the sailor?' Josiah asked.

'He'll live. We better get you into some dry clothes. You are a hero, sir.'

*Perhaps better if I had gone down.*

The voice.

*What are you trying to prove? You can't bring McPerson back to life.*

He went below to change, and wrote up the incident for the log.

After he had changed his clothes Josiah went below to visit the sailor in the small hospital bay.

The man fumbled for words of thanks. 'It takes a bold man to jump into the sea in a storm, sir.'

'I would have expected you to do the same.'

'I have seen men left behind even when the weather is good. You saved me in a storm. That I have never known happen before.'

'I had the good fortune to have a rope around my

waist. Still I am grateful to God you survived. You know, you look familiar. Have we served together before?'

'Indeed we did, sir. On *Dolphin*. Years ago. In the Tagus.'

'My old hospital ship!'

'We had been just a-layin' there before you showed up. You was keen as mustard and had us sailing that old ship, mustering the men, firing the cannon. As if she were a ship of the line!'

He laughed and Josiah laughed too. He had been barely seventeen. The reward for saving Horatio's life at Santa Cruz. He'd wanted a fighting ship but got the *Dolphin*.

'How did you come to be aboard *Thalia?*'

'Captain Kent brought me with him.'

There was a silence as they recalled far-off years.

❧

The accident helped. His despair over the duel lifted. He set to, reviewing the rules of the ship, studying the log, interviewing the warrant officers and creating a schedule to meet each department and their crew. He assessed their skills for the forthcoming battle. He had no idea what they might confront. But he knew they had little with which to defend themselves. Twenty of the thirty-six cannon they had once carried were gone. But they still had a carronade and enough ordnance to discourage a privateer or even a corvette. The shortage of men was the biggest problem. They barely had enough crew to sail the ship, never mind to fight her.

And what could they expect to find when they reached Gibraltar? The French had a month's start on the British, who had another month's start on *Thalia*. Chances were good the French were snug in harbour at Brest or one of the Spanish ports, blockaded by Horatio's fleet. Still, Josiah remembered Horatio's conviction that the final battle was in the offing. He was seldom wrong.

Every day he held gunnery practice and he watched the crew steadily improving. There was a palpable excitement aboard after months and years of boring fleet duties, transporting thousands of troops from one posting to another.

At one of their regular meetings, Mitchell presented the punishment detail. Josiah cast his eye over the short list. The minor misdemeanours could be dealt with easily enough, but there were two more serious matters: insubordination and drunkenness.

'This man has gone too far this time. He's bought a flogging,' the master asserted.

'Very well. Five lashes after church on Sunday.'

'That is a too light if you mean business.'

'I see it differently, Mr Mitchell. The man overboard matter has raised morale. While this man has committed an offence for which he will be punished, I see no reason to create fear.'

'If I'm not mistaken, sir, you made a name for punishing offenders fiercely. They are expecting it.'

That remark made Josiah pause but he did not change his mind. He stood impassively as the sailor was lashed to the grating and the bosun took out his red baize bag and laid into the offender's back with all his strength. After the first blow, blood flowed down the scarred back. But five lashes were a trifle to someone who had experienced this ritual many times before. After they had thrown a bucket of salt water over him, they untied him and he stepped away smartly without a defiant glare, as if he knew his punishment had been unusually merciful.

Later on Josiah thought about the scene: the short church service that he had read from the prayer book, a shortened version of the Articles of War, the punishment detail – and then dinner. It was so familiar, a foundation stone of the navy's fighting tradition: hard discipline. Yet, he mused, love had as much to do with discipline as fear. Which were more important in battle? He had no doubt. That was why his father had been so successful.

He remembered witnessing the terrible flogging

on Nevis. It was the time he had seen McPherson's overseer attacking his slave. It had been horrible to watch because it had ended only when he grew tired and his victim was unconscious, perhaps dead.

Once again he found himself asking whether the world was not changing. It was no longer so simple – 'us' versus 'them'. Tyranny against rebellion. So much of the whole affair had to do with the management of hundreds of men in small ships. The close confinement bred resentments and irritations. Perhaps in this new world of machines it would be possible to fight a ship with half of the crew.

Dining with the Master, he was confronted by the realisation that his emerging views were at variance with his own reputation.

'I don't see you as the Captain of *Thalia* for long, sir. As like as not you'll make have command of a Ship of the Line.'

'I will recommend your promotion to Captain when it's time for me to leave *Thalia*. But in the meantime we have work to do.'

'The fleet won't want us anywhere near a battle, sir. We'll be helpers. Help pick up the pieces afterwards.'

'Then let's be prepared now. Extra training in lowering the boats and how we are going to bring the injured on board. Best prepare the troop quarters as hospital wards. Our surgeon will need help. We'd better give a few lessons to some of our stronger crew. The surgeon will need them to hold his patients while he operates.'

'Still, it's unlikely we will find the scene of the battle.'

'I have a feeling in my bones. Did I ever tell you I arrived in Alexandria the morning after the Battle of the Nile? Too late for glory, just in time to clear up the blood and gore. I had to help with the dreadful aftermath.'

'No, you haven't told me that story. I'd like to hear it.'

❦

By mid-month they were more than halfway across the Atlantic, and a week after that they were approaching the coast of Spain, the crew alert for enemy ships.

'Ahoy!'

It was the lookout calling from the crow's nest. 'A British frigate, *Sirius*.'

'A flurry of flags, twenty or thirty.

The signal midshipman was busy translating the code.

'Sir, there is a battle over the horizon.'

Josiah was gripped with disappointment. He was too late.

They continued until, in the distance, they saw a great cloud of mist. Smoke! The wind had dropped, and the moist air carried the sound of sporadic gunfire.

'The battle is over,' Josiah said. 'That is the sound of surrender. A few ships still resisting. We are too late.'

Another signal from *Sirius*. The midshipman read it aloud:

'The victory is ours! The French are surrendering. We are looking for survivors.'

And then the flags fluttered up and down again: The midshipman said: 'Lord Nelson is dead.'

The enemy ships were distinguishable only by their flags. Fifty ships in a few square miles off the coast of Cape Trafalgar. Masts gone, sails in shreds, smoke and flames. Everywhere carpenters swarmed about the mighty warships, patching and fashioning make-do spars and rigging. From the decks men were dropping bodies into the water. And everywhere, apart from the occasional report from a cannon, a dreadful silence. Josiah thought he should stay aboard but he needed to be there. To rescue, to help. To do something – anything which would assuage his misery.

The seas were full of debris. Bodies floated amid wreckage: broken bodies, sailors who had toppled from falling masts, refugees from shattered ships. Josiah came upon three sailors clinging to a spar and helped them into the boat. Spaniards. They rowed on, filling the launch with injured and frightened men. The English were jubilant despite their injuries, the French sullen and the Spanish cowed.

'These men don't look like sailors,' someone said, pointing to a Spanish sailor.

'They are dogs,' said a voice in French. 'The Spanish fleet was manned with criminals and soldiers, scarce a sailor among them!'

They returned to *Thalia* and unloaded their sad cargo and set out again. It was late afternoon. The English ships were getting organised. Prize crews were in place. Josiah saw *Victory* in the distance, battered beyond belief and under tow. He longed to go to her, but duty and common sense kept him working.

When it was dark and almost impossible to see, they returned to *Thalia*. After the calm of the day there was a stiff breeze blowing. The sick were being tended and the uninjured sailors were being fed. Mitchell was well organised, settling men in the troop quarters and organising the crew to assist the surgeons.

As they made way for Gibraltar, Josiah called for dinner to be served. He invited the officers they had picked up to join him. There were five – three Frenchmen, whose ships had sunk, one Spaniard and an Englishman. The Englishman had been found in the sea unable to locate his ship.

The Englishman could not speak French, nor the French English. Josiah became the translator.

The French were eager to talk. 'It was foolishness from the very start. Villeneuve said he was ordered to make for Naples. The truth was we all knew he was being replaced, and he chose to fight this battle even though we knew it was suicidal.'

The other French officer took up the story. 'The Spanish fleet was not ready. They had too few sailors, so they filled their fleet with men who had never been aboard a ship before.'

The Englishman gave a different tale. 'Lord Nelson had the battle plan completely ready. He had his frigates probing enemy defences. Every move made by the enemy was transmitted back to the fleet, which kept over the horizon until all the enemy ships had left Cadiz. Then the trap was sprung. *Victory* and *Royal Sovereign* crashed through the ragged French line. They drew tremendous fire. Oh, the courage of Nelson and Collingwood! They could take their punishment – and that is what broke the enemy.'

Tears filled the officer's eyes and his voice trembled. 'The greatest admiral we have ever known drew the fire and was shot to death by a sniper.'

There was silence around the table.

Josiah said quietly, 'He was my father.'

As he said farewell to his guests, he noticed the wind was still rising. There was going to be a storm. He put on his greatcoat and made his way to the quarterdeck.

'Mr Mitchell, it's going to be a rough night.'

'I've given the order to take in the topsails and have reefed the main.'

'Better take it all down. Leave a small sprit sail to enable steerage.'

By now *Thalia* was pitching through the seas. As the night passed, the storm grew with it until the winds were at hurricane strength. *Thalia* ran before the wind, her drogues slowing her as waves broke over her stern.

It required every ounce of seamanship from Josiah and Mitchell to keep the old ship from broaching or being beaten to pieces. The seas raged through the next day, and it was another two days before they limped into Gibraltar.

The remains of the fleet were there, and a heavy wetness hung over everything. Josiah recognised it immediately. The triumphal moment had passed and the cost was being reckoned. Still, the momentous events of the battle were forefront in every conversation in the officers' mess.

Josiah met with Fleet Captain Murray in his dockyard office. He gave a short account of the events in Nevis, including the duel he had fought and his work at the scene of the recent battle.

'Josiah, may I say how deeply sorry I am at the death of your father. What a great loss … Thank you for returning *Thalia* back to the fleet. I promised to get you back to England, and I have a passage for you on a transport that leaves tomorrow.'

'Thank you, sir. Where is my father's body? Can I see him?'

'I am afraid not, Josiah. We have had to preserve the body in a barrel of spirits. It is sealed until it reaches London.'

Josiah shuddered.

'What do you plan to do now?'

'I will return to London and bury my father. I will then be at their lordships' disposal.'

'If I may say so, Josiah. You are a man of great potential. You have enemies, but you also have the sympathy of many. In my report I will make some of my thoughts known. Who knows the result?'

He raised his eyebrows, reached across the desk and shook Josiah's hand. Then they saluted and Murray escorted Josiah to the door. He watched as Josiah walked through the busy dockyard, where the battered battleships were being patched and painted and prepared for sea again.

# CHAPTER 32

She was a converted merchantman, and she was slow, cumbersome and rode the waves like a cart-horse: rolling and pitching clumsily. Though he rarely suffered from seasickness, even Josiah succumbed as they wallowed their way through the Bay of Biscay.

A few officers of the victorious fleet kept the ward-room occupied throughout the journey with their tales of the great battle. Josiah had plenty of time to prepare himself for England. He often wondered about his friends in Nevis. How did Elizabeth fare after the death of McPherson? And Jefferson? Sometimes he ached for their company.

In Gibraltar he had learned there were new people at the Admiralty. Pitt's government had replaced St Vincent with Charles Middleton, now Lord Barham.

The fiasco at the dockyards had been reversed. England was building more warships than ever. But after Trafalgar, he asked, would the country need such a huge fleet?

He learned that Napoleon had expected the French fleet to arrive at the Channel ports two months earlier and had his army ready to invade England. But Villeneuve had not risked the Channel after Sir John Orde had intercepted him, and had retreated to Cadiz. Instead Napoleon had turned his attention to the resurgent Austrian army – which he had defeated at the Battle of Austerlitz.

The implications were not lost on Josiah. It meant that Britain's victory at Trafalgar had given the British outright control of the seas. The struggle for naval supremacy was over.

⚓

He had written ahead to advise Viscountess Nelson of his imminent arrival in England. His letter read:

*My dear Mama,*
*I am taking sail tomorrow for England. It will be a slow journey so this will reach you before I do.*
*I was present at Trafalgar a short time after the battle ended. The devastation was awful to behold – not least the condition of Victory, which*

*had received a terrible battering. I was not able to
see father before his glorious death but when we meet
I will tell you about our last meeting – in the West
Indies. I can imagine this is a very hard time for you.
I know you continued to love him from afar.*

*When I arrive in England I will take an express
coach from Portsmouth to London. I have missed you
and have been a poor correspondent. I hope to put that
to rights when I am in London.*

*Your loving son,
Josiah.*

When he rang the bell at his mother's home, the maid
answered the door and let him into the morning room,
where Fanny was waiting for him. They kissed gently
and she held him at arm's length and marvelled at
how he had matured. She was still a beautiful woman,
but her hair had grey at the temples and her eyes were
saddened by her losses.

She said, 'I lost Horatio, but I found my son.
Tell me everything, absolutely everything that has
happened to you. I want every detail – from the very
beginning.'

He told her the whole story from beginning to
end. But it was at the end, as he described his reunion
with Horatio, his journey back to Gibraltar and the

scene at Trafalgar that she began to weep – hot tears of both joy and sorrow.

At length, when the story ended, the maid brought them dinner. This time Fanny recounted all that had happened in London from the time he left to the time she received a visit from Commodore Hood.

Fanny was devastated by Horatio's death and over-whelmed by the miraculous news of Josiah's return. Nonetheless, when she knew he was coming she had taken steps – through her circle of friends – to alert the Admiralty. They had received Commodore Hood's letter as well as the official notifications from George Murray. They had heard nothing from Horatio himself.

In consequence when Josiah appeared at the Admiralty to make his report, they were expecting him and told him his appointment to see the First Lord was within the hour. The meeting was in the very same room his father had described to him when, years ago, he was given command of *Agamemnon*. It was high-ceilinged, decorated in the baroque style with grey silk hangings and a view from the windows across to St James's Park. The First Lord rose to his feet when Josiah was ushered in.

'My dear fellow, I am so pleased to see you again.

Do sit down,' he said, indicating a chair next to his own. They both sat and paused while a servant poured them tea.

'Your lordship is kind to see me so quickly. Perhaps I can let you know—'

Lord Barham held up his hand. 'We have our own ways of finding what has happened, and we know more or less everything you have done.'

Josiah looked at him uncertainly.

'Cheer up. We know about the duel too.' He smiled. 'Everything has advanced our cause. Your work in the dockyard alerted us to the problems being caused by my predecessor's witch hunt. Your involvement in the slave revolt was raised in parliament and has helped us to bring the Slave Trade Bill close to approval. We are confident it will pass. Your work with the island militia was reported by Sam Hood, who also told us about Diamond Rock. And when your father was in this very room only three months ago, he told me about his meeting with you and *Thalia*. I have Charles Murray's report on the sterling work you undertook at Trafalgar – rescuing over a hundred stranded seamen. I believe even our enemies are inclined to give you a medal.'

'I had no idea.'

'Someone else made a personal report to me.'

Josiah suddenly felt nervous.

'I received a letter from my dear friend, Charles Grey. His work in Nevis is of the highest interest to me and my friends. Perhaps you know of William Wilberforce?'

Josiah thought of the book with the long title that James Nisbet had given him so long ago, when they had first met at the Methodist Church in Nevis. He still treasured it.

'We need more people like you, Josiah. You have been trained by the navy and you are proof that whatever the circumstances our best officers always rise to the top. Indeed, in your own way, you are a lot like your father.'

'Are you suggesting I return to sea?'

'I have something better for you'

'Better?'

'A better way of using your skills.'

Josiah's heart was pounding. He could get command of a seventy-four. But *something better*? Perhaps he meant more suitable?

'Yes. You are someone who can operate "incognito". It's a rare ability. Together with your fluency in the French language you are able to operate with local people whatever their position. You are the man we need to begin a new division of the navy. A secret service.'

Josiah had always thought of himself as a man of

action – a man in command. This seemed to be very different. A spy, an agent of the government operating on his own in enemy territory? He felt flattered and puzzled.

'I want you to meet the other members of the Admiralty Board. They know of the plan and wish to meet you. I have booked a room at White's Club. Would you be free in – shall we say – an hour's time? At 2.00 p.m.?'

'Yes, sir. I'd be honoured.'

'There is someone else who wants to talk with you as well. My esteemed wife has arranged a dinner with Mr Wilberforce. We will send you a note.'

# EPILOGUE: JANUARY 1806

Horatio's funeral was on 9th January 1805. Fanny was invited to attend, but it was a pro forma invitation, because ladies were not expected to attend funerals. Instead, Captain Hardy escorted her, by boat, to Greenwich Hospital, where Horatio lay in state, and she said her private goodbye to him there in the Painted Hall.

The funeral procession started in Hyde Park. The funeral car built in the shape of a ship was escorted to St Paul's Cathedral by troops and seamen and fifty mourning coaches. The family was represented by William, the new earl, his son Horatio, and his brother-in-law Matcham. Horatio's lawyers and Davison the prize agent were there too. Josiah saw them all from a distance. He was not included in the seats set apart for the family and instead sat towards the back of the cathedral in seats for members of the public.

St. Paul's was filled to capacity, and those without reserved seats had been sitting in the cold building since seven in the morning. In his long black cloak, the chief mourner, Sir Peter Parker, led the procession to the altar where the coffin was reverently laid. He was followed by the Duke of Clarence, 'Sailor Bill', brother to the King and an old friend of Horatio's from the West Indies days. There were government and opposition politicians – Charles James Fox, aldermen from the city and nearly two hundred naval officers. His band of brothers from the Nile were represented by Commodore Sam Hood, captain of the *Zealous*. The others were all away at sea.

Josiah had queued with the rest of the ticketless for the 7.00 a.m. admission of the public to the cathedral. He was dressed in the captain's uniform Horatio had given him in Trinidad. When the coffin – made from the timbers of *L'Orient* – was carried down to the crypt for committal to the grave, he rose as if to join in that intimate ceremony, but changed his mind and subsided into the pew. He watched as young Horatio, with his father William, followed the coffin to the crypt.

Anthems were sung, prayers offered, and by mid-afternoon the great candelabra was lit as darkness came early. Eventually the service came to an end, and the mourners departed in a melee of coaches.

In the cathedral, as the crowds disappeared, Josiah remained, his face in his hands. As Sam Hood passed Josiah, he reached out and grasped Josiah's arm.

'Hello, Josiah. My respects to you and your mother.'

The procession swept Sam away, and Josiah sat down again, weeping.

The following day, Haslewood, the family lawyer, came to visit Fanny and Josiah to explain the terms of Horatio's will. The maid escorted him to the sitting room. His face shone with the pedantic dignity of experienced legal servants.

The will had been drawn up some years before, but had been amended to take account of the changes in the family situation. In an earlier version Fanny and Josiah had been executors and heirs. No longer. Haslewood, seated at a small writing table to which Fanny had escorted him, drew a copy of the will from his satchel and started to read the document aloud. It took five minutes or so. Then he stood up and, moving over to where she sat, he showed her the uneven left-handed signature and the seal of her lord. The sentiment of the will perpetuated Horatio's sense of personal obligation to her, while somehow managing to spite Fanny with its conditions. The sum of £1000 per annum had been settled on her, continuing the grant made to her in his lifetime but terminating on his death if, before that event, a grateful nation should decide to settle a pension on his widow. Parliament, under the gracious guidance of the Admiralty and Treasury, had awarded her £2000 per annum *after* his death, so this callous clause was of no consequence; Fanny had her thousand and the government's two – she would be very comfortable. Parliament, Haslewood explained, voted an earldom to the heir – brother William – as well as annual endowments of five thousand pounds in perpetuity. In addition they had endowed the family with funds sufficient for an estate worthy of a hero. Parliament's largesse extended to Horatio's siblings, leaving them comfortable for the rest of their lives.

Fanny said, 'What I am most concerned about is whether some of the personal artefacts that I treasured so much – paintings, mementos of the campaigns and such like – will be afforded to me or to Josiah?'

'My dear lady'—Haslewood's voice grew quiet with embarrassment—'there are no provisions for anything beyond what was settled three years ago. Earl William was most adamant about that, and as far as I know the division of those things that will not remain at Merton has already been agreed if they were not specified in the will.'

'And what about my lord's son?' There was an edge to her voice.

'I assume you are referring to Josiah?'

'That is correct. My lord over the years was quite definite that he regarded Josiah as his son and would make full provision for him in that regard.'

Haslewood stood up, drawing the papers together and putting them in his black satchel. 'There are no longer any provision for Josiah, my lady.'

Fanny stood, smoothing the black silk of her dress. 'Thank you for your professional service, Haslewood. I am sure that in the years to come, there will be more congenial times for us to meet.'

She escorted him from the drawing room to the hall and bent her head to his polite bow. The door closed, and she returned to the sitting room.

Josiah stood and put his arms around her. 'Mother, the will means nothing to me. What counts to me is that Papa and I reconciled. He loved me.'

～

Matcham and Josiah met a few weeks later to settle outstanding issues. Josiah could not bring himself to deal with the pompous earl, whose friendship had given Emma so much power in the times following the breakdown of Fanny's marriage to Horatio. The two men met in Hyde Park and strolled around the Serpentine.

Josiah asked, 'What has become of Emma Hamilton?'

'The earl couldn't wait to ditch her.'

'Ditch her?'

'Yes, he and Sarah always despised her, but she was important in cementing William's position as the heir. How she must have regretted her friendship with that hypocrite!'

'And now?'

'Merton is in chaos. The last time I saw Emma she was drunk and hysterical, face down on the carpet. Empty bottles everywhere. She must have swept them from the table. Mrs Cadogan, Emma's mother, tries everything. Emma's moods swing wildly – either unfounded optimism the government *will* recognise her claim to a pension, or to grief, pessimism and fear about her future. Sometimes she rallies and talks of her friendship with the Queen of Naples, and even about a future in the theatre. But only for a few moments and then her hysteria starts again. Pathetic, really!'

'And the child – the baby I saw when I visited Merton those years ago?'

'She is still there, but what is to become of her?'

'And what will become of this great country of ours?'

'The death of William Pitt is a blow to all of us,' Matcham said. 'It has stirred hope that Fox will return – his followers, the great Whig landowners, believe *he* could make peace with Napoleon.'

'What about the new moneyed classes? The war has been good for them. Will *they* want to make peace?'

'The manufacturers and ship builders who make the guns and build the ships have a great deal to lose.'

'What about the sugar interests?'

'They are still reeling from the end of the slave trade and are making common cause with the East India traders to close ranks against the abolition of slavery itself.'

'They make me sick!'

'Josiah, you are sounding like a Jacobin!'

'If the war doesn't end soon, the poor will starve. The country can barely feed its population.'

'Well, Josiah, whatever else *may* happen, thank God we are one step closer to ending the war.'

'Yes, George. Trafalgar has changed the future of our Nation. Thank God for my father!'

# AUTHOR'S NOTE

For those who have read "Nelson's Folly", you will be aware that the principal characters in that book – Fanny Nelson, Horatio and Josiah, were part of my own story. I am descended from Fanny and her son, Josiah, who was born to Fanny in an earlier short-lived marriage. Although I am not related "by blood" to the great Horatio, he is nonetheless part of my family lore. I have long been fascinated by the larger story of Horatio's place in history and how this affected my family. "Nelson's Lost Son" is the second book about this heroic figure and his wider family.

The first book in the trilogy, "Nelson's Folly" is the account of Fanny and Horatio's marriage and careers over eight years from 1793 to 1801. Included is the account – largely accurate – of Josiah's early years aboard *Agamemnon*, his education as a Commander in the Royal Navy and his brief career as a Post Captain.

By 1801, Josiah had lost the patronage of his father and the support of senior officers in the Navy. He had made enough enemies to ensure his career as a Captain was at its end. I imagined Josiah, only twenty one years old; desperate to get back to the only life he ever knew. He would have been bored senseless in London and frustrated beyond measure by his fate at such an early age.

This is the seed of the idea. The rest is my imagination. The contextual stories in the plot – the Great Dockyard scandal, West Indian Slavery, the French fleet sailing to the West Indies pursued by Nelson, the fight for Diamond Rock, and Trafalgar, are all true. There are some details which were true in part. While there was no Battle of Brimstone Hill – at least in 1804-5 – the planters *were* threatened by the French and paid "protection money" to deter them from invading the islands. Nelson *did* sail to Port of Spain thinking the French must be there. There *was* an uprising in Haiti which terrified the white settlers of Jamaica. Sam Hood *was* the Commodore of the Leeward Islands Squadron. But the majority of the plot and its characters are entirely fictional. Jefferson, Colonel Smith and Nisbet (Josiah's cousin), Elisabeth and Reverend Grey may be similar to real life figures but none of them actually existed.

Josiah is a wonderful subject for a story of this nature. From what I have learned he was enterprising, courageous and had good intentions. He was also introverted, gruff and had a tendency to feel sorry for himself. His ambitions would have been common to young men at that time and would have centred on winning respect, marrying a wealthy woman and making money to cement a place in Society. This would have been finished by the ending of his career as a Navy Captain. But, the world was changing, as the aristocratic oligarchy of the eighteenth century, whose wealth and power rested on their possession of land and investments in Colonial projects like the East India Company, American Plantations and Sugar interests, were superseded by industrialists and financiers enriched by their banks and businesses which prospered as a result of the Napoleonic War. Privileged families and Patronage networks were soon to be replaced by Capitalism in which individual enterprise was a more important attribute than birth. After the Napoleonic wars politics changed as well; political and social reform was long overdue. Josiah lived in this transitional period of history and his thinking reflects this change.

I apologise unreservedly if I have misled any reader

as to *who* Josiah was and what he actually accomplished. I am not trying to glorify a historical figure with false facts and narratives. I am rather, taking liberties with my ancestor, Josiah, to see how a young man with a powerful father *might* behave if he was stripped of his patronage and reputation and forced to confront the world on his own. Actually, later in life, Josiah became a wealthy investment banker and lived and died in some opulence in Paris. He is buried in Exmouth in the same Church as his mother, Fanny.

Some readers may be shocked by my narrative of the Slave society I have portrayed. St Kitts and Nevis are peaceful islands today whose population is largely descended from the enslaved. This novel poses the question; suppose the white planters needed help from their enslaved population to the point when they would give them fire arms? This actually happened in the earlier years of the eighteenth century when the French invaded St Kitts and Nevis and attempted to kidnap local people and transport them to the largest and most brutal sugar enterprise in the West Indies – Saint Domingue, now known as Haiti. The story also asks whether there were local institutions opposed to Slavery. There were – among them the Methodists whose faithfulness to the Gospel challenges the established church. The Methodists also helped by establishing self-help institutions, thereby reducing the risk of poverty for those no longer living as slaves.

As Josiah sees it, slavery was an exploitative enterprise that enriched the British moneyed classes. It was a crude early capitalistic system that was corrupt and decaying even before the Slave Trade came to an end in 1807 and Slavery was abolished later on. Josiah's decision to use his inheritance to set up an agricultural cooperative, foreshadowed a way of dealing with a major problem of the time as these Societies became free; finding ways for the enslaved to become self-sufficient.

All of this is set in the context of the great sea battle between the French and British Fleets at Trafalgar. I have not included an account of the battle – there are enough already - but the aftermath of the battle is not as well understood. The French and Spanish fleets were annihilated and what was not lost in the battle was devastated in the brutal storm which followed.

For Josiah, though, his part in the struggle is over. He has communicated vital intelligence, settled his affairs in Nevis and now returns home in the aftermath of the battle. What will become of him? It seems as though he has won new friends at the Admiralty. They always need courageous and resourceful men. We will see.

I would like to thank the many friends who have

helped me write this book. I single out for special praise the members of my "Boys Own Writers' Group" who have read and critiqued my work chapter by chapter, fortified by plenty of Australian Red. Ollie, Andrew, Steve, Walter, Rob and Indrek, thank you! Others who have helped me include John Gilbert, a retired Royal Navy Officer who reviewed the manuscript with a keen eye for maritime details and naval history. Ian Palmer, who is the reader in the Audible version of "Nelson's Folly," read the manuscript and offered many useful suggestions. Roger Henderson QC who read the manuscript, has an abiding love of Nevis and suggested many important corrections. (Thank you for Barry and Karen for introducing me to Roger). I would also like to thank Ann, Michele and Danielle at Independent Ink for very professional assistance in publishing this book. I owe Nadja Leffler a debt of gratitude for helping me promote my work and for helping set up and manage my website – Fannynelsonfan.com. Lastly, I am ever grateful to my wife Susanne who has lived with this book from conception to final edit. Her advice – especially regarding the perspective of women readers – has been of the greatest value to me.

Fannynelsonfan.com

# Also by Oliver Greeves
*Nelson's Folly*

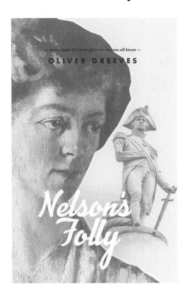

*Nelson's Folly* is a compelling, vividly portrayed tale that is well grounded in a sense of the changing times, yet also nicely rooted in memorable characters. Historical novel and political history readers, as well as general-interest readers who enjoy stories of British society in 18th century England, will find it an accessible, thoroughly involving saga rich in psychological, political, and social inspection.

— **Diane Donovan (Senior Reviewer, Midwest Book Review, USA)**

 **OLIVER GREEVES,** a direct descendent of Fanny Nelson, lives in Sydney. He is a historian and sailor who spent many years working on Wall Street. He is currently working on another story about Josiah. Set at the time of the war between Britain and the USA, known as "The War of 1812" it is the last novel of the Trilogy.